PRAISE FOR T...
OF TOBY...

HAPPY ANY DAY NOW

"*Happy Any Day Now* is a charming read for women of any age, especially those who have mothers, fathers, boyfriends, former lovers, or careers. Judith Soo Jin Raphael is unique and also completely like your best friend, facing decisions and doubts with courage and lots of LOL humor. I learned so much from reading this book, and had such fun!"

—Nancy Thayer, author of *Summer Breeze* and *The Hot Flash Club*

"A smart, funny novel that explores the midlife angst of Judith Soo Jin Raphael, a half-Korean, half-Jewish classical cellist. Caught between two cultures, two lovers, and an errant father who reenters her life just as her professional and personal lives collide, Judith struggles to accept that what she wants might not truly be what she needs. Fast-paced and witty, with great dialogue and three-dimensional characters, *Happy Any Day Now* will ring true for many women."
—Cathy Holton, author of *Beach Trip*

"If you're looking for smart, upbeat fiction with snappy dialogue and a fun peek into ethnic traditions, *Happy Any Day Now* is perfect. A lively read that offers an interesting behind-the-scenes look at a symphony orchestra and a midlife heroine who is all grown up but still capable of being comically and poignantly bewildered by life." —Nancy Martin, author of *Little Black Book of Murder*

continued . . .

Written by today's freshest new talents and selected by New American Library, NAL Accent novels touch on subjects close to a woman's heart, from friendship to family to finding our place in the world. The Conversation Guides included in each book are intended to enrich the individual reading experience, as well as encourage us to explore these topics together—because books, and life, are meant for sharing.

Visit us online at www.penguin.com.

"Judith Raphael is half-Korean and half-Jewish, and full-on fabulous! Toby Devens's novel is warm, witty, and wonderful."
—Wendy Wax, author of *While We Were Watching Downton Abbey*

"Never has a midlife crisis—or actually a perfect storm of them—been treated with such charm, insight, and smart, sardonic humor. Judith Soo Jin Raphael, the heroine of Toby Devens's engaging new novel, is half-Korean, half-Jewish, and facing her fiftieth birthday, she is carrying enough emotional baggage and family history to last several additional lifetimes. With a deft touch, Devens spins a tale of lost opportunities and rediscovered romance, second chances and second thoughts, family secrets and lasting friendships. Set in the fascinating world of classical music—with all its pressures, rivalries, passions, and loyalties—Devens's *Happy Any Day Now* is a virtuoso performance which is bound to win Devens a host of new fans."
—Liza Gyllenhaal, author of *A Place for Us*

MY FAVORITE MIDLIFE CRISIS (YET)

"An excellent read! Toby Devens weaves an intricate tale of lust, deceit, divorce, and face-lifts, as her unique protagonist navigates her way."
—Ben Mezrich, *New York Times* bestselling author of *Sex on the Moon* and *The Accidental Billionaires*

OTHER NOVELS BY TOBY DEVENS

My Favorite Midlife Crisis (Yet)

Happy Any Day Now

Toby Devens

NAL Accent
Published by the Penguin Group
Penguin Group (USA) Inc., 375 Hudson Street,
New York, New York 10014, USA

USA | Canada | UK | Ireland | Australia | New Zealand | India | South Africa | China

Penguin Books Ltd., Registered Offices: 80 Strand, London WC2R 0RL, England
For more information about the Penguin Group visit penguin.com.

First published by NAL Accent, an imprint of New American Library,
a division of Penguin Group (USA) Inc.

First Printing, August 2013

LIBRARY OF CONGRESS CATALOGING-IN-PUBLICATION DATA:
Devens, Toby.
Happy any day now/Toby Devens.
p. cm.
ISBN 978-0-451-41898-2
1. Middle-aged women—Maryland—Baltimore—Fiction.
2. Women musicians—Maryland—Baltimore—Fiction.
3. Self-actualization (Psychology) in middle age—Fiction.
4. Life change events—Fiction. I. Title.
PS3604.E885H37 2013
813'.6—dc23   2013000045

Printed in the United States of America
1   3   5   7   9   10   8   6   4   2

Set in Stempel Garamond
Designed by Elke Sigal

For the next generation of strong, talented women—especially Felicia, Sarina, and Elizabeth

Happy Any Day Now

Chapter 1

❧

Every five years my mother had her fortune read by Lulu Cho, the owner of the Golden Lotus Massage Club for Men. She didn't find it strange that the old gods, in their mysterious wisdom, had elected to send their portents through a sex parlor shaman. I thought it was crazy, but it was a Korean thing. It made her happy, no harm done.

Then last year she set *me* up with Lulu. "My fifty birthday present to you, Judith. Count from birth, you already in fifty year. Time just right for reading."

Even if Lulu Cho was a true *mudang* and could really predict the future, I had zero desire to hear what was coming up for the rest of my life. I was just as glad no one had warned me about the past before I had to deal with it.

I protested. My mother insisted. "No argue. Reading is booked. Lulu has policy. No return, no exchange."

Which is how I came to be sitting in a cramped apartment with a scotch-sipping *mudang* across from me and my mother next to me, rapping her knuckles nervously on the kitchen table.

I have to admit, I got caught up in it at first, the spooky stuff. I'm half Korean, half Jewish, so I inherited the superstition gene from both sides. When Lulu Cho rang a small brass bell and scattered rice and coins across a lacquered tray, I held my breath. When she chanted in Korean, a thrill ran up my spine. But the spell vaporized when she announced in a dramatic doomsday voice, "Now we begin."

She'd been reading my mother's fortune for decades, so I figured she probably knew a lot about me and she'd start with the obvious stuff like any fraud.

The first half of my life had been stormy. "Bad weather, much thunder for little girl. Ten birthday, you be so angry. Heart feel hard like stone." True . . .

She lifted her glass, took a swig of the Johnnie Walker Red she claimed helped her make potent connections with the spirits, and licked her lips.

"Twenty okay, but thirty birthday not so hot. Love signs crashing."

She nailed that one. I'd whipped up something of a hurricane for my thirtieth birthday. That was the year I was totally obsessed with marriage and my lack of same or prospects related to. By the year's end, I stood under the wedding canopy with "Rebound Todd," regretting it even before the rabbi said the final blessing.

"Forty, very very sad. You feel empty inside," Lulu said.

On target again. The big four-oh was mainly about my ovaries, specifically their age-related deterioration. The dimming prospect for babies. There was a lot of weeping that birthday.

"Blessed with talent, but cursed with much trouble in past, Judith." The *mudang*'s eyes were squinched in concentration. Mine were open and rolling, earning a pinch on the arm from my mother, who hung on to every word.

"Ouch." I rubbed the spot above my elbow.

"Be nice, Judith."

I stage-whispered, "Oh, come on, *Uhm-mah*. You told her all about me. Filled in the details."

"Not true. Not say one word. She hear all from . . ." Grace pointed upward, ostensibly to heaven, really to apartment 3C.

"Grace tell you the truth," Lulu pronounced. "And now we look to future. Fifty is *pok*, good luck. I hope I find good luck for you." She gave me a quick smile, reached across the table, and took my hand. "Okay. You have love now. More love ahead. Maybe too much love. Bring problems. But"—she squinted—"I think you solve."

I shrugged. Who needed more love? I already had Geoff Birdsall, six years younger, Australian, hunky, a talented musician who was also very gifted in bed. Our connection was heavy on pleasure, light on commitment. The last thing it brought me was problems.

"Music important. Music in your life until the very end." I was a cellist with the Maryland Philharmonic Orchestra. My mother bragged about my job to everyone. A no-brainer. "And you never go deaf." That was reassuring.

She guessed right about my problem with acid reflux and my desire to lose five pounds—like the rest of the known world. And then, right in the middle of forecasting the onset of menopause, Lulu froze, her stare fixed on a spot in the distance.

"What? You see roach?" my mother asked.

The *mudang* had lapsed into a trance. Maybe thirty seconds went by.

Then, roused by a shudder, Lulu clapped her hands to her head and hissed as if she were speaking for an evil spirit. "Judith, *ayyyy*." She called out my name in a thin, high-pitched voice not her own. "Judith!" Her eyes slid to white, then closed.

Cradling her temples in her hands, she rocked back and forth. "Ay, stop the pain. Head split like lightning hit. Worst pain." She moaned. She cried out as a wild spasm shook her body.

Then, suddenly, all was quiet. She slumped in her chair. Her eyes opened and focused. I figured she was back from the spirit world. The bony finger that had just wiped spittle from her mouth pointed at me. "You listen, Judith. Danger coming close. You have to see doctor soon. Soon as possible. Matter of life and death. Black crows circle round your head. I see—" Her hand shot out to touch my hair.

"No!" My mother toppled the tray with the rice and coins as she stood up. "Reading over. Enough for now. Judith, get up." Trembling, she reached into her wallet, peeled off five twenties, snatched back two of them, and tossed the rest on the table. "Not worth more. Not worth nothing. Very bad fortune. You should be shamed, Lulu. You are lousy *mudang*."

The following week, as I walked to my car after a rehearsal of Verdi's *Requiem*, half a block from the musician's garage I was struck by what neurologists call a thunderclap headache—the worst pain in the history of pain. A minute into the agony, I collapsed with the aneurysm that almost killed me.

Chapter 2

❧

A year later, one week short of the anniversary of my aneurysm and a brilliant Johns Hopkins neurosurgeon saving my life, I made the stupid decision to risk it.

Blame it on spring fever. Or on the cherry blossom trees that were currently turning the dowdiest parts of Baltimore into a pink blaze of glory. The flowers bloomed for a few days of gorgeousness and then faded away. But oh, how they lived when they lived. Maybe they weren't the best inspiration for making a dangerous decision.

I checked my watch. Ten of two. For the umpteenth time, I skimmed the page ripped from the *Goucher College Quarterly* that had been slipped under my door by my best friend and neighbor, my favorite lesbian yenta Marti McDowell. The article was titled "Justice Pruitt to Discuss American Elective Process." Far left, where God knows he'd never have placed himself in real life, was a recent photo of Charlie Pruitt, man of my dreams, man of my sleepless nights.

I'd met Charles Evans Pruitt when I was at the New England Conservatory of Music and he was a student at Harvard Law School. A scholarship kid from Brooklyn and a Brahmin from Manhattan were an unlikely pair, but we were madly in love—

okay, I thought it was we; maybe it was only me—for more than two years. Then he told his family about his half-Jewish, half-Korean girlfriend, Judith Soo Jin Raphael, and *boom!* It was over.

Except not for me, not for a very long time. Keeping a vow to my therapist, I'd forced myself to stop Googling him years ago. Now I stared at his image, searching for landmarks of the Charlie I'd known and loved.

Decked out in his robe, he looked somber and weighty, both judicially and figuratively. He had to have gained twenty pounds since the last time I'd seen him, thin and drawn at our horrible breakup. But the eyes were the same, a brilliant magnetic blue. And his hair was polished silver. He looked like a more distinguished version of the young, irresistible Charlie: smart, pedigreed, and for a second—as the old sad song played in my brain for the first time in decades—totally out of my league.

A paragraph was devoted to his credentials, dazzling of course: Harvard Law, with honors. Name partner in Pruitt, Bryce and Summerville, LLP, a prestigious Park Avenue law firm, until his appointment thirteen years earlier as a justice on New York State's highest court, Manhattan branch. And the public was invited to a free lecture at Goucher, Sunday afternoon, two p.m., where he'd be addressing the topic "Pros and Cons of the Electoral College." Riveting. There was nothing about his personal life in the article, but Marti had scrawled in the margins, "I Googled. He's divorced."

I shouldn't have cared. Charlie was no longer a part of my life, which was infinitely better for that. I was perfectly happy with Geoff. Well, not perfectly, but close. I shouldn't have come to Goucher. But, of course, in a classic case of heart over head so you land on your ass, here I was approaching the entrance to Kelley Hall, fingers trembling as I jammed the article back into my handbag. Then I heard a jumble of loud young voices and turned to check out what the excitement was all about. That's when I saw him.

Not his face. In the crush of students who made a walking barrier, protecting him as if he were the Dalai Lama, all that was visible was Charlie's back. But I'd have known the slope of it anywhere. And underneath the Hickey Freeman suit, I could connect the spatter of freckles below his right shoulder blade into a map of Venezuela. For a second, I was aware of my inability to swallow. Then, amid a flash of silver hair, an angle of jaw, I found spit and he vanished into the lecture hall. His audience drifted in. I waited until the coast was clear, then walked slowly up the steps, as if it were the last mile. On the landing, I halted. This outing was absurd. Charlie might not even remember how special we were, given how time erases life and life erases time.

Then again, he might have bookmarked those excruciating last moments when I'd deliberately dumped his law texts on the floor—the vilest insult I could think of—and mocked his family as a cadre of fascist snobs. Why did I even want to meet him again, this traitor who had snubbed me because my ex so-called father sold lox and my war bride mother had a checkered past? I was starting up so I could stop? Talk about circular reasoning. Talk about bullshit. Turn around and go, for God's sake!

And I would have. But I caught a snatch of conversation from inside Kelley Hall. The words were muffled through the closed door, but when you've heard someone tell you he loves you, he adores you, you're the best thing that ever happened to him, sorry but good-bye, you remember that voice forever.

So fine, I'd see him. Now or never. I'd gripped the door handle, ready to push, when a student, some kid in an Orioles baseball cap and a camouflage backpack, came up behind me.

"May I help you with that, ma'am?" Polite enough to charm an old lady, which he obviously thought I was. *Oy!* and its Korean equivalent, *Aigoo!* I almost turned on my heel then, but the kid was holding the door, waiting. I took a deep breath and barreled through. Charlie was already striding to the lectern, his back to me. My intent was to slip into a seat in the last row, but it was packed, so I wound up in the only empty seat, second row, dead center. It took me a while, concentrating on my hands, which I'd folded into the prayer pose to control their tremor, before I felt I could look up. When I did, my glance met Charlie's and locked. Brown eyes to blue, we held that stare for maybe five seconds. Then I blinked. First, dammit. But he managed to knock into his stack of notes and send them flying. So I called it a draw.

Charlie had always been an accomplished public speaker. He was quick on his feet and, more important, he had nerves of steel and the confidence of a man born to an established trust fund.

That afternoon at Goucher, once I heard all I ever needed to know about the electoral college, I tuned out and treated myself to nearly an hour of just watching him, with that voice, its timbre as mellow as a Guarneri cello's, playing soothingly in the background.

Maybe I wasn't objective—we had a complicated history—but to me Charles Evans Pruitt was still handsome, even with the extra weight, which in his well-cut suit seemed less blimpy than under the robe in the photo. His hair was now parted left, instead of right—more a barber's decision than a political statement, I figured. Beyond the hair issues, the Cotton Mather sharpness of his features—I used to think I could slice Aunt Phyllis's challah with the knife-edge of his nose—had softened with more padding; the angle of his jaw had become less Superman. These I counted as improvements. Yes, there were the wrinkles around the eyes and the chin sag, but no major facial erosion. And when he paced up front with a bounce in his gait, I could see hardly any paunch beyond the unbuttoned suit jacket. Charlie was fifty-four and I'd bet he was still a runner. *Aigoo*, was he a runner.

After he'd nimbly dispatched with the Q and A, it was over. By the time I stood to work my way toward the aisle, a crush of admiring students had surrounded him. There was no way I was going to take a ticket to talk to a man I had once screwed. I didn't have to. Charlie called out, "Judith!" I waved. Nothing fancy. And then I heard him excuse himself. Next moment, he was leaning over the first-row seats to clasp both my hands in both of his. Thus linked, I made my way to the aisle.

His eyes were sparkling. "My God, it *is* you." As if there were hordes of big-bosomed women with almond-shaped eyes and gold cello charms hung from their necks to choose from. "What are you doing here?"

"I figured it was my chance to learn the intricacies of the electoral college. Just in case I ever decide to enroll."

He chuckled. "Well, for whatever reason, I'm delighted you're here. Good God, Judith, it's been how long? Twenty-five years?"

"Soon to be twenty-six."

"Let me take a look at you." We were still hands-in-hands and now he pulled out for a body-riding appraisal. *Thank you, Nordstrom's, for the miraculous tummy-tuck jeans.* "Still beautiful. It's amazing. You really haven't changed."

"I have actually, but now's not the time to go into detail." The restless buzz from the students gathered at the lectern was spiraling.

"Right. We must catch up, though." His forehead wrinkled. "Damn, I wish I were free tonight, but Manhattan calls. I've got a meeting I can't miss. My car should be here"—he checked his watch—"about now."

Before he gave me back my hands, he ran his thumb over the ring finger of my left one. Typical Charlie move. According to Emily Post or his mommy dearest, Kiki Pruitt, or whoever had taught Charlie the minutiae of etiquette, it would have been crass to cop a glimpse of my finger, so he'd found a discreet way to establish that the old girlfriend wasn't wearing a wedding band.

"You're in the phone book?"

"Well, no actually." I managed to get that out just as a large woman with a Goucher name tag touched his shoulder.

"I hate to interrupt, Your Honor, but your fans are waiting."

"I play with the Maryland Philharmonic," I said.

"I'll find you," His Honor answered. "May I call you?"

Now that got me—the request for permission that was pure Pruitt. I was doing just fine until that exquisitely polite expression of noblesse oblige from the haves to the haves-less. A ridiculous notion of power, *my* notion yanked from my insecure old times in Boston. He was just being his natural charming self. I nodded, feeling a lump bob in my throat.

"We'll talk" were his last words before he was led away. Correction: "Judith," with a smile and an incredulous shake of his head, was his actual last word.

Back at my car, I had second, third and fourth thoughts. Did I really need this foray into the past? If Charlie said he'd call, he'd call. And where would that lead? Nowhere was the best option. Somewhere was the worst. Final destination for both: dead end.

As I gazed morosely at a cherry tree that had just begun to shed, a Lincoln Town Car drove up and parked. Charlie's ride. To ferry him to the airport or Penn Station or all the way to New York and his Park Avenue apartment, transmogrified in my mind to a penthouse with a John Singer Sargent portrait of Great-

Great-Grandmama Pruitt over the sofa and a butler on call in the pantry.

So there it was. All laid out for me in living color. Charlie and I moved in different worlds that would only collide if we tried to nudge them closer.

What had I been thinking?

Chapter 3

On Monday morning, my only guaranteed day off in the week, I was in my neurologist's office for the first of my post-aneurysm yearly checkups.

I was fine. Dr. Creswell, God bless him, got that out of the way fast.

"We had a look at the 3-D angiogram of your brain and the radiologist and I concur: Everything looks just the way it should in there. No surprises. Coils are sitting pretty." He showed me the computer image of the platinum coils and the stent sealing off the vascular bubble that could have killed me. "Nothing remarkable like baby aneurysms hiding out. You should be good as new."

After exhaling the breath I'd been holding since waking up that morning, I grumbled—just for effect—"Some new. I'm going to be fifty in a few months." He and I were both aware there had been a time when we weren't sure I'd make it through the surgery, let alone to this milestone.

"Fifty, huh?" He checked the chart. "Could have fooled me. Well, there's no reason to believe you don't have another fifty ahead of you."

I thought of Lulu Cho and said, "I'd like that in writing, please."

He laughed. "And I'd like to give it to you. But what I've learned in my thirty years of practice is there's no such thing as a sure thing in medicine. No guarantees. I'm a doctor, not a fortune-teller."

Under the circumstances, ouch.

"What I *can* say is that everything looks good at the moment. I wish I could tell that to all my patients. This was a positive report, Judith. Go out and celebrate, and I'll see you next year."

When I called Marti to tell her that Creswell had given me an all clear, she whooped and said, "Fantastic news. Couldn't be happier for you and your empty head. And perfect timing—we can follow doctor's orders and celebrate at Tio Pepe's."

Marti patched together a respectable income from a number of part-time jobs—contributing editor at *Toque Blanche* magazine, food columnist for *The Gourmet Travel Digest*, head honcho at the blog Hot and Juicy, and her favorite: restaurant critic for the Baltimore *Herald* newspaper.

"Tio's is long overdue for a review," she said. "You can have your gastronomic orgasm. The sole with bananas." It was the restaurant's signature dish, decadently rich and my downfall.

I loved Tio's, but it was a low-ceilinged whitewashed grotto with the worst acoustics in town, which meant that everyone shouted and everyone heard what everyone was shouting. The regulars tended to know one another and table-hop nonstop, so it was like a bar mitzvah, only with shrimp. The place was jammed when I arrived. I waved to a Maryland Phil flutist as I made my way to our table. Marti was dressed in her restaurant reviewer's mufti, a large shadow-casting black straw hat and sunglasses that fooled no one, including the staff. Grinning, she gave me a thumbs-up, which might have triggered what happened next. As I slipped into the seat across from her and the waiter handed me my menu, I felt swamped by a wave of unadulterated joy—the first in a long time—which I attributed to having been given the green light on life that morning. *Probably* given. My grandma Roz would have been muttering kinehoras from the grave. But my live mother, quoting Buddha, overrode Raphael ghosts knocking on the wood of their own coffins: "Not dream of past, not dwell in future, live in present. This is true happiness, Judith."

"Earth to Judith, hell-*o*? You all right, kiddo?" Marti was tapping her spoon to her water glass for attention.

"Huh? Fine. I didn't realize it until I smelled the garlic, but I'm starved."

"Yeah, taking a pass on death will do that for you."

We ordered half the menu to sample.

"Save enough room for dessert. Gotta have dessert. Which reminds me . . ." Marti flung down her napkin. "Be right back."

When she returned wearing a cryptic smirk, we settled down to the serious business of journalistic eating, passing tastes and opinions to each other while Marti took notes under the drape of the tablecloth.

Nearly an hour and eight dishes later, as the busboy began to clear the table, she said, "Bueno. Three stars. Some things never change, thank God. Okay, now that your tummy's full and your mood is mellow, tell me how it went with you and The Barrister. Did he ravish you on the steps of Haebler Chapel?"

"How did you—?" The woman confounded me.

"Oh, puh-*leeze*," she cut me off. "As if you could have stayed away. He's like cream to your cat. Talk."

"Not much to talk about. We had maybe two minutes with students milling around. He's still charming. Attractive."

"Uh-oh."

"He was happy to see me. Stunned, but in a good way."

"And you?"

I shrugged. "It was a dumb move, stirring up all that old Charlie shit. I probably should have left well enough alone."

Marti scowled. "I've always hated that phrase. 'Well enough alone.' If all of us left well enough alone, life would be incredibly boring. But maybe in this case . . ."

I stared into my wineglass.

"Stop second-guessing yourself, Judith. If you hadn't wanted to see him, you wouldn't have gone to the lecture. Don't evil eye me. A woman's heart knows a woman's heart. Maybe you and I don't march to the same drummer sexually, but the heart is not the pussy. Speaking of which, I'll bet you didn't sleep with Geoff this weekend."

"I couldn't have been less in the mood. I had my period." For the first time in months, after I thought it had vanished forever.

"Well, aren't you Britney Spears. You do know Geoff's going to be heartbroken if you run off with The Barrister."

I played with my knife. "If you're so concerned about Geoff, why did you bait me with the article about Charlie? I don't get it. I thought you liked Geoff."

"Me? Hell, I love Geoff. If you loved Geoff, I never would have brought it up. But you don't seem to take him seriously and—"

"It's Geoff who doesn't take *me* seriously," I interrupted.

"—appreciate him. Maybe there's unresolved Charlie stuff in the way. So I figure you stop by, say hello, see what he looks like with a fat ass from sitting on the bench for thirteen years, get a whiff of the *Hah-vad* accent that can't possibly impress you anymore, say 'Nice meeting you again and thanks for most of the memories' and be done with him forever. Finally flush him out of your system so there's room for Geoff. But it didn't work that way, did it?"

I slugged the last of the white sangria. "Charlie wants to get together. To catch up." Marti gave off a low hum. "Please don't read more into it than old friends having a reunion."

"Oh, definitely and positively. And you won't go, of course. When is this so-called, never-to-be-realized reunion taking place?"

"He said he'd call."

"Nothing worse than waiting for a call from a once and/or future lover. Don't you dare let me catch you mooning by the phone like some teenager."

"Not to worry. I haven't been a teenager since . . . Come to think of it, I was never a teenager. Not the way you mean, with the dating and the phoning and the acting goofy. On the other hand, maybe I should make up for it now. Turn sweet sixteen instead of freakin' fifty."

"Now *that* is a brilliant idea!" Marti exclaimed.

As if on cue, a server emerged at my elbow with a slab of pine nut roll the size of a cedar shingle crowned with a single lit candle. I shot my lunch partner a poisonous arrow of a look. She'd done this dirty deed behind my back.

"*Feliz cumpleaños, Señora*," the handsome young waiter said, placing the pinwheel of custard and cake in front of me.

"Señor*ita*. And she's going to be fifty—can you believe that?" Marti drawled in her Georgia accent.

"Oh jeez," I said through gritted teeth. "Thanks a lot."

The waiter managed a reserved smile.

"Blow, honey." She glanced up at him. "Her, not you. Come on, Judith, make your wish."

I closed my eyes and fervently wished the waitstaff wouldn't burst into the happy birthday song.

My wish was granted, but after the server backed off, I hissed at Marti, "I can't believe you did this. My birthday's not until June."

"Big whoppin' deal. A few months." She extended a finger, plowed a line of pine nuts off the custard, and sucked. "Basic rule of thumb: Never turn down cake. And you can consider this your first party. Your pre-party. Didn't your mama ever tell you there's no such thing as too many parties?"

Grace Raphael (née Ryang Yun Mi), the former party girl, no longer knew from parties after my father skipped town two weeks after my sixth birthday. His business as a purveyor of lox and whitefish was floundering when he went west for a national smoked-fish conference, caught a live one—a rich, older woman—and never looked back. Lorna Chippendale aka "the chippie" aka the second Mrs. Raphael wasn't inclined to share her bounty with Irwin's first family and he wasn't punctilious about child support. Right after the split, he sent some money, some herring, a few presents. Then he faded away.

On her salary as a sewing machine operator at a bathing suit factory, my mother made sure we had enough to eat and a roof over our heads. And music lessons for me. Which were, in her mind, as much a necessity as milk and bread. There wasn't much left over for indulgences.

"I never had a birthday party in my life. At least none I can remember," I said, not uncheerily thanks to the sangria.

My confession precipitated an astounded whisk of breath. Then Marti said, "You never told me that. If that isn't the most pitiful thing I've ever heard. Makes me want to cry." She was a tough broad; tears were generally off-limits. She wasn't crying now, but her classic features were squinched in sympathy. "You never had a birthday party. We've got to rectify that." Her eyes were way too bright. "Lordy, Lordy, I am so ready to rectify."

"Marti . . ."

"Okay, I'm thinking fifty guests. One for each year of your life. And a theme." A warning tingle fired through me as Marti waxed enthusiastic. "You have to have a theme. Hawaii is hot this year. Leis, mai tais with the little umbrellas. And the men could wear those tacky flowered shirts."

She was putting me on with the Hawaiian business. Maybe. You never knew with Marti.

Oh God.

"Of course you have birthday party," my mother said later that afternoon. "First-year party, *Tol*, very important in Korea. Baby survive so we celebrate. In Korea, party held in banquet hall but I have only few Korean friends so we hold at home. Many balloons. Many gifts. You wear *hanbok* and I put makeup on you, like tradition. Aunt Phyllis try to make cake like *saeng* cream cake with canned fruit." She threw her head back and laughed. "Oh, so awful. But she try."

We were in the activity room of Blumen House, the assisted living complex where my mother lived. Really, the activity room was *where* she lived. She dropped into her fourth-floor apartment for sleep and breakfast, and took lunch and dinner in the communal dining room. But mornings were spent in the activity room playing gin rummy and canasta, afternoons were dedicated to mah-jongg marathons, and betweentimes she gambled online on one of the computers provided for residents.

I'd waited fifteen minutes for her to finish her mah-jongg game, which was conducted with all the fervor of a blood sport. Because she'd won the two-dollar pot, she was in a good mood.

"You pick out violin, remember I tell you."

I did remember the story of how I reached for the miniature violin over the stethoscope and the thread of long life on a table of objects set before me, but not that it happened at my first birthday party. I thought the choice that predicted my future had been made at one of my mother's fortune-telling sessions with

Lulu Cho. My childhood memories were spotty, a protective device, no doubt.

"Okay, first birthday," I said. "Were there any after that with friends my own age?"

"You were not friendly girl, Judith. Not many friends."

It was tough making them, I refrained from telling her, when you were shuttled to five schools in twelve years.

Every time the landlord raised our rent, we downshifted to an apartment for less money and the bonus of a free month. Lulu Cho's husband had a truck. He moved us, looking sadder and sadder as the neighborhoods got seedier and seedier.

"You have just one friend. Brenda Himmelstein. You love Brenda Himmelstein. Only one."

Third to fifth grade. My longest stretch in one school, PS 139, and my happiest because of Brenda Himmelstein with her normal family, her salesclerk mother, her bookkeeper father, even a brother who was a pain in the ass. She called me Mutt for my mixed background, but affectionately, and I called her Rusty for her red hair, and we lived in each other's pockets. Then the landlord raised the rent on our one-bedroom walk-up a block from the Himmelsteins and we tumbled way down to Bedford-Stuyvesant. Junior high school was hell. The few white girls on one side of the cafeteria, the majority black on the other—everyone ready to rumble—and me in no-man's-land, the Chinese (they never made the distinction; I let it ride) dork in thick glasses who had to leave early for her cello lessons and raised her hand in class too much.

Brenda and I tried to stay in touch. We phoned each other a few times a week, but her father wouldn't drive her to Bed-Stuy, we didn't have a car of course, and the subway stations in my new neighborhood were a mugger's paradise. By high school, Brenda was already only a bright memory in the prevailing gloom.

"Just the one party on my first birthday," I said, musing aloud. I should have been aware that my mother, an immigrant even after fifty years, was always on guard, listening carefully, eyes wary.

"What you expect? After your father left, you think have money for birthday parties? I put food on table. You have music lessons. You know how long I wore same winter coat?"

Back at Tio Pepe's I'd squirmed off the birthday party hook. I'd hosed down Marti and thought I'd closed the issue. But now I thought, *I'm giving myself a party for my fiftieth*. The thought made words, a string of them that detonated like firecrackers, jolting a table of Scrabble players across the room, snapping my mother's gaze from the solitaire hand she was laying out.

She closed her eyes and her lips moved silently as if she were a *mudang* like Lulu Cho taking messages from the spirits. Then she opened them to say, "Good for you. You deserve."

This is how she surprised me, my mother. Just when I thought she came close to matching her ex-husband's talent for self-absorption, she came through.

"But you give party for self? You have friends now. The people from orchestra and the . . ." She couldn't bring herself to say "lesbian," though she watched *Jerry Springer* on TV and had seen them pulling hair.

"Marti will take over," I said. "She's good at organizing things."

"I help, too," my mother said. "I pay."

"No, Mom, that's okay."

"I'm your mother. You listen to me. I pay. You don't have big wedding." With Todd, I'd hastened to wed so I wouldn't change my mind. "At this age, no chance. This your wedding money. Sky is limit. Up to three thousand."

My mother lived on social security and a small payment from

the Korean-American Benevolent Society. The whole thing sounded as fishy to me as *aek jeot*, the anchovy sauce we use in kimchi.

"How come I never heard about these savings? Let me get this straight. You're telling me you stashed away my wedding money and you never spent it in all these years? You didn't declare it when Blumen House added up your assets to figure out your rent on the sliding scale? You're saying—"

"Okay, okay," she interrupted. "You win, smart girl. Truth is I make killing at craps table last time in Atlantic City." She was staring at her hands in her lap and her complexion was flushed pink, but this correction might have been the truth—it was just the kind of jackpot my mother would come up with. She looked up, eyes faking hurt. "My money good. You make nice party. And take advice from me, Judith. Brenda Himmelstein probably still in Brooklyn. Look in phone book. Invite her."

My mother used present tense for all tenses. In this case, I think she meant past, or maybe she knew more than I gave her credit for. Because she said, "Invite her. You love her."

I phoned Marti on my way home. "I've changed my mind about the party."

"No kidding. Well, I guess it's a good thing I started working on the guest list. You'll help me fill in names. I should have some invitations for you to choose from midweek. And I've got a few ideas about the venue."

"I can't believe you've already . . . and I'm not even sure I . . ."

She cut off my stammering. "You don't have to be sure of everything, Judith. I know you play classical, but, honestly, it's okay to improvise once in a while. Relax." She took a deep breath as an example. "It's going to be wonderful."

Chapter 4

❧

At Tuesday morning's rehearsal, Vijay Patel, the concert-master, approached as the stage door closed behind me. "You're in first chair again tonight."

It took me a moment, but I got it. "It's Richard, right? Oh God, what now?"

Richard Tarkoff, our principal cellist, my stand partner, my mentor, my dear friend, was seventy-two and battling melanoma. Two years before, a nasty black mole had surfaced on his cheek. Months later another appeared on his leg. As new lesions cropped up, his Johns Hopkins surgeons hacked off pieces of him until, he joked, all that would be left would be his bow hand and two kneecaps. He'd finished his third round of chemo the week before and this was to be his first night back.

"He came in, began his run-through and stopped eight bars in. I'll tell you, Judith, he scared the hell out of me. He was swaying as if he was going to pass out. His wife drove him in. She's on her way back to get him. I hope I'm wrong, but this could be it."

Richard's fondest wish was to die in the chair. Some musicians signed off when they noticed flagging technique, but many wanted to play until the bow had to be pried from their cold, dead fingers. Making music was a passion, one of the last to go.

The concertmaster cast a grim glance at Richard leaning on his cane, hobbling a path between the men's room and the artists' exit, and breathed a sigh. "No one wants to say the words none of us want to hear. But from the looks of it, we'll be posting auditions for his seat sooner rather than later. I'm assuming you . . ."

I knew what he was assuming. As associate principal, I was in a prime position to advance to the top spot. But I wasn't a shoo-in. I'd have to compete with our own musicians and with cellists from around the world if I wanted the job. Did I want the job? Right now, watching Richard panting to a stop, I didn't even want to think about it.

"Later," I said to Vijay.

I walked across the room into the embrace of my friend's one free arm.

"Can you believe this shit, Judith?" Richard's face appeared steroid swollen and as fragile as porcelain, but he managed a smile, as thin as a spider crack. After years together, we'd become expert at reading each other's subtle signals, a knack that made for a successful professional partnership but sometimes produced TMI personally. As in, I didn't like the look in his eyes. Behind the battlefield of anger and frustration, I thought I detected the white flag of surrender.

"I was so ready to get back in the harness. I felt great when I woke up this morning. Then, just as I start going through the Schubert here, I get light-headed, shaky, and my fingers won't work. I can't get the bow under control. That's a new one. Goddamn chemo kills the good cells, too. It keeps you alive, but for what?"

I gave him nothing creative, only what could have been the

truth and what I wanted to believe: "I think you jumped the gun coming back. This will pass. You just need more time."

"Yeah, my better half, smarter half told me the same thing. Too much, too soon. But I was sure I was okay to play." He pulled a handkerchief from his trousers pocket and mopped his forehead. "I don't know anything for sure anymore. Maybe I'm deluding myself. Maybe the time has come to hang it up."

"Maybe it hasn't," I countered. I needed to keep the delusion going too.

A horn sounded outside. "Sarah. Coming to fetch me. Thank God I didn't marry an I-told-you-so woman." He'd lost his eyebrows to the chemo, but the exposed skin furrowed. "You handling that bastard Schubert with no problems?"

The Ninth's second movement was a killer, but I'd done fine with it the night before. I nodded.

"Of course. Never had a doubt. Get the feel of the first chair, Judith. It looks like it's going to be yours from now on."

Sarah leaned on the horn. Richard waved off my offer of a supporting arm and straightened his spine. The mind-body connection must have kicked in because he paused, then said, "On the other hand, a few more days of R and R, and I could pull a Lazarus. So don't get *too* comfortable."

"I'll keep the seat warm for you," I promised.

"With that little tush?"

Ah, the witty, sparring Richard was still in there behind the suffering. I loved hearing him laugh.

In the musicians' lounge, Geoff Birdsall (my lover, significant other, whatever you're supposed to call your boyfriend after your acne has cleared) added milk to my tea and handed me the cup. "Sorry about Richard. Damned shame. But at least he knows the principal seat will be in good hands."

"If I make it."

He took a deep swig of his coffee and peered over the rim of the mug. "Do you want it?"

"I want Richard to stay alive and keep the seat," I said.

"Come on, Jude, that's not going to happen."

I sighed. "Then I want first chair more than anything in the world."

"And knowing you, you've been wanting it forever."

"No, not all the way back. When I was a kid, especially a teenager, my dream was to be a star, in the spotlight, solo, famous. That's what teenagers want. Fuck-you fame."

"Fuck-you fame. I like it." Geoff chuckled.

"On my street, the girls wanted to be Pam Grier. I wanted to be Jacqueline du Pré, without the MS of course. But you know what happened in my twenties."

I'd screwed up the finals of a competition that meant more to me than it should have. How I lost it made me wonder whether I was cut out to be a solo artist. As in not being quite good enough. Or not having the temperament or the ego for it. But that reaction had been knee-jerk, and might have passed if I hadn't fallen in love with being a part of an orchestra.

The thing is, an orchestra is a family, and beyond my mother—all credit to her—I'd never had one. Never experienced that jumble of love and hurt, intimacy and irritation, the craziness, the caring, the mess of it. I'd never even met any of my Korean relatives. Occasionally, when she got tipsy on rice wine or gin, my mother would reminisce about her family in North Korea.

As a teenager, she'd had big dreams, too. Leaving her parents and brother behind on their small farm in the north, she and her sister had fled south to the city to find work. Then the war hit and Seoul changed hands four times. In the chaos the girls got separated.

"My sister get trap behind north line. Never see her again. Have photo of parent but not her. So beautiful, Min Sun. You look like her. Who knows if she still alive? Life so hard there. Very bad place." And she'd blot tears for her vanished family, for herself, for me and our loss.

As for my father's clan, the center hadn't held. I could count on his sister, Phyllis, to keep me attached, but I'd always felt like the outsider, the not-quite-one-of-us, the oh-poor-Judith.

It was only after I'd joined my first professional orchestra that I felt the presence of family. And when I needed a larger home, the Maryland Philharmonic took me in. A move that had turned out far better for me than any fuck-you fame.

I'd been associate for nearly ten years and would have been comfortable in the second chair for as long as Richard held the top slot. But now, with the impending vacancy, I was being given a chance to reclaim some of the old dream. The principal got the solos. So, God yes, I wanted it. But there was a risk. If I didn't win the seat, I would feel too humiliated to stay on. That would be a loss I wasn't sure I'd survive. Take the Maryland Philharmonic from me and . . . honestly, I didn't know what or who I'd be.

But I wasn't going to tell Geoff that.

The big, handsome Aussie gave me an approving nod. "You need to want it heart, gut, liver, and lights. I give management a day or two to post the opening. Nothing to stop you. You've got a clean bill of health, so there's no worry about taking on more than you're able."

I'd phoned him right after my neurologist appointment the day before, eliciting a "Hurrah for you, Jude" at my good report. Now he pecked the spot on my temple above the life-saving coil. "I have to keep reminding myself you're fine. That every headache isn't an aneurysm."

"Yeah, and I have a bitch of one now." I should never have mentioned it. The color drained from his face.

With a singular exception, Geoff Birdsall had no fear. He'd wrestled a fifty-pound squid off the Great Barrier Reef and his idea of fun was cliff diving into the Loch Raven Reservoir. But the possibility of my suffering another aneurysm terrified him. "We're ten minutes by car from the Hopkins ER if you want to check it out," he said.

No, I assured him, there was a difference between this hormone-driven throbbing in my temples and the blinding pain of a hatchet sunk into my forehead signaling an arterial bubble was poised to burst. "A couple of aspirin and I'll be fine."

He looked doubtful and kept watch on me throughout rehearsal. He really cared.

I nailed the Schubert. Technically and creatively. I played and the world fell away. Richard's illness. The impending big birthday. My mother with all her craziness. Charlie. The dull tail end of my headache. God, I loved my work.

The audience did too. Baltimore audiences are incredibly generous. Give them the flimsiest reason, a show-off cadenza, daring inflexions, and they're on their feet yelling bravos. And the Maryland Phil's second female conductor, Angela Driscoll, was, in the tradition of her predecessor, a gracious commander. She motioned for me to stand not once but twice to acknowledge the applause. Among the approving *tap-tap* of bows on instruments from my peers, a voice stood out: Geoff rumbling, "Well done, well done."

"Brava, Jude," he said when he caught up with me on my way to the women's dressing room. "Not bad for a night's work. Headache all gone? Splendid." He was also interested in weather conditions in my southern hemisphere.

"Your visitor still in town?"

It took me a moment, but when he raised his eyebrow salaciously, I got it.

"Vanished, without a trace." In perimenopause, your period's here today, gone tomorrow.

"The perfect guest." He smiled.

"Who wore out her welcome a couple of years ago."

Secretly, though, I was pleased she hadn't left for good. For some reason, the idea of menstruating even once every so often was reassuring. How many AARP women still got their period? I had no illusions about making at fifty the baby I'd longed for at thirty and forty. My eggs were more poached than the ones they served at the Café Hon under hollandaise. No, this was just a reminder that the tap on the juices of youth hadn't shut down entirely. There was life in the old girl yet.

"Let's do a special dinner tonight to mark your two standings," Geoff suggested. Our usual postconcert supper was bacon and eggs at the Double T Diner. "I'm thinking mussels at Petit Louis. How does that sound?" Like a shellfish aphrodisiac, I thought. "Dessert at your house." I knew Geoff's idea of dessert. Something incredibly delicious that burned off the calories from dinner and then some.

It was Tuesday, two days past Sunday, and Charlie hadn't called. Obviously, he wasn't in any rush. Rush for what? For—with the exception of an absurd fantasy on my part that I was loath to admit even to myself—nothing. On the other hand, I had a very real fantastic something peering at me questioningly with smoky eyes.

"You're on," I said.

"On is good," Geoff responded. "Actually, I have a feeling on will be exceptional this evening."

. . .

It was. Geoff was a pleasure maven, an expert. It wasn't just the sex, which was spectacular. It was much more.

Home from dinner, he stood at my kitchen window, one hand clutching a chilled bottle of Foster's, the other, warmer, creeping under my sweater to stroke my back as he stared at the cherry tree on my front lawn. Its blossoms were lit iridescent by a full moon.

"Bloody glorious, isn't it? And look, a rabbit!" There was indeed a small brown bunny sitting under the tree.

What knocked me out about Geoff was that he took pleasure from what slipped by most people. He'd point out to me how savory garlic smelled when the olive oil was at a perfect temperature in the pan. The rough elegance of some hip-hop artist spinning street poetry. "Come," he'd call, "you have to see this." And *this* would be a battalion of ants marching across the kitchen table. I'd run for the Raid and he'd marvel at their strange little bodies working together to haul crumbs.

Maybe because when I was a kid and the world around me didn't offer me much of anything I wanted, and too much of what made me scared or sad, I'd gotten into the habit of blanking it out with music and books. But Geoff Birdsall had the luck of a happy childhood and he'd evolved into that rare creature, a happy man. Pretty soon I began to see small wonders the way he did, and lately I'd been edging toward happy myself.

How long would it last? I hadn't a clue. After my nasty breakup with Charlie and the hasty, weird marriage to Todd, I'd dismissed the possibility of anything permanent. And Geoff was king in the land of the uncommitted, so we were a perfect match. I took the relationship for what it was, as something I understood: Geoff and I made beautiful music together, but music fades. I decided to appreciate his easy charm, inexhaustible energy, and sky-high libido for whatever time we had together. He also made a succulent lamb stew. The man could cook. Who could ask for anything more?

Now he kissed the pulse in my neck and held the kiss for two beats.

"I'm thinking we could go to Japan this summer," he said, seemingly out of the blue, but I got the drift: cherry blossoms/Japan. "Not Tokyo, which is just another big, crowded city, but a country inn with the shoji screens and futons. How's that for my birthday gift to you?"

"A trip is a wonderful gift, Geoff. But Japan?" I wrinkled my nose. "Not to be piggy, but do I get a choice of where?"

"Your birthday, your choice." He pulled me tight against him. "I'm up for anything." Yes, I could feel he was. He pressed harder to underscore the point.

We were facing an exhausting schedule at the orchestra. "Maybe just kick back on an island somewhere? Antigua. St. Martin. Only a few hours' flight and the pace is easy and slow."

At the mention of slow, his hand tugged my skirt up to bunch around my hips, then traveled to my thighs. "Right, I like easy and slow." His voice had gone silky.

"Beaches." I was into it now. I heard my own response, thick with desire.

"Good beaches on the Riviera."

"Too many fat Russian mafia in Speedos."

"Hmm. The Greek islands? Santorini. White sand. Cliffside nightclubs where we'll drink ouzo and dance in the moonlight. Maybe we can get in some hang gliding." Forget that. "And long afternoon naps where I'd . . . and you'd . . . and we'd . . ." He whispered a menu of appetizers more spicy than taramasalata. "How does that sound?"

It sounded exactly like Geoff. Felt like him, too, after I unbuttoned his shirt. He worked out and his chest was as glossy and muscular as those airbrushed pecs on the covers of romance novels. My hand skimmed its smooth surface and he groaned and inched me toward the kitchen table. For Geoff any flat surface would serve. Failing that, he'd make do with a broom closet.

"Not here. My lower back's been acting up."

"I love older women." His laugh was husky.

"Sofa?" I mumbled.

"Bed," he said. Bed was best. He did this incredible trick with pillows and a rolled-up quilt. And other jazzy moves. He had a large repertoire, sweet and hot.

"So good," I said when it was over, when I could catch my breath.

"Just *good*?" He was propped on his elbow, gazing at me in mock alarm. "Not exceptional?"

"Exceptional," I agreed. And it had been, in spite of a minor interference during the blissful post-orgasmic decrescendo when The Barrister's face had surfaced.

"I can't allow a blot on my record. Give me twenty minutes and we'll try again," Geoff promised with the assurance of a man in his prime.

We did. It was even better the second time. No ghosts.

Chapter 5

On Thursday, I still hadn't heard from Charlie, but Marti had called three times and then stopped by with a loose-leaf notebook crammed with party-related materials she'd collected over the last few days. First, we chose the invitation. I passed on the one with a cartoon Maxine bitching about support stockings and droopy boobs for something blandly tasteful in ecru with engraved lettering. Done.

Next, she briefed me on the venue. She'd narrowed the choices to the Parthenon, the Hamden Rotary's clubhouse, "and"—she consulted her notes—"there's the Belvedere," naming the Baltimore landmark that had once been the city's most famous hotel. The building had been converted to condos in the nineties, and its two gorgeous ballrooms on the twelfth floor were perfect for weddings and other celebrations. "The Belvedere will give me a twenty percent discount because the catering manager and I went to culinary school together, but it's still pricey, probably out of your range."

"The Belvedere, definitely." It wasn't even a horse race. "My mother is footing the bill."

Marti's face brightened. "No shit? Gracie came through. Your father die and leave her guilt gelt?"

"We should only be so lucky. No, she struck it rich at the craps tables. Or maybe baccarat. I can't remember."

My mother was—had been for as long as I could remember—a gambler. As an Asian, she had gambling in her blood, she told me. "Korean people love to bet anytime, anything."

In my childhood, she'd given me—a kid—sucker's odds on the outcome of cockroach races she set up on our kitchen floor. And she'd pocket my pennies, too. "You always pay off, Judith. It is honorable thing to do."

"Well, good for Mama," Marti drawled on. "I guess this means I strike Irwin Raphael's name off the guest list."

"Not funny, Marti."

Without my father-in-name-only, she still insisted on fifty. Fiftieth birthday, fifty guests. Propitious.

"That's a lot of people. I'm not inviting the whole freakin' orchestra," I grumbled.

"Of course not. You'll cherry-pick. You'll want the fifty who loomed largest in your life. The ones who made a difference. Current, past, whatever."

"Brenda Himmelstein," I blurted. "My mother gave me strict instructions to invite Brenda Himmelstein."

"Then by all means invite your grade school best friend. *Only* friend in your pathetic antisocial childhood. Just joking." Marti flicked me a semi-penitent glance.

"I've searched for her on the Net but I guess she's married with a new name," I said. "And she probably left Brooklyn. How can you track someone down after all these years?"

"Leave it to me and my laptop. There are all kinds of Web sites out there willing to tell the world your deepest, darkest secrets for a price. I could turn up Jimmy Hoffa with enough time and money. I'll find Brenda." Marti was like a multi-armed Hindu goddess with an inspired energy and a divine will you really didn't want to cross. The pen, in one of her eight hands, was poised. "Okay, who else?" Her eyes lit with a wicked twinkle. "How about Eloise Flint?"

"How about the head of al-Qaeda while you're de-scumming the universe?" I snarled. "Eloise Flint. Over my dead body. Or better yet, hers."

Acclaimed cellist, five-time Grammy winner for best classical performance, international pain-in-the-ass renowned for her arrogance and her hairspring temper, Eloise Flint had been my personal and professional nemesis for almost half my life. She'd been a classmate and pseudo-friend at the conservatory, but when Charlie dumped me, she moved in on him like a spider on a fly, rendering my humiliation complete and very public. Five years later, she and I had met up again. And I'd had a chance to even the score.

Marti had heard the story ad nauseam, so she should have known better than to joke about Eloise, but for Marti a good laugh took precedence over the pain of faded heartbreak any day. This time, though, she saw my face and must have deduced she'd gone too far because she quickly said, "Strike the bitch. Bad joke. On the other hand, I was thinking you'd like to include Tim Beckersham, son of the late Florence."

That worked. I smiled at the memory of the plump English woman, my intrepid cello teacher who had followed me into the bowels of Bed-Stuy for my after-school lessons. Fiercely determined not to let my talent go under, Florence Beckersham had managed to tack together bus transfers and subway routes and make her way to whatever high-crime neighborhood my mother and I had landed in on our downward spiral. But she was equally committed to connecting with me, the girl who—except for my brief friendship with Brenda—had no one to talk to or be heard by.

My mother had been depressed and exhausted most of the time. Circumstance had stripped life pretty much to its essentials. Communication beyond the directives—"Take bath now, Judith"—and the interrogatives—"You finish homework? How long you practice?"—had been limited.

Only while tucking me in at night did *uhm-mah* make time for me. Grace sat on the side of my bed in the room we shared and, as her mother and *her* mother before *her* had, she sang the traditional Korean folk song *Arirang* in an enchantingly soft voice. In winter, tucking the quilt under my chin, in spring, as a fresh tar-scented city breeze blew the sheets-made-into-curtains into ghost shapes in the half dark, she smoothed my bangs back from my forehead and crooned *Arirang* for my lullaby. I lived on that nightly sliver of song, that precious, comforting stroke of affection from my mother.

Otherwise, it was Mrs. Beckersham who guided my emotional life. Mrs. Beckersham who explained that ignoring the taunts at school would make me a stronger person. Mrs. B who scrubbed away at my lack of confidence and helped me polish the essay that got me into the New England Conservatory.

After my graduation, Mrs. B and I stayed in touch. Then I moved to Baltimore and she retired to California. The last time I saw her, I was playing a Mozart festival in Berkeley and her son drove her over from San Francisco. Backstage, while Tim beamed, she and I hugged and wept.

"I knew it from the first, Judith. You were just so special—as a musician, yes, but more importantly as a child," she'd said.

Six months later, she was dead.

"I have Tim's address," I said to Marti. "He sends me a

Christmas card every year. I remember him as a kid doing his homework at our recital rehearsals. Now he's a doctor living on the West Coast, so he probably won't come in for it, but, sure, invite him."

"Okay, who else? Charlie Pruitt?"

"Ah, the Harvard Houdini. Vanished! He said he'd call and he hasn't." So much for tracking me down. Nothing had appeared in my mail cubby at the Berenson Concert Hall, and the orchestra's webmaster confirmed that no one had attempted to trace me through the musicians' page. "Screw Charlie Pruitt."

She gave me a measuring look. "Maybe you should call him when you're in New York this weekend. Casual like. That is, if you want to follow up." The Maryland Phil's annual performance at Carnegie Hall was Saturday evening.

"Forget it. If Charlie wants to reconnect, he's going to have to come after me."

Fat chance, but Marti said, "Atta girl. You're not nineteen anymore and bowled over by the fancy background. I gotta tell you, Jude, your story, outie impressed with innie, is never going to be made into a major motion picture starring Lucy Liu. It's a new day, and you're not the same old wannabe, and all that snooty Episcopalian bullshit doesn't wash anymore. Trust me, honey, I was a Southern Baptist before I expelled myself from the fold for lusting after women—WASP is *très passé*. Check the demographics. And can you imagine anything more fashionable than the Jewish-Asian mix? You're finally in style. Now *you're* in, *he's* out."

"Right," I said. "And we only met for five minutes on Sunday and it was so superficial. He probably thought it over and decided we really had nothing to talk about. Polluted water under the bridge and all that."

So why did I feel so—I don't know—dumped? Again.

. . .

The first time, back in Cambridge, had been orchestrated by his parents. Not that he hadn't played his part brilliantly, but Kiki and Don held the baton, the purse strings, the power, and Charlie's balls in escrow.

I was astonished when my romance blew up after two years. What an idiot! With my head in the clouds, you'd think I'd have noticed the thunder rumbling around me. Almost from the beginning, Charlie had dropped hints that I wasn't what Mum and Dad had in mind for the son they called Chip. There were hundreds of girls more appropriate than I, daughters of his mother's bridge partners, daughters of his father's colleagues at the law firm and chums from the Fenwick Club and the New York Athletic Club.

Donald Pruitt was principal senior partner in the law firm of Pruitt, Bryce and Summerville, LLP, with offices in New York, London, Bermuda, and Hong Kong. The firm had been founded by Charlie's great-grandfather, who'd married a Rockefeller cousin and sired eight children, every one a winner. Charlie's mother, Kathryn with a K and a Y, she reminded me twice during my visit to their Sutton Place apartment, was a direct descendant of Willem Van Tiller, who'd helped settle Manhattan Island. She was known as Kiki by those closest to her. I would never call her Kiki, I knew by the time I left that afternoon.

On that visit, my own ancestral tree was shaken until every nut and rotten apple had hit the ground. "Tell me about your family" didn't mean just the immediate or the current. I put the best slant I could on what was essentially unslantable. I was a direct descendant of Chaim Rafalsky, milkman of Lvov, and his wife, Malka. On my paternal side, the family history didn't go back more than three generations; Hitler had seen to that with the destruction of all Hebrew records. On my mother's side, I came from a long line of peasants and shopkeepers from North

Hwanghae Province. Irwin Raphael had fought in the Korean War and that's how he'd met my mother. One boozy evening—I was about seventeen—while Mom and I played gin and she also drank it, she let slip that back in Seoul she'd been an entertainer of unspecified talents. "Sang, danced, all kind things." (Probably a bar girl.) Needless to say, my father's mother took one look at the skinny Asian chicken of a woman standing in her kitchen, one listen to my father's intro of the chicken as his wife, and had to be forcibly restrained from turning on the gas and shoving her freshly permed head into the oven.

"Once our family marries we stay married," Kiki Pruitt had informed me on my first and only visit. There was no record of divorce in the family back to William of Orange on one side and just after Henry VIII on the other. In other words, Charlie had better nip this in the bud or I'd be his mistake for life.

In the apartment on Sutton Place the day I met Kathryn with a K, if she could have put her head in *her* oven, she would have, but she wasn't in charge of her kitchen. A black woman named Reba ran the household. Reba helped bring Charlie up. Correction: it was Reba who raised Charlie. She'd taken the newborn from the nurse's arms for the drive home from the hospital and never let go. Six months after my introduction to the Pruitts, she retired, having put in twenty-two years of service.

She moved back to her rural South Carolina home, where she lived on social security and the small pension Kiki and Don doled out. From his spending money, Charlie sent her an extra hundred dollars a month. He also sent her photos of himself, some including me, which, her daughter wrote, Mama passed around as if Charlie was "her own flesh-and-blood son. And the girlfriend is right pretty."

Every August, Charlie visited Reba, stayed the weekend at a cousin's house, and treated the whole family to dinner at the local barbecue restaurant. When her daughter called to report the housekeeper's death, he sobbed in my arms. Then he cut classes to fly to South Carolina for the funeral, where he gave the eulogy. He'd adored Reba. His mother, not so much. But Kiki wielded serious influence. I had a feeling that if Reba had been there to drum some common sense into Charlie's head, we would have stayed together. But Reba wasn't there, Kiki was, and we didn't . . . stay together.

The last couple of weeks with Charlie had been hell. By then, I had a premonition of what was coming, but was helpless to deflect it. And I loved him with every nerve ending in my body.

He was smart—*really* smart, a deep thinker, not just clever. He was a brilliant bridge player. He taught me bridge and never yelled. He was charming. Generous in bed, a deft and tender first lover. Witty, but without the brittle edge of sarcasm. He had this trick of raising one eyebrow that cracked me up. Reba had taught him how to cook, and he made the best French toast, which he served me in bed Sunday mornings after we made love. He recited case law to me as if it were poetry. I dreamed of him at night after we'd been together the entire previous day. I was saturated with Charles Evans Pruitt.

He was equally besotted, but he couldn't make up his mind about the relationship. About next steps. I tugged one way. His parents tugged the other. We were living together then, and one afternoon I walked in from a lesson to find him stinking of scotch and packing his books. I sat quietly in our only living room chair, half jury/half condemned woman, as he told me we weren't right for each other. It wasn't just his parents. Dr. Joyce Brothers said matches in which the parties came from significantly different backgrounds were doomed to failure. He loved me with all his heart, he declared. He would die for me. But he wouldn't, couldn't marry me.

"They cut you off, right?"

He sat staring at me, holding a copy of *The Devil's Alternative* by Frederick Forsyth.

"Okay, disinherited you. Whatever people like your people do when they want to twist their kid's arm."

"It's not just the money. I need the connections. My father knows everyone who's anyone in New York law. He can pull strings."

"You're brilliant. You can do it on your own—you don't need his strings."

"You don't know the profession, Judith. I love the law. It's my passion. I'll need help if I want to practice it at the highest level."

"And I'd make a lousy wife for a United States Supreme Court justice."

"You're wonderful. I love you. And you're going to make someone the absolutely right wife. God knows, I wish it were me."

Were, not *was*. That Choate education.

"But it's not going to work for us."

And that was it.

Or not, because for decades after, Charlie was with me. I subscribed to the *New York Times* so I could check for articles about him. I read his father's obituary. The engagement announcement with the photo of his wife to be. She was gorgeous. Blond and not dumb, a psychologist. I didn't see a wedding announcement, though I scoured for it. I read Chloe's birth announcement, cut it out, and put it in an unlabeled box I'd dedicated to Charlie stuff. Then I went into the bathroom and threw up.

Ten years ago I canceled the *Times* subscription. My shrink and I agreed Google was too much of a temptation, but by now I was driven by mere curiosity. The fire had burned itself out finally.

From the lack of interest since the Goucher meeting, I figured Charlie had no intention of stirring the embers. Me either. I didn't see the point in raking dead ashes. And yet, there seemed to have been a spark between us in that lecture hall. With Charlie, it had been a long time since I'd trusted my judgment. Yes? No? His silence told me no.

Chapter 6

Old joke: Woman stops policeman to ask for directions. "How do I get to Carnegie Hall?" Cop answers: "Practice, lady, practice."

My mother didn't get it. "Of course practice. How else you get to Carnegie Hall?"

The first time I went there as a solemn little girl of nine, I'd been playing cello for two years. My aunt Phyllis, a social worker with the only cultural pretensions in the Raphael family, had bought tickets for her and my uncle Arnold for a Sunday afternoon performance. Last minute, they couldn't go. So Mom and I inherited the seats. The Cavendish Quartet sat in a pool of light onstage and played their collective heart out and I thought I was in the balcony of heaven.

It took me another twenty-five years and a contract as tutti cellist with the Maryland Philharmonic, but I finally got to play Carnegie Hall. I've played there once a year since, fall or spring, and nothing—not sex, not even crème brûlée—gives me more of a high than walking onto those brushed oak floorboards to warm up.

That's what I was doing that sultry-for-April Saturday evening and the scene evoked the same swelling in my chest as it had the first time I'd set foot on that stage. Only tonight was bittersweet for me. It was Richard's illness that had led to my solo debut here. I stopped to take it all in, and that's when I heard Geoff, whose embouchure—the position his lips shaped around the trumpet's mouthpiece—gave him a signature sound. He was working through a tricky part in the Stravinsky.

I turned and nodded. He winked. Then it was down to business.

People can and do approach the musicians in this nether time. Mothers haul little Dylan or Tiffany to the proscenium to ask the nice lady with the cello questions about how many hours a week she practices. Acquaintances walk up to say hello. Old boyfriends appear out of nowhere.

From the stage with the houselights on, you can make out individual faces to about the tenth row. But I was focused on warming up, and even as he approached I didn't see him coming. After I finished tinkering with my cello, I looked up and there he was. My heart lurched as if it had been jump-started.

"Jesus, Charlie, you scared me!"

He gave a low laugh. "Sorry, Ju-ju. I didn't mean to startle you. I was aiming for a pleasant surprise."

Ju-ju. Holy God, I hadn't heard that name in twenty-five years. Charlie had coined it at the height of our heat. I was his Ju-ju, he'd murmured in bed, his fetish, his lucky charm. I hadn't had the heart to tell him that Ju-ju meant "breast milk" in Korean.

"I said I'd find you." He looked up with a Stan Laurel smile. Totally innocent. I wanted to say, *Actually, you said you'd call,* but I didn't.

He tapped his rolled program against his palm. "Looking forward to this. You know how I love Stravinsky."

Had I known? If so, I'd forgotten.

"Look, I realize this is shamefully last minute, but I'm hoping you might be free for dinner."

"Tonight?" I said. I thought I saw Geoff's large shadow looming. Someone behind me coughed baritone.

"Tonight. And I apologize for not contacting you earlier to suggest it. This week was a killer. In any event, if you don't have previous plans."

Now, had Geoff and I made a date for dinner, one on one, I like to think I wouldn't have ditched him. But when the orchestra plays New York, a large group of us goes out together afterward to grab a bite. So . . .

I waited a beat, wanting to make Charlie sweat for it. Charlie Pruitt, in his impeccable pin-striped suit and silk tie with a pattern of Harvard crests, was no schvitzer. He was a first-class lawyer who relished winning an argument. "I'll buy you the best steak in the city, or if you've converted to vegetarian, the most succulent white asparagus this side of the Loire. And the place I have in mind does a mean crème brûlée." That last was to let me know he remembered my favorite dessert. To clinch the deal, he broke out the dazzling Pruitt smile.

At twenty, I'd found the slight overbite irresistible. Pushing fifty, I managed to resist it for about ten seconds before succumbing with a stammer: "Dinner. Yes, fine. Sure. Of course." I caught a breath and moved to an articulate finish. "Give me twenty minutes after curtain and I'll meet you at the artists' entrance."

Charlie bobbed a little bow to convey his gratitude. Then he said, "You've made an old guy very happy." He was only fifty-four. That old-guy crapola had to be an affectation or his idea of a joke. But if it wasn't either . . . I was forty-nine. What did that make me?

In spite of my advanced age, I had no problem with the *Don Juan*, which can be a little dodgy in the middle. For just a moment in the second movement, I lost my focus. *Oh God, Charlie is out there!* But I lassoed it back. Twenty-two minutes after the last bravo faded, seven after I made hurried excuses to the second violin who'd organized our group dinner, and five after I scribbled an explanatory note to Geoff, I walked, Charlie guiding me with his hand on my elbow, from the Fifty-Seventh Street exit to the curb where his driver waited.

"I hope you like this surprise better than the first," Charlie said ten minutes later.

He'd taken my hand to help me exit the Town Car and now it was folded into his very warm one as I stood on the sidewalk, peering through Manhattan's fragrant spring darkness.

"Your mother's place?" We were in front of the apartment building where Kiki had grilled me like a burger that first/last time I met her. I shivered at the thought of resuming our acquaintance.

"Look up."

The Pruitt co-op, the approximate size of a football field, was on the nineteenth floor.

"No." Charlie tipped my chin with his finger to guide my gaze. "Way up." And suddenly it became clear.

"The roof garden?"

"One and the same. I hope you don't mind. The steak and the crème brûlée were bait and switch. I thought a picnic would be nice."

Based on our history, that could have been the most romantic gesture since *Romeo and Juliet*. Of course, considering how that pair ended up, maybe not the wisest. I felt myself losing it, so I leapt over the messy emotions to my sense of humor.

"Again? We had a picnic up there twenty-seven years ago. Can't you come up with anything new?"

When the tipping finger brushed my cheek, I said, "It's a lovely idea, Charlie."

On our first date in New York, spring vacation of my senior year, Charlie had arranged dinner for two up among the trees in planters and the pots of impatiens on the building's roof garden. There were no tables, so he'd spread a blanket, and as the moon rose over the East River we ate pâté, lobster salad, and chocolate mousse and drank champagne. I'd wanted to make love under the stars, but Charlie was afraid the doorman might stumble upon us during his nightly rounds, so we did it his way, the conservative way. We went down to the Pruitts' apartment—Kiki and Don were at the house in Maine—and made love in his parents' bed. So sinful. So heady. So nauseating. A half hour later, wine, butter, and chocolate churning, I raced to his mother's bathroom and threw up in her bidet. You can take the girl out of Brooklyn . . .

Tonight there was a wrought-iron table set for two.

"This is a common area. But a little baksheesh, a little shmear"—he rubbed his fingertips together—"for the doorman and the cleaning crew buys a lot of privacy." A descendant of the founding fathers shmeared. I loved this country. "No one will bother us, I promise."

Charlie hooked up his iPod to a portable speaker and lit a couple of fishnet table candles to augment the soft light cast by the torchieres. He emptied the contents of the picnic basket and arranged napkins, silverware, and the food: roast chicken, green salad, whole-wheat baguettes. Dessert was two chocolate-dipped strawberries.

"Les Palmiers?" I asked, remembering the French restaurant around the corner that had provided the food first time around.

"Ah, long gone." Les Palmiers had been our restaurant.

Spring break, summer, Christmas—when they dressed a tree with antique French ornaments—we celebrated there. Our three-month anniversary, six months, one year. At first Charlie seemed proud to show me off—an exotic, almond-eyed, small-boned brunette, not your standard blond thick-ankled Mount Holyoke deb. I was the perfect weapon for a postponed adolescent rebellion. But when things started going downhill between us—as his mother hammered away at the inappropriateness of his choice— we stopped going to Les Palmiers. By that time I suppose I'd become an embarrassment to him. Or maybe he just didn't want to sully the good memories with the grime that love picks up on the slide.

Now he piled my plate with salad. "I hope you don't mind the menu. I've got to watch my cholesterol. Those strawberries are for you. I know how you love your chocolate."

He played with the iPod and released the damaged voice of Édith Piaf. Just as we'd had our restaurant, Charlie and I also had our song, plucked from its background music: "Non, Je Ne Regrette Rien."

"I have burnt my memories, my sorrows, my pleasures. I don't need them anymore. Swept away the love affairs and all their tremblings," the Little Sparrow sang. *Oh, brother.*

Halfway through the salad, Charlie presented the requisite photo of his daughter. At seventeen Chloe was a stepped-up version of Kiki—same retroussé nose that made her look as if she were sniffing something slightly off, and the mouth was unadulterated Van Tiller.

"She's beautiful," I said, handing it back. "Sorry. I can't reciprocate. I used to have a cat. Oedipuss. But he died four years ago and I don't carry his picture." I smiled to show this was supposed to be witty, not bitter.

Give him this, Charlie laughed. He reached across the table

and stroked the back of my free hand. The one that wasn't lifting the glass of pinot grigio for another sip. The rest of my wine went down while we caught up. His ex-wife and the amicable divorce. Rebound Todd got a mention from me. Charlie's parents—Don dead of pancreatic cancer, Kiki alive but on the verge of gaga. My mother. I never should have told him she'd been a bar girl in Seoul. That had been the beginning of the end. "You ever see your father?" He knew that piece of history, too.

"Once, twenty years ago, when he came east for Grandma Roz's funeral. I pretty much kept my distance. But he ambushed me as we entered the cemetery and tried to make conversation. I wasn't interested. Too little, too late."

I didn't go into what we'd exchanged on that knoll at Beth David. Irwin had retorted, "Life's short, Judy. How about you and me try to pick up the pieces?"

"Judith. Don't call me Judy. And you can pick them up, but you can't glue them together, Irwin, so what's the point?"

"Very philosophic. You're a smart girl, kiddo. *Judith*. Brains are good—you got that from your mother's side. Okay, maybe Aunt Phyllis. But you gotta be careful about not outsmarting yourself. I'm not seeing too much heart here. And what's with the 'Irwin'? Is that the way you talk to your father?"

Bad move. I'd wheeled on him then, drilling my heel into the loamy earth. He was so close to the open grave and it was such a temptation to give him a shove. "Enough," I said. "Really. You don't want to start. Not here."

"Where then? Life's short, as I said."

"Very philosophic. I'll let you know."

Charlie refilled my glass and his own. "You're not strong on forgiveness, then?" Which cued us to the chicken and The Apology.

He removed his blazer. We were going at this in shirtsleeves.

"I appreciate your meeting with me, Judith. I wasn't sure you would because, God knows, I treated you shabbily. It took a while for me to comprehend how shabbily.

"You need to hear— No, that's not true. I need to *tell* you that I did love you. You *do* know that? I loved you as much, more probably, than I've ever loved anyone."

Wow. I leaned against the chair's cushion to remind me I had a backbone. Also to support my head, which might have fallen off my neck from shock and bounced over the railing onto Sutton Place twenty-two stories below and, well, there goes the neighborhood.

"I was a kid, a selfish kid. What did I know about loyalty or the pain I'm sure I caused you?"

Oh no, he wasn't getting off the hook that easily. The alcohol gave me courage. "You knew what was important to you, Charlie. The law. Your family. That's what you traded me in for. And it worked out for you." His face had drained to white. "You're a prominent judge with all the trimmings. I'm sure you picked the perfect wife for the job. Maybe the marriage didn't last, but it was good for a while, right? And it gave you Chloe. Your mother must adore her. Does she—your mother—know we're having this little tête-à-tête?"

"*I* wasn't sure we were even having this tête-à-tête. I took a major risk you'd send me packing. Besides, I doubt Kiki would know who you are, Ju-ju. It was a long time ago and her memory's dicey."

"I remember *her*. What a character." I toyed with my chicken. "She would have been hell on wheels as a mother-in-law. I ducked the bullet on that one."

"You did indeed." Charlie chuckled, but when I looked up, I

saw his eyes were filled. I'd seen him cry only once in all the years
we were together, and that was when Reba died. "I just want you
to know I am sorry. Deeply sorry. You'd been abandoned once; I
did it to you again. What a bastard I was. So I guess I deserve to
be in Irwin's spot. I can't ask you to forgive me."

Dear God, how long had I been waiting for this? "Sure you
can. You just did, Charlie."

And that's the way I left it because, what the hell, he *did* deserve to wonder if I forgave him. It was the least I could do. The
great unanswered hovered between us, but he knew better than
to push.

I took my strawberries and moved toward the railing. Charlie
followed me. We stood together gazing at the East River, silver in
the moonlight, with the lights from the Queensboro Bridge
arcing a spangle of stars over Roosevelt Island. Charlie's shoulder
brushing mine charged the still air with an electricity I hadn't felt
in twenty-five years. More than that, I felt something around my
heart give way. After the breakup, when he'd left the Cambridge
house schlepping the last of his books, the semipermeable cardiac
membrane that allows love and trust to filter in had hardened into
my shield. Emblazoned with "Never Again," it stayed tough
through Todd, through Geoff. As I stood there with the apology
still fresh, I felt it give a little.

I bit into a chocolate-dipped strawberry. There's nothing like
chocolate to haul you into the moment.

Charlie stared down into the anonymous city. "I'm not sure
why I'm telling you this, but I ended a relationship recently. You
may have read about it in the tabloids. No? Well, that's refreshing.
I was seeing Carolyn Brinks."

"The newscaster?" How did I miss that with gossip-hound
Marti around? Carolyn Brinks, star reporter, famous for her in-

ternational coverage and interviews with heads of state. I re-called hearing somewhere her father had been busted for running a Ponzi scheme in the downturn a few years back. Got jail time. Now here we had a scenario that sounded vaguely familiar. Accomplished dark-haired woman with a disreputable background. Hmm.

"For the record, it was an amicable, mutual parting of the ways. Carrie really had no time for extracurricular activities. And when we managed to find some, the paparazzi were all over us. I'm uncomfortable in that kind of limelight. In case you forgot, I'm a pretty conservative guy." No kidding.

He turned as I did. We traded stares. He asked, "And you, are you involved with anyone?"

"I have been."

Okay, so I didn't think before I spoke. It was all uncensored and Freud would have had a field day. *Have been*, I'd said. Not as bad as *had* been. But not nearly as honest as *am*.

Charlie might have requested details; I might have elaborated. But we each caught a breath, and on our simultaneous exhale his cell phone rang out the theme to *Brideshead Revisited*. He'd loved that PBS show. *Our* show. "Damn," he grumbled. He checked the screen. "Sorry. I have to take this."

It really was an emergency. His mother's housekeeper, talking loud enough for me to follow, advised him that Mrs. Pruitt had passed out in the middle of watching some liberal pundit on CNN. She'd regained consciousness, but was still light-headed. The 911 responders were on their way.

"Her doctor's been working on regulating her blood pressure medication," Charlie said as he hustled us toward the door. "That's probably what's going on, but just to be sure it's not a ministroke, it's a good idea to have the medics check her out."

In the elevator, he called down to arrange for the driver to take me to my hotel. At the nineteenth floor, before he exited, he said, "I'm sorry the evening had to end on this lousy note."

"It's okay. I've played my share of lousy notes in my lifetime."

He gave me the weak smile the weak pun warranted. Then he got serious. "Thank you for tonight, Judith. I can't tell you how much it meant to me." He kissed me, Philadelphia style, as in brotherly love, on the cheek. And then he was gone. Back to his mother.

Chapter 7

*M*y mother flashed me a glance as I arrived at the Blumen House activity room Monday afternoon. "You look tired. Face too pale." Then she went back to scanning the numbers on the four bingo cards spread before her. The announcer called out, "I-23."

"*Hop'ung!* I-23 not on any my boards. Say hello to Mrs. Doyle. She win two games today. Lucky, lucky. You not sleeping, Judith? You take red ginseng tea I give you? Natural estrogen. No horse pee. Good for hot flash, good for sleep."

The announcer called out, "B-39."

"Bingo so close. Need one more number. You have bags under eyes. Look bad."

"Thank you," I said. "And you look different. What did you do to your hair?" I tried to peer around her to see whether I was hallucinating the wispy bangs and what appeared to be razored tiers in her glossy black hair. My mother had worn the same style forever. Thick bangs, length chopped uniformly to her jaw. Pyongyang chic. This was a major change. "What made you decide to do this? It's beautiful. I like it."

"Cut this morning. No reason. Time for new. Stop annoy me, child." She flicked away my fingers fluffing the new layers. "Take seat near window. This last game for big prize."

She always won something—a trinket, a candy bar. The winnings didn't matter; it was winning itself that had her hooked. My biological father also liked to gamble. Not me. The universe was haphazard enough without games of chance.

Bingo over, she was all smiles as she crossed the room and tossed a lipstick into my lap. "Not so big prize today, but okay. Cober Girl. You use Cober Girl. Coral no good for me, but your skin it work. So—" She sat herself in the club chair across from me. "New York weekend. Want to hear all about it."

The thing is, growing up, I didn't get much of my mother. She managed to check the progress of my schoolwork and music lessons, but after spending grueling days bent over a sewing machine and then doing her homework of cleaning, cooking and laundry, there wasn't a lot of her left for me. Since coming down to Baltimore, though, and especially since moving into Blumen House, where nearly everything was done for her, she had the time for me and, to my surprise, the interest.

"You and Geoff went to fancy restaurant? Manhattan, *aigoo!* Tell me, tell me everything you eat. What you see."

"Actually, I didn't see much of Geoff. He drove both ways because he was taking an extra day to help a friend from Australia move into a loft in SoHo."

The orchestra provided a bus to haul us to off-site venues, and Geoff and I always sat together. I'd missed having him next to me on the way up. Not so much on the way back, with the previous night still on my mind. And no, I hadn't heard from him since the concert, but I figured he was probably exhausted from carrying all those cartons.

"Do you remember Charlie Pruitt?" I asked my mother.

"Sure. The one who dump you because you not good enough. With crazy mother who think she's Martha Washington."

"That one. He showed up at Carnegie Hall Saturday night and we had dinner together."

"You had date? He can't have date. Charlie Pruitt is hot item with girl reporter. I read in *Enquirer*." My mother was the only person I knew who subscribed to the *National Enquirer* rather than thumbing through it on the supermarket checkout line.

"You read about Charlie Pruitt and you didn't tell me?"

"Why? To make you jealous old boyfriend have new girl?"

"His romance with Carolyn Brinks is over," I said.

"No kidding? And he start with you again? Very rich boy. Judge high up. Good catch. Why not?"

"Why not? What about Geoff?" It was the question that had kept me tossing in my bed the night before. And what was it with my friends and family? Marti had just about thrown me in Charlie's path. My mother was ready for me to make a quick U-turn back to an old boyfriend and leave Geoff sitting on the curb.

"Geoff fine man. He visit me. We play cards, laugh together. Drink beer." Geoff stopped by to see my mother once or twice a month. He got a kick out of her. She was a survivor, he said. He had a lot of respect for survivors.

"I like Geoff, but he is crane. On one foot, then on other foot. Someday he spread wings and fly away. And Lulu Cho read *I Ching*. She say he never marry you. Wasting your time."

Lulu was back in favor. When I was in the Johns Hopkins hospital having the stent inserted near my brain, my mother called her to apologize and say she was a first-class *mudang*.

Reportedly Lulu had said, "Surprise she alive. Very lucky girl. You owe me forty bucks, Grace. Already discount, half price because you regular customer."

"I send you check for one hundred. You deserve," my mother had told her.

Now Lulu was casting Geoff's horoscope? "I don't think I want to get married, *Uhm-mah*."

"Even to judge? All that money. Big condo in New York, I bet. You be in *Enquirer*. Top-rate musician marries big-time judge with nine-carat diamond." She threw her head back and laughed, exposing three gold teeth.

"Very funny. But don't stop the presses. Charlie won't call. He just wanted to apologize for the way he broke up with me back in Cambridge. Clear his conscience. That's all."

"What you mean? You sell short always, Judith. You smart, pretty, good job with famous orchestra. Healthy if you watch step. Nice package. He has your phone number?" I'd given him my card in the elevator. "Will call, I promise."

"I can't believe you'd even want him to. He left me because our family wasn't good enough for him. That means you." Furious after the split, I'd told her everything.

"Maybe he different, better now. You different, better. Sometime can go back. It happen. I hear on *Dr. Phil*. Old boyfriend, old girlfriend from high school get together. Sometime even in nursing home. And marry, ninety with no teeth. Men, women change, Judith. Your heart like ice. I understand. But maybe melt a little when you see him?"

Melt. Exactly what had happened on that roof garden.

My mother leaned toward me. "You forgive him?"

I thought about it. "I don't know. He was so apologetic. But I can't forget. He hurt me so much."

She reached across the space between us to pat my hand. "You be nice when he call. See what happen."

Maybe my mother had some of Lulu Cho's *yuk hak* magic in her, because when I got home, there was a message from Marti on my voice mail. Very trilly for a lesbian. "I've got something for you. They wouldn't leave it so I took it in. Call me and I'll bring it over."

I'd filled her in on the weekend situation that morning, so her eyes were glittering when she handed over the floral delivery. "You haven't heard from Geoff yet. What do you think, Geoff or Charlie?"

"Geoff," I said. He was very competitive and had the rugby scars to prove it. Charlie's appearance would be just the thing to stir him to action.

But the flowers were from Charlie. A dozen yellow roses, our flower, with a note, a single line from the Piaf song, in French. *"Car ma vie, car mes joies, aujourd'hui ça commence avec toi."*

I knew the English. "For my life, for my joys, today, they start with you."

Chapter 8

"I'm glad you liked the flowers." Charlie Pruitt's voice came through loud and clear on my cell phone. It was nine forty-five Tuesday morning and he'd called just as I was making my way to the stage for our first rehearsal of the week. Behind me a bass player was tuning up, a timpanist let loose a riff, and a few violinists drifted toward entrance right. Within minutes I would be playing a bitch of a solo and I noticed that my hand clutching my cell was trembling. The maestra would not be pleased.

"I hope I didn't go overboard with the inscription on the card. I downed a couple of scotches before summoning the courage to write it." This was coming from—what had my mother called him?—the big-time judge. Pretty damned charming.

"I thought the sentiment was sweet," I said. "Sweet" was actually the word I'd used in my thank-you call the night before. "Thanks for the roses and the sweet note," I'd said to Charlie's voice mail, kicking myself for sounding like Dottie the Dork.

"I was afraid you might be offended by my dragging up the old stuff. Aside from Saturday night's abrupt ending—Mother's doing fine by the way, thanks for asking." Oh yes, in my message to him, I'd also asked after Kiki. Ugh. "Aside from the scare with her, the evening was so . . . uh . . . enjoyable, I'd really like to see where we go with this. You and I."

"Charlie . . ." I was about to fill in the blank on Geoff, the one I'd leapt over like Evel Knievel vaulting the Snake River, when who should emerge from the musicians' practice room but the cipher in question, trumpet in hand. He raised it in salute as he walked toward me.

Trapped! I lowered my voice for Charlie. "Listen, I'm backstage and it's kind of chaotic here. This isn't a good time to talk. But we should."

"We should indeed. I'm heading into chambers now. I'll phone later this week. Evenings good?"

"Fine. Except Thursday. We have a performance Thursday night." Geoff was maybe three feet away. I held up my index finger asking for a moment. It was also a gesture that could be interpreted as "stop." That's what he did. In his tracks.

"Just one more thing," Charlie said.

I wondered whether Geoff could make out the other end of the conversation. At the very least, he'd peg the voice as masculine. Geoff had perfect pitch. As I checked for a sign that he recognized my caller, his glance flew to his shoes. I backed away a few steps, but there was a wall.

Charlie was saying, "Before you take off, I've got a quick question. Time sensitive. There's an RSVP involved. I'm going to be in D.C. in a couple of weeks. Tuesday the twenty-ninth to be exact. A retirement party in Georgetown for Justice Braithwaite."

The story of U.S. Supreme Court Justice Edwin Braithwaite's surprise resignation was all over the airwaves. Diagnosed with terminal lung cancer, he had only months to live.

"I don't know if you remember, but he's a friend of the family." Uncle Ed and Aunt Kay, of course. The Pruitts' and the

Braithwaites' summer homes on the Maine coast were within hallooing distance.

"Anyway, what I seem to have a problem getting to is I'm wondering if you'd like to accompany me." He stuttered out the *cuh* in "accompany," a nervous faltering that, under less stressful circumstances, I would have found endearing. All I could think of was, *Hurry up, spit it out, the man I sleep with is listening.*

Or not. I couldn't tell because Geoff was staring at his shoe as if he'd stepped in something brown and odiferous. "Well, it sounds very tempting." Dottie was back in action. "But I'm not sure. I'll have to check . . ."

"Your calendar, of course." Charlie faded for a moment, then returned. "Sorry. I'm being summoned. I really have to go. I hope you can make it, Ju-ju. I think you'd have a wonderful time. In fact I guarantee it."

"I'll let you know," I said. And then for Geoff's benefit, so he would think Charlie was—who, my auto mechanic? I ended it, "Nice talking to you." Already I was into duplicity, and my emotional circus, featuring juggling and tightrope walking, hadn't even begun.

After I turned off my cell phone and slipped it into the rear pocket of my jeans, Geoff moved in. He patted it familiarly, then draped an arm around my shoulders and we began walking toward the stage. I allowed for maybe twenty seconds of silence before I felt compelled to speak.

"Long time no hear." It had been a grand total of sixty hours.

"Yup. I'm sure you have lots to tell me. We'll talk at break."

An hour later we stood at the soft drink machine. "You played flawlessly. Bloody confident bow work. I was worried there for a while." Geoff held out a hand and deliberately made it tremble.

He shot me a questioning look, which I ignored. "No caffeine for you."

I dropped my seventy-five cents into the slot, punched the button for a Sprite, took a sip, and gave him my brightest smile. The best defense is a good offense. "So, the move went well? You have fun with your old mate?"

"It did. We did. Worked hard, drank a lot of beer, hauled a lot of Aussie ass. You?"

"Excuse me?" Buying time.

"Did you have fun with *your* old mate?"

In the note I'd left him after the Carnegie Hall concert, I'd written "meeting a New York friend." No name. But his question sounded loaded. Could he have known? How?

Ah, my mother. They were pals. It would be just like Grace to add a pinch of jealousy and stir the pot. See whether she could cook up a happy ending.

He was shifting his weight from one foot to another. Waiting for my answer.

"Fun. Oh sure. We spent the evening catching up."

I was aiming for nonchalant, but Geoff had the keenest ear. He picked up a sharp that should have been played flat.

His voice went tight, tone testy. "And are you sufficiently caught up?" When I didn't answer immediately, when I vamped by taking a swig of my Sprite, he recanted, "Sorry, Jude. Not to pry. I'm a clod."

There you go: the perfect example of everything that was screwy about our relationship. Which boiled down to one thing, really. It was unyieldingly superficial. Geoff and I could talk about music, politics, mutual friends, but what we felt for each other? How we defined our relationship? Our future? Off-limits. We'd established the ground rules early on. Geoff had laid it out: many ties, no strings. I'd agreed. Eagerly. Because it fit seamlessly with my own mishegoss, my personal nuttiness having to do with trust issues. So far it had worked for us. It was working for me right now. So why was I having second thoughts about this cushy arrangement? And how come Geoff, with only the shadow of Charlie in the picture, looked so miserable?

"Change of subject, then. You saw the posting, I take it? No? Check your mailbox." The musicians had mail cubbies downstairs near our locker rooms. I'd been heading for mine when Charlie's call had knocked me off course. "Richard's position is now officially up for grabs."

That hadn't taken long. Richard was well liked, highly respected. Everyone was sad, management included. But for them business was business.

"It's also posted on the job Web site. Auditions are scheduled for the first week of June. That gives you almost two months to prepare. And prepare you must, because you've already got stiff competition."

Shit. "Really, who?"

"Burt says Vince DeGrassi's going to try out."

According to our timpanist Burt Silverman, his friend Vincent DeGrassi, principal cello with the San Francisco Symphony, had decided to jump ship in the wake of the recent collapse of his marriage to the SFO's concertmaster. I knew Vince DeGrassi from a summer stint at Jacob's Pillow. He was a cellist of prodigious talent and unquenchable ambition.

"Messy divorce. Burt says Vince would like to put a continent between them. This spot would be perfect for him."

"I am one dead Oriyenta." The nickname my sensitive lox-slinging father had given me as a toddler. No wonder I was so screwed up.

"I'd be glad to help you train for the ring," Geoff said. "I'll whip you into shape. Figuratively, of course. We can start next

Monday at ten a.m. and do an hour or two every Monday thereafter until June." He paused for a frown. "Unless you'd rather not."

I realized there might be potential complications with the arrangement, but for the moment it was an offer I couldn't pass up. "I'd rather. And thank you."

Geoff gave me the twisty smile that I found so sexy. That it probably resulted from all those hours of trumpet practice perfecting his embouchure made it no less hot.

"Brilliant. We can talk it out over lunch."

"Can't today. Marti's coming over to go through the party plans. I brought her a pastrami sandwich from New York."

"Ah."

I thought for a moment. I'd have three hours with Marti in the afternoon to tap into her cut-to-the-chase wisdom. I'd lay out the Charlie/Geoff situation and by the time I got to see Geoff that night I'd have all my ducks in a row. Or I'd be a dead one. Either way, decision made.

"Free tonight?" I asked.

"Shame, but I've got a few lads coming over to watch some Ozzie football on the telly. Here's my final offer—" He hitched up the smile. "Tomorrow, dinner. My house. I'll cook."

"It's a date," I said.

The twisty smile unraveled into a grin.

"There you go. That's my sheila."

Chapter 9

When I told Marti about Charlie's invitation, she let loose a long, low whistle. "Well, isn't your stock soaring through the roof."

"Would it constitute a date, do you think, going to the party with Charlie?" I asked.

"Constitute a date. Yeah, you'd be stepping out on Geoff if you screwed Charlie in the coat closet. That's what you really want to know, huh?"

"I could use some advice here. I can't see the forest for the trees," I conceded.

"Well, sure, but before I take out my little ax, lunch and a rundown of your party so far."

She wolfed down the pastrami on rye and crunched through the half-sour pickle that, in a moment of knish-induced psychosis, I'd had the counterman at the Carnegie Deli bag along with her sandwich. It had dripped garlic juice on my shoes during the bus ride back from New York. Such is the power of friendship.

She insisted it was an abomination to eat Jewish deli without beer to wash it down and made her way through the first bottle as we reviewed the caterer's menu. Heavy hors d'oeuvres. Assorted pastries. Our budget was beginning to nudge the limits of my mother's donation and I wasn't about to dip deep into my savings for hard liquor. Bottom line, wine and beer only. I did spring for champagne for a toast and a cake that Marti had planned on setting ablaze with fifty candles. Over my baby boomer body. We compromised on five, one for each decade. The invitations were ready to be picked up at the printers. The guest list was presented for additions and deletions. So far, there was no sign of Brenda Himmelstein, last known address Parkside Avenue, Brooklyn. Marti had Facebooked, MySpaced, Classmate dot commed, PeopleFindered, and Googled her way through cyberspace with no luck. Her last hope was to trace Brenda through her birthday on some esoteric site she'd dug up. "You know your best/only childhood friend's birth date?"

"March twenty-fourth. Same year as me."

"You can't even say it, can you? It tears your heart out to say out loud the year you were born because why? You think your life is slipping away and you haven't accomplished enough?"

I had an answer. Marti knew about Richard Tarkoff's retirement, but not about my decision. "Richard would dearly love for me to take over his spot and I think my time has come. I'm going to audition for principal cello."

She broke out a congratulatory smile. "Good thing too, or I'd never speak to you again."

"And Geoff offered to work with me to get me in shape. He heard the principal cellist of the San Francisco Symphony has his eye on the seat. Stiff competition."

"You've got Geoff in your corner, so that's an edge."

"Well, there could be a problem."

"Isn't there always?"

"He might not want to mentor his ex."

Marti's gray irises went steely. "Did I hear 'ex' or were you just clearing your throat?"

"I've been thinking about converting my relationship with Geoff from sexual to . . . I don't know . . . fraternal."

"Really? That's what you've been thinking?" Never taking her eyes off me, the crazy lady, she said, "Oh, that's going to be well received." Marti shook her head disapprovingly. "I can't believe you're serious about dumping Geoff and, without a breath between, picking up with Charlie. You just can't move people around on the chessboard of your life without regard for their feelings, Judith. Do you not realize how self-absorbed that is?"

I said, "You could look at it that way." *I* had. Over the past few days, I'd examined this triangle from every slant. In the end I came up with a decision I could live with, though it was probably half rationalization, half truth. I explained to Marti, whose chiseled features had taken on a dubious cast, "The way I see it, it's worse to dangle Geoff while I explore the potential of the Charlie thing. In my book, that's cheating and Geoff deserves better than me two-timing him."

She thought about that for as long as it took to polish off her sandwich. "You've got a point," she said seriously. Then she drawled, "In fact, it's very noble of you, shafting Geoff."

At least I'd knocked her off her moral high horse. And Marti being Marti, as soon as she was on foot, she took the low road.

"But listen, Jude. Wouldn't it be fun to get it on with both of them? Not at the same time, though; that might blow your delicate circuits. Rotate. Like the sultans used to do. Men shuffle women like cards all the time. Wives and mistresses. Multiple girlfriends. It really pisses me off that women can't manage it. Not even my fellow vagitarians. Okay, my opinion: I think you need time off from both your charming suitors. Listen, I know Jews don't do convents. But there are Buddhist nuns, right? You need to be alone for a while. If it takes wind chimes and incense, so be it. My advice is to back off from men in general, a couple in particular, until you're sure you know what you want."

"I hear you. But how do I find out if I back off? And Charlie needs an answer about the Georgetown reception the next time he calls."

"You're not even listening, are you? You knew damn well what you were going to do before you asked me. I think you're crazy cutting Geoff from the lineup this early on. And you're going to lose a cello coach in the bargain. That may not be the smartest move on the planet, Judith."

"But don't you think it's smarmy to string him along just so he'll prep me for the audition? I could probably pick up a coach at Peabody." The prestigious music school downtown had a slew of faculty members who were eager to earn some extra cash.

"You've really thought through all these moral issues, haven't you?" I couldn't tell whether she was being serious or sarcastic. "Anyway, I'm not sure why you called me in on this. Your mind is made up. Proceed with The Barrister at your own risk."

"No, really, I bounced it off you to figure out what I really want. And it worked. Thanks. You're the best." I leaned over and popped a kiss on her cheek.

"Wow. Kissing. Now you've fallen in love with me too? Nasty habit, Judith, all this falling." She had eyes only for the slab of New York cheesecake I'd brought her for dessert. "And I'd say you have enough on your plate at the moment."

Chapter 10

The talk at Wednesday afternoon's rehearsal was about Richard. Angela made an announcement before we got started. She'd just had a call from Sarah Tarkoff, who asked her to inform us that Richard's last round of chemo hadn't been successful. His most recent MRI had picked up melanoma metastases in a part of his brain that couldn't be reached by surgery. He and his oncologist were considering next steps. In the meantime, Richard was home trying to regain his strength.

"He's up for visitors as long as you phone first." Angela took a vibrato-edged breath before going on. Our tough musical director had her soft side. "She asked that we pray for him and for their family."

I sniffed my way through the run-through of the Tchaikovsky.

Rehearsal over, I stored my cello, phoned the Tarkoffs, and went looking for Geoff. He was digging out his car keys as I approached. "I just called Sarah. Richard would love to see us."

"You mean today?" he asked.

"A quick stopover. Sarah says we'll do him a world of good."

Geoff jingled his keys. "Then let's go. And, Jude, bring the

Dvořák music. I think he'd get a kick out of discussing your approach to the second movement. Make him feel useful."

It was just like Geoff to be eager to extend a hand. He was such a decent man, I almost had second thoughts about dropping my breakup bomb at dinner.

Sarah and Richard Tarkoff lived in a handsome Tudor home in Roland Park, one of Baltimore's most beautiful neighborhoods. At the front steps, a gardener was fussing with some early tulips and hyacinths, perennials that would bloom next year when Richard was gone. Inside, the atmosphere was timeless as my colleague's personal clock tick-tocked down his remaining days. Sarah, having overtaken the housekeeper on the way to the door, briefed us on the ground rules. Briskly, like the attorney she was. Richard had just awakened from a snooze, she told us, so he was in good spirits. Beyond a polite "How are you doing?" she asked us not to talk about his illness. Orchestra gossip, on the other hand, was good medicine. When Geoff asked her, waving my sheet music, whether Richard's consulting on the cello concerto would pass muster, her dark eyes lit up. "He'd love that, Geoff. Just the thing to engage him. But no more than a half hour with him, please. He tires easily."

We stayed for more than two hours. The patient wouldn't let us go. Twice, Sarah tried to intervene. "Be gone, woman," Richard shooed her. "Would you deny a dying man his pleasure? This is the first real fun I've had since the grandkids were here on Saturday. Judith, try this chocolate-covered marzipan."

The spacious bedroom overlooked a back garden and an open window captured the scent of lilacs and the fluty trill of a Baltimore oriole late on an April afternoon. In the corner, Richard's priceless cello stood idle but watchful. The instrument, built by the Venetian luthier Matteo Goffriller in 1729, had been Richard's guardian and his companion for decades. Now it presided over his death watch.

With my music in hand, he pointed a skeletal finger at the instrument. "Damn thing needs more exercise. Play that second movement for me."

The Goffriller was slightly larger than my own cello, but slender with a rich, full sound that flooded the room. I'd played it a few times before and was familiar with the adjusted touch it required.

Richard's critique zeroed in on the fine points. "A little too much fire there. Hold something in reserve." And, "Ah, yes. Much better, darling."

"There, you've nailed it," he said when I'd finished. "I'm proud of you, my dear. Look at that face. Always so hard on yourself. You're much better than you think. There's no doubt in my mind that you're ready for first chair." He stared at the ceiling for a long minute, plucking at the quilt pizzicato as if he were working something through. Geoff and I exchanged glances. With a groan, Richard shifted so he was talking directly to me. "The hell with it. I hate secrets anyway and this one you should be a party to, Judith. This one should light a fire under you."

In the ten seconds of silence that followed, a dark-feathered bird landed on the windowsill with a loud caw. From where I sat, with an old maple tree casting deep shadows, I couldn't tell whether it was a crow (bad omen in Korean folklore) or a magpie (lucky).

"Well, that fellow seems to agree. You—" He raised an eyebrow to Geoff. "You're only included in this cabal because I know Judith would tell you anyway. It's all very hush-hush. In fact, I think the reason Angela let *me* in on it is because she wanted to give me something extra to live for, to fight for. You need to keep this to yourselves—is that understood?"

Geoff and I nodded in unison.

He smiled impishly. "It looks like the orchestra is heading for North Korea next spring."

"What?" That was my voice with only enough strength to manufacture a whisper.

"The idea of a cultural exchange was initiated by the State Department. Something about stalled nuclear talks, but relations between the two countries are especially shitty these days. This cultural outreach is supposed to thaw the situation as much as it's thawable. Negotiations are under way and Angela is hopeful." He took a sip of his bedside water through the straw. "It's not a done deal by any means. The North Koreans are famous for reneging last minute. They make unreasonable demands, the project falls apart, and they blame us. However, if we get there, it would be a helluva coup for our merry band." His eyes twinkled when he said to me, "So, do you want to visit North Korea, sweetheart?"

I was caught between stunned and delighted. "Incredible" was all I could muster in reply. I was a loyal, oh so grateful American, but Korea would always own half my genes. I shook my head in disbelief. "My mother will go ballistic."

"No telling Grace," Richard admonished.

"Not now. But if and when it goes through, she'll be thrilled."

"I thought your mother was from Seoul," Geoff said.

"She moved south right before the war, but she was brought up in a farming village in a place called Hwanghae. If I have any relatives left, they're in the north."

"And so will you be next April." Richard grinned, obviously pleased with himself.

"You too," I lied.

"I can't fool myself. I don't expect another year. Maybe I'll make it through the summer. No guarantees. Now give the old man a kiss, Judith, and you two get on your way. Mmm, chocolate and perfume. Why do women smell so delicious? Well, it's nice to know I ain't dead yet."

Stuffed on chocolates and tasting the lilac fragrance that seemed suddenly like funeral flowers in the back of my mouth, I wasn't hungry. It was too late for Geoff to roast the rack of lamb he'd planned and I wasn't up for the noise and hustle of the Mt. Washington Tavern. What I really wanted was to go home alone, make myself a bologna sandwich, and later climb into bed and daydream that Richard's chemo had worked and he was in the first seat as we played the orchestral arrangement of *Arirang*, the Korean folk song my mother sang me to sleep with when I was little. At the end of the Pyongyang concert, the audience, comprised of people who looked a lot like me, stood and cheered. Lovely fantasy.

The reality was Richard was dying and I had a life ahead of me. Which meant moving on. Only, to move on, I'd have to undo history, starting with the most recent past. The big talk had to be tonight so I could get myself in fresh trouble immediately.

"Follow me. My place. I'll rustle up something simple," Geoff said as we left the Tarkoffs'. His territory. Not the best choice for the conversation I had in mind, but I was too preoccupied and too sad to protest.

Geoff lived in a downtown high-rise with a panoramic view of the old Domino Sugar factory and the Inner Harbor. The condo's décor was Australian sports/ethnic/music. Lots of aboriginal drums and didgeridoos among the soccer and rugby shirts hung like tapestries and framed autographed photos of his favorite dames: Joan Sutherland, Edna, and me.

In the kitchen he rummaged through the fridge. "Let's see

what I have in here. Uh-oh. Sorry. I forgot to restock on bologna."
He turned to give me a fond and knowing smile.

It was more of a joke now, but back in elementary school I'd
been obsessed by bologna. While the other kids unwrapped
Oscar Mayer on Wonder Bread or PB and J, I emptied my lunch
box of leftover squid and vegetables, kimchi or cold-by-lunchtime
seaweed soup packed in Tupperware knockoffs. The aroma in-
variably drew a crowd. "Chink-stink," the little bastards called it,
pinching their noses and ostentatiously gagging. I was mortified.
By middle school we were living in Bed-Stuy, where I could have
had my ass whipped for lesser infractions than smelling up the
cafeteria. The shape of my eyes alone got me deliberately and re-
peatedly bumped in the hall by Tylana Haynes and her gang. So
I made my stand, and my mother didn't protest; she knew when
it was futile. I made my own all-American bologna sandwich on
the days I didn't eat pizza or chicken nuggets off the cafeteria line,
a free lunch for which I easily qualified along with most of the
kids, then hit the vending machines for a Snickers dessert with the
money Mrs. Beckersham slipped me every week after my lesson.

I loved that lunch meat. How it tasted, what it symbolized.

While Geoff puttered in the kitchen, I was in his living room,
drawn to his trumpet, spotlighted like sculpture, its brass glowing.
As I traced the sensual flare of the bell, ran my finger over the
curve of a slide, I picked up a resident energy, as if the music were
coiled within, ready to spring to life. Leafing through the sheet
music on his stand, which wasn't really like going through someone's mail, I shuffled classical pieces coming up on the orchestra's
schedule as well as some standards and jazz, the stuff he played for
fun. A man of multiple tastes and talents, he also composed. Brilliantly, of course. Under the score for "Stompin' at the Savoy," I
recognized, with its corrections and marginal scrawling, a piece
he'd been writing for two of the three years of our relationship.

The title, Geoff's loving pun, was spelled "Suite for My *Seoul*mate."
I was his muse, he'd confessed before playing the half-finished
version for me a few months before. Its beauty had left me
speechless, breathless.

After tonight, like some symphonies of note, it would
probably remain unfinished, crumpled and pitched into the trash.
My sense of Geoff was that—unlike Charlie—he did not look
back.

I replaced the music with trembling fingers and moved to the
window to stare out at the water shimmering in the harbor light
and ponder how I was going to start The Conversation. And then
he came up behind me, encircled his arm around my waist, and
handed me a glass of Shiraz. "How about I fry us up some eggs?"
he asked.

"I'd just as soon skip dinner," I said. "Do you mind?"

"Fine with me. I haven't much appetite either. Not for food
anyway."

His right hand cupped my right breast. He'd once told me he
loved that I was this slender Asian reed with boobs like a Wag-
nerian soprano.

He rubbed his thumb over my nipple and I felt it stiffen in
spite of myself and my thoughts of extinction. In spite of the
looming conversation. That was what we did, Geoff and I, buried
the deep feelings under the easily reachable ones. Sex was our cure
for everything. Geoff was hiking my skirt with his left hand,
making passage for the other one to migrate down to my panties
and burrow.

Sex and death, an odd duo and one you never expected to
work but did, like Sonny and Cher or Yoko and John. Maybe the
pairing had to do with schadenfreude—someone's dying, I'm not,
let's make love to prove we're alive.

I didn't bother to resist as he slipped his hand into my panties.

For a moment, I thought he was fingering the trumpet part in the Brandenburg No. 2, which would have been outrageously insulting, but then he found my rhythm and we tumbled onto the IKEA sofa that groaned under our weight.

Geoff always made me hot. No one, including Charlie—there he surfaced again; *down, boy*—had ever turned me on like Geoff Birdsall did. And as he tried to do that night. Fingers there. Lips here. In, out, up, down. The man tried every trick in the book and some that had been edited out. And yet. So close. And yet. And yet.

"Enough," I said finally. He looked up from between my thighs and blinked. I didn't have to repeat myself. His mouth, which was his livelihood, was at risk.

"We have to talk," I said.

"Yes, well, I'm not sure I can." He rubbed his moist bottom lip.

"I'm sorry about that," I said afterward, while he was getting into his boxers. "I know it's a cliché, but it really wasn't you. It was me."

"Yes, it was." And then he did something he hadn't done in our three years together: he cued me into a talk about us, past the mantle and into the core. "What's going on, Judith? Not just this short circuit—that happens—but something's brewing beneath the surface. I think I know, but I deserve to hear it from you."

"It's not Charlie," I said, giving myself away smack out of the gate. Nerves must have scrambled my censoring mechanism.

He gave a short laugh. "Come on, Jude. You think I'm that lamb-brained? Give me credit."

"Okay, maybe it's partially Charlie. But just because of the timing. Lots of things—my upcoming birthday, my good report from the doc—got me to thinking about how much time I have left and what I need to make the most of it."

"Charlie Pruitt is not what you need," he growled. "A judge. At the concert—Christ, what a bloody stuffed shirt." Geoff ran a hand through his longish hair, glossy dark blond without a wisp of gray.

It occurred to me that the man I was trading in would be snapped up in a heartbeat by someone willing to settle for looks, charm, wit, and—if her mind wasn't two hundred and fifty miles away in Manhattan—fabulous sex. With no strings—a sentiment I'd fully subscribed to. But now, maybe I wanted more. Or maybe I wanted my knot tightened by someone else. The truth was I didn't know what I wanted, except the freedom to find out. I told him that, editing out the knot part.

But Geoff was no fool. "Charlie. That three-button suit and the necktie of his with the Harvard logos? The man is a tight-ass, Jude; you think he can make you happy? But—hell, whatever floats your boat, darling. If it's freedom you want, it's freedom you'll have." Chin jutted, he was taking it like a man.

We dressed, the silence broken only by his phone ringing as I shrugged on my sweater. Except for a flat smile in my approximate direction as I gathered my jacket and car keys, I was ignored. My good-bye wave was met with a casual answering wave. And then, with one foot into the hall, I heard him say, "Hold on a minute, Jacko."

He padded over on the hardwood and turned me around to face him. "Whatever you decide, I hope it works out for you, Judith. My blessings."

Charlie checked in by phone that night from a black-tie fundraiser for the Museum of Modern Art. He was a busy boy. He'd chaired a six p.m. meeting of the New York State Bar Association's ethics committee and now, he told me, he was standing in the MOMA sculpture garden between the Lachaise nude and a massive steel Richard Serra installation, sipping a vodka martini and thinking of me. Sweet.

"Also, I don't mean to press you, but I have to RSVP the retirement party for Uncle Ed."

"I'd love to go with you," I said. The magic of Charlie was powerful enough to cast out any residual social phobia of mine.

"Really? That's wonderful, Ju-ju." He sounded surprised, elated. "Do me a favor. Call my secretary tomorrow and give her your social security number. You'll need to be cleared."

"For a party? Who's doing the clearing?"

"When the party is for a Supreme Court justice, one who's been the swing vote on a number of highly controversial decisions over the last forty years, they have to take precautions. Especially post 9/11. I'm assuming it falls to the FBI to review the backgrounds of the guests. It's not our old, cozy, uncomplicated world out there, as you know. But you'll enjoy the crowd. All the Washington stars will be out. I'll tell Diana to expect your call." His voice peeled away and I heard him say, "Yes, very well. Thanks, Mr. Mayor. And you? Wonderful." He was back with me. "Better return to the party. Sleep well, *ma belle*." Hokey, but that had been his sign-off on our phone calls twenty-seven years before when I was still living in the campus dorm.

After I clicked off, I kicked off the coverlet. April weather in Baltimore was erratic. It had been in the seventies until a few hours earlier, when a cold front swept down from Canada. But Charlie's call had made me sweat. Or maybe it was my first hot flash of the night that left me wringing wet. At forty-nine, I found it hard to tell the difference.

Chapter 11

Geoff was coolish at rehearsal on Thursday. All I got was a thin smile he sent like a paper airplane over the heads of the brass section into the strings. Before it crashed, I smiled back, but he was already occupied with tuning up and had his eyes closed. At break, not finding him in the musicians' lounge kibitzing with the poker players, I figured he was ducking me. I did get a shoulder clap and a quick "Thanks, Judith" after Friday night's performance, but that was in response to my compliment on his brilliant solo in the Gershwin. Geoff was unflappable onstage. Off, he carried the strained look of a man with an untrussed hernia.

Saturday evening, before we went on, he finally approached, brow wrinkled. "I just want to know, uh . . . thought I'd ask if, under the new rules, I need to send my regrets to your aunt Phyllis. Because if it would make you uncomfortable to have me at the table Tuesday, I can skip it. No problem, really."

Oh God, the Seder. With Jewish holidays governed by the moon and the dates fluctuating year to year, I had to be reminded when to feel guilty about not observing them. Except for Passover. Though I sometimes had to be reminded, I always observed it.

Credit to my mother—even after Irwin scrammed for warmer climes, she never failed to bring me to Seder with his family. First at Grandma Roz's apartment in Flatbush. And what an apartment! It was tiny and dark, but in a twist of irony I didn't appreciate until much later, this old lady who wasn't thrilled to have an Asian fusion granddaughter had, long before Grace was in the picture, decorated her home with cloisonné lamps, red lacquered tables, and a large screen painted with flying cranes. The place resembled Sun Yat's, my grandmother's favorite restaurant down the street. She even kept a canary in a bamboo cage, a feathered surrogate who twice nipped my finger, drawing blood. My grandmother had a yen for Oriental. As they said in Korean: *Go know.*

After Aunt Phyllis got married, she took over the Seder. But because my grandmother's cuisine was legendary—read: notorious—she brought jars of her homemade gefilte fish and matzo ball soup out to Long Island. According to my aunt, this had nothing to do with tradition; Grandma Roz just couldn't give up what was known in the family as the "in-laws' surprise." In a triumph of passive-aggressive gastronomy, she managed to serve *only* her son-in-law (whom she'd dubbed "The Rug Salesman," although he owned the very profitable Feldmesser's Magic Carpets chain) and her Korean daughter-in-law portions that contained a little something extra. One year it was a single gray hair in the fish, another it was a pared fingernail in a matzo ball, and in her most memorable coup, Uncle Arnold picked a staple from between his teeth that had been buried in her hand-grated horseradish.

"An accident," she'd said with a shrug.

"Some accident," my uncle had responded. "Like Hitler was an accident."

My mother let it ride. "Because family most important. Your grandma love you, Judith. Don't know how to show, but she love you." I wasn't sure about that, but I suppose I kept trying to make it true, because I flew in from Boston during spring break at the conservatory, and from Atlanta, where I settled first after Charlie and I had split. The only years I missed Seder with the Feldmesser/Raphael clan was when I was married to Todd. Todd Grossman was a cantor at the synagogue I attended, which was how I'd met him. A year into our marriage, he had some kind of epiphany that prodded him to upshift from Reform to Orthodox Judaism. I wasn't willing to make the journey by his side. I looked lousy in hats. The last Seder we attended together was incredibly meticulous and interminably long. My family's version tended toward the *Haggadah Digest* condensed edition.

Geoff had come with me last year. He'd trained up to New York with my mother and me on the Acela Express and charmed the Long Island family. Raised eyebrows were exchanged around the table—*Judith has finally landed a mensch, a good one.* It didn't matter that he wasn't Jewish. In my gene pool, precedent had been set.

Phyllis swooned—the upscale version of plotzed—because Geoff had read the Haggadah story of the Exodus in rich tones that made him sound like, according to her, "an Australian Charlton Heston." My mother heaped his plate with brisket. Arnold and he talked sports. Geoff, who was Church of England, ate it all up, including the gefilte fish, which was an acquired taste. On the spot, he was invited for the following year and he accepted then and there, as if it were dead cert he was going to be in my life in twelve months. So, no . . . No way was I going to deprive him of his pleasure, or the rest of the guests of his company.

"Of course you're still invited. My mother would kill me if you didn't come."

"She knows about us, then? And your family? That we're not us anymore? Because it could be awkward." He gave me a wry smile. "Talk about the Last Supper."

"I'm telling her today. I promise she won't sling the soup at you."

"I wasn't worried about me, Jude." He paused for a moment. "I'm carting in a rug for my mate in SoHo, so I'm driving up. Care to join me?"

I hadn't thought about the travel. Talk about awkward. "I've already bought my Acela ticket," I lied. "But thanks."

"Well, see you over the bitter herbs, then."

As it turned out, when I broke the news to my mother, she fluffed it off. "Time for change. He never marry you. Good boy, but too young. Not ready to settle down like at your age."

"He's young? We're only six years apart."

"Korean fortune say six year bad spread for couple. Six bring *sang chun sal.* Not so good luck. You be happy together, but poor like beggar."

I waved off that craziness. "Plus, who says I want to settle down?" I internally counted to ten. "I'm leaving it to you to tell Aunt Phyllis about Geoff and me." That way I'd avoid the lecture about what a find Geoff was, how grateful I should be for such a wonderful man, and where did I get off being so picky? "And no talking about it at the Seder."

"Don't worry. Was going to tell you, Judith. Seder off this year. Aunt Phyllis call last night. She sick. Has UFO."

When I gave her a quizzical look, she gave me an exasperated one back. "You know, pee-pee backed up."

"Ah, UTI. She has a urinary tract infection."

"That one. Always in bathroom. Can't do Seder." I breathed a deep sigh of relief. "And don't call her to say sorry. Big secret. Down there." She pointed to her own crotch. "She so embarrassed. Now tell me, dress look good, yes? Ah, *aigoo*, very nice."

Almost as interesting as Aunt Phyllis's canceling Seder because of her UFO was where my mother was telling me this—on a Sunday morning, in a Loehmann's dressing room while she was doing the unthinkable: trying on dresses. She'd left a message that morning to meet her there.

Grace had never been one for shopping, especially for clothes. Every couple of years I dragged her to Chico's, where I'd treat her to three or four outfits at a clip so we wouldn't have to go through the torture again for a while. She'd find a look she liked and would buy it in different colors so she'd only have to try it on once.

"Who want to look in mirror that show everything? *Aigoo!* Gain so much weight. I skinny till I have you, Judith. Now fat old lady."

That's what she used to say. But today she said, "Not bad, I think. You like black better? Or green? Winnie, come look. Tell me truth."

Winnie Chang, a well-educated third-generation Chinese-American and the only other Asian at Blumen House, didn't have much in common with my uneducated immigrant mother. But Winnie loved to shop and she still drove her ten-year-old Mercedes.

"Say hello Dr. Chang. She bring me. What one you think, Winnie, green or black?" My mother smoothed the skirt over her hips.

"Hello, Judith. Grace looks good, doesn't she? The fifteen pounds makes a difference." Winnie checked out the mirror image. "Personally, I like the black."

My mother turned slowly and peeked over her shoulder at her reflected behind. "Fat *ko* not so big now."

I stared at this woman whom I saw every week, sometimes twice a week, wondering how I hadn't noticed she'd dropped fifteen pounds. To be fair, it wasn't evident in her face, which retained its pretty roundness, and the drapey fabric of her Chico's outfits had hidden her exact shape. Who was I kidding? I'd fended off Marti's accusation that I was insensitive where Geoff was concerned, but maybe she was on to something. Maybe the rankling truth was I was so caught up in my own suddenly shifting life that I didn't really see anyone but me.

"Green more young, but black make me look thin. I take black. Also two pair trouser pants and nightgown. Mine all torn. These only ten dollar. Good buy." She emitted a delighted laugh at my stunned, slack-jawed silence. "Winnie, you got no kid, but I tell you they make you nuts. Look at Judith face. She think *I* go crazy. A dress, few nightgown, and I need funny farm. Time is spring, Judith. Flower boom." She reached out and stroked my cheek. Her fingernails were freshly manicured. With red polish yet. She never wore *any* polish. "I know. You make big change with Geoff. Even if turns out right, you sad. But you buy something new, you cheer up. Don't say no. Buy something new. I pay."

She insisted I try on a black crepe sleeveless Donna Karan from the Back Room. Size six, marked down hundreds, final sale. "So beautiful, Judith. Meant for you." She was right. It was elegant, classic. Charlie's kind of dress, perfect for the Georgetown party.

"Look how happy," my mother said to Winnie Chang. "Look at smile just for dress. Worth twice price."

Chapter 12

It was weird spending Passover at home alone. My mother had invited me to the Blumen House Seder last minute, but I decided I might as well skip the whole shebang this year and eat a bologna sandwich, watch TV, and go to bed early. As it turned out, this night really *was* different from all other nights; it had some kind of hold on me. So I spent the few hours before sundown brewing chicken soup according to Aunt Phyllis's recipe and making matzo balls from scratch. Then I sat myself down at my dining room table with a nice place mat and a glass of Manischewitz wine, the teeth-achingly sweet concord grape syrup that's the madeleine of the holiday to American Jews, and read the Haggadah story of Exodus straight through. Crazy lady, but at least I didn't recite it out loud.

The phone rang twice that evening as I nibbled my way through a box of chocolate-dipped macaroons. First time was a hang-up, probably a wrong number, but without caller ID.

I could speculate it was Geoff checking to see whether the Seder really had been canceled. He'd expressed regret when my mother informed him it had been called on account of the host's flu.

"I couldn't tell him pee-pee." She'd wrinkled her nose in distaste. "And he say maybe next year."

"He said that? Maybe next year? Oh Lord, what did you say?"

"I say maybe. You no *mudang*. You don't know, Judith. No one know what future bring."

Wonderful. That could have been just enough encouragement to spur him to make a Seder night call. Then, when he heard my voice, he lost his nerve or realized my mother had been telling the truth, so he hung up. Or it could have been someone looking for a plumber.

The second caller didn't even know it was Passover and wasn't surprised to find me in. Charlie sounded much less ebullient than during his last call from the MOMA party. I thought perhaps the social security number I'd provided to his secretary hadn't cleared. My mother probably had family in North Korea. Had that raised a red flag?

I found out soon enough that the problem was worse than international espionage.

"Kiki's coming." Charlie's voice was funereal. "To the party for Uncle Ed. She was invited, of course—Ed and Kay were my parents' closest friends. Everyone assumed in her current condition Mother wouldn't think of making the trip. But dammit if she didn't decide to attend. Can you believe that?"

I believed it. I remembered how she'd interrupted Charlie's and my tryst in the moonlight with her fainting spell. Either the old lady was a witch or you had to laugh at my lousy luck. For the time being, I laughed.

Charlie exhaled a kind of woof at the other end. "I'm sorry, Ju-ju. This was totally unexpected. You're not going to back out on me, are you?"

"Charlie, you know I was never a social butterfly. That hasn't changed. A room full of strangers, I'd rather hide out in my cocoon. So if you're going to have to chaperone your mother all evening and that leaves me on my own, then for everybody's sake I'd rather pass."

"No," he said. "That's not the way it's going to be. I've got a nurse coming along to keep an eye on her. And if Mother gets out of line, the nurse has strict instructions they're gone one-two-three. Whatever happens, I'm with you. Leading the way. By your side."

"Anatomically impossible."

"Not at all. I'll split myself in half for you. Whatever it takes."

The Charlie who'd once dumped me was willing to do whatever it took to win me back. In front of Kiki. If that wasn't irresistible, I didn't know what was.

"In that case . . ." I said.

"Kiki wins round two on points and the fighters haven't come out of their corners yet," Marti said when I told her Charlie's news.

"Don't be so sure. I called Lulu Cho for a consult. The fortune-teller? She came up with Kiki's birth date online and crunched the astrological numbers. She said Kiki is losing her strength while I'm gaining. My magpies are chirping. They symbolize good luck. Kiki's birds are crows and they're plunging from the sky."

"Meaning?"

"According to Korean voodoo, crows are bad omens and their fall signifies her *haeng-un*—her luck—is on the descent."

Marti snorted. "Kiki's between eighty and death, so, yeah, she's descending. But what kind of collateral damage is she going to take out on her way down? That's the question. Now, my feeling is the woman isn't altogether—what did you call her, gaga? Say she's only half out of it, barely ga, and she managed to get a sneak peek at the guest list. When she saw your name on it, she got a sudden urge to party." She shrugged. "Just a theory."

"So you think as soon as I heard about Kiki coming I should have hiked my skirts and run?"

"No way, girl. This is going to be interesting. A test of sorts. How much has Charlie severed the apron strings? Does Mommy still control him by a thread? Does she jerk him around like a Tennessee walking horse on a tight rein?"

"Charlie says she probably won't even remember me. What if she does? What if you're right and it's a setup? What if she makes a scene?"

"That kind won't make a scene. Restraint has been bred into her bones. She might cut you dead, though." Marti's eyes took on an evil glint. "Then again, if she's well and truly gaga, all bets are off. My grandpaw pulled a gun on my grannie when he was eighty-two. Loaded, but not cocked. Of course, she had to forgive him since he wasn't all there." When Marti saw my face, she said, "Come on. Lighten up, kiddo. Everything will be fine as long as you remember your birds are flying and Kiki's are crashing."

Maybe. I'd read that morning on the *Huffington Post* that senators from both sides of the aisle were expected to attend the party for Justice Braithwaite. Sandra Day O'Connor was flying in from Arizona. The Braithwaite kids, who'd shared Charlie's childhood summers in Maine, would be there. What if they were expecting him to bring Carolyn Brinks? She'd just won a Peabody Award for her series on domestic violence in Afghanistan. I'd Googled her age. Forty-three—a young Botoxed forty-three. Oh God, this crowd was way out of my league. And Kiki, the loose cannon, would be rolling around. What had I been thinking? Okay, I'd simply phone Charlie and say I'd changed my mind or I just remembered a previous engagement.

"I know what you're thinking," Marti interrupted. She probably did. Sometimes she was a better *mudang* than Lulu Cho. "Stop playing 'Ain't Nothing but a Hound Dog' in your head. Because you're not. And if you ever were, you sure as hell aren't anymore."

Suddenly, her face lit with glee. "Oh Lordy, I almost forgot. I've got news about another former unworthy rival for The Barrister's affections. Last night, I caught one of those interview shows on CNN. And guess who was in the hot seat? None other than your old pal Eloise Flint. Yup, the world-famous cellist from hell who, lo those many years ago, slid into your spot in Charlie's bed before it had a chance to cool down. She was on for a full fifteen minutes and they even took questions from the viewers. Quite illuminating. Sorry you missed it." Marti was playing me, enjoying watching my pupils dilate. "Not that you give a rat's furry ass about what Eloise Flint is up to these days, right?"

I managed to say, "Right. Couldn't care less. Did you DVR it?"

She gave off a giant guffaw. "Not interested, huh?"

"Whatever. What was she doing being interviewed? Is she a suspect in an ax murder?"

"*Tsk-tsk.* I wouldn't want you as an enemy. She was promoting her new book, an autobiography titled *Different Strokes*. Get it? Strokes? Cellist? That's supposed to be witty, I guess. You might want to check the index to see if you're in there. Maybe in the chapter called 'How I Spent My Summer Vacation Screwing My Girlfriend's Boyfriend.'"

I winced. Eloise had done exactly that.

In a classic, almost Shakespearian betrayal, my classmate at the New England Conservatory—another Brooklyn kid, which made it all the more painful—had stabbed me in the back straight through to the heart.

Add up the hours I'd spent over the years trying to figure out what Charlie had seen in her and I probably lost eight months of my life. Eloise wasn't even his type. Working-class background. Fixer-upper looks. Great hair—thick, curly, and auburn—pretty little nose, good cheekbones. But hippo hips and the legs of a Steinway. If she tweezed the unibrow and got hold of a good dentist, she'd be attractive, neck up. By our senior year, she'd ditched the New York accent and had begun to sound vaguely like Judi Dench, though her voice was still the texture of a potato grater. And then, when Charlie and I split, she sprung for the complete makeover—caps, electrolysis—and went after him. No one was better at realizing—no, wringing out every last drop of— her potential than Eloise Flint.

After they'd hooked up, she and I stopped talking, of course, and I never heard from him—he *should* have been ashamed, going back to the same sandbox for his next playmate. But I'd see flashes of them around town, or walking across the Common. And then it was summer and I went home to eat my heart out in private. By October, their mismatched affair was over. The scuttlebutt was that it was Charlie who'd ended it.

It might have been over for him, but I wasn't finished with Eloise Flint. Five years later, I got the chance to take back my own.

Marti used her elbow to nudge me out of my reverie. "Trust me, Eloise Flint's man-poaching days are over. High-def TV is ruthless. She looked old enough to be your mother. As for Carolyn Brinks, the media dish is she jumped straight from Charlie's arms into the bed of that horndog—what's his name, the Italian prime minister. So no threat there. And if your Charlie did any growing up in the last twenty-five years, he knows pâté when he tastes it. That's you, girl. If you ask me, you're way too good for him."

Which is what friends are for. To say that when it's obviously not true.

"Anyway," Marti continued, "it's Kiki you really have to worry about. She'll duel you to the death for the soul of her son. I'm warning you, Jude—this time, watch your back."

Chapter 13

Friday afternoon, I brought two containers of my homemade chicken soup and a ziplock bag of the matzo balls to my mother. I was a good daughter.

As a kid, I was good because I had no choice. By default, Grace was all I had. If she'd died, what would have happened to me? My father, sunning himself in Arizona, showed no interest and even if, pricked by conscience, he decided to rescue me, I doubt the chippie would have allowed him to take in his half-caste daughter. Grandma Roz, who thought of me as part of her meshugena son's biggest mistake, couldn't take on such a responsibility. By the time I was ten, she was in her seventies and bent nearly in half by osteoporosis. The only haven left for me would have been with Aunt Phyllis, who actually liked me and would have been constrained by her social worker's principles and her good heart not to let me slip into foster care. But life with her daughter, my bitchy cousin Staci, would have been hell. So my mother couldn't die.

Her dying was the central theme of my nightmares and most of my anxious daydreams. I was consumed by all the ways she could bite the dust and leave me alone in the world.

As I'd read through the *Getting to Know Performers in Music* series, the biography of Isadora Duncan always stopped me cold. The book ended with Isadora strangling on her own scarf while driving a French sports car. How many times did I reread that gruesome paragraph, obsessing? We didn't own a car, my mother didn't drive, but she worked with sewing machines every day and her long hair could get caught in the handwheel and . . .

In fourth grade, we covered New York City history and learned about the Triangle Shirtwaist fire. The image of the women sweatshop workers tumbling from the windows like tossed rag dolls was etched in my memory. My mother labored in a clothing factory. The building was old and high. What if . . .

After Mrs. Beckersham intervened because I was throwing up before my lessons, my mother took me to visit Slimline Swimsuits. She pointed to all the brightly lit exit signs and introduced me to Mr. Hersh, her boss, who told me he would personally keep an eye on Gracie so nothing would happen to her on his watch. "We love your mom here. Now you stop worrying. Such a serious little girl."

I needed to save my mother. When she went to the market for our dinner after work, I met her at the subway station so I could help carry the grocery bags. When she sniffed with only the possibility of a cold, I dosed her with aspirin. I unlaced her work shoes and brought her slippers and tea before I set the table for dinner. Anything, *anything* to keep her alive.

Only after Charlie ditched me and I survived the most pain I'd ever known was I able to let go. If anything happened to my mother now, I knew I could make it on my own. With that knowledge, I rebelled and married Rebound Todd. Probably so I wouldn't have to make it on my own. My mother had warned me. "Not for you. He very strange boy. You love Charlie, he don't want you, so you think Todd better than nothing. Sometimes nothing better than something."

For about twenty years I didn't worry about her dying. I was busy; she was still relatively young. Then perimenopause unleashed its crazy-making changes in me at the same time she began to show her age. It was a toxic combination. I insisted she get out of Bed-Stuy just as the neighborhood was turning around. I found her a small apartment fifteen minutes from my house in a predominantly Jewish section of northwest Baltimore. Grace had an affinity for Jews. She'd been in the Pikesville apartment for four months when she slipped in the shower, and that's when I moved her to Blumen House.

Finally, I could exhale. But habits, especially death-defying ones, were hard to break.

Two days into Passover, carting a cool pack with containers of soup, I drove to my mother's. In case she got the flu or a sore throat or frostbite in April, she'd have chicken broth available for a microwave zap.

I always knew where to find her on Friday afternoons. Not that she wasn't in the activity room most days, but she never missed "Pimlico at Blumen." This game—residents bet on DVDs of horse races run years ago, but new to them—always drew the biggest, rowdiest crowd of the week. Out in the parking lot, I could hear the shouts whipping the ponies through the homestretch. Inside, the room was pandemonium.

God forbid you should distract the Blumen Housers when the field was in motion. Asking Mrs. Botansky if my mother was in the ladies' room evoked a backhanded shoo. "Upstairs."

My heart sank when the apartment doorbell went unanswered on the second ring. The time my mother took the fall in her Pikesville apartment, I'd let myself in to find her sprawled against the tub, unable to hoist herself up. Blumen House had grab bars in the bathroom and didn't allow scatter rugs, but you never knew.

I used my key. One step in, I sensed something was off and just as quickly that it wasn't an emergency. The table in the dinette held a glass of iced tea, cubes floating. My mother didn't drink iced tea—hot, yes, cups and cups of pale green *nok cha*, but never iced. The apartment was too warm. And humid, as if someone had just showered. Dance music filtered from behind the bedroom's closed door, and—ugh—the stink of cigarette smoke hung in the air.

As I stood in the tiny foyer adding it all up—I'd never been swift at arithmetic—the mystery solved itself by emerging from the bathroom. I hadn't seen him in two decades, but he hadn't changed much. Still a putz. Irwin Raphael, wearing only pajama bottoms, a fake orange tan, and a smear of shaving cream on one cheek, peered at me with a nearsighted squint.

"Judy. Jesus," he said. "You don't knock? You could give someone a heart attack."

Chapter 14

⁓

"What the hell are you doing here?" I stared pop-eyed and disbelieving.

My father-in-name-only came up with a jaunty response. "I was invited." He smiled with exaggerated innocence.

That did it. I barked, "Where is she? Where's my mother?"

She exited the bedroom, her almond eyes chestnut round, to see what the noise was all about. Canny as a fox, the old man retreated to the bathroom to let her deal with me.

"*Aigoo.* Be nice, Judith." She stood before me, making *calm down* waves with both hands.

"No, I will not be nice. He's in his *pajamas*. A married man."

"Not married anymore. Lorna die six months back. Irwin is widow."

"Widower," I said automatically. I'd been giving my mother English lessons for most of my life. "Irwin is a widower." Hearing myself say it made it real. "And look at you."

At least she wasn't in her nightgown, one of the new ones she'd bought at Loehmann's. Damn. I should have known. Her fancy haircut. The weight loss. The sudden interest in fashion. I wanted to kick myself, but I was wearing my Spanx and my ass wasn't low enough to meet my foot.

She was all dolled up in something I hadn't seen before, and I knew my mother's closet. The neckline was scooped way too low for a woman of seventy-eight. Dangling in a cleavage that I swear to God could only have been made by a push-up bra was not her Life Alert lavaliere, but a delicate chain suspending a diamond pendant that had to be a full carat.

"He gave you that." With a trembling finger, I pointed to the jewel in the cleft. "You know where it came from, don't you?"

My mother's hand flew to the diamond.

"From you know who, the dead wife."

"No, not true."

Irwin's voice issued from the bathroom. "Don't talk what you have no idea about."

"He took it off her corpse," I said.

"No, it your grandma Roz jewelry. Your aunt Phyllis give him."

"You believe that?"

That brought Irwin out of his den, dark eyes shining. He'd changed into chinos and a T-shirt with a Brooklyn Dodgers logo. Not only had he shaved, but he'd slicked his dyed hair into a pompadour circa 1950. Back in the day, on the mean streets of Brooklyn, my father had been what they used to call a "hood," a bad boy. Leather jacket, garrison belt, huge Star of David on a rope chain so the Italian gang he hung with would never forget they had a ballsy Jew in their midst. I'd seen the pictures. This was my heritage.

He walked up to my mother and draped an arm around her shoulders. They stood there, the two of them, as I'd never seen them standing before. A united front. Sure, now it was easy. There was no me to bring up, no chippie with the lure of easy money opening the escape hatch from responsibility.

I ignored him and said to my mother, "You—just *you*—talk to me."

"You make big deal, but small deal, Judith. He come in for Seder to Aunt Phyllis. No Seder. But here already, East Coast, so he stop by."

"You knew about this how long ago?"

"Okay, maybe month."

"We've been e-mailing," Irwin said, unbidden.

"You e-mail?" I stared at my mother, astounded.

"Winnie Chang teach me. Easy. I join Facebook soon."

"Holy Mary, Mother of God," I said.

"None of that," my father admonished.

"And he's sleeping here? Of course he is."

"Listen, kiddo. I can afford the best hotel in town. That Harbor whatever? I could take a suite there if I wanted. But your mother said, Why not stay here? and I thought, Yeah, why not? We got lots to catch up on. We're making up for lost time."

"I'm going to vomit," I said. I actually felt close to heaving.

"You so high-stringed, Judith. Always like Shakespeare." Grace proclaimed dramatically, "I go vomit." She made gagging sounds. "You need calm down. Almost fifty. You give yourself new aneurysm."

Instinctively I massaged my temple. I turned to Irwin. "How long?"

"A week or two." He pulled a nail file from his pocket and proceeded to dig away. "I want to see the sights. That old boat in the harbor." The *Constellation*. "Go to D.C. and stop by the White House and all. Eat crabs. I never ate a Baltimore crab."

"Very good. Baltimore crab best," my mother said, looking up at him. She showed her teeth smudged with lipstick. A new color, pink, like a young girl's.

"I'm out of here," I said. I placed the jars of soup on the *Sun* newspaper laid out on the dinette table.

"Whoa, girlie. I'm a different man now," Irwin said. "You oughta give me a chance."

He ambled—actually it was more like a hood's swagger—to the sideboard and lifted a shirt-sized box wrapped in silver paper. He held it out with both hands. "I brought this for you. A peace offering. What, no? You have no idea what it is."

"How many birthdays did you forget? How many?"

I caught a quick visual exchange between him and my mother, his eyebrows up, her head waggling a negative cue.

I turned on her. "Boy, you forgive fast. Well, I don't. All those years he didn't know I was alive. Left you without a dime." I tapped my temple. "I can't imagine what's going on in there. Have you lost it? Do we need to see Dr. Wolf?" I pointedly named her geriatrician.

She stepped in front of me. "Don't talk like that, Judith. So rude. I'm mother, you child. No matter how old."

"Fine. You're right. I need to stop worrying about you." A proposal I didn't believe for a minute. "We're both grown women. But this, I can't deal with. So call me when he's gone."

Irwin was snapping his right thumb and third finger noise-lessly. It was obvious I made him nervous and he was jonesing for a cigarette. I lobbed my final shot. "For your information, it's against the rules to smoke in the Blumen House units. They find out, they'll evict her."

"I smoke on the balcony," he said. But he stood his ground.

My mother held a jar of my soup in each hand. "You wait one minute, Judith. I have stuff for you too."

"Next time."

"No room in freezer. You take now. Don't insult. One more minute only. I have *japchae* in kitchen for you." I couldn't resist her sweet potato noodles with veggies.

"I'll wait outside in the hall," I said, which was juvenile of me, but the brat I never had a chance to be as a child exploded every once in a while from my adult self.

"See ya, Judy," Irwin said as I closed the door behind me.

"You don't give kiss?" my mother asked at the elevator a few minutes later as she handed over a shopping bag.

I never left my mother without pecking her on the cheek. But I couldn't. I stood there, a block of ice, thinking I'd probably be visited by a plague of locusts and boils for this fifth-commandment transgression. But I just couldn't.

"I know you so angry. But he be gone soon. Sad man. Pity. Wife dead. He need family now."

I snapped, "I'm not his family and neither are you. He made sure of that long ago."

No one could sigh like my mother. She pulled it up from her feet and as it passed her heart it picked up a quaver. At her voice box it added a thread of soprano sorrow.

"Okay. I call you later. Or I send you e-mail address and you write after you calm down."

I was nearly hyperventilating when I reached the parking lot. As I clicked my remote, a huge cheer surged from the Blumen House activity room. I checked my watch. It was the last race of the afternoon and someone had just won the trifecta, the big jackpot. My mother had pulled that off twice the year before and had taken home expensive prizes: a juicer and a certificate for a massage at a local spa. A gambling woman, she bet long shots. Not me.

I popped the Toyota's trunk and, maneuvering the jars of *japchae* to stand upright in the shopping bag, caught a flash of silver paper at the bottom. My sly mother had tucked Irwin's gift in the bag. Or maybe he had. I removed the box and shoved it to the back of the trunk, next to the emergency kit and an old blanket. Out of sight, out of mind.

Chapter 15

Maybe if Marti had been around to hammer some sense into me, I would have kept my family drama contained. But she was somewhere in the Caribbean doing research for a *Herald* article about food service on cruise ships departing from Baltimore Harbor. And she swore she was going incommunicado on her assignment cum windfall vacation.

On my own, I phoned my aunt Phyllis. After her unsolicited report on the current state of her bladder, I brought up my most recent surprise.

"It was entirely Irwin's idea to see your mother," she explained. "I didn't recommend it, but now that he's there, maybe it isn't altogether off the wall. I know you're in shock, Judith. So take a deep breath and don't make any rash decisions."

"I've had forty-three years to come up with my decision, Aunt Phyllis."

"Very clever. Look, I'm not saying my brother is a perfect person, but who is? Not you, Judith. Though you've done well for yourself in your career, you're not an expert in the romance department to say the least. Which says to me you're not well equipped to give relationship advice to Grace, especially considering your last move."

My mother, with her big mouth, had told her about my split with Geoff.

"Frankly, your track record stinks." Unlike that of my cousin Staci, divorced from a two-timing orthodontist, now married to a proctologist who was a walking, talking advertisement for his medical specialty. Seth Cohen-Shenker, MD, was a certified asshole.

"Also, where your father is concerned, you don't know the whole story. Believe me. And I'm in no position to tell you. But take it on my say-so—he's not the terrible, awful man you think he is."

"Meaning what?"

"Meaning ask your mother. My lips are sealed."

I would, but before Aunt Phyllis hung up, we had one more of Irwin's lies to confirm.

"He gave her a necklace. With a diamond. He told my mother it was from Grandma Roz, but I'm sure it was the chippie's."

"You're sure? See how you jump to conclusions. It *is* from your grandmother. She left me her engagement ring and my brother got the diamond drop. I was executor of the will and I held off handing it over to him until the chippie . . . until Lorna died, because I was afraid he'd give it to her."

Okay, he'd told the truth about that. But there was a Korean proverb: "Even into a mouse hole, light shines." I didn't quote it, but I was certain it applied.

"Grandma Roz had diamonds?" Not much money in that household, and I strained to recall if I'd ever seen her wear anything around her neck other than her reading glasses on a lariat. Her knuckles, swollen with arthritis, had been bare. Of that much I was sure.

"Only two pieces and they were in and out of hock during the Depression. When she got them back for good, she kept them in a bank vault. Well, well, so Irwin gave the jewelry to Grace. This is what I mean about a basically good human being." I heard the muffled click of call waiting, but my aunt ignored it. This was serious business. She wouldn't be interrupted.

"If you're smart—and no one can deny you're book smart—but if you have *seykhl*, common sense, you'll let your mother make her own decision as to how to deal with my brother. What you decide for yourself is your business, but I hope you make your judgment based on facts, not speculation. I can't say more than that."

Again with the sealed lips? It must have been one hell of a secret she was hiding. On the other hand, I could make a case for her inflating some minor Hebraic drama into Greek tragedy. "And my last word is, you ought to rethink getting rid of the Australian. His quality doesn't come along every day and you're not getting any younger, Judith, if you know what I mean."

I knew what she meant.

"Which reminds me, we got your party invitation and we're a yes, your uncle Arnold and I. I'm not sure about Staci and Seth. They may be in Israel that week."

I'd included my aunt and uncle on the guest list. But Staci and Seth? Was this Marti's idea of a joke?

"And one very last word, my dear niece—whom I love in spite of her hardheadedness, and I wonder where you get that from. Irwin Raphael is your father. Whatever else he may be, he's your father. And when he dies, and he's not so young, you don't want to be left with regrets."

"The regrets will be all on his side," I said. "I promise you."

I'd told my mother to phone me when Irwin was gone. No word on Saturday. And tightening the screws, digging in my heels, I didn't call her. In the last five years, we'd rarely missed a day talking either in person or by phone, but it was fine. *She* was fine. She had him.

I had no one—not to think through the new situation with anyway. Charlie's message on my answering machine Friday night was thirty seconds of firming up plans for meeting in D.C. Besides, even if he had the time or the interest, there was no way I was going to discuss my family problems with Charlie Pruitt. I'd learned my lesson the first time around.

Geoff, who really was skillful at analyzing relationships as long as they weren't his own, did a good job of keeping his distance. In the musicians' lounge pre-performance, he stood off to one side sipping coffee and conversing with Deena Marquis, our on-call harpist, whom I'd always suspected of having the hots for him. Now she had a clear path, which she'd scurried up as fast as her long legs could carry her.

Well, good for her. And him. This was a couple made in magazine-cover heaven—he tall, buff, and handsome; she model slim and glossily attractive, if you liked the perfectly made-up, surgically refined, breast-enhanced type. Geoff must have. He seemed captivated by whatever she was telling him, though I did catch the flick of his gaze toward my general vicinity.

As I drained the last of my Diet Dr. Pepper, he pretended to be seeing me for the first time and waved. Deena swept me with a blank, uncomprehending stare as if I were a stranger, which at this juncture I pretty much was. When the five-minute warning buzzed, I left them still chattering away.

The performance that evening was less than brilliant. Brass held up, but strings seemed listless to me, and my stand partner gave me a roll of her eyes at the lackluster violins in the first half. Only the harp was in top form. Deena's glissandos were positively ecstatic.

On my way out, Geoff caught up with me. "Shit performance, wasn't it?"

I nodded.

"Just a reminder," he said. "I'll be at your place Monday morning. You've forgotten, haven't you? We need to get cracking. Your audition will be here before we know it. Schedule two hours this time. We'll go over the selections and then, well, we'll see."

So Marti had been wrong. Me too. I knew him better than she did and *I* hadn't figured he'd hang in after I'd strung him up. Amazing. He was going to make good on his coaching offer. Which was beyond even Geoff's everyday Aussie generosity. Or maybe, just maybe, he'd decided that keeping a hand in and an eye on me was his best chance of a) getting the inside scoop on my revised love life or b) being around to pick up the pieces when it collapsed.

I scanned his expression. Open, genuine, pure Geoff. No trace of a self-serving motive. More likely, I was the cynic here. Suddenly my life seemed infinitely, depressingly complicated.

I tried to uncomplicate it. Match him noble gesture for noble gesture. "I'm really very grateful, Geoff. But under the circumstances, I'd understand if—"

"Ten. Promptly. All I ask is coffee on the boil and a melody in your heart. Ah, the infamous Raphael lip curl. Very well, just the coffee will do. Joining the gang for dinner? No? See you Monday, then. Cheers."

And he was off. To where and with whom, I didn't know or care. All that much.

My mother sent me an e-mail on Sunday night. A first. It had been posted by seoulfulgirl@hotmail.com at seven p.m. I didn't get on my computer until nine.

Why yu not call. Mean chile. No matter what I luv yu.
Who yu think I luv more. Father. No. Yu always. But
yu need grow up. Judith. Yu be like kid. So stupid.
Grow up. Call.

I luv yu.

Momi

I called her home phone and got my own voice, the incoming message I'd recorded on her answering machine. She must have been out with Irwin. I phoned her cell. She didn't pick up. Maybe she was in the apartment but otherwise occupied. *Aigoo!*

I left a message. "Call me, please." I didn't include the "after he's gone" this time. Aunt Phyllis's hint about some deep, dark family secret had been nibbling at me, so I added, "You're right, time for a chat." Then, quickly, "Love you too." Because I really wasn't a mean chile.

Chapter 16

After my divorce from Todd, I'd landed a job with the Maryland Philharmonic and relocated to Baltimore, where I bought a 1920s colonial in a leafy Mt. Washington neighborhood. The house was probably too big for me, with four bedrooms and a dining room big enough to swing a cougar in, but back then, having fled an increasingly cramped marriage—when God moved in with all the prayers and the koshering and the other baggage, it got really tight—I craved space.

Friends used phrases like "rattle around" when they visited, but I loved the place. The kitchen was flooded with sunlight in the morning, and I'd made a high-ceilinged hexagonal area on the ground floor into my music room. It had incredible acoustics.

So there was no excuse Monday morning for the sounds I produced as I mangled two solos required for my audition. After an hour of this torture, punctuated by Geoff's increasingly impatient commentary, he tossed down the sheet music in disgust.

"What the hell's going on with the Bach, Judith? You were rushing that last passage. And the intonation was sharp. I know it's technically a killer, but you've done it well before. Worst of all, the feeling's missing. You're playing cello, but you're not playing music."

I leaned my cheek against the fingerboard, the cello's neck. Beautiful instrument. Smooth, cool body. Sensuous curves. Warm response. Great love of my life, it never caused me the heartache my men did. All I had to do was give it my best and it gave me its best.

I exhaled a groan. "It was that bad, huh?"

"Try to slide through on that crap and I guarantee you'll crash and burn in front of the committee. You've got serious competition for this post. We're talking heavy hitters here. So you can't cut even a single corner."

He was right. An opening for principal in a major city brings out the top candidates from around the world. The good news was I had an initial advantage. As associate principal with the home orchestra, I automatically leapfrogged the preliminary trials. The bad was that from then on everyone was on an equal footing because the semis, as well as the prelims, were performed behind a screen, the musicians identified only by numbers.

Numbers that fell like pins. The first round cut maybe sixty contestants to around twenty; the next produced a final three, who played in full view of the audition committee. If I didn't step up my game, I wouldn't make it past the second round—a colossal embarrassment when you played for the home team.

"My best guess is you're not concentrating." Geoff slumped back in the chair. "Is it me? Am I throwing you off? If so, get over it. Or get someone else to work with you."

"It's not you." The truth was, it probably was partly him, though I wasn't going to risk losing his sharp critical judgment by confessing that, now that we'd split, his closeness—a few feet away observing intently—made me edgy.

"Not me is good. Is it your dad, then?"

I felt like I'd been sucker punched. It took me a moment to regain my breath. "My . . ." My tongue locked on the d-word.

"Irwin. His sudden surfacing knock you for a loop?"

If I'd gripped the bow any tighter it would have fused to my fingers. "How did you know? Wait. My mother told you, right?"

Geoff played with a loose thread on the arm of the club chair. "Actually, I kind of ran into him yesterday."

"You ran into Irwin. Kind of."

"At your mum's." He looked up then, brow furrowed. "It was all very accidental, Jude. I'd bought a box of Passover truffles as a gift for your aunt Phyllis. With the Seder canceled— Well, I know how much your mother loves chocolate, so I thought to drop it off at Blumen House. I figured Mum would be playing cards in the activity room. But she was in the apartment. And so was dear old Dad. A real character, Irwin. Fancies himself the charmer."

"Yeah, your average sociopathic charmer." A gong of pain rang behind my temples. "Really, Geoff, when were you planning on telling me this?"

He checked his watch. "About now, actually. I didn't want to rattle you before you began playing. I thought we'd break halfway through and over coffee we'd talk. So let's. Come on." He rose and extended his hand. "Coffee break. You're no good anyway until we have this out."

For the next fifteen minutes we sipped coffee and talked. Actually, I mostly listened while Geoff provided insights I probably could have dug up on my own had I been able to summon the courage to crawl solo into dim places.

"I don't know if your father-in-name-only"—his mouth went wry—"has changed. Maybe, maybe not. Some people never do. But from everything you've told me about your childhood, your mother has. She's a different person now, right?"

"Very."

My childhood coincided with Grace's early years in America. She'd been much more introverted back then, made shy by the bewilderingly foreign environment and her lack of English. Turned cautious by the shock of Irwin's leaving. Depressed by poverty, responsibility, loneliness.

I knew even back then that she'd once had a zest for life. I saw it in the few photos she'd brought with her from Seoul. One, especially, captivated me preadolescence when I was fumbling for my own identity. Grace leaning against Private Irwin Raphael in the Lucky Time Bar. He wearing his uniform and an uncommonly tentative grin. She, tarted up in a slinky dress slit to the thigh, hoisting a shot glass filled with what the GIs thought was whiskey but really was tea. Her smile seemed pure, unforced. The camera exaggerated her wink.

She'd never been a prostitute, she'd sworn, and I believed her. "Never *ch'ang-yo*." But she'd come close. "Lot of fun even with war on. I pretty girl. Many GI want marry me. I pick your daddy. Not so good choice."

I took a pensive bite of bagel. "Back in Brooklyn, she was always working to keep us afloat. When she wasn't working, she was tired. But once I was grown and on my own, she blossomed."

"You need to respect that, Jude. Stop treating her the way you did as a child. As if *she's* a child. Or some doomed creature tumbling off a fourth-floor fire escape."

I'd told him about my terror of the Triangle fire. I'd told him so many things, trusting he'd never betray me or my nightmares. And so far he hadn't.

"She's upset that you're angry with her. 'Judith throw tantrum because of father. Won't call me.'" He had Grace's shorthand English down pat. "Come on. That's a three-year-old's response."

I nodded. "I admit it. But I left a message, and when she didn't get back to me I called again first thing this morning. I had maybe two minutes with my mother before he was bellowing for her in the background."

"Go see her, Jude. Take her for a walk in the garden, just the two of you. She loves that garden. So what if he's there?"

"He'd better not be around," I fumed. "He did say he'd be gone in a week or two, didn't he?" I grasped for that sliver of hope.

"After he's finished seeing the sights," Geoff said.

"After he's made my mother fall for his bullshit again. Then he'll take off like he did before."

"Say, for the sake of argument, you're right. Say he does and she does. You know what? She'll survive as she did before. The way she's done all her life. And it *is* her life, Jude."

"Yup. To screw up."

"Maybe to screw up. We all have that right," he said, gazing into his coffee. "As I don't have to tell *you*."

Our kitchen shrink session must have worked. I played much better in the second hour.

I did an okay job on Strauss's *Don Quixote*, then gave my all to the chunk of Brahms. Its serenely gorgeous cello melody seemed to emerge liquid from the strings. Geoff applauded at the finish. For the last piece, I'd made a sprightly start on the overture to *The Bartered Bride* when the phone rang.

"Focus," Geoff warned above my voice on the outgoing message.

The nearest phone, the one with the answering machine, was in the next room. The volume was set louder than I'd remembered.

"Get used to it. You'll have distractions," Geoff was saying above my recorded voice. "When I auditioned for my first job, a light crashed from the rafters onto the stage. I soldiered on and won the seat. Don't stop. Play over it."

But this distraction wouldn't be played over. It came through loud and clear and nearly toppled me from my chair.

"Hi, Ju-ju. It's Charlie. Listen, slight change of plans for to-morrow night. I'm hoping you can meet me at the hotel at six instead of six thirty. I'd like to get to the party a little early to see Uncle Ed before the crowd arrives and swamps him. I left the same message on your cell phone. I'm a belt-and-suspenders kind of guy. Looking forward to a wonderful evening. Call only if the time change presents a problem. Otherwise, see you at six in the lobby of the Mandarin."

I played on throughout. Wildly, badly. Geoff never took his eyes off me. Not my fingers. My face.

When the passage was over, he rose, expressionless. "Out of control," he pronounced. No kidding. "We'll need to work on that. Next week, same time, same station. Yes?"

So we were going to ignore the Harvard-educated elephant in the music room. Disregarding large, disturbing obstacles in our relationship was quintessential Geoff. For once, that was fine by me.

When we were a couple, he'd come in and out of my house at his pleasure. Now, as if he were a guest, I walked Geoff to the door. On the threshold he turned, his smile tightly wound. "Well," he said, "looks as if we're off to a decent start, Judith." He leaned forward to kiss my cheek, then thought better of it.

I backed up a step. "Thanks for everything," I said. "I really appreciate it."

"Sure. Ah, yes, almost forgot, and now is as good a time as any. Excellent time in fact." He reached into his pocket and pulled out my house key, the one I'd given him a year earlier, when we'd been at a high point. He pressed it into my hand.

It was a plain metal copy of a common key, but it lay in my palm as heavy as a stone, carrying the weight of lost hope, I suppose, or regret. But hope for what? Regret for what? Entering our relationship, I hadn't known exactly what I wanted from it. Now I was exiting and I still didn't know what I wanted. Except something more. Had I ever told Geoff that? No, I'd just added it to the stacks of words unspoken, risks untaken that both of us were so skilled at building.

Even now, we weren't exactly saying good-bye—he was still a part of my musical life—so what was there to say?

He thought of something, but it took him a moment. I'd pocketed the key and he was halfway down the path to his car when he called back over his shoulder, "Don't forget. Work on that focus, Jude."

He'd timed it so I didn't have to look in his eyes.

Chapter 17

I passed on the Donna Karan sheath my mother had bought me at Loehmann's and wore my lucky dress to the Georgetown reception. Of course I had a lucky dress. Superstition had its very own gene on my chromosome string. Two, in fact.

My mother consulted a *mudang*. As a kid, I hadn't been allowed to shampoo my hair on the morning of a school test because I would wash away my memory. And no cutting of your nails at night. Animals might eat the clippings and thus consume your spirit. Such Korean mishegoss. Craziness.

On my other crazy side, Aunt Phyllis wouldn't sew a loose button on Uncle Arnold's shirt while he wore it for fear of stitching up his brain. So it wasn't farfetched for me to choose for my date with Charlie the dress I'd worn the night I played for the Dalai Lama at a benefit for Tibetan earthquake victims, and at a Blair House chamber concert for the vice president of Malawi. Also on my first day back with the orchestra after my aneurysm. That it was the same dress Geoff had frenziedly unzipped the first time we made love never entered my zone of irony.

Besides, I looked great in it. I have super narrow Korean shoulders and bountiful Jewish boobs that at forty-nine were only beginning to lose their lift. The deep V of the neckline made the most of my cross-cultural configurations. Needless to say, the dress was black. As an orchestra musician, my closet contained the wardrobe of a perpetual mourner—one from America, not Korea, where death calls for something chic in white. So it was a matter of which black dress, and this one had always given me a boost. Plus, it gave me a waistline, which was something of a menopausal miracle.

"You look stunning," Charlie said as he rounded one of the marble columns in the lobby of the Mandarin Oriental, a foyer that looked like the entrance to Xanadu. Charlie was the only straight man I knew who could get away with using the word "stunning."

He looked pretty stunning himself. Okay, dashing. He did not drop women in their tracks the way Geoff did with his height and naturally blond streaked hair. But Charles Evans Pruitt cut a fine masculine figure. Dignified. Obviously moneyed. His suit appeared custom-made and, like its wearer, classic. It could have been purchased yesterday or twenty years ago. That kind of disregard for time was an emblem of those who could afford to buy it.

Charlie took my hand and led me through the lobby. "I'm going to leave the car in the garage. We'll grab a cab. Parking in Georgetown is hell."

We walked the final block of the cordoned-off street and, IDs checked, got wanded on the steps of a handsome town house. In the hall, an obvious agent—they were all so much of a type that the secret in Secret Service seemed a misnomer—extended his hand. "Your Honor. A pleasure to see you, sir."

"This is all for the big boss, I presume," Charlie said on the shake.

An almost imperceptible nod from the agent.

"The president?" I whispered as Charlie moved me along. My

heart gave a flutter. I was a commander-in-chief groupie. I identified with our fearless leader. We were both half-castes.

Charlie said, "I heard he and the first lady might drop in, but I didn't want to get your hopes up."

Drop in. Not quite like Mrs. Santos, our neighbor in Bed-Stuy, who'd show up at our door to borrow our Raid.

The home's sunny front rooms were handsomely furnished and filled with a galaxy of the brightest stars in the Washington universe. We got maybe a minute of face time with Justice Braithwaite, a tall New England aristocrat brought to emaciation by his lung cancer. He nearly bent in half to hug Charlie. He laid a hand on my shoulder as he told us he was eager to return to private life in Amherst, was looking forward to sailing with Charlie in Maine that summer, and hoped to see me again. Not a word about his illness, of course, and then we were absorbed into the crowd.

There were senators I recognized and congressional reps Charlie pointed out. Celebs of a higher order. Nobel-winning authors, film stars fighting hunger and land mines worldwide. And there was Yo-Yo Ma, who waved hi to me, impressing Charlie. In turn, he nearly bowled me over by introducing me to the secretary of state, Eleanor Aldridge, who just happened to be his first cousin on his father's side, a fact he'd never bothered to mention.

We wove our way through a majority of the Supreme Court justices. Bumped shoulders with media pundits trying to appear harmless while nibbling hors d'oeuvres and listening for dropped gossip. After a while I lost count and then interest. More tantalizing was my first sight of Kiki Pruitt, who stood in the dining room balancing on a cane. Behind her, a middle-aged woman in a white uniform leaned forward to catch Kiki's nonstop commentary. The private nurse, I presumed.

Smaller and thinner than Ruth Bader Ginsburg, who up close

and in person was prettier than in her photos, Kiki with her deep Palm Beach tan and a shar-pei's worth of wrinkles resembled nothing so much as an animated prune. There's a saying that by the time you reach sixty you've earned the face you deserve. There was no doubt in my mind that over her lifetime Kathryn Pruitt had accumulated more creases, crumples, and puckers for nastiness than the puny pile she'd netted from her treatment of me.

Charlie spotted her, I was sure of it, and made a sharp turn into the library, where he introduced me to one of the lock-jawed Braithwaite cousins. For the moment, I let the detour slide, but my date was now on probation. Did he have the guts to present me to his mother or was he still scared shitless of her? As much as I'd been dreading meeting up with the witch, as soon as I'd seen her, as wrinkled and irrelevant as an old love letter, I knew I could take her.

The Braithwaite cousin faded into the crowd and I turned to Charlie.

"Where to now?" I asked, giving him every opportunity.

He inhaled a deep, steeling breath. "Well, it's rude we haven't said hello to my mother."

He'd passed the first test. "Then let's do it," I said.

He looked at me admiringly, as if I'd passed mine. Then, simultaneously, we swiveled our glances toward the dining room. Kiki had us in her sights. "I have to warn you, the strokes have done their damage. There's no censor between her brain and her mouth. She's been known to make very inappropriate comments."

"Some things never change," I said, and heard his shaky laugh. His hand in mine was clammy as he threaded us through the crowd.

Kiki arced forward, her patrician nose inches from my cleavage as if she were inspecting produce. I expected her to reach in, grab one of my boobs, and squeeze it for ripeness. Charlie, buzzing alarm, insinuated a shoulder between us. My hero.

She strong-armed him out of her way. "And who is this pretty thing?" She cackled. Okay, so she didn't cackle. Her voice was still musical. Maybe not the elegant flute of middle age, but a rich oboe. I backed up and thought I caught a flash of recognition in those colorless eyes as she took me in. One spark only; then they settled into a pleasant daze.

"Mother, I'd like you to meet Judith Raphael." He made it sound as if she and I were meeting for the first time. I slid him a look that said, *Yellow belly.* Quickly he tried to make up, but from his face I realized even this small concession was painful. "Judith is an old friend."

Kiki seemed to have spun the attitude wheel and landed on charming. "Lovely coloring. And what pretty eyes you have. Such an interesting almond shape." And slipped a notch to fairy tale wicked. Oh, she knew me all right. The strokes hadn't wiped out the memory center.

"That's from my mother's side," I drawled. "The Ryangs. Of the Hwanghae Ryangs?" She looked confused and I immediately felt contrite.

But not for long. As clear and strong as the glass of vodka I held, she then asked, "What *is* your background, dear?"

"I'm half Korean." As she processed that, I added, without mercy, "And half Jewish."

Kiki's nurse reached for her charge's elbow, but the old lady stayed steady on her feet. Charlie was another matter. He swayed slightly.

"What an odd combination." She turned to her son. "Wasn't that awful girl you used to see up in Cambridge half Jewish and half some kind of Oriental?"

"Mother, for God's sakes." It was embarrassing to hear

Charlie croak. He hadn't been drinking, abstaining to keep his wits, I suppose, to be able to referee the play-off between Kiki and me. And for what? She'd rendered him speechless. I handed him my glass and he drained it.

"*I'm* that awful girl," I said.

Kiki's eyes remained narrow, calculating, unsurprised. Of course she'd known all along.

She reached out and placed her talon over my free hand. "But you're lovely, dear. Much more attractive as an older woman than as a young one. Isn't she, Chip, very attractive for an older woman? Not even a wisp of gray in your hair. And so straight. None of that kinkiness from your other side."

Charlie had begun to laugh. The chuckle was low but maniacal. This was completely out of his hands and he knew it. From outside, growing closer, the sirens of the president's escort cars spiraled a warning.

"Yes, Korean hair turns gray late," I said sweetly. That's how I'd just decided to play this. Sweet. Let him see sweet.

Kiki removed her hand from mine and swept it over her hair. It was silver, still youthfully glossy, pulled taut from her forehead to reveal every age spot along the horizontal rails of wrinkles— like the notes on a staff—and drawn into a chignon at the back of her neck.

"But your brains are pure Jewish, aren't they?" She smiled, ivory teeth showing. Beside me, Charlie's laugh escalated into madness. "I've always respected the Hebrew culture. Such a clever people with—"

Her critique of my heritage got drowned out by a call for attention from the front of the room. A path had been cleared down its center and lined with Secret Service. "Ladies and gentlemen," our host announced, "the President of the United States and the First Lady."

Chapter 18

Henry Kissinger once said, "Power is the ultimate aphrodisiac," and you knew he had to be speaking from experience. I mean, come on. The man had a thickly accented growl, accordion-pleated hair, a major paunch, and duck-splayed feet, but as Nixon's secretary of state he'd become the hottest piece of Washington property since the White House burned in the War of 1812.

To clarify, I wasn't turned on by the current president, who, as we moved down the makeshift receiving line, clasped my hand for approximately five seconds. Charmed, yes. Impressed, of course. But those lanky, long-lashed looks just didn't do it for me in the sizzle department. Now Charlie Pruitt—that was a different story. I'd always been drawn to Charlie in part—probably my worst part—for his proximity to power and privilege. Even better, for the easy grace bred though generations of American aristocracy. Of course, those were the same attractions that did me in once upon a time, but I told myself we were in a new fairy tale here.

When the president clapped Charlie's shoulder and said, "Good to see you, Judge. How's the tennis game coming along?" and Charlie said, "Holding my own, Mr. President," it was enough to make my legs go soft and my nipples hard. Not right there, but potentially.

"Very modest of you, but Rob Griffin told me you cream him on the court with regularity." Robert Griffin was New York's senior senator, a Republican. "I'd like to take you on myself one of these days." Oh God. Tingling.

"I'd be honored, sir, but not enough to rein in my backhand."

The president reared his head in a burst of laughter and I fanned myself with one hand.

Then again, I chalked up some points myself as we faced the first lady. Her hand swooped from a brisk handshake to thumb the material of my sleeve. While Charlie looked on, foot tapping nervously, she said, "Love your dress. Is it an American designer, I hope?"

"Vintage Galliano."

"Shame." Her brown eyes warmed. "You're with the Maryland Philharmonic, right? I spotted your entry on the guest list. I love the cello. I only play campfire guitar, but I think every child should learn an instrument. Our older daughter is taking cello lessons. She's not big on practicing, though. She says she'll never be really good at it, so what's the point?"

"I felt the same way," I said. "But my mother used to quote a Korean proverb to me. 'After three years in the village school-house, even a cat can recite a poem.'"

It took the first lady a moment to get it. Then she flashed a radiant smile. "Wonderful. I'll use it. A very wise woman, your mother."

"Yes, she is," I said. As we got nudged on, I thought of how thrilled my mom would be to hear *that* comment from *that* source.

Charlie was also pretty happy. "Nice going." He was beaming. "*Very* nice going."

. . .

When the president of the United States is a guest at a party, you're stuck there until he leaves. The Secret Service wants him clear of the site before you can even duck out for a pee (although, in this case, the bathrooms had been checked out by sniffer dogs before he arrived). So we waited.

Kiki waited less patiently. Citing weakness in her legs, she declined to make her way down the receiving line—for which blessing Charlie was going to slap an extra hundred bucks in the offertory tray at St. Bart's on Sunday. She sat ramrod stiff in a Queen Anne chair, casting a disdainful eye at the mixed-blood liberal president. When he made a touching little speech praising Ed Braithwaite, she bit her lip and stared at her cuticles. And when the door closed behind the presidential party, she was the first one up, a bit wobbly on those spindly sclerotic legs, to peck the justice good-bye.

Charlie had fetched my shawl on the way back and now he draped it around my shoulders. "Come on, we can get out of here now. And I've got something to show you back at the hotel."

That line uttered by any other man would have sounded like sexual innuendo. To my raised eyebrow he said, "Come on, Ju-ju, you know me better than that."

Funny, for the last twenty-five years I'd been thinking I hadn't known him at all.

Charlie's hotel room at the Mandarin was actually a suite. While I took in the breathtaking view of the Tidal Basin, he went to the safe and extracted a large manila envelope. He'd brought it from his Manhattan apartment, he told me as he sat next to me on the sofa, and could trace its provenance over decades. It had been with him in his rooms at Oxford, where he'd gone as a Rhodes Scholar after ditching me, then shelved in a brownstone at his bachelor digs in Brooklyn Heights, and even tucked away in the

Pound Ridge megamansion he'd shared with the shrink wife and the daughter.

"Memories. All I had of you, of us." He swallowed hard, then gave it over. "You open it," he said, watching my fingertips. "But take care handling the contents. Some of this stuff is fragile."

As I sorted through, I felt my throat tighten. The cache contained photos, notes, and letters we'd exchanged, programs from concerts I'd played as a student, a matchbook from the Union Oyster House, a scorecard from a Red Sox game. Incredible. Who knew Charlie Pruitt was a romantic pack rat, a nostalgic squirrel?

I'd kept no souvenirs of our time together. Correction: I did for a while and tortured myself sifting through them when the compulsion overcame me, typically when I was premenstrual. But just back from my honeymoon with Todd, I'd schlepped a plastic bag to the front of our apartment complex and finally and literally kicked what was left of Charlie Pruitt to the curb. After which I got drunk on cheap chardonnay and slept on the living room sofa for the night so my new husband couldn't touch me.

Charlie plucked a photo from the heap. "This one's my favorite. See if you know why."

"Good God." I held it at arm's length and squinted. "The Cambridge house. Wendell Street. Is that me? I don't even remember you taking this."

"Here, use my reading glasses," Charlie said. Ah, the gallantry of middle age. I still squinted. The hotel room was lit with a gentle, flattering light, but there was a desk with a reading lamp. I carried the photo into its brightness.

Now it was clear, and what struck me was how happy I looked. What was the phrase Marti used? Happy as if this was the day the world was created. In many ways, for me it had been. Two hours after the picture was taken, I lost the virginity I'd held on to way past its pull date.

"Now that was a party," Charlie said. "In every way." He'd come up behind and was peering over my shoulder. "Look at all those ashtrays. Everybody smoked in those days except you. You used to lecture me on the perils of tobacco. A woman ahead of her time." In the background, the huge back porch was a shambles of smeared dishes, dropped napkins, overloaded ashtrays.

"And there's Alan behind you, the last one to leave, remember? He wanted to talk Middle East politics all night and I wanted to get you into my arms."

As president of the Harvard Law School Forum, Charlie had been in charge of handling its programs. That night's speaker, Alan Dershowitz, had been Charlie's criminal law professor the year before, and despite their polar opposite political views, they'd liked and respected each other. Charlie had decided to host a postevent reception for Dershowitz at the house.

We'd brought in a maid service and the place shone. There was turkey and Caesar salad from a caterer, and I'd filled in with my own recipes. Dershowitz complimented me on Aunt Phyllis's chopped liver. As the evening wound down, he and Charlie drank scotch together in a corner. Heady stuff for two kids, even over-achievers like us. After we'd cleaned up, riding the high of our success, we fell onto the bed covered with fresh sheets for a change and made love for the first time. Not Charlie's first—there'd been a summer girl in Maine—but mine and ours.

"You remember the song that played as we washed dishes together? And I tossed the towel and swept you off your feet. 'Endless Love.' Diana Ross." Charlie stroked my hair.

"And Lionel Richie. His voice was so hot."

"*We* were so hot. What got to me was that up till then you'd been such a good little girl. Five dates and you only wanted to argue about Iran-Contra and busing, but no sex, not even serious fooling around. And then it was as if someone had struck a match to you."

"You did. I thought I was in love with you," I said.

"*I* thought you were in love with me. You weren't?" he murmured close to my neck.

"Before we made love I thought I was. Right after I wasn't so sure. You have to admit, that first time was a disaster. But then you brought me tea, remember, and the steamy towel because I could hardly walk. And that's when I knew. Really knew."

He was nuzzling me now. "I almost set fire to the microwave heating up that towel. But I would have done anything, I was so crazy about you. More in love than I'd ever been before or—" There was a God-forgive-me pause. "Since."

I have a pretty good ear and that note sounded like a clinker to me. Then again, it was possible he really believed it. And I wasn't angry. So much time had passed. Still, for the record, I had to say, "Before and since, but not enough."

That's when Charlie did what Charlie always used to do to shut me up. He turned me around into his arms and kissed me quiet. Nice. Oh yes, wonderful. "My sweet Judith," he whispered as we came up for air and the whiff of oxygen cleared my head. Suddenly I knew I wasn't going to be shut up by one of Charlie's kisses, no matter how thrilling. What had worked at twenty didn't work with me pushing fifty.

I disengaged and stepped back.

"I've been wondering," Charlie said, blue eyes catching, then searching my dark ones, "how many times a man can fall in love with the same woman in a single lifetime."

Okay, so *that* worked.

For about two minutes we kissed with all the old passion. He pressed his lips to the hollow of my neck. My knees went rubbery. I traced the outline of his jaw with my finger. He pulled me tight against him and I felt the hardness behind his zipper. Then his BlackBerry chimed.

He hadn't bothered to turn it off and he reached for it. Though he gave it only a glance before slipping it back into his pocket, the spell was broken, thank God.

I had an early rehearsal the next morning. I was home and in bed by eleven. Alone.

Chapter 19

"Girl, if common sense were lard, you wouldn't have enough to grease a skillet," my closest friend and neighbor chided me the next day. My revelation that I'd pulled a premature evacuation of the Mandarin suite had stopped Marti dead in her tracks. She was back from her Caribbean cruise, tan, fit, and ready to smack me upside my head.

"Honestly, Judith, I can't believe you went to Charlie Pruitt's hotel room unsupervised after downing two vodkas. You think that's the smartest move, considering you weren't sure you wanted to sleep with him? Huh? Do you?"

I shrugged.

"And then, when he makes the expected pass, you take off like a scared jackrabbit. What were you thinking?"

"Nothing profound—believe me. His BlackBerry went off and after that, the moment had passed."

"Moments come and go; you can make a new moment. Next."

"I don't know. The setting? We're going to make love for the first time in twenty-five years and it's in a hotel room? Somehow that seemed so tawdry."

"The Mandarin Oriental," she sneered. "A suite. At least a thousand dollars a night. So, bullshit. Try again."

"How about having just slept with Geoff, I would have felt like a slut jumping in the sack with Charlie."

"Jumping in the sack? I haven't heard that hip turn of phrase since 1970. And may I remind you, 'just' was two weeks ago. You told me, remember? So, nah. Reach down deep, kiddo."

I thought for a long moment. "Because I don't know what the hell I want?"

"Excellent. Very insightful. I just wanted you to hear yourself say it so you don't jump into anything too fast. If Charlie is all he's cracked up to be, he'll let you take your time. And if he's really into you enough to want more than just to be into you, if you get my drift, he'll call."

"He already did, last night, to make sure I got home safely."

"Okay, a good beginning, but only a beginning. So is there another date with the judge on the horizon?"

I nodded. "He's coming in next week with his daughter to look at colleges. The rite-of-passage campus tour. She wants to major in international relations."

"Georgetown," Marti said.

"And Hopkins has a great program. But the lure of D.C. is stronger. So one night Chloe's going to test out the Georgetown dorm and Charlie and I get to see each other."

"Very neat. And not to add to the mass confusion, but how's Geoff taking all this? Does he know about Charlie?"

"He gets the basics. I don't think he's hurting that much." I didn't mention the harpist who might have been kissing his boo-boos. "He'll be fine. Men always are."

"Are they really?" She faked a reproachful finger. "I might expect such a comment from one of my feminist terrorist lesbian comrades, but from a certified heterosexual of the lacy panties variety—why, I'm shocked by your insensitivity, missy."

"Go screw yourself," I said.

"Trust me, screwing yourself is highly overrated and I'm an expert." She caught a breath. "All right, enough of this. I'm reviewing a new Asian fusion place down at the harbor and I've got to hustle if I'm going to drop off your mama's check at the Belvedere first. If we pay the remainder of the fee by the end of the month, which is today, we'll get a fifteen percent discount."

"May I see the check?"

Not what I'd feared. The signature in a loopy hand was Grace Raphael's. But as I stared at the inked numbers—$3,000—I felt a wave of queasiness wash over me. My mother's underwriting of my birthday party was incredibly generous, but she'd never in her life had three thousand dollars in her checking account. And if she was supposed to have dipped into her jackpot winnings from the Atlantic City craps tables, why hadn't I heard about the windfall when it happened? The woman called me to brag when she pulled off a ten-dollar to-show bet at Pimlico.

"Grace didn't happen to mention my erstwhile father in connection with this largesse, did she?"

Marti reached out and nipped the check back. "She didn't. And he didn't. In fact, when she dropped off the check he muttered something about not understanding why people would want to spend all that money to celebrate growing older."

My heart took an express elevator to my stomach. "Irwin was with her? At your place?"

"Yes, sugarpie. In madras Bermudas and a pink Ralph Lauren polo shirt. Very senior fashion forward. She was wearing jeans. I don't think I've ever seen your mom in jeans. And a kerchief, so the wind wouldn't ruin the new hairdo on the drive over. He had the top down on the Jag."

That stalled me out. "My father drove her over. In a Jaguar. What idiot would lend him a Jaguar? Mrs. Chang drives a Mercedes and she doesn't lend it out. Oh God, don't tell me he rented a Jaguar." That would be so like Irwin Raphael. The quintessential salesman. Keep the image top of the line and all shined up.

Marti was watching me warily, as if I were wired with explosives. When she spoke it was barely above a whisper, afraid, I suppose, that her voice could set me off. "You didn't know about the XJ8? He bought it over the weekend. Used. It was advertised on Craigslist and he got a helluva deal. His words."

It took me a moment to process the implications. "Do you realize what this means, Marti?"

Eyes bugging, she shook her head.

"He's not going back to Arizona. He's staying in Baltimore. Settling in." I had begun to pace in circles.

Marti had backed off. "Wow. You know this from his buying a car?"

"He's eighty years old. You think he's going to drive cross-country in a secondhand Jaguar? No, he's not going home. Why should he when my mother is laying out the welcome mat?" I wiped a bubble of spittle from my lip. I was actually foaming at the mouth, but I couldn't seem to control my fury. "He's so sharp. He becomes her wheels, and suddenly they're off to Atlantic City or the racetrack, and he's got her under his thumb, that bastard. Wait till I get my hands on him. On her. What is she thinking? I know what she's thinking. But it's not going to work, not after all these years. He shows up out of nowhere and shoves himself back into our lives as if the past never happened. Well, it did and I've got the therapy bills to prove it. And God is my witness, it's not going to happen again."

Marti rolled her eyes heavenward. "Good grief, Scarlett. Get a grip."

I didn't, couldn't. Backstage later that morning, my colleagues steered clear of me. Musicians' senses are fine-tuned to pick up the smallest variation in tempo and pitch, and my back-off vibes were not exactly subtle. Geoff waved me a hi from afar, though his smile was skewed into more of a question mark than a greeting. Angela drove us through a galloping no-holds-barred rendition of "Ride of the Valkyries," which couldn't have been a more appropriate piece for my mood. I played as if spurred, not wanting to lose my pissed off, wanting to save it to unleash on my mother and her boy toy at Blumen House. Buying a Jaguar at his age! Con man. Jerk.

At break, Geoff approached. "What's up, Jude? Everything okay?"

"Fine."

"You look tapped out. Long night?"

It sounded harmless and politely casual enough, but I heard all kinds of questions behind the question. As in: Was my foul mood due to lack of sleep because I'd been writhing on sweaty sheets with Charlie? Or maybe: Had I realized my date with Charlie had been a mistake? Had we ended the resurrected relationship before it got serious and now it was all clear for former lovers to reenter the picture?

I looked up and snapped, "What? What does *that* mean?"

He raised his hands shoulder high, palms exposed in a gesture of surrender. "Nothing," he said. "Not a damn thing, Judith, if that's who you are these days. Bugger! Forget it."

I did. Promptly. Okay, not promptly; I spent a moment watching his retreating back, realizing I'd probably just burned that bridge down to the waterline. Chalk the destruction up to a classic Raphael overreaction. I'd apologize, of course. But not now. Now I had more important things on my slightly cracked plate to deal with—my mother and you know who.

Chapter 20

Blumen House was considered the finest assisted living facility in the Baltimore area, a place my mother wouldn't have been able to afford on her income. But I was determined that the last phase of her life would be free of roaches and sour smells in dim hallways. In a convenient coincidence, just as I decided to move her out of Brooklyn, I got promoted to associate principal cellist, so there was a little extra money to contribute to her care. Aunt Phyllis and Uncle Arnold generously came up with the rest, and we managed Blumen House's smallest one bedroom. Gracie was happy there, happier than I'd ever seen her. This naturally gregarious woman now had enough time, energy, and English to make friends. The other women, especially the Jewish ones, got a kick out of her. True to Blumen House's brochure, she bloomed in her golden years.

"What not to like?" she'd reassured me, picking up her closest friends' inflection. It was a relief not having to cook every day. My mother developed a taste for the chef's blueberry blintzes. The recreation staff worked overtime to keep the residents on their feet and clot free. There were field trips, lectures, classes. Arts and crafts, sing-alongs, bingo. And on the last day of every month, a party for all the residents whose birthdays had fallen in the previous one.

On this April 30, four celebrants sat at the birthday table: three women and one man, which was less depressing than the real residential ratio of about eight to one.

Grace, at a far table, spotted my entrance, rose, and headed me off midstride. Her party hat, a polka-dotted paper cone, was perched jauntily on the new hairdo. "Why you here, Judith? Not your day to visit."

"Well, that's a warm welcome. Happy to see you too. We need to talk." I pecked her cheek.

"About time kiss." She hadn't forgotten the scene at the elevator. She thrust her lower jaw pugnaciously. "So talk."

I scanned the room for signs of Irwin. "He's not here?"

"Very disrespect how you call father. He. He. Always he. Very bad manner. I brought you up to respect. Where that all go?"

"It followed your ex-husband to Arizona. Where is he?"

"*Aigoo!* You so mean. He want us all taste special ice cream. Ben & Jerry. So he go to buy for everyone and pay for all."

"He took the Jaguar?"

Miriam Botansky, a little gray bird of a woman, had flown to my mother's side. No doubt the subject of my reaction to Irwin's reappearance was a hot topic at the mah-jongg table. Mrs. Botansky slid me an appraising look. "Beautiful car. He's going to buy a GPS next week, but in the meantime Sonia Applebaum went along for the ride to show him the way to the supermarket." She stroked my mother's shoulder consolingly.

Sonia Applebaum was Blumen House's brazen hussy. A stiffly coiffed platinum blonde, she lip-lined, wore two-inch heels in a one-inch society, had outlived two very wealthy husbands, and the scuttlebutt was that more than one Viagra-infused male resident had taken liberties. My so-called father was alone with her, only a stick shift separating them. *Oy!* Or maybe, just maybe, Mrs. Applebaum was the answer to a daughter's prayers, and

Irwin and the blondie would skip town together and live happily ever after in Boynton Beach.

"They're taking a long time to buy ice cream." Mrs. Botansky's eyes were overbright. "But I'm sure everything is all right. Gracie can hold her own. Can't you, darling?"

My mother shook off the old lady's bejeweled claw and dragged me by two fingers to a corner. "Private here." She folded her arms and waited.

I folded mine and tried to keep my voice steady. "Is there something you're not telling me, *Uhm-mah*? Something to do with the family? Maybe from long ago? A secret I'm not supposed to know?"

She looked innocent. A little less so when she backed up two steps. "Like what?"

The problem was Aunt Phyllis hadn't given me a clue. Since our conversation, I'd been sifting through all kinds of possibilities. I laid out the one I liked the best. "I was thinking Irwin isn't my real father."

"What!" My mother clapped her thick peasant's hand against her chest. "Not your father!" She almost lost her balance as she rocked with the hilarity of it. "Of course Irwin your father." She couldn't contain her whoops of laughter. "This what you want to be true, different daddy. Ay, so funny. We do paternity test?" *That* phrase she knew, thanks to *Jerry Springer*. "Fine. Can prove with paternity test."

The response was too spontaneous to be a bluff. And she'd called mine. My last, best hope for a disconnect with that loser had just gone down the tube.

"Then you're hiding something else from me," I said. "What is it?"

That shut her down as if a plug had been pulled. "What else? Secret about your father? Why you think that?"

Answering a question with a question. Three, actually. The

cross-cultural contamination was getting serious. Also, it was a clever evasive move. She didn't look at me. Her stare was fixed on her bright red fingernails. Her lips, which had been parted a moment before, pursed as if she'd been sucking a lemon. She made a half turn away. Gave me a cold shoulder. Oh yes, she was hiding something, and she wasn't about to give it up.

I had no more to go on. I said, "Okay," meaning for now, and switched to a more pressing issue. "Marti showed me your check for the party."

"You're welcome," my mother said. Koreans are not big on sarcasm, but living among the Jews and Italians, she seemed to be picking up the knack.

"Yes, thank you. However, before the check is handed over to the Belvedere, I really need to know if that money was from you or him."

She flared. "First Irwin not your father. Then Irwin-not-father pay for party." She shook her head in wonderment.

"Come on, *Uhm-mah*. If you'd won three thousand dollars at the craps table, you would have been on the phone to me in a heartbeat. But not a peep. You never mentioned it."

"You want me call you every time I pee. This so stupid. So stupid and crazy, Judith. I be nice and give money. You be . . . what word?"

"Ungrateful?"

"Ungrateful. So stop ungrateful. Enjoy party. No more questions. *Chungbun!*"

When my mother said "Enough!" she meant it. At fourteen I'd obeyed. Not so much at forty-nine. "One more, an easy one, and then I'm finished. Is he planning on moving in?"

"Here? Apartment too small. He don't know where he live. Free as bird now. Thinking maybe move to near Aunt Phyllis. Great Neck."

No subways on Long Island. That might explain the Jaguar, which would be perfect for Great Neck.

I was finished with my mother, but she wasn't finished with me. "Why where he live your business? Maybe you move to New York with judge. That my business? No. Don't insult. So many insult today."

I was still basking in the Great Neck moment when Irwin walked through the door carrying a Wegmans shopping bag. Sonia Applebaum followed, arms empty, eyes clouded with maybe cataracts, maybe adulation.

He searched the room for my mother. When he found her, he lit up.

I looked at her when she found him. Radiant.

Irwin handed off the ice cream to the activities director and made his way toward us. He walked briskly for an eighty-year-old man. With the entire room now watching, I found myself stuck facing him.

He shifted his gaze from my mother to me and assumed a salesman's eager expression, as if he had a pound of the finest kippered herring up his sleeve. With my name on it. Half price. Today only.

"Hiya, Jude. Long time no see. You look good. I hope you're staying for the party because I just bought this gang some Ben & Jerry's Chunky Monkey. You ever tried that? The best. It's bananas and nuts and these big hunks of chocolate. I know how you love chocolate. I remember once, when you were a kid around two, I brought you Hanukkah gelt. You know what that is? The gold-wrapped chocolate money." His mouth never stopped working. "What a thing you had for chocolate. Didn't she, Gracie? You went through that chocolate money like Grant took Richmond."

From the doting-father routine, you'd think he'd never left.

It was too much. My mother must have known I was ready to tell that old bastard where to shove his Chunky Monkey, because she slung a restraining arm around my waist and drew me close.

"Go away, Irwin. Now. Help serve ice cream. Not for me. Tea for me. No sugar."

"I know no sugar, Grace. For fifty years I've known no sugar."

"Go." She shooed him off with her free hand.

And the amazing thing was, he actually listened to her. "Sure," he said, "glad to be of assistance." To me he said, "We're at table four. I'll put an extra chair out for you," and took off.

She loosened her grip on my waist. "I'm boss now. Big difference. Feel good."

I had only a few foggy memories of the time before he left, but even *I* knew that back then the balance of power had weighed heavily on his side. He ran the show. *Big* difference.

We both watched him strut to the front table, where Sonia Applebaum was waiting with the scoop.

"Ha. Look at how she push herself on him. Such slut. *Shibal nyon.*"

"Mother . . ." Shocked, I laughed at the language. "But what if she and he—?"

"What if, what if, you always what if. No matter what if, I be fine. You think so hard, Judith. Not healthy. Bad for more aneurysm. Go home, take hot bath. Drink ginseng tea. *Kok-tchong ma-se-yo*—don't worry. Everything be okey-dokey, you see."

Everything wasn't okey. It didn't even approach dokey. I called Marti on my drive home. "Listen, I want you to cancel the contract. Get in touch with the Belvedere. Back us out."

"Calm down, sugarpuss, you're going to burst another blood vessel."

"Fine, I'm calm. Very calm. I'll say this slowly and distinctly: the money is from a tainted source. Probably from the dead chippie via Irwin. Now cancel the damn party."

There was a brief pause before Marti said, "No can do. Sorry, honeychile. I signed a contract. I pull out now and we lose everything. Including the down payment, which was my contribution."

"*You* made the down payment?"

"A thousand bucks. My gift to you. And don't give me any shit about it. The party's a go. You think your father's the moneyman? Well, hurrah to that. I say it's time he paid up. Dance on his dime, have a ball."

"You don't understand. I can't deal with the—"

"Sure you can. You can deal with anything you decide to deal with. Problem is, you need an attitude adjustment. Judith, I have to tell you, your mental state lately has been worrisome. You're way overdue for a tune-up with what's her name, Gottlieb, your therapist."

"I don't need therapy. I need Irwin Raphael to vacate the premises and slink back to the other slimy, belly-crawling sidewinders in Arizona."

"Oh boy. Hang up now and call Gottlieb. Do not pass go. And have her send the bill to Irwin." Marti gave a throaty laugh. "Now wouldn't that be a nice touch."

At home there was a message waiting. Geoff had called me before I got to him with my apology for snapping at him at rehearsal.

In our history, I'd heard him angry only a few times, furious once or twice, which churned his voice into a thunderous rumble. But I'd never heard this flat chill, like a glacial plain, as he informed me he wasn't going to be able to make our Monday morning practice session; something had come up. Yeah, his hackles over my treatment of him. So I figured unless I did something fast, that was pretty much the end of our friendship, which had lasted about two weeks after I called time on the sex part of it.

Oh God, everything was coming apart on nearly every front. But there was a Korean proverb I kept in mind: "Even when the sky is falling, there's a sunny hole to climb through."

On Monday, only six days away, with Chloe at her sleepover in the Georgetown dorm, Charlie and I would have an extended evening together. Alone. No Kiki doing her diversionary routines, no Jiminy Cricket conscience on my shoulder. I'd called Charlie Pruitt many names in my lifetime, but never a "sunny hole." I guess there's a first for everything.

My plan was to get to Berenson Hall early, ambush Geoff before rehearsal, and make a short, dignified apology for my unseemly behavior the day before. Unfortunately, he was otherwise occupied with Deena Marquis, the stunning blond harpist with turquoise eyes only for him.

There didn't seem to be any hanky-panky or what Aunt Phyllis called mufky-pufky going on between them, but Deena, who'd been literally waiting in the wings through our relationship, was now center stage.

Her fingers cruised Geoff's sleeve between his elbow and wrist. His profile was handsome, stoic. I moved in close enough to cast a shadow and maybe the scent of my Chanel because I thought I saw him flinch. But there was no follow-up with eye contact, so I backed off.

We didn't connect onstage or at the break, but after rehearsal, when I came out of the locker room, there was Geoff packing up his trumpet. I waited until he turned to say, "Geoff, hi."

"Hello, Judith." Formal. The smile was flatlined.

I barreled full steam ahead. "About yesterday. I have no excuse for my bad behavior, but I do have an explanation."

It was obvious from the speculative angle of his head that whatever I had better be good.

"This situation with my pseudo-father is exploding all around me and you just happened to walk into the fallout." Not quite the way it had happened—I was playing with the sequence of events—but a little revisionist history seemed in order.

"It wasn't enough that Irwin screwed up my life by leaving it; now he has to screw it up again by coming back. The man is bad news in forward and reverse. And I'm picking up signs he might stay for good. With my mother. Which is driving me crazy. Unfortunately, you got in the way of that crazy. So, my apologies."

Geoff ran his hand through his Redford hair. Finally he said, "Apology accepted. Consider the matter closed." He slung his backpack over a shoulder. "Gotta go."

He went. But then, one foot on the stairs to the exit, he stopped and executed a half spin. "This thing for Monday morning is important. I can't pass it up, but you could use some polishing on the Mendelssohn, so if you're free in the afternoon . . ."

"Afternoon works for me. Two?"

"I'm driving back on I-95. I don't know what kind of traffic I'll hit. Three?"

I calculated a couple hours of cello with Geoff. That would give me more than enough time to shower and dress for dinner with Charlie. As long as everyone knew his place, I'd be fine. As long as I knew everyone's place, I'd be fine.

"Sold," I said.

Chapter 21

I never saw it coming. I should have, of course; there'd been signs all week—four a.m. wake-ups, loss of appetite. To be honest, there'd been signs all my life.

For example, my childhood aversion to peaches and plums. It had kicked in a few months after my father moved out. The fruit had "strings" that made me gag.

"Strings represent attachments. What you had was a symbolic transference," my intermittent shrink, Theodora Gottlieb, MD, had diagnosed in retrospect. "You couldn't swallow your father's abandonment, ergo the classic anxiety response." My mother, who'd never heard of symbolic transference, had simply switched me to bananas. Case closed.

Reopened, perhaps, when I went through a spell of binge eating in college that ceased abruptly the night Charlie told me he loved me. I wiped chocolate syrup from my mouth, whispered on Hershey breath that *I* loved *him* and never looked back on the jumbo bags of M&M's, the cans of Pringles, the boxes of Mallomars stashed in the back of my closet.

In adulthood, I adopted full-blown phobias. I dreaded driving through tunnels. Clowns gave me the creeps, even Ronald McDonald, despite his good work with the sick children. And the mishegoss related to my mother were magnificent in their variety and originality. They waxed and waned. The worst was after I'd left for Boston and she lived alone in the Brooklyn flat. Three hundred miles away I obsessed over her. Pilot lights, boiling water, scatter rugs, flip-flops, open windows, closed windows, electrical cords and outlets—all had their individual niches, like the relics of medieval saints, only these didn't promise salvation; they promised death and destruction.

Stable I wasn't. Over the years, I'd dipped into Dr. Gottlieb to help me cope. We managed to get most of my fears under control, though the clowns and the tunnels hung tough. But this new phenomenon, in all its nauseating, heart-galloping glory, this exquisite mind-bender of a neurosis that threatened to destroy my livelihood, it just blindsided me.

Marti might have inadvertently played a part in setting it off when she stopped by to tell me she'd found Brenda Himmelstein.

As soon as I saw Marti's face, I knew. "Damn," I muttered. "She's dead, right?"

"Sorry to be the bearer of bad news."

"What did she die of?" All the diseases of aging spooked me. Cancer, the big sneak. Heart attack. Stroke. Oh, please God, don't let it have been an aneurysm.

"She fell off a mountain. A climbing accident. She and her husband were on some peak in Albania, I think he said. Last August. She lost her footing."

Given the alternatives, it was a happy ending. Quick, no chemo, no tubes.

"We spoke on the phone yesterday. He's also a high-end lawyer, but he sounded like an okay guy. I don't think he pushed her."

"That's comforting."

"He overnighted some photos."

She pulled a file from her briefcase and shoved across the dining room table the picture of a well-preserved middle-aged woman. Big smile, tanned and wrinkled face framed by a cloud of red hair. I wouldn't have known her if I'd bumped into her; it had been nearly forty years. But she looked nice. Brenda's essential goodness still shone through, the nature that had made her the perfect playmate for the needy little girl who'd followed her around like a puppy.

I sighed. "So I missed her by less than a year. That is so cruel."

"Yeah, life is cruel. Just when you think you've got your feet on the ground, it pulls the rug out from under you." Slippery rugs, one of my phobias. "She tried to find you, by the way. When her Googling Judith Gabriel turned up nothing, she figured you got married and changed your name."

"Gabriel?"

"Gabriel, Raphael—she knew it was some angel at least. But her husband said she talked about her best friend Judith from grade school. And she saved this."

Up and out of her seat, Marti moved around and gently placed another photo in front of me. She laid a hand on top of my head, as if she needed to baptize me into pain. "Turn it over. See what she wrote on the back? 'J and B in front of Rube's Candy Store. Eight yrs. old.'"

That night, getting ready for bed after an exhilarating concert, I propped the photo on the side table. My last waking image was of Brenda and me, two innocents holding hands on a summer afternoon. When I startled up on sweaty sheets at three a.m., the night-light was spilling just enough glow to catch Brenda's haunting green eyes. Adorable at eight. Dead at forty-eight. Happiness, life, everything can go just like that, I thought, and for a split second I got slammed by the astonishment, the dizziness, the weightlessness Brenda must have felt flying off that

Albanian mountain with nothing beneath her except air and oblivion. Funny, though, I felt no fear. That came later.

The weekend program at the Berenson was an odd combination of the sublime, Brahms' Piano Concerto No. 2, and the sublimely ridiculous, a new work by the brilliantly erratic Baltimore-born composer John Briscom. His *Bi-Polar Suite* had been written during his latest stay at Sheppard Pratt, a local private psychiatric facility. The piece's cello solo bounded from a depressive threnody to manic passages that jumped pitch, position, and strings with breathtaking speed. You really had to concentrate not to slip up.

Premieres are always challenging and this one had a few dings, but the audience loved it. They were on their feet at the final note, and when Angela flourished me up for a solo bow, a chorus of bravas flew at me.

The second half, the Brahms, was old hat—beautiful, elegant old hat. One of my favorites, and as Geoff might have said, I could have played it with my toes.

The following evening, we nailed the *Bi-Polar*. We got a standing, though no bravas for me this time. I told myself some crowds were just more demonstrative than others.

At intermission, Angela clapped me on the shoulder as she walked past. So the boss was pleased at least. Still, I remembered the shouts of the night before and wondered whether I'd missed something. Messed something.

Everything was spot-on for the first movement of the Brahms. But the second movement, a scherzo, has moments of tumultuous energy, and tonight as the storm whipped up, something in me suddenly went frantic. Without warning, my pulse took off, thrumming wildly, my mouth went dry, and my right leg began to twitch. What nonsense! This was good old Brahms, for God's sake. Sure, I'd been nervous in our earliest encounters, but we'd been married for years, Johannes and I, and the fires had long since banked. What was my problem?

I was perspiring rivers and we weren't even up to the cello solo that kicked off the third movement. Well, not kicked, glided. And not exactly solo, but it might as well be, with the principal playing the most rigorous top lines and the rest of the cellos filling in the background for a very romantic lyrical effect. The lead part wasn't particularly challenging in terms of fingering; it was executed at its best, I thought, when instinct and experience took over. I'd been fine with it Friday night.

As the second movement ended, a few overenthusiastic members of the audience applauded, and Angela smiled at Raffi Shimon, the guest pianist. I was up next. In the silent pause, I could hear my breath huffing shallow and quick. As I leaned forward to grasp the bow, a wave of dizziness swamped me, followed by a surge of nausea. I tried to swallow it back. Couldn't. Mouth was a desert. Tried again and up jetted a spurt of sour liquid.

That was the moment I knew I was in real trouble.

My cello was a David Tecchler built in Rome in 1712. I'd been playing it for twenty years and it took me nearly that long to pay it off. Humidity affects it, of course—it's wood—but I can count on one hand the times it's produced a squeak. That's what I heard on my first stroke. The squeak of a steroidal mouse. I couldn't see my own eyes widen in panic, but I caught a flash of uneasiness flit through Angela's. I plunged ahead. What choice did I have? My entry was off, much too brisk. The movement was andante, Italian for walking, not jogging.

A minute in, my bow slipped on another stroke. I focused on

my clammy hands, focused on my clumsy fingering, focused much too much on what I was doing.

Playing recklessly, trying to distract myself from the terror, I forced myself to look up and out. Second row center, a man was squirming. Somewhere behind him, a cougher erupted at the decibel level of an atomic blast. A white-haired woman on the aisle gave me the fish-eye and scowled. A rustle swept the audience. They knew. Oh, believe me, they knew.

As my nightmare first solo gave way to the oboe's, I caught a quavering breath. The squirming man settled down.

My gaze was still stuck in the audience as Raffi came alive at the piano. That's when I spotted third row far left—oh God—Irwin Jerome Raphael, his dark-dyed pompadour, scimitar of a nose, soft chin unmistakable even in the dimmed houselights. What the hell was he doing here? And who the hell was sitting beside him? Female. Not my mother. I squinted. Not Sonia Applebaum. Some other floozy he'd picked up. This one with flame red hair.

Except Irwin wasn't the bow tie type. He'd taken to wearing bolos in Arizona and I could imagine his closet-hanging polyester neckties splashed with cacti and tropical flora. So maybe it wasn't my alleged father out there in the semidarkness. Maybe blazer-man was a cardiologist from Towson. All I was sure of was my urgent need to pee, and that the half-moons staining the fabric at my underarms had to be visible from the audience. Oh yes, and that I was light-headed and on my way to passing out. No, not just passing out. I was entirely convinced I was going to die, right there, a few seats away from the concertmaster who knew CPR but would be too late to save me.

Then, suddenly, my cue for the second and last solo jerked me back into the living, torturing moment. The audience was a sea of faces staring expectantly.

No turning back now. Trembling, I drew the bow and played. It was awful. Adequate. I had no idea. I just got through it.

The next thing I knew Angela was waving me up to take the applause. As I stood halfway, as far as my jelly legs could carry me, I thought I heard, of all things, a decent smattering of bravas from the back of the house. Pity praise, of course. If they'd had fruit, they would have pitched it.

Chapter 22

"Performance anxiety," Geoff pronounced at the start of our Monday practice. "You got hit by a blast of stage fright. It happens."

"Not to me, it doesn't. This is a first."

I'd fled the scene right after Saturday evening's concert, trying to get away before Geoff could tag me. I didn't need him telling me what I already knew: that I'd made a bloody spectacle of myself in front of hundreds of paying guests.

Minutes before the performance Sunday afternoon, he'd ambushed me. I hadn't even set foot onstage and I had the shakes.

His eyes were sharp with alarm. "What's going on, Jude?"

"I don't know. I really don't know." Every musician knows about stage fright; the horror stories abound. But if you haven't experienced it, you really don't *know*.

"Not a headache, right?"

No, not an aneurysm. For me, fully conscious, this was worse.

Onstage, I was a basket case. Same symptoms as Saturday, maybe a little worse. I got through it, but I saw Angela conferring with our concertmaster after the performance. They were sending sidelong glances my way.

Geoff, stirring his iced tea in my music room, denied having heard anything off.

"You sounded fine to me Saturday. Yesterday, a mite hurried at the beginning of Brahms, but nothing jarring. As for the panic attacks, you're a late bloomer, Jude. Consider yourself blessed. I had a problem in my twenties. My first year in Brisbane? I got a case of the woo-hoos that nearly drove me into teaching. Seemingly out of the blue, though my mum was going through a cancer scare at the time and I felt I should have been home in Sydney doing some hand-holding."

He added a third packet of sugar to his tea. "I gritted my teeth, ruined a few dress shirts, and pushed through it."

Yes, but you're Geoff. You swim with sharks and skydive out of moving planes. Courage is your default.

"I was thinking more in terms of Inderal," I confessed. "Just to get me over the hump."

Inderal is a beta-blocker used on-label effectively to control blood pressure, but it also has the power to diffuse the adrenaline rush that makes for sweaty hands and the hyperventilation that sabotages the best players. It's an open secret that a subset of musicians all over the world pop Inderal preperformance to quell paralyzing bouts of nerves.

"Happy tablets." Geoff's mouth screwed with distaste. "I know musicians who swear by them. Inderal can help get you through a crisis, but it isn't magic, Jude. And the trick is to begin to trust yourself again without it. Because, personally, I think it flattens one's affect, and in my opinion a slight edge of anxiety brings extra energy to the music."

I sighed hopelessly. "This wasn't simple stage fright. May I remind you that I hallucinated my father in the audience?"

"You mistook one old man for another in poor lighting and you're ready for the straitjacket. The mind in panic mode plays horror film tricks. Speak to Dr. Gottlieb. She'll give you some behavioral exercises to keep the nerves in check while you dig at the root causes."

He put the tea aside and began shuffling through sheet music, selecting my pieces for practice.

"Hold off a sec." I swiped the papers from his grasp and rattled off, tremolo, "Maybe we ought to skip today. Because until I get a handle on this, what's the point of working my ass off preparing for an audition I may never have? In this shape, I can't see myself trying out. I'll never make it through the initial round."

He retrieved the music. Slowly, patiently, he instructed, "The point is, you will if you tell yourself you will. Fear is all mental, and mind-set can be changed. You're under a lot of pressure now with the dad in town. And you have other bloke-related issues stressing you out, I expect." This last was said with broad innocence.

"Of course, we need to alter the shape you're in. We need to infuse you with unshakable confidence so when you get before those judges, you're on automatic pilot. Cool as a cuke." He handed me my music. "Now let's get going. The morning's drive was tough, I'm seriously knackered, and I don't want to fall asleep on you." There was a *ba-boom* beat and he said, "Well, that last isn't strictly true . . ."

That had me reaching for my bow.

We started with the solo in the William Tell Overture. Not the Lone Ranger gallopy part, but a slow, soulful melody in a minor key. And with only Geoff watching, all was serene. This time, to make sure we wouldn't be disturbed, I'd muted the volume on the phone in the next room, both the ring and the message center, and quieted my cell. We got through three pieces in ninety minutes with no break so Geoff could go home and catch a nap.

As we walked to my front hall, I said, "I think I'll be okay at rehearsal, but I'm dreading the next time I face an audience." I shuddered. "What if I can never play again? I mean *perform*."

"Oh Jesus. Get to Gottlieb fast. Nip this thing in the bud." At the door, he turned to me. "You'll be fine, Judith. You've conquered worse."

My reaching out was spontaneous. "Right," I said. "Thanks. I needed to hear that." And I kissed him.

No big deal. It was a chaste brush of my lips against the cheek of a mentor who was helping me secure my footing on the next step, at my age the *final* step up the career ladder. And if that made me completely narcissistic, try this on for self-serving: I still wanted Geoff in my life. In a limited edition, of course. As a colleague, friend, and coach. But not as a lover. Because the bed in my head wasn't big enough for three, and if Geoff was tried and terrific, Charlie was . . . well, Charlie. Who might be *as* terrific, given the chance. Besides, I couldn't resist the old pull.

I'd told Marti I didn't know what I wanted. Wrong. Suddenly I knew exactly what I wanted: everything.

And I suppose that's what I got when I opened the door and found the old pull himself, tieless, in shirtsleeves, attractively rumpled, standing on my doorstep. "Charlie," I managed to choke out. "It's not even five o'clock. You're two hours early."

"Yes, I know. But, Judith," he said, eyes exclusively on me, "I've been out here listening. And you're wonderful. Absolutely wonderful."

The next few minutes were a rerun of Rodan vs. Godzilla. Geoff moved forward, assuming a place by my side. An obvious power move.

I almost laughed as the two men sized each other up. Literally. Geoff unchinked his spine, vertebra by vertebra, apparently having more than the standard thirty-three. As he became six feet four of towering, glowering inferno, Charlie stretched himself to his full height of five-eleven, maybe only ten—he was in his fifties now, the decade when you start to shrink.

Geoff knew about Charlie, but not vice versa. I introduced them.

"Pleasure," Geoff said on the handshake.

"All mine," Charlie responded. The judge seemed to be checking this large miscreant for a criminal record.

"Well, I'm on my way," Geoff said into the air. But his feet were stuck to the planks of my porch.

I gave him a mental nudge. "I really appreciate the cheerleading. And that you took the time after your long drive. You must be wiped," I added, reminding him his nap waited.

Charlie, too, was eager to get the Geoff show on the road. He leaned forward. "Nice to . . ." he began.

". . . have met you," Geoff finished the sentence. And then they traded places. Simultaneously. Charlie just about leapt to my side. Geoff paused for a moment in the spot where Charlie had been. Long enough to send me a pained look. Then he turned and hurried down the steps.

That's when Charlie placed both hands on my shoulders, swiveled me around, and steered me through the front door.

"Well, that was awkward," he said in my hall. "He's the ex-boyfriend, I assume. The *newest* ex-boyfriend."

"Very funny. How did you know?"

"You've got to be kidding. He's also—what, your teacher?"

"There's an audition coming up. He's coaching me. Really, that's all."

"Good. Bottom line is, he's gone, I'm here." Men are so competitive. He gave me his bad boy smile.

I wasn't falling for it. "Yeah, you're here two hours early. Not to be inhospitable, but . . ."

"I screwed with your schedule, huh? I forgot how women hate that. I *am* sorry. Chloe decided she wanted to be dropped at Georgetown early and I thought, Great, this gives Judith and me some extra time together. I tried to heads-up you. I called, but you didn't pick up either phone.

"I figured you weren't home but you might be by the time I got here. And you were. First thing I heard when I got out of my car was your music. I didn't want to disturb you, so I set myself up on your patio and got in a little work with you playing in the background. It's nice out there. Cool in the shade. And with all the flowers, it smells good." He moved closer. "So do you."

Hardly. I was a sweatball from the heat and the tension of watching the two men go at it. Wearing jeans and a tee and scruffy sandals, no makeup and my hair pulled back in a ponytail, I figured I looked about as appetizing as a cheese sandwich, but Charlie stared at me as if I were caviar. He cupped my chin in his hands and kissed me lightly on the lips. A breeze of a kiss, but sparks flew. Then he drew back.

"I left my jacket, my laptop, and some other stuff on your patio. Let me get them. It will only take a minute."

"Stay there and I'll bring out iced tea."

His premature arrival hadn't given me time to prepare for him actually being in the house. I needed to take this slowly—Charlie in my garden, Charlie in my living room—or I'd get the bends.

When I got to the patio with a tray of tea and cookies, I found him pacing and mumbling into his BlackBerry. He held up a one-minute finger and I tabled the tray, sprawled in the wrought-iron chair closest to my herb garden, and watched him at work. Shades of Cambridge, when one of my greatest pleasures, one of the world's most potent aphrodisiacs, was watching Charlie totally immersed in what I knew he loved best, the law, even before he proved it beyond a reasonable doubt.

"Sorry," he said when he clicked off. "That's the downside of my job. It's not usually quite this intrusive, but I'm in the midst of a major case. One that could set an important precedent. At this level, appellate, you don't want to screw up. That was my law clerk updating me on some research." He shrugged, as if helpless to stop the onslaught. "These days, I'm almost never unconnected."

Of course.

He took my hands in both of his, backed away, and just looked at me. The tenderness of his gaze made me flush. "I've missed you," he said.

"It's only been a week."

"Twenty-five years," he corrected.

And if that didn't make me go all gooey inside, the next bit reduced me to syrup.

"Before I forget—" He unlatched me, found his briefcase, rummaged through it, and extracted a wrapped rectangle. "Time you had this back in your collection. Go ahead, open it."

It was one of those small, thin volumes you pick up near the cash register at card shops or at airport news kiosks. I recognized the cover, an abstract red rose. *Love Is a Poem.* Charlie had given it to me at the height of our relationship and I'd thrown it back at him at the end. Now slightly bruised, it sat on my palm like a wilted flower. "You kept this all these years?"

"Wouldn't part with it."

He moved close as I read the inscription. "Before you, these poems had no meaning. Now they articulate feelings much deeper than words on paper. I love you, my Ju-ju. Charlie." By the time

I got to "feelings" my eyes had clouded. "You really were a romantic back then."

"Still am. Maybe more so now. When you're on Lipitor you pay more attention to the workings of your heart." He patted the book balanced on my hand. "You hold on to it," he said.

But I didn't. I carefully placed it on the glass-topped table and turned into his arms. This time he really kissed me. Hard, soft, hard again. Ben Franklin could have harnessed our electricity to run his printing press.

We had full frontal engagement and . . . liftoff, Houston!

"Oh God," Charlie murmured into my sweaty hair and next thing I knew his hand was under my "Musicians Play for Keeps" T-shirt that Geoff, who never played for keeps, had given me last Christmas. I'd asked the Aussie then, half joking, "Is this your idea of a proposal?" He hadn't panicked but retorted, "You'd run like hell, Jude, if I ever tried to pin you down." And I'd nodded, thinking he was probably right.

But it was Charlie who crushed the cotton of my shirt getting to skin and Charlie who managed—much better at it now than in his frantic twenties—to unhook my bra.

He was right about the scent of the garden. The aromas of mint, basil, and early roses made an intoxicating mix. We clung like two drunks. Then I felt him stiffen, not around his zipper, where the bulge had suddenly collapsed, but head to toe. "Looks like we've got a visitor," he whispered.

It took me a moment. "What?"

He disengaged and, backing off, hitched his eyebrows at something behind me. "Were you expecting more guests?"

I turned to see Marti standing at the break in my privet hedge, having taken the shortcut garden path between her place and mine.

She carried a shopping bag and wore a highly amused expression.

"Don't let me stop you," she said in that honeyed Southern drawl that attracted gnats. "This is waaay better than HBO."

"Oh God," I muttered as I struggled to rehook my bra.

I couldn't blame her for the intrusion. She worked mostly out of her home office, so I never knew when she'd take a break from writing and drop by. If she heard cello music on the wind, she retreated, respecting my practice time. Today, no music and no way of knowing Charlie had arrived early. Besides, she was delivering on a favor. I'd asked to borrow a particular bra that was constructed like a Gothic cathedral, with flying buttresses and suspension grids. I thought it might do the job of holding up my assets in the halter top I wanted to wear for my date with the man she was currently eyeballing with unabashed interest.

Charlie shot me a questioning look.

"Charlie Pruitt, meet Marti McDowell," I said. "Marti's my neighbor and friend."

Marti said, "A pleasure to meet you, Your Honor. I've heard all about you."

"No, you haven't." I was already mortified.

"Okay, I've heard so much about you. All of it highly complimentary. Is that better, Judith?" She tsked. "Shame on you. Embarrassing me in front of the judge."

"Call me Charlie. Please."

"Okay, Charlie." She ambled over to the table and perched one butt cheek on its glass top. "So, Charlie, what do you think of same-sex marriage?"

I saw his double take segue into a second, more appraising look. Marti was wearing cutoffs, a schmutzy tank top, a Ravens cap, and combat boots, standard attire for working in her garden.

"Marti, for heaven's sake." But by now I was laughing. Charlie's mouth was drawn into a tentative smile.

"Honey, he's a judge, isn't he? I just want a judicial opinion. You know, like on CheapLawyer.com. You can ask one question about anything legal for twenty bucks."

"It's fine," Charlie reassured me. He leaned toward Marti. "This isn't for publication, because I'm not supposed to express opinions without my gavel, but between us, I'm all for civil unions. A contract between two consenting adult parties. I say give them all the nuptial benefits. It's only fair. Marriage, on the other hand, is a sacrament. Goes back to Genesis. Did God say Adam and Bruce? Eve and Ellen?" His eyes were twinkling. He'd caught on to her. Smart Charlie. But I bet those views were, under the humor, solid convictions.

Marti waved a finger at him. "Hold on one cotton-pickin' minute. We need to debate this, Charlie, my newest dear friend." She pulled a chair out for herself. At which point I intervened and shoved it back. "Court will be in session some other time," I said. "Charlie and I have dinner reservations." We didn't, but the ploy worked.

"To be continued, then." She handed me the shopping bag. "Wear that"—she pointed into its recesses—"and it will change your life. Okay, my aphids are waiting." She snapped an order, but finished with a smirk. "As you were, troops."

After she marched off, I exhaled. "She has boundary issues, but she's really a good person."

"Funny lady. And very attractive. Great body. She *is* a lesbian, right?"

"Card carrying."

Once she was out of sight, Charlie moved behind me and wound his arms around my waist.

"She ever hit on you?"

Was he proposing a threesome? No, not Charles Evans Pruitt, Mr. Conservative. And he knew better where I was concerned.

"Never. We're not each other's types."

"Am I your type?" He rotated me into his embrace. "Because, oh girl, are you ever mine."

Girl? I was almost fifty. I didn't know whether to be insulted or flattered.

He resumed his nuzzling, but for me, at least, Marti's appearance had broken the spell.

Okay, maybe the spell wasn't broken. Maybe it was just chipped and able to be repaired with wine, oysters, crab cakes, and a little sweet talk for dessert at Petit Louis. We'd find out.

Chapter 23

❧

It wasn't clear what was on the menu for after dinner. In spite of my architecturally buttressed bosom and Charlie's obvious fascination with it, conversation at the restaurant was all about Chloe's SAT scores and her college options. No sweet talk.

Time was also a factor. My date had an hour's drive back to his hotel in D.C. and an early meeting at the Justice Department the following morning. Part of me was relieved it looked like we weren't going to consummate this reunion. The other part was disappointed.

Disappointed won out when he surprised me by asking, "How about a nightcap at your place?" He reached across the table and with a single finger drew a sinuous trail from the base of my neck down to my décolletage, from which he fished out the gold cello pendant Geoff had given me. Yes, I'd worn a gift from one man on a date with another. Sounds as if my reservoir of chutzpah ran deep and cold, but the truth was more neurotic. Since Geoff had first snapped the closing catch for me, I'd taken off the protective necklace only long enough to dip it in jewelry cleaner. You don't screw around with Miss Fortune.

"Lucky charm," I explained.

Charlie fingered the talisman, then let it fall against the prickling skin of my cleavage. "I'll say." He hiked his eyebrows suggestively. Which was so frat boy.

Now, this was where I could have turned back. Instead, a half hour later, a scotch-mellowed Charlie was on the last stop of my house tour, in my bedroom, a place I'd never thought would hold Charlie Pruitt. It seemed smaller for containing him.

He stopped to examine the large oil painting of a blond, green-eyed, shirtwaisted Victorian matron that hung over my dresser. "Pretty. She's your grandmother?"

"My Caucasian grandmother, you mean? You're talking Grandma Roz, whose apron always smelled of herring? Grandma Roz, who made a single chicken last from one Sabbath to the next? Grandma Roz, whose fingernails—?"

"Okay, okay, I get it. You came from poor but hardworking Eastern European stock."

"Jews. Outcasts. That was one side. On the Korean side, I'm descended from radish farmers and shopkeepers. And you know what? I'm not ashamed of that anymore. Most of the world is made up of people who toil with their hands and earn an honest living."

"Unlike my folks, who lived off the sweat of their exploited workers on one side and plundered the judicial system on the other." He chuckled. "You don't need to be so defensive, Ju-ju. Scratch the surface and we're all human beings."

Hardly a Rush Limbaughian sentiment. It was either the booze mellowing him out or him doing what it took to soften me up for the seduction.

He moved on, sipping scotch as he went. He picked up the photo I'd propped on my night table. "Is this you?"

I nodded.

"The child with you is Brenda, right? Your grade school girl-friend."

I had no memory of telling him about Brenda, but I must have. That's what I had with Charlie that I didn't have with Geoff. The bond of shared memories. Some of them horrendous, though with him massaging my right shoulder I wasn't thinking that way.

"You were a cute little thing. Incredible eyes. But it's hard to look at. You seem so sad."

"I was. I'm not anymore."

"I can see that." He replaced the photo but kept staring at it while he said, "I want to make you happier. I hope I can."

"You can try," I said.

Even I wasn't sure whether that was a challenge or an invitation.

We made love. An act that probably raised more questions than it answered.

One minute we were sitting on the quilt, feet on the floor, discussing whether Israel could take out the Natanz uranium enrichment plant; the next Charlie was overcome by lust or geopolitics and began to undo my top. Everything else came off quickly, propelling us toward the moment of truth: how I'd look to him after all these years.

Foreplay for a forty-nine-year-old woman involves stroking the light dimmer, but even in shadows I could see he'd changed. Well, of course he had. Could I have expected the abs of a twenty-five-year-old? He had a bit of a paunch. The freckles that had been just a spattering near his shoulder were now raised and darker, and one below his collarbone really needed to be seen by a dermatologist. His runner's thighs had held up, but his calves had sprouted rivers of varicose blue. Why did I find all this erosion so endearing?

"God, Ju-ju," he whispered, then backed off to appraise me as if I were something old but valuable on the block at Christie's. "You're as spectacular as ever. How did you make time stand still?" Obviously his midrange vision was beginning to go. Very gallant, nonetheless.

I rewarded him by pressing my lips against his. He tasted the way I remembered. Of Glenfiddich. He kissed the same. Magically. I didn't want him to stop. Ever. Why did he have to stop?

Apparently because he'd misplaced an appendage more important than the one that swung between his thighs. "My Black-Berry. Damn. So sorry. Really. Be right back. Promise."

He dashed downstairs stark naked. He dashed upstairs. You had to laugh. Naked man carrying briefcase is an automatic giggle. I controlled myself while he rolled through his e-mails; then it occurred to me that I ought to be furious. This was a serious case of coitus interruptus.

"I really do apologize," he said, not glancing up from the tiny screen. "Terribly rude of me. But it's an exceptional case. If I reverse the lower court decision, it would break precedent and all hell could break loose. I'm expecting a call from the White House."

And so we made love to assorted dings and dongs, none of which signaled the leader of the free world was calling. Only once, when the device sounded an identifying warble, did he reach across me to the night table and check the text message. "Mother's nurse. Ah, one of Kiki's prescriptions is running low."

Ugh. Just the mention of her name and all my residual estrogen vaporized into thin air. Charlie had to work hard after that to get me back into high gear.

The sex itself? Charlie's psychologist wife and globe-trotting reporter girlfriend had inspired innovations in his technique. It was notably better than the old basic insert Tab A into Slot A, which had been good enough twenty-five years before. Now, as soon as we got over our initial nervousness and found our old rhythm, it was *very* good. Okay, so maybe the man wasn't as creative as some I could name, but who was? The musician in me was certain it would improve with practice, and for what was really a debut, he more than got the job done. And it was Charlie. *Charlie!* I had schlepped a ton of emotional baggage for him. I bit back tears afterward.

For the record, no one said anything about love at any time during the proceedings. But after a respectable twenty minutes of recovery with me nestled in his arms, Charlie said something I knew Marti would think was even better:

"We need to do this again soon. See each other. Though the other should be a project as well." He kissed the top of my head. "Next weekend is a washout. It's Mother's Day and I'm taking you know who to dinner at a restaurant that still serves tomato aspic. But the following week, I'm taking Friday off to make it a three-day weekend. I'm going to fly up to the Landing, the place in Maine."

The Landing was the family's summer compound situated at the end of Cove Haven Island on Penobscot Bay.

"I'd love you to join me there."

I had vacation time coming. At the Maryland Phil, you bank days to use at your discretion. And God knows I was due for a break.

"The water won't be warm enough to swim, but we can go sailing. You've never seen the Landing, have you?" He'd never invited me. Had he, no doubt Kiki would have barred the door. "It sits on a bluff overlooking the sea. The scenery is beautiful.

We could eat lobster three times a day and make love four. How does that sound?"

"Like wishful thinking." I laughed.

He ran a fingertip down my cheek. "Don't be so sure. You make me feel young again, Judith. Like old times."

New times are never like old times. Even *I* knew *that*. "I'll let you know," I managed to say just before his BlackBerry chimed.

Chapter 24

Theodora Gottlieb, MD, leaned back in her oversized chair, the thready cascade of her blond-growing-out-to-silver hair almost lost in the buttercream leather. She steepled her fingers in a contemplative arch. This was my first appointment with her in months and although I was in dire need of a tune-up, what I'd really come in for was a fix.

I'd been hitting the Internet full throttle since the panic attacks, searching for advice from fellow sufferers. Not the best idea. The cellist chat rooms were filled with accounts of careers killed, lives ruined by stage fright. Anxiety, it seems, has a way of spreading. First the terror centers on playing solo; then it might expand to playing ensemble, then maybe leach over to other areas of your life. Today I couldn't hold a bow. Tomorrow I could have a phobia about anything long, hard, and pleasure providing. Oh no, I had to nip this in the bud pronto. And that would take the magic pill.

Not so fast, was my shrink's unspoken message. I'd been filling her in on how I'd been doing since we last met, including the bouts with stage fright. Now she scrutinized me with her savvy gaze. "Interesting, this need to end your relationship with

Geoff as soon as your former boyfriend entered the picture. You rushed to cut him loose because . . . ?"

The same question Marti had asked evoked the same answer. "Because I thought it was better than stringing him along while I worked out my feelings for Charlie. A process"—Theodora loved the word "process"—"that included screwing. And I couldn't, *wouldn't* do that with Geoff in the picture." That *was* the reason, and not a scummy one either, but in Theodora's huge, panoramically windowed office it resounded as smug and self-righteous.

I sneaked a glance at my watch. Twenty minutes of psychobabble and we still hadn't gotten to the real reason for my visit. "An interesting rationale," she was saying. "You might want to probe beneath the surface here."

Well, no, I really didn't want to wade in much deeper. She'd redecorated since my last visit and the new sea blue walls and shelved artifacts of Israeli Roman glass, so liquid, already made me feel as if I were drowning.

"Not to be rude, Dr. G, but I came here to talk about my stage fright, not my sex life."

She had been twirling a spiral of Botticelli curl, but now she stopped and leaned forward, her face a caricature of incredulity. "You think your personal and professional crises are unconnected? Come on, Judith, we've been working together too long for that." She paused for a reaction.

I gave her a prickly one. "If there's a connection between my performance anxiety and anyone else, it's Irwin. It was Irwin I hallucinated in the audience."

"A father who wasn't around to give you approval. But he's only one in a cast of characters playing the roles of judge and jury. There's Charlie, who left you because, in your own words, you weren't good enough. Might his appearance revive those old

feelings of inadequacy? Feelings that translate into panic in precisely the arena where excellence is most important to you: onstage. Just a thought."

A ridiculous thought. "So far, all signs point to Charlie
thinking I'm more than adequate," I snapped.

"So far." Theodora plucked that note. "This relationship is all
very new. Please remember you're in the first stages of rediscov-
ering each other. And then there's Geoff, still in your life, mar-
ginalized romantically but acting as your coach, someone to
whom you've granted thumbs-up/thumbs-down authority. This
anxiety might be about a healthy reluctance to give up your
power. What do you say?"

I said, "I guess."

She scribbled a word on her ever present legal pad and underlined it twice. Probably "Resistant."

"And now one more challenge: Richard's terminal illness.
How are you dealing with that?"

I was trying *not* to deal with it and shamefully succeeding
until the day before, when Angela gave us the latest report. The
metastases in Richard's brain were screwing around with his oc-
cipital nerve. His sight was going.

At her announcement, a hush had settled over the orchestra.
I'd squirmed in the silence. And deserved to. It had been three
weeks since Geoff and I had been to the Roland Park house. I'd
called a few times, but the conversations were always brief. Which
was my doing. I told myself I didn't want to wear out a sick man,
but that was crap. What I didn't want was to hear the details that
added up to his dying. Not Richard. So I put distance between us
because I couldn't bear to see, to feel the pain of it.

What a selfish clunk I was. What a lousy friend, mentee,
whatever.

After rehearsal, I'd taken my guilty self to the closest Barnes

& Noble, filled a shopping bag with large-type mysteries and audio books, and went to see him. The housekeeper stopped me at the door and took the bag. Mr. Richard was sleeping and not to be disturbed. "Holding his own," she'd told me with a pitying shake of the head.

Now I pulled a tissue from one of the pale blue boxes scattered over every flat surface in Theodora's aquarium of an office. She gave me an empathic smile.

"Richard has been more than just a stand partner to you, hasn't he? A friend?"

I sniffed, tying to hold back the tears.

"Stand partners can be like family, close as siblings," she proposed.

"Some are," I acknowledged.

"Go with that, Judith."

It had been her "that," not mine. I shrugged, stalled halfway down the path to enlightenment.

Theodora prodded, knee in my behind. Richard was twenty-some years older than I, not a good fit for a brother. But the daddy spot was vacant. *The daddy spot was vacant!* My mermaid shrink nearly flipped herself out of her chair with delight over her discovery.

"I don't buy it," I said, throwing cold water on her theory. "Richard always treated me as an equal. Plus, it's not as if he's looking to play papa. He has kids." Sons only, but still. A tone-deaf commodities broker and a physics professor at Stanford whose musical tastes ran to Coldplay. And grandkids. Twin boys. But still.

Theodora shot me a frustrated look. "In any event, he's been a potent male influence. And now this accomplished and caring man is dying, and waiting in the wings is Irwin, whom you know only for abandoning and subsequently neglecting you. Not a fair trade, is it? A transaction that might very well elicit a need for denial on your part."

My denial was undeniable. I blew into my scrunched-up ball of Kleenex.

"The point is, you've gotten past it. You've self-corrected. You made phone calls. You went to his home yesterday with the intention of seeing him. That tells me you're showing compassion even while adapting to the inevitability of his moving on." As if he and his furniture were being hauled to New Jersey. "And you're preparing yourself to take over his seat, I assume."

"Yes, but if I can't perform solo, I won't be able to do that. Will I?"

She gave that a moment's thought and took pity, I suppose.

"Very well." She scrawled and tore off the scrip. "I have to tell you, Judith, Inderal will help you get a handle on the physiologic manifestations of your stage fight, but it may not cover the emotional panic." She reached for a clip of papers on her desktop and handed them over along with the prescription. "You can begin to practice the breathing and relaxation techniques on these handouts. They should help. Long term, though, you'll have to deal with the underlying issues that are sapping your confidence. All right, next week same time?"

Not good. I'd be just returning from Maine. Among the details I'd skipped with Dr. G.

I mumbled something about a heavy schedule and calling to fit something in and watched her face crimp with disapproval.

"Don't wait too long," she warned.

"I won't." I was already on my feet and moving toward the door. I flipped her a good-bye with my precious prescription.

·   ·   ·

A half hour before curtain Friday evening I popped my first Inderal. Fifteen minutes later, my heartbeat, which had jolted at my first glimpse of Berenson Hall and pounded with each reluctant step toward my doom, had slowed and evened out. By the time I finished my warm-up, I'd lost the tremor in my hands and my salivary glands had kicked in. In my chair onstage, I closed my eyes against the terrifying audience taking their seats and visualized myself floating high above the concert hall, clouds supporting me, sun warming me. Deep breath. Sun. Clouds. Breathe from the gut, not the lungs. Hold to a count of three, exhale slowly through the nose. That's what Dr. G's handouts instructed. I'd been practicing.

My solo in the first half of the program was brief. I felt a twinge of unease as I drew the initial bow stroke; then I timed my breathing to the leisurely rhythm of the music and I was fine. Slid right through it. Better living through chemistry. *Woohee!* as Marti would have exalted.

I wanted to share my triumph with Geoff. He managed to avoid me all evening. But after the concert, on a survivor's high and just about dancing to the exit, I crashed into him.

"Judith," he acknowledged. The last time we'd seen each other had been on my porch with Charlie. My lingering image of Geoffzilla was from the rear, scaly tail dragging, monster claws retracted. Rodan had thrashed him. "You seemed to be handling the anxiety up there. Crisis overcome?"

"I saw Dr. Gottlieb and she agreed I could try a little Inderal. She said . . ."

While I babbled on, his attention drifted to his watch. When I came up for air, he said, "Yes, I thought you might be on the meds."

"You could tell? How could you—?"

He cut me off. "We'll have to talk some other time, I'm

afraid. I've got people waiting." Deliberately vague, but what wasn't vague at all was his impatience to be gone and the chill in the air.

What had I expected? A liege lord ready to do my bidding when I decided to bestow my royal favors? That wasn't Geoff.

"We're on for Monday?" I hooked him with that.

"*I* am."

"See you then."

"Right."

"Great." We had work to do. I had an audition to ace.

I rode that surge of euphoria until the drug wore off.

I got home at eleven to find my answering machine flashing three messages. Charlie clocked in at nine fifty-two, oblivious to my anxiety issues because I hadn't shared them. Would he, a civilian, have understood? Also, we hadn't reached the point in our relationship where I was willing to show weakness. Would I ever? Who knew? I'd been there, done that, got the T-shirt . . . and the boot, first time around.

He was sorry he'd missed me. I needn't call back tonight. He was early to bed, figuring he'd better bank as much sleep as possible to face that Mother's Day lunch with Kiki on Sunday.

I'd sent my own mother a card, though this year it had been a half-hour project at the Hallmark store looking for something that didn't gush, because I was still exasperated with her. Also it had to be a simple sentiment—she missed subtleties in English—and not funny. Greeting card humor eluded her.

The day before, I'd e-mailed her to see if my presumed father might be persuaded to take a powder for the holiday so just the two of us could have brunch at Miss Shirley's Café. It wasn't a time-honored tradition, but we'd done it last year. She'd e-mailed back: "You don't say we do something Sunday you and me, so I make other plan. Tomorrow morning good time to come. Father not here after ten."

When I listened to the next message, I was reminded of the Korean saying my mother recited: "When you're healthy, have many trouble. When you're sick, have only one. Be happy for many trouble."

Richard Tarkoff's voice was slushy and he spoke slowly, but I could hear him straining for the old lilt. His labored breathing was a sure sign of slippage.

"Sorry I missed you yesterday, my dear. Sleep seems to be my default these days, but I do want to say thanks for the books. The large type really makes a difference. Just what the doctor ordered. They tell me loss of coordination is next on the list of top ten plagues for mets to the brain," he said. Then a beep sounded and the message cut off. I pressed for the next one.

"Apologies," he resumed. "I'm simultaneously short-winded and long-winded. What I was about to say is I can still manage around fifteen minutes daily on the cello, but that's not going to last without working fingers. And just as I was getting the hang of Paganini's twenty-fourth Caprice after fifty years—" A dry laugh led to a cough. "I may have to ask Sarah to move the damn cello where I can't see it. The idea of that beautiful Goffriller sitting ten feet away taunting me to play it—ach, it's just too much to bear."

And then he surprised me. Although he'd announced after the last futile round of chemo that he was finished with treatment, and vowed to spend whatever was left of his life without an anti-nausea suppository shoved up his ass, now that the time had actually come to give up the fight, he'd changed his mind. He was nudging his medical team to find a miracle. His oncologist was turning over every rock to come up with a clinical trial that admitted the most desperate cases.

"If I'm lucky, I'll live to regret my decision." He sighed. "I'm just not ready to surrender." Proving once again that the life force is stronger even than the gravity of death. "So them's my parting words for now: Never give up the ship. Be well, sweetheart. Speak to you soon, I hope."

"Yes, you will," I promised the glowing zero on my phone. Promised myself.

Chapter 25

❧

Irwin Raphael, decked out in white duck pants, a blue-and-white-striped T-shirt, and a white cap embroidered with a gold anchor, emerged from the elevator into the Blumen House lobby. Spotting me, he doffed the cap. Behind him, struggling to keep up but encumbered by the fishing gear he carried, was another surprise: Geoffrey Birdsall. Geoff was suddenly fishing buds with my . . . with *Irwin*? Oh no. Definitely no.

Irwin approached, checking his watch. "You're early. I hope you're hungry because Gracie's got a feast prepared. By the way, kiddo, I'm sorry I screwed up your schedule with her. We're going to AC tomorrow. They have a special Mother's Day promotion at Bally's." As if he were royalty, the Emperor of No-Goodniks thumped the grip of his fishing rod on the tiled floor.

"Lovely. If you'll excuse me—" I just short of snarled. I wanted to get my hands on Geoff, preferably around his throat. How dare he barge into my family, cozy up to Irwin the Invader!

I strode over to the traitor, who was trying to juggle a tackle box, his own rod, a cooler, and a couple of windbreakers.

I snatched the cooler from his arms so he was forced to look directly at me. "What's going on here?"

"Trying to get organized. Not very successfully, it appears."

"You know that's not what I mean. What are you doing with—?" I hitched my neck toward the Saturday sailor.

"I'm taking him down to Sandy Point to land some croaker. After that, we're heading for the Inner Harbor. We'll tour the *Constellation*, then grab the water taxi to Fort McHenry. If he isn't tapped out by then, we'll go for high tea Dundalk style. Crabs and beer. I'll have him back here by five so I can get to the Berenson by seven." He gave off a satisfied vibe. He'd answered his version of my question.

"I repeat. What do you think you're doing?"

"Ah, you're going for motivation. Two things: a) giving you some time alone with Grace to do your Mother's Day's thing, and b) showing him as many sights as I can cram into a single day, which might hasten his return to the desert from whence he came."

He took my measure and produced a thin smile. "You seem to be unhappy with my involvement in the Raphael family." He was tapping his foot, a sure sign he was irritated. "Let's get something straight, Judith. We may have split, you and I, but you didn't get custody of Grace in the settlement. She's my mate, my chum as well."

So was he being manipulative, trying to stay attached to me through my family in some twisted way? Or was he just being a mensch, a man of high moral character? Geoff was a musician, used to waiting a few beats. He vamped as I considered whether to give him the benefit of the doubt.

"Go," I said finally. "Catch a fish. Ride a boat. Maybe he'll fall overboard."

Geoff threw me a disappointed look as if to say, *Beneath you.*

The ancient mariner hollered over to us, "Nu, Geoffrey? Time is a-wasting and the fish are a-biting. And if we're going to fit in hang gliding, we'd better hustle."

"Hang gliding? He's eighty years old."

"And strong as an ox. Don't worry, we won't get to it today. Maybe next time." Geoff called back, "Be there in a jiff, Irwin." He nodded at me. "Enjoy your mum. We should be gone all afternoon."

"Thanks." I'd decided finally that thanks were in order. "Really. I owe you."

"Put it on my tab," he said.

My mother had prepared brunch.

I stood in her cramped dining area, awed by the spread, feeling as if I'd stumbled into some fantasy Disney park Herringland where any moment Mickey Herring would descend from Mr. Herring's Wild Ride to offer me maybe a glass of tea with a sugar cube to suck between my teeth. And some herring.

Plattered and bowled on the plastic lace tablecloth were herring in wine sauce, in sour cream, chopped with onion, chopped with beets and apple. Also nova lox and kippered salmon. Hard-boiled eggs. Bagels, bialys, and three kinds of cream cheese, one low-fat.

Incredible. All the more because there was no such thing as brunch in Korea. Maybe in a trendy neighborhood in Seoul there was an imitation New York luncheonette offering blueberry pancakes, but Koreans traditionally ate the same foods for breakfast, lunch, and dinner, the only meals they acknowledged.

"That kipper herring. Kipper mean smoke. Very good." My mother smacked her lips. "Lox. I don't like, but maybe you like. You love lox when you baby. Daddy bring home."

What she didn't remember was that as soon as Irwin took off for points west, we never had lox in the house. And after finding out he'd made half a living selling it, I'd always turned up my nose when Aunt Phyllis served it.

"We go to deli on Liberty Road owned by Russian people. Your father know all about lox. Russians very impressed."

"Did he pay for this?" The bagel would stick in my throat.

"No, why should he pay? I pay. I have money." She sat herself firmly at the head of the table.

I parked myself in the chair next to hers, speared a bagel, sliced it, and shmeared cream cheese. I took a sip of my mother's homemade *horicha*, barley tea with honey.

The conversation was surprisingly easy, as if there'd never been a breach, until I mentioned Geoff's trying to cram in Baltimore's sights to nudge Irwin's return to Arizona.

"That so stupid. He not go back so fast. Maybe not go back at all." She concentrated on peeling the white from the yolk of a hard-cooked egg. "Maybe stay here."

"Here?" I had a serrated knife in my hand. The question was in which direction I would plunge it.

"Not here in 4C," my mother clarified. "We look for big apartment in Blumen House. Two bedroom. For hobbies. He make Indian doll. Ka-chi-na." She pronounced it carefully, as if she'd been coached. "He have space. I have space. Bigger kitchen so I cook more."

I felt myself flushing. "The idea of having you here was so you'd cook less. Oh, for heaven's sake, *Uhm-mah*, you can't be thinking of taking him back. What are you, *dol dae ga ri*?" Literal translation: stonehead. Colloquially: a dolt, a dunce.

Now she slammed the bagel on her plate. "Don't insult. Terrible to insult mother on almost Mother's Day. And I *am* smart, Judith." This was an important enough statement to warrant the use of the verb.

"Yes, you are, Mommy. But he's smarter," I said, not meaning to insult her. "In a sneaky, underhanded way. Can't you see now that Lorna's dead he needs someone to take care of him? Cook for him. Do his laundry. Look at him with goo-goo eyes."

"What goo-goo eyes?"

I rolled an adolescent lovesick glance.

"That not me." She laughed. "Old days maybe, but not now. My heart also smart. Even sneaky a little. He make me laugh. Buy me things. Show me good time. We go places. Atlantic City. Arizona. Maybe we go to Seoul. I never been back. He promise Seoul end of summer."

"So this is about money. He has money and . . ." I couldn't finish as my rage bubbled up to my throat. I forced a deep breath and found my voice. "He left you, a stranger in a foreign country, to fend for yourself with a six-year-old daughter who loved him, who thought she was crap because he left and he didn't care enough to even stay in touch . . ."

Now, I have been known to tear up in my time, but full-out weeping with torrents of splashy sound effects? That I usually saved for films featuring dying lovers, doomed mutts, or abandoned kids. Abandoned kids—*bingo!*

My mother eased herself out of her chair and came around to me. "Nonono. Judith. Judith."

She tried to stroke my hair, but I jerked away. "How can you take him back?" I sobbed. "He's a real bastard, to his core."

"Not to core, Judith. You don't know." She patted me helplessly on the shoulder.

I whirled on her. "You tell me I don't know. Aunt Phyllis tells me I don't know. What's the big secret? What's to know? I'm forty-nine years old, for chrissakes. Whatever it is, isn't it time to tell me?"

She pressed a fresh napkin on me. "Blow nose. Wipe eyes. Okay? Okay. You right, you big girl now. I tell you." She settled herself in the chair next to me and took my sparrow-boned hand in her dove-soft one. "Ay, *aigoo*." She expelled one of her incomparable sighs. "I tell you, but don't throw fit.

"At beginning, I very mad at your father. Leave me for chippie.

First month he send stuff. Then I don't hear from him many months. When he make phone call, I hang up. He call again, ask for you. I hang up. Bad mother. But I very, very hurt inside." She was nervously peeling the nail polish from her left thumb. "He send card from California. Card from cruise. He go with her to England, send card. Address: Judith Raphael. Sign, 'Love, kisses, Your Daddy.' I find in mailbox and tear up. So bad mother."

I'd sunk my head in my hands when she mentioned the phone calls. Covered my eyes. What I really wanted to do was stuff my fingers in my ears.

"Aunt Phyllis tell me I do wrong, but he hurt me very, very bad here." She banged a fist against her chest. "I don't want this bad man in your life. I think you do okay. After year or two you stop asking question, Where my father? Why Daddy not call? Why not visit?

"He stop calling after I hang up so much. But he keep writing. And start sending checks."

At that, I snapped my head up so hard I gave myself one of those teeth-jarring shocks to the jaw.

"When you in six grade he start sending checks." The rest I heard in a state of heightened awareness, my mother's voice coming through magnified, the colors in the room shining bright and sharp, the sentences running into one another like streams converging.

Irwin hadn't been working until then. The chippie wanted him at her disposal. To dance with her on the cruise ships, hold her handbag on their world tours. The globe-trotting stopped when Lorna was diagnosed with lupus. From then on, they were home in Tucson for long stretches, which meant he was able to hold a job. Not a full week, just part-time. "Your father very good salesman. Sell cars, sell Amway, work different places. Not steady, but he send me check here, check there from what he make."

He'd never held on to any job long enough for Grace to rely on his payments for rent in a better neighborhood, but she'd squirreled the money away. "And he pay for your cello lessons."

I was still reeling from the first revelation, but this one—striking so close to my kishkes, my vitals—made me see stars. "He don't know I use it for that," my mother amended, and I released a breath. "He want me buy you clothes, toys, like that, but I think Mrs. Beckersham very important. Also, he buy your first cello."

At which point I lurched to my feet. My mother kept a bottle of *soju*, a Korean rice vodka, in the china cabinet. I poured her a shot and me a shot and, in the old-fashioned way, turned from my elder out of deference and gulped down the slightly sweet liquor. It made fire in my throat, warmth in my belly, anesthetic in my brain.

Fortified, I faced her. "You never told me," I said. I wasn't accusatory, just trying to understand.

"Tell you? I tell you, you stop lessons, throw cello in garbage. When teenager, you scream if he ever come back, you kick his ass." Thanks to my Bed-Stuy peers, I'd had a way with words. "You say nothing he do make up for run away, remember? He leave us for rich lady and you hate him and his lousy money, you say. So I don't say nothing."

"When did the checks stop?"

"Not for long time. How you think you go to Boston? Korean spirits, *yo-sansin*, come down from mountain and help? Only part scholarship to conservatory. You think Aunt Phyllis and Uncle Arnold so generous? Sure, they buy school clothes and books, but not made of money and cousin Staci in college same time. Your father's check pay rest for school. And I can't tell you or you quit. You be so mad."

She was right. That's exactly what I would have done.

The kicker was that even knowing his daughter was in the dark about the source of her tuition, Irwin continued to send checks when he could.

My mother groaned, lifting herself from the chair. She poured herself another shot of *soju*, watching my eyes with the caution of a low-flying bird eyeing a rumbling volcano. But I was too overwhelmed, too tapped out to blow.

"Now maybe time come for you to stop so angry inside. Make you crazy. You can't even play music. Geoff tells me you scared and nervous onstage. All from bitter and angry." She tossed the liquor down and followed it with a long *Ahhh*. "Okay, so Irwin not best man in world, but not so bad either. He try. I take much blame too." That was a first. "Time to forgive, Judith. You almost fifty. Nice present for yourself, for everyone."

By the time I got home I had a raging headache. Maybe it was the three shots of *soju*, the two and a half cups of coffee plus the revelations I could barely swallow, but my temples were pounding as if our timpanist had taken a mallet to them. It wasn't an aneurysm headache—that pain was more a screaming atonal assault by Christopher Rouse—but it was a bruiser. The nausea had hit as I turned into my driveway. Upstairs, I'd dosed myself with a couple of Advil and a swig of Pepto-Bismol, collapsed on my bed, and lay there, teeth chattering, stomach roiling, staring at the ceiling, playing my mother's betrayal over and over in my brain.

I called the Berenson at five to tell them to have Joan Farley, our assistant principal cello, sub for me that night, then dozed fitfully until intermission, when Geoff phoned.

"What's going on? You looked fine this morning. Pissed off, but healthy."

"I think it's some kind of flu," I said. I took a deep breath and made my chest ache trying to be nice. I told myself that in spite of my snitty performance in the lobby, he'd called to check up on me, so he deserved a little nice. "How did your excursion go? Catch anything?"

"We did. Irwin caught a mess of croakers. He seems to be a natural on the water. Then he ate the first steamed crabs of his life and drank two beers. He was quite the mellow fellow when I delivered him back to Grace. Actually, we had a fine time. He's not bad company, the old bloke. Has a sense of humor. A bit Henny Youngman, but funny."

"Funny."

"After the first beer. After the second he got serious and told me how he'd been a bastard to you and your mother and how much he regretted it. His eyes filled."

"Yeah, cheap beer, cheap talk." Oh, please. I really didn't want to hear any more about how funny and sensitive Irwin Raphael was. I delivered my punch line: "I'm going to say good-bye now, Geoff. I'm feeling really lousy. Maybe this is that forty-eight-hour bug that's going around. If so, I'm not sure I'll be up for our session Monday."

"Understood. Well, if you wake all bright and sunshiny, I can do last minute. Otherwise, if you like, I can pick up some Attman's chicken soup and drop it off."

"Thanks. I have some of my mom's in the freezer." A white lie.

"Ah. See you at rehearsal on Tuesday, then."

Well, no. Since I was taking the following weekend off for my trip to Maine, I wasn't going to be rehearsing at all that week.

"Maine," Geoff said, after I'd explained. "What's in Maine?"

Had I ever told him about Charlie's place up there? I couldn't remember.

"Beautiful scenery and not my father," I answered, the second half-truth tripping off my coated tongue.

"Sounds like just what the doctor ordered," Geoff said, signing off.

After hanging up, he phoned Marti to have her check in on me. Within ten minutes, she was sitting at the edge of my bed spoon-feeding me ice chips. My headache had dulled down, but I was still fighting nausea.

"He wanted to drop off chicken soup for you. Well, isn't *he* gooder than grits," she said.

"Oh, right, all the men in my life are just paragons of virtue."

"What you told me about your dad before—" Marti held up a hand. "And honestly, babygirl, I'm about fed up to my gullet with the erstwhile, so-called, purported, alleged father bit. The man sired you. You are genetically linked to him, like it or not. And now with Gracie's herring confession, you have to deal with the possibility that Irwin wasn't the monster you spent your life believing. Okay, he abandoned you and your mom and took off for warmer, richer climes. Pretty shitty. But . . . he made payments, he sent presents, he tried to contact you."

I was seized by a furious spasm of chills.

"That really throws you, doesn't it? Of course it does."

I glared at her as she tucked the quilt under my chin.

"It shakes your entire belief system down to its roots. Maybe that's why you're shivering. An old dead tree is about to fall. About time, too. All I can say is *tim-berrrrr!!!*"

Chapter 26

I began to have second thoughts about the Maine trip about twenty minutes into the flight. The idea had been to escape from the gaggle of demons chasing me. Hanging out with Charlie was supposed to be a bonus, but when I was almost there, the thought of spending three days on an island with a man I hardly knew anymore . . . Well, the plane hit a rough patch over Philadelphia, but that wasn't what made my stomach lurch.

It didn't help that, succumbing to curiosity, I'd picked up Eloise Flint's memoir at the airport bookstore and was thumbing through it. What a crock! The fake had shifted her rough Brooklyn childhood to tonier Manhattan. Her father had been upgraded from a guy in the subway token booth to a railroad executive. No mention of the Charlie interlude, of course, and her years at the conservatory read like a novel, the blossoming of a musical genius.

I flipped to her account of the Balakirev competition, when we'd met up again after a five-year hiatus. I was twenty-seven years old, in top form, and itching for retribution. Eloise was already considered the up-and-coming successor to Jacqueline du Pré, but my sense was I could beat her, that whatever I lacked in talent I'd more than compensate for with a burning desire to even the score.

We both got through the first two rounds. I was psyched to take the last one, really show her up and also show Charlie, whom I fantasized would read the details of my triumph in the *New York Times*. I was cruising along until ten minutes before my slot onstage, when I turned into one of the Moscow Conservatory's labyrinthine corridors and nearly crashed into Eloise. All I wanted to do was free myself from her tentacles, but as I pulled away she tightened her grip on my arm and said in the accent that was no longer British but some cloudy international concoction, "I just want to wish you good luck, Judith." We both knew that wishing someone good luck in our profession meant bad luck. I shook her off, but I couldn't shake off the curse.

I blew the final round. Little glitches in the Hindemith Sonata and a loss of control in Lutoslawski's Sacher Variations added up. Eloise took the grand prix and went on to a blazingly successful solo career while I decided, after some thought, that my calling was playing tutti cello in a world-class orchestra.

Don't get me wrong: I loved my work, loved the embracing Philharmonic family and the anchor of a regular paycheck. But the idea that the bitch had *twice* bested me big-time—that rankled.

In her book, she awarded the Balakirev competition a single self-serving paragraph. In retrospect, it had been no big deal to her. To me, the event had been life-shifting, the first time my nerves had derailed my ambition.

When the flight attendant came around collecting trash, I tossed the book in with my empty Coke can and half-eaten cheese crackers.

At the airport, Charlie hardly seemed in the mood for any kind of face-to-face conversation. He gave me a peck on the cheek as he mumbled into his Bluetooth headset. On the drive to Rockland, he took two or three more calls.

And then a magical transformation—he set foot on the deck of the ferry taking us across Penobscot Bay and his spirits lifted. He clicked off the BlackBerry, pocketed the headset, and turned garrulous. "Ahh—" He inhaled deeply. "Freedom." He wound an arm around my shoulder. "When I was a boy, this trip was like falling down the rabbit hole. You left the mainland, the real world, and twenty minutes later you were on Cove Haven, wonderland. No set bedtime. On or in the water all day." A gust of spray spewed up from the bay to whack us hard. Charlie laughed and tightened his grip. "It's hard to explain, but you know what I mean."

"In theory," I said. We didn't have air-conditioning in any of the Brooklyn apartments until I was maybe twelve and Uncle Arnold installed a window unit in the flat on Moore Street. Summer was always a killer.

"Here we are. The Landing," announced the lord of the manor ten minutes later. His eyes sparkled taking in the view under a cloudless sky.

The Pruitts' Maine estate sprawled on the longest point of Cove Haven. The Landing, as Charlie's great-great-grandmother Eliza Pruitt had named the expansive New England fieldstone and shingle house on the property's rugged rim, had been built by her husband, Harrison, to afford his young family escape from a predicted epidemic of typhoid fever in the fetid New York summer of 1904. With bacterial fevers roaming the cities, an island off the coast of Maine seemed like the end of the world to Eliza, and that's exactly where she wanted her brood to be.

"She was a pip, Eliza was," Charlie declared. "Strong woman. My mother claimed to have met up with her ghost in the attic. Maybe she hung around to haunt us, because Kiki dumped the original furniture in 1958. Come on." He took my hand as we rounded the boathouse to the Landing's front entrance bracketed by pine trees. "I'll show you around inside."

I'd been in larger homes because I'd been hired to play in them. And God knows I'd wandered through better-appointed ones. The living room was furnished in scratched-up whitewashed oak and peeling rattan. Two sofas and a brace of chairs were draped in slipcovers of gray ticking that was also a little ratty, and the few upholstered pieces had deteriorated way beyond shabby chic and into threadbare. Aunt Phyllis would have taken one look and called in her decorator to do a complete makeover, in seven shades of blue no doubt, the desert tribe's favorite color. On the other hand, the Landing's atmosphere was pure summer house, with slatted louvers and ceiling fans, and I felt its pull. Charlie had called in one of the year-round people to come by that morning, clean the place, and open all the windows. The breeze that blew in from the bay was tangy sweet and wistful. Or maybe the wistful part was me.

"Aside from the overhaul of the kitchen, which we did a few years ago, the house is pretty much Kiki," Charlie told me. Upstairs, she'd gone wild with chintz. Only the master bedroom had been spared the flower explosion. That room was a gorgeous, spacious retreat in lavender and purple against white.

"Betsy finally prevailed upon me to let her do her thing in here."

The ex-wife. "She had lovely taste." I fingered a cloudy Lalique sculpture.

"Expensive taste. We spent a fortune on this room."

"But you and Betsy ended not because she had expensive taste . . ." I paused so he could fill in the blank. Sure, I applied a bit of chutzpah here, but I felt I had a right. He'd been mine before he'd been hers. And I was going after some insight that might be useful later.

He sighed. "We grew in different directions. That was the party line anyway, and she was the shrink, the PhD. That she also stepped out on me with a thirty-five-year-old ski instructor in Aspen she claimed was irrelevant because the root causes lay with me, apparently." He sounded bitter. I left well enough alone. We had an entire weekend ahead.

The remainder of the afternoon was spent on the balcony off the bedroom—I engrossed in a musty Perry Mason I'd dug out of the bookshelf in the guest room, Charlie doing legal work on his laptop. He was taking calls again. Occasionally, he reached over to squeeze my hand.

"Time for a drink," he announced, around four.

"Just water for me," I said.

When he came back with a glass of water for me and a tumbler of Glenfiddich for himself, I put down my mystery. It seemed an appropriate moment to solve another, more private one. I gave him a few minutes to stare at the sea and make a dent in his scotch. Then I said, "After we split back in Cambridge, you started dating Eloise Flint."

He twirled a finger lazily in the liquid, apparently unalarmed. "Eloise Flint. So long ago."

"I was even longer ago. So you and I had just broken up and suddenly you were a hot item with Eloise. She and I were friends. But you knew that."

"You were dormmates, not friends. Acquaintances. That's what she told me." He put down his scotch and removed his sunglasses to squint at me. "I don't ever remember your mentioning Eloise when you and I were together."

Probably true. Certainly true after I'd moved out of the dorm and into his place on Wendell Street.

"So tacky," I said. "Sleeping with someone who lived across the hall from the woman you'd just ditched."

"Come on, Ju-ju. I was a jerk, but not so much that I would have dated your close friend. But you're right in a way. I did see a connection between you two. She was also brainy and good looking, except for the legs. A New Yorker. A cellist. At first I thought, Okay, a reasonable facsimile of Judith."

I snorted.

"No, really. When you and I split, I went into a deep funk, angry with myself for buckling to my family, and still in love with you. And then Eloise came on to me, all engines firing. She said just the right flattering things at a time when I was really vulnerable. Don't get me wrong. I didn't push her away. I figured, Well, I've got the Protestant version of you, only this time with the required papers. Her father was a railroad executive—did you know that? And her mother was descended from some obscure Irish baronet." More Eloise bullshit. "Though Kiki couldn't find him in *Burke's Peerage*."

"You took Eloise Flint home to Mommy?"

"Never. But I mentioned the noble lineage in passing. So she got the Kiki Pruitt seal of approval." He slugged the last half inch of scotch, eyes on me. "Of course, it didn't work. Couldn't have. It was all built on an impossible fantasy. On wanting the woman I couldn't have."

"Wouldn't," I corrected. "So who ended it?" Somehow that still seemed important.

"I did. And she was very ticked off indeed. I received a venomous letter. Quite a long letter for such a short affair. Also I got a rash of hang-up calls. Not a pleasant ending."

"Most aren't."

"Right." He inspected me first for damage and, not finding any obvious signs of it, checked his watch. "Well . . ." I could almost hear the relief in the released breath. "We have a little time yet before we have to dress for the club. I think I'll refresh my drink. You sure I can't interest you in a very fine cabernet?"

No, I wanted to assess his tale of Eloise with a clear head. Also—here I took up my glass of ice water—it might be prudent to keep my wits about me since I'd be facing a jury definitely not of my peers at the club later.

Smart decision all around.

As the sun began to fade, I came down with a nasty case of the jitters and there wasn't a cello in sight. Six of Charlie's friends had flown in from Boston on a private plane piloted by one of their own just to meet me. Talk about pressure.

I'd known about the Cove Haven crowd as far back as Cambridge. They'd romped together through golden childhood summers on the island and as adults returned every season to the family compounds. They were a loyal, protective, insular band, and I was, as I'd always been, the quintessential outsider. So of course I dreaded this dinner.

However, there was one member of the crowd I was dying to meet. Ginny Forbes Carlin was Charlie's first girlfriend. At seventeen she'd enthusiastically awarded him her virginity behind the boathouse at Maweshenook Harbor. She'd been a beauty back then, patrician, a direct descendant of Ralph Waldo Emerson, and she had a talent for giving incredible head, a combo that seemed to me, when I first heard about it back in Cambridge, the most blatantly unfair distribution of DNA since God gifted Michelangelo. She was a drunk now, Charlie told me, which sounded like the universe was just trying to balance out the goodies.

Ginny with a snootful I figured I could take. The rest of them? Well, I knew I was facing one tough audience and that I had a couple of big-time acts to follow: Betsy the gorgeous PhD wife, Carolyn the TV reporter girlfriend. Oy, *aigoo*, I'd never pass muster.

"You're kidding, Ju-ju," he reassured me after he'd spotted

my left eyelid twitching as we mounted the steps to the Cove Haven Yacht Club and I confessed how intimidated I was. "You're an accomplished, charming woman. You're going to knock their socks off."

Possibly, had there been any socks to knock off. It was mid-May and the men were all in loafers or docksiders sans socks, the finishing touch to the uniform of khakis and blazers. The women looked like a stable of long-necked, long-maned, long-legged racehorses. They wore slacks with twee patterns like anchors and cherries, topped with blouses and cardigans to hide the kidnapping of their waists around menopause. I wished I had the headband concession.

I elicited a few *Isn't she the exotic flower?* looks. But after the first few minutes, I faded into the wood paneling, sipped my gin and tonic—no chocotinis or mojitos here; time stopped at the bar around 1937—and listened, smiling blandly, while they caught up.

Twenty minutes and two rounds in, we drifted out to the deck and sorted ourselves by gender. Well oiled with yet another round of drinks—thanks but no, I demurred—the talk at the women's table turned to what interested the wives almost as much as creeping socialism: their kids and grandkids.

This effectively shut me out for a while, the way the subject of labor and childbirth had exiled me from female conversations in my twenties and thirties.

Of course, this wasn't the first time it occurred to me that I could have had grown children, maybe even grandchildren by now had I married Charlie as planned. My plans, not his. When he and I were dating seriously, I'd daydreamed our kids: straight haired, with a talent for music and debate. Our daughter Rose Pruitt, named after Grandma Roz, would be loved lavishly, the way the old lady hadn't loved me. Little Rose had almond-shaped eyes, but in hazel or blue. The boy was named Isaac Solomon

Pruitt just to flip the bird to Kiki, who would have secretly had him baptized Ian Scott. Truly, I wouldn't have put it past her.

As for my short-lived marriage, Rebound Todd had been eager to fulfill the Talmudic injunction to go forth and multiply—exponentially as he became increasingly Orthodox—which might have been one reason I checked out so fast. And I was okay—more than okay—with my biological dead end. "I have my music" was my answer when the question popped up. Not that I ever had the guts to say it aloud. But it was true. I had my baby of a cello, which was sufficiently demanding, usually rewarding, and didn't require orthodontics.

But I wasn't going to get out of this conversation unscathed. Ginny Carlin made sure of that. "How about you? Any grandkids yet?" Though her diction was blurry, her gaze was on point.

I worked to make my expression neutral. "I never got that far. I'm happily child free." "Child free" would have worked among my liberal musician colleagues and the "happy" modifier might have bought me some smiles among Marti's older lesbian pals—the ones before the in vitro fertilization craze hit same-sex couples. Here the words drew wondering looks all around.

Just as I was about to be sacrificed to the God of Family Values, Charlie intervened. I didn't know what he'd heard or whether he'd heard, but he sidled over and curled a defensive, proprietary arm around my waist. Take that, Ginny Forbes Carlin, you slut.

"Time to do battle with some lobsters," he said. "I swear, Ju-ju, you've never eaten a lobster until you've had one fresh from the waters of Penobscot Bay."

He was right. The lobsters looked like specimens of a giant new species and they were sweet and briny and just about danced out of the shell pleading to be eaten. Between bites, I gritted my teeth as the talk around the big table returned to bashing the administration in Washington. About twenty minutes in, one of the women, a second wife who wasn't steeped in the history, asked, "Where did you two meet anyway?"

"In college, right?" Ginny Carlin said. "They were engaged back in the day." She took a gulp of her endless martini.

"Not quite," Charlie said. "Close, though."

Had we been close to engaged? I wondered. Really? News to me.

"And now you're dating again—that's so sweet." Ginny's voice was sugary enough to trigger diabetic shock. "Long distance is a bummer, though. You in Baltimore"—she lifted her glass in my direction, then swung it toward Charlie, spilling a little—"you in New York. But that should be rectified soon when Chip moves to Washington. And then there'll be smooth sailing ahead."

"What's this about moving?" I turned to Charlie, who was fishing the tiny onion out of his Gibson. He looked up to glare at Jack Carlin, who was a partner at Pruitt, Bryce and Summerville, Charlie's old law firm, the one he'd left when he assumed the bench.

"Sorry," Jack said, sending Ginny a withering stare. "Pillow talk. My fault. Never trust a woman who can't hold her liquor. Not that any woman—or man or beast for that matter—could hold as much as Ginny puts away."

Dead silence. Then Charlie said, "All right, who wants dessert?" And aside, to me, "We'll talk later."

He was moving to Washington without telling me? Damned right, we'd talk.

On the drive home, I confronted him. "What Ginny said—when were you going to tell me about that?"

Charlie pulled the car off the road onto a spot overlooking

the ocean. "It's warm for May, and there's a full moon. You game for a walk on the beach?"

Warm it wasn't. But Charlie removed a Harvard-crested throw from the trunk and draped it over my jacket. He took my hand and as we walked along the sand, cool and damp from the last tide, he talked.

"I was going to tell you about this after the partners' vote. My old firm, the one my great-grandfather founded and where I practiced for nearly twenty years, is considering opening an office in D.C. Right now, the idea is in the talking stages. That's probably how Jack Carlin got his information. But if it gels—and I have reason to believe it will—I've learned from a reliable source that I'll be asked to head it up. Which, of course, would involve my relocating."

"You'd leave New York? Resign from the bench?" I tried to make out his profile in the glimmering dark. Inscrutable. "I thought you loved your work."

"I do, very much, but I'm thinking it may be time for a change. On many fronts." We took simultaneous deep breaths before he resumed talking. "I'm about to write decisions in two cases that carry enormous implications for major social issues in this country. Hence the umbilical cord to my BlackBerry." His silhouette patted his blazer pocket. "Yes, the work is exciting and rewarding. But it's also exhausting. I've been doing this for a long time and burnout's become an issue. I'm up for reappointment next year, so maybe the gods of serendipity are telling me it's the right time to get out of the judge business. Return to practice, take up the legacy. It should be invigorating to launch a D.C. office." Long pause. "And then there's you. Finding you again. But in Baltimore."

Here he turned to gauge my reaction. I was listening, not talking. We stopped and stared at the moon. Silvery white and poised high over the water, it was as kitschy as calendar art, but it inspired Charlie to croon, "I know Washington isn't Baltimore, but we'd be a lot closer. A few beltway stops away. Is that something you might want, Ju-ju?"

I wished people would quit asking me what I wanted. Among the few things I'd known for sure was Charlie. My feelings for him. But that was twenty-five years before, and if there was one certainty in life it was that life ground away at certainty.

With no answer at my fingertips, I gave him the only thing I had handy. My lips, still scented with the flowers of gin. I kissed him. Passionately. He slipped me his tongue. And then he did something so out of character, so removed from any experience I'd ever had with him, I wondered whether lunacy wasn't more than an old wives' tale. He unwrapped the throw from around me, spread it on the beach, and pulled me down on top of him. Charlie Pruitt. Mr. Conservative. At fifty-four!

For an Ivy League school, Harvard was very skimpy with its fabric. The crimson blanket almost immediately balled up into a pillow so the bottom half of Charlie lay flat against the cold, moist sand. We kissed valiantly a few more times and then he groaned. "My back's killing me. And something just bit me on the ankle. Shit." He swatted.

"That's what you get for not wearing socks." I rolled off him.

"Maybe this wasn't such a great idea," he said, struggling to sit up. "Ugh. I really need to get to a physical therapist for my back. It's always been my weak spot."

Yes, but not enough to hamper acrobatics in our twenties, which Charlie hastened to remind me we weren't in anymore and maybe we needed to find a more hospitable spot for sport. "Like an old-fashioned bed," he said.

I'd known all along he could never go through with it. To my surprise, he was able to resnag his focus back at the Landing, where we made age-appropriate, perfectly lovely love on Betsy's six-hundred-count Egyptian cotton sheets.

All very comfortable. It occurred to me, maybe too comfortable. I knew it wasn't cricket to conjure up one man while another was poking about inside you, though I'd done it vice versa at the wind-down of the Geoff romance. Nonetheless, I couldn't help thinking how the daring Australian would have turned that beach scene into a *From Here to Eternity* moment. His ass could have been bitten to a lunar landscape by sand fleas, he could have been nearly swept away by the tide, and he would have been baying in ecstasy under the full moon, counting it as a marvelous adventure.

Geoff while I was with Charlie. Charlie while I was with Geoff.

What was it with me? Was I never satisfied?

Chapter 27

Saturday morning I woke at seven thirty-four in a different bed than the one in which I'd fallen asleep the night before. Sometime after midnight, I'd moved out of Charlie's arms and staggered woozily from the master bedroom down the hall and into the guest room.

I know, I know, we'd made love, Charlie and I, which involved the juxtaposition of highly personal body parts, but even my subconscious got that I wasn't ready to take the next step, which was to sleep—as in snore and drool—through the night next to him. The geography of intimacy draws illogical borders.

Charlie had told me the night before that he ran first thing in the morning. I was invited to join him, but he was heading out at six, which was too early for me on vacation. He'd be back by eight and on the way home he'd pick up coffee for me at the Daily Grind on Matinicus Avenue.

I'd been instructed to help myself to orange juice in the fridge and bagels in the freezer. It was too early for solid food, so no to the bagels. But my mouth tasted like the bottom of an owl's nest from the gin, so yes, oh yes, to the juice waiting to quench me downstairs.

From my suitcase, I withdrew and slipped on a pair of silky

baby doll pj's that were duplicates of the ones that had turned Charlie on long, long ago. You can buy anything on eBay. I was hoping the lingerie might inspire a matinee, because I hadn't given my all to last night's toss, what with the static from Geoff, and I wanted to try again, clearheaded.

As I was checking my thighs for cellulite in the guest room mirror I heard banging around downstairs. Charlie scrambling eggs, probably. If he would do that for me, then I had a delicious breakfast treat for him. I descended the stairs stealthily—nothing like a bit of surprise to add spice to seduction—and tiptoed into the kitchen.

Uh-oh. Standing, back to me, at the far counter, methodically stashing bottles of Sam Adams into the refrigerator, was not Charlie. It was, I assumed from the jeans, pink tank top, and baseball cap turned round, the cleaning woman who'd gotten her days mixed up.

Time to retreat. Not wanting to embarrass either of us, I took a few steps back, heading for the hall, the stairs, and my escape. On the fourth blind step I tripped and knocked against a steel trash can, which clanged resoundingly. The cleaning lady wheeled.

Her hand flew to her chest. She made a woofing sound and yelled, "Shit!" Then, softer, "Oh God, you scared the crap out of me."

Both of us were breathing hard. Her stare was frozen on my bare thighs. (Thank you God for my last-minute decision to wear the bikini bottoms—it had been a close call.) Only when I muttered, "Sorry," did her gaze swoop up to mine. We were now in a contest to establish whose eyes showed more white. At the beginning I'd have said hers. Fifteen seconds in, as everything clicked for me, mine.

When she got her huffing under control, she snarled, "Who . . . the hell . . . are you?"

Not very welcoming, but under the circumstances forgivable.

"Hi, Chloe," I responded with a little wave, the way you'd show a dog the back of your hand to let it know you meant it no harm. "I didn't mean to freak you out. No one told me you were coming." I was going to kill Charlie. Slowly. Torturously. "I'm Judith Raphael. Your dad's houseguest."

"You're who? What?" She squinched her face into something resembling a French cruller. "Ugh, my father's . . . Ugh, that is *so* gross."

And that's when Charlie called out from the hall, "I'm back, Ju-ju. Got you a latte grande and picked up some muffins." Then he walked in, brown paper bag in hand, stopped dead, and looked from one of us to the other, horror growing. He decided to ignore the strange lady in his kitchen—all right, maybe not such a lady, considering the baby dolls—and cooed to his daughter, "Sweetheart, you okay? What's wrong? What are you doing here?"

"I'm fine, Daddy. Really."

"You sure, Clo-Clo?" As in Ju-ju? My empty stomach flipped.

He gave her a parental once-over. "You look okay. What's up?"

"Not much. I've got this monster exam next week and I just couldn't focus in the dorm. Here I can study in peace and quiet."

Oh, come on. Granted, I never had a child, much less a teenager. But if any kid of mine laid that story on me with half a case of beer sitting on the counter, my bullshit needle would be off the meter. I couldn't believe Charlie went for that academic alibi. What she had on the agenda was party time.

"You never said you'd be here this weekend," she scolded, on the offensive.

Her father disregarded the bait. He also overlooked the carton of Sam Adams inches from where he placed the bag with my container of coffee.

"Whatever. It's good to see you, Cookie. How did you get here?"

"Andy gave me a lift. BU's on the same finals schedule."

"Andy Bowen? He drove you?"

"To Rockland. We caught the ferry."

Charlie checked his watch. "Not this morning, you didn't. The first ferry doesn't get in until nine."

"Yesterday, Daddy. We took the last one in."

At that point, I made a discreet lunge for my coffee. As I grabbed the bag, Chloe lowered those heavy Van Tiller eyelids at me and I was catapulted twenty-plus years back. Kiki was standing in the Sutton Place living room, arms folded, taking my measure. I was the fly in the fruit bowl, the staph in the petri dish, beyond nothing and into pestilence.

I lifted the paper cup from the bag and inhaled deeply. Hazelnut. Blessed caffeine.

"Where did you spend the night, Chloe?" It seemed Charlie had given some thought to the timing. His voice was so Mr. Cleaver stern it was laughable.

I took a sip of coffee, which in my eagerness emerged as a slurp. Loud.

Chloe turned to me. "Do you mind? And can we have a little privacy here?" Her voice was bathed in loathing.

I shrugged. "Sure."

One word. Which was one more than Charlie had uttered to me throughout this entire exchange. It was as if I didn't exist. I did for Chloe, though. As I padded through the hall, I heard her say, "Jeez, Daddy, at least you used to have some taste. But this one with the hooker nightgown and those pigsty manners? Incredible."

Charlie—and I waited a good thirty seconds at the bottom of the stairs listening—responded with *moo-ka-chi*: nothing. Deep silence. The man might have graduated from Harvard Law magna cum laude, but a defense attorney he wasn't. He was, however, a fourteen-carat wuss.

Surprisingly, the rest of the weekend worked out—the way it works out when you go to the dentist expecting a root canal and she tells you it's only a cavity. A deep one that involves a double shot of novocaine and copious bleeding from the gums.

I slipped away to a room Charlie had introduced the day before as "Dad's office." Its only concession to the modern era was a clunky old desktop computer that I'd been given permission to use. It took me a good three minutes to summon up the Internet, but I managed to find my way to US Airways.

I was waiting for the Web site to cough up its Saturday flight schedule when Charlie snuck up behind me. "What's going on?" He made a twist of my hair, lifted it, and kissed the back of my neck. I shook him off.

"You're really pissed. Understandable." Just then the page limped on. He peered. "Wow. *Really* pissed. So you're going to jump ship on me, are you?"

The old oak chair had a hundred years' swiveling practice. It spun me around to land on the master of the house.

"Charlie, you don't want me here. Trust me. We'd both—all three of us would be better off if I left today." And then, unlike old times when I let things slip, trying not to turn one of Charlie's waves into a tsunami, I didn't surf over it. I plunged right in. "Look, I heard what Chloe said. The hooker slur and that I had the manners of Miss Piggy. I can't believe you let her get away with that."

I picked up a letter opener. It made me feel good to heft a sharp object.

"Then *don't* believe it. I'm not an idiot, Judith. I figured you were listening in the hall." When I showed no shame, he said, "You had a right, but I didn't want to dress Chloe down within your hearing. According to the psychologist I consulted, public humiliation is a very destructive response for both parent and child. For your information, I gave her hell in private. She's grounded for the rest of her stay. No TV. No computer. No cell. Cut off. And she'll apologize to you."

That seemed like a reasonable penalty for an abusively fresh mouth, but there was more.

"Do you have any idea what she was planning for tonight?" he asked.

On tap, literally, was a Saturday night party at the Landing. Students were on their way in from assorted Boston prep schools and colleges. Chloe promised Charlie she'd head them off at the pass.

"Kids," he said, finishing with a hint of an indulgent chuckle. The chuckle was what set me off.

"Kids, exactly." I felt my cheeks flush. "A horde of underage and, in case you've forgotten your misspent youth, horny kids. In your house. Unchaperoned. Without your knowledge." I paused to let that sink in, resumed with, "And you've laid down what consequences for this betrayal of your trust?"

Charlie had backed away during my tirade. He was literally up against the wall when he stammered, "I haven't really . . ." He finally found words. "The thing is, honestly, I don't know what the hell I'm doing. A teenage girl. This is entirely out of my area of expertise. Chloe's basically a good kid. But she's seventeen with all that implies. Add in the stress of the divorce. Plus her personality, which, with the hormones surging, has become a junior version of my mother's, and I don't have to tell *you* that Kiki Van Tiller Pruitt genes could take out Osama bin Laden genes anytime. I love my daughter more than life, but these days she's a handful. And I'm on my own here. Lost." He threw up his hands in surrender and looked at me for mercy. Found none.

He reached over and hit the X on the airline site. "Don't go, Ju-ju. She's under house arrest, which I'm definitely going to enforce. I guess we need to hang out here today and tonight to keep an eye on her. But she'll be on her way back to school tomorrow morning. That leaves us with an afternoon to play. We could bike the island, I'll show you the sheep farms, or, better yet, they're promising perfect sailing weather. We'll take out the *My Mayflower*."

He'd named his boat the *My Mayflower*? Oh, give me a break.

"Have you ever made love on the deck of a sailboat? No, me either, but I have a feeling the rocking motion enhances the experience. And with the sun warm on your bare skin, what could be better?"

Screwing on a sailboat. That was a stretch for Charlie, a stretch and his law-abiding version of a bribe. Also a diversion. Well, it wouldn't work. The old charm had lost its mojo, at least temporarily.

I pointed with the letter opener. "You haven't changed. This is history repeating itself. You're letting your daughter walk all over you the way you let your mother trample your backbone the first time around. But I'm not going through it again." I placed the letter opener on the desk, Cove Haven Yacht Club insignia facing down. I stood up. I really was ready to walk.

That's when he got down on one knee. Pleading. Funny, but serious. He clasped his hands in front of him. "Come on, Ju-ju. Give me a chance. You're right. I've been taking the easy way out. She's been playing me since the divorce. I saw it, but now I'm going to deal with it. I promise." When I answered him with a skeptically raised eyebrow, he said, "No, really. For her sake as well as mine. Ours."

"I don't know . . ." His admission had caught me off guard. This was a new Charlie, and the latest model hadn't come with operating instructions.

He caught me wavering, grabbed my hand, and crooned over-dramatically, "Stay, Ju-ju," working to suppress a grin. "I beg of you. Please don't leave me alone with her. *Please.*"

That made me laugh, and the laugh did me in. For the moment—subject to reversal, I assured myself—judgment for the plaintiff.

Late afternoon, I returned to the computer to check my e-mail. There was a note from Marti that listed the yes responses to our party invitation, thirty-three so far, and a message from seoulfulgirl sent at eight ten a.m.

> Father out with Geff today. High in sky. He say very
> safe. Hope you like Maine.
> Love Yu

Hang gliding? No way. Maybe driving over the Bay Bridge. Whatever they did, they survived, because a breezy three sentences from Geoff flew into cyberspace at four forty-six: "Watch how he handles the pizzicatos in the middle movement. Hair-raisingly brave. Let's work on this," with a hotlink to Yo-Yo Ma performing the Debussy Sonata for Cello and Piano.

I was halfway through the YouTube clip when I caught a rustle behind me. Chloe was standing at the open doorway. Face bare of makeup, blond hair pulled into pigtails, she looked like a little girl, a sulky little girl, for about ten seconds. Then my gaze slipped to read her T-shirt: "I Could Be a Bitch if I Was Nicer." The grammar was off, but the sentiment was spot-on.

"My father thinks I was out of line before. So, uhm, sorree." As if the grudging attitude might not adequately convey her real feelings, she rolled her eyes to let me know just how sorry she was.

There was no way I was going to accept that bogus apology, so I just nodded "received and acknowledged" and thought the moment was over. But no. Chloe had another grenade up her short shorts. She stood there brazenly, hand on her hip, and announced, "I spoke to my grandmother a few minutes ago." On what? Her confiscated cell phone? "When I described you, she knew exactly who you were. She said she never liked you." She watched me for a reaction. I'm proud to say I gave her not even a twitch, not a sign she'd drawn blood. "It's funny. Everyone thinks Grammy's lost it due to strokes or whatever. She hasn't. She's sharp as ever." She tossed her head like an unbroken colt before trotting off, calling behind her, "I just thought you'd like to know."

Charlie and I never did wind up making love on the deck of the *My Mayflower*—on Sunday, the bay was crowded with beer-swilling three-day-weekend sailors who might have hooted. Besides, within twenty minutes of casting off, the sky turned gray, the water began to churn, and I got a touch of mal de mer. Blame it on my landlocked childhood. The closest beach to Bed-Stuy was Coney Island, where the only objects that sailed were used condoms and Nathan's hot dog wrappers. Still, despite the queasiness, I held my own on the boat, winching and tying and being seaworthy. So much so that I earned the kind of respect that translates into passion for men who equate sheeting the mainsail with foreplay.

Back at the empty house, we raced each other to the master bedroom. I was ready to dive onto the bed, but he made me wait, folded back the spread, arranged the pillows, and only then drew me to him. He kissed me deep, nipped my bottom lip in farewell, then moved on to my right palm, flicking his tongue against flesh. I heard an animal growl. Surprise—it was coming from me.

He moved on to suck my middle finger rhythmically, sending the message he'd like some of the same at a different location. "Yes," he moaned when I complied. I made him gasp again and again, finally with a plea to stop. "No more. I'm too close. Not this way."

As I came up for air, I licked his thighs tasting of salt, his shoulders sweet with coconut sunscreen. "You," he murmured, "taste of . . ." Something I didn't hear because I was already too far gone.

This time there was no sign of the Australian intruder. The only distraction was a nagging phone, probably the Cove Haven crowd hunting us down. Forced to guard Chloe, we'd missed the Saturday night gathering—thank you, Buddha. Charlie, for once, passed on the calls and stuck with me, inside me, until he had me whimpering with pleasure. Twice.

It was a nice memory to take back with me to Baltimore. Charlie had never worked well for me as a memory. Now he had a second chance.

Chapter 28

 ❧

Straight from the airport, I drove to Blumen House to make up with my mother. Those long, boring hours passively guarding Charlie's daughter from hell had given me time to think about my own parent-child relationship. My conclusion was that whatever Gracie had done, whatever decisions she'd made, be they good or bad in hindsight, they had been motivated by the best intentions. I had always—*would* always—come first with her.

One Father's Day in my early adolescence, I'd had the bright idea of giving her a card: "To a Wonderful Dad." Above my signature I'd written, "Because you are a father and mother to me, Mommy. And I love you."

"So crazy, Judith. What this mean?" she'd said, making a cuckoo sign, finger twirling at her ear. But she knew. She was all I had. And I was all she had. Back then.

Even now, when we both had more, I couldn't bear to lose her.

I found her in the garden. Tended by the residents, it was the brainchild of the facility's occupational therapist, who contended that all the planting and weeding would strengthen muscles, improve balance, and, most important, connect old folks to the earth and the cycles of life.

Miriam Botansky's response had been, "I'll be close to the

earth soon enough when *my* life cycle is over. Don't rush me." But my mother loved to get her hands in dirt.

When she squinted me into focus, she cried out, "I can't believe. Look who's back from Maine. Ay, so surprise." And she broke out her best smile.

Gracie made her way toward my outstretched arms. I'd passed her height when I was twelve, but she was thicker boned than I and heavier. Fully grown, I still thought of her as bigger. But now she seemed—with the weight loss and under the large-brimmed straw hat—tiny, more fragile. Inches away from my hug, she nearly lost her balance and my heart jolted as my hand shot out to steady her.

"I'm fine," she reassured me, peeling my fingers from her elbow. "Wrong. I lie. Not fine. I miss you. Not just in Maine. Since we fight."

"I missed you too." Realizing how much, I removed her hat and pulled her into a hug.

"You not still mad with me?" Her whisper carried the scent of mint. My mother liked to chew the herbs she planted.

"Did I ever say I was mad at you?" I backed her away so she could see the reassurance in my eyes.

"Don't have to say. Show. Beside, I know in my bones. You hate me over Daddy. Now and before. You think mean mother like in fairy tale."

"I could never hate you and you're a wonderful mother."

"So all I told you that day, you forgive?"

I patted her layered hair. "Nothing to forgive, *Uhm-mah*." Not exactly true, but the love and the need were strong enough to overcome the disappointment.

She exhaled a relieved breath and smacked her chest, unseating Grandma Roz's diamond pendant. "Ahh, feel better. Friends again. Very happy, Judith. Come, we sit. I need to catch breath. Hot out here, but the porch have shade."

There were no rocking chairs on the verandah—too symbolic—but we settled on a cushioned bench and ordered lemonade—"good for digestion"—and cookies.

"So now we can talk like old times. I want to hear what happened on weekend. You and Charlie hot item, yes? Tell me everything." Her dark eyes glittered.

Did I mention my mother liked to play in dirt?

I gave her the censored version of my weekend. But enquiring minds wanted to know more. She interrupted my description of the lobster dinner at the Cove Haven club. "Who care about lobster? How romance go?" Her eyebrow hitched salaciously. "You sleep in same room?"

Totally inappropriate, but close questioning went way back with my mother and me. In fact, interrogations had comprised most of our conversations during my childhood.

Talk about sex? That was another story. When it came time for the Big Reveal, Mrs. Beckersham had taken over. It was she, not my mother, who bought me my first box of sanitary pads. She who handed down her own copy of the Kotex puberty bible, "As One Girl to Another," a slim booklet written in the slightly stilted language of the forties.

No, Grace had claimed no part of that discussion when it really counted. Now, though, she was a fountain of sexual advice. "It all right you sleep together," she assured me. "You big girl now and this twenty-one century, Judith. Sex not much shame. Nothing much shame anymore." Then she came up with something that was either a plug for her eighty-year-old boy toy . . . *ugh* . . . or more tabloid philosophy. "Sex no big deal, though best if you love him."

"I appreciate your stamp of approval, *Uhm-mah*. But I don't know if I love him."

She shook her head impatiently. "*Make* love all right anyway."

Would she understand that this thing with Charlie wasn't all about sex? It wasn't even about love the way the poets wrote it. What rhymed with do-over? (Except screw over, but why go there?) My best bet was that it had something to do with closing circles, righting wrongs, seizing opportunities. The universe, having pulled the rug out from under me twenty-five years before, had shown up at my door with a once-in-a-lifetime deal on wall-to-wall carpeting. I ask you, do you turn the universe down when it decides it might have shortchanged you? Or do you hang around to see what it has in store this time? You hang. One way or another.

Sitting on the verandah as an errant breeze ruffled the leaves of a nearby birch tree, I was ambushed by a hot flash. My lemonade floated ice cubes. I rolled the chill glass over my forehead.

"So have good time, but don't marry him. That daughter, nasty girl, ruin your life. Fresh mouth. Don't care age. Need smack on tookass."

"You never smacked me on my touchas or anywhere else. Not once—and I'd remember."

"You good girl. No need. She spoil brat. You want such rude stepdaughter? And her father let her insult you? Watch out. Charlie is wimp, like with Kiki."

That was close to what Marti had shouted into my cell phone when I'd phoned her from the airport. "Why, that little shit! I would have spun Miss Chloe's ass around and kicked it into the next county."

"Charlie said it was the shock of her finding me there. That's why she was so rude, but that we'd grow to like each other, given time."

"Right, I'd give it time. How about till hell freezes over?"

"You never know. He promised to get the two of them into counseling as soon as he can find a shrink who'll fit his schedule."

Going back into therapy had been my suggestion, but he'd bought into it. Maybe. This breathless transaction had been made during foreplay, so I wasn't sure the deal would stick.

Marti wasn't buying it. "Oh, honeybunch, you're falling for someone who has more baggage than Lady Gaga on tour. Lace up your Nikes and run for your life."

Now my mother held out the plate of Mint Milanos, her version of Xanax. "More cookie? Or maybe stay for dinner? Tonight lamb chop on menu. You like lamb chop."

"Oh my God—I'm glad you reminded me. I brought you something from my trip."

Charlie and I had toured one of Cove Haven's sheep farms, where the gift shop sold sweaters knit from their wool. I'd bought my mother a heather purple V-neck, very stylish. It was in the car's trunk with my suitcase.

"You think of Mommy all way up there." She stroked my cheek. "Very nice. Come on, I want to see what you get me."

Presents had been rare in Grace's impoverished childhood. As an adult, she greeted them with childlike wonder and delight. She walked with me to the car and stood watching as I popped the trunk.

"Ay, *aigoo*." In her eagerness, she edged me aside, poked her head into its recesses, and shifted its contents. "Your car so messy, Judith." She clucked with disgust. "You always so neat. Now so slob. What happen to you? Oh no, this still here?" She'd caught a brash flash of silver wrapping paper and snapped around to look at me, eyes wide. "Gift from your father? You not open yet?"

I hadn't. I'd forgotten it was there and hadn't missed it. Or I'd buried it in my brain, camouflaged and shoved as far back as I'd stashed it in the trunk.

I blinked against the insistent silver.

"Very rude, Judith. Your father give you special gift. You *must* open."

"Later, at home," I promised.

"No, I don't trust. We open now."

She reached in and snagged the box. And so we marched—with me first, Grace behind me carrying both boxes, to prevent me from bolting, I suppose. Back on the verandah, we took new seats, away from the parking lot and the potential of prying eyes.

Still in command, she tore through the metallic paper, opened the box, and removed a large leatherette book with ALBUM stamped in gold on its cover. She placed it on my lap. I reared back as if it were an infant—something live and demanding.

"Read note." She plucked an envelope from the box and handed it over. What was the use? The damage had been done. My father was brilliant at insinuating himself where he wasn't wanted. An intrusion maven. Even if I stopped the process now, he'd already gotten to me.

I read. Aloud, because I refused to go through the pain on my own and Grace had pushed me into it. Irwin's handwriting was fluid and elegant for an old man with a limited education.

> *Dear Judith~*
> *Been collecting these pix and articles for a while.*
> *Here they are along with some pix of your mom*
> *and I. Now that I've seen you and her, I don't need*
> *them as much to remind me. I kept a few doubles,*
> *so this album is all yours.*
> *I know you don't think so, but*
> *Love,*
> *Your father AKA Irwin*

I'd never seen a photo of my parents' wedding. I hadn't known one existed. It turned out to be a Polaroid, its colors faded to washed-out orange, its edges curled with age.

Irwin Jerome Raphael and Ryang Yun Mi, who'd taken the American name Grace, had eloped to Elkton, Maryland, and were married by a justice of the peace while my grandmother remained blissfully unaware—okay, maybe not blissfully; Grandma Roz didn't know from bliss—back in Brooklyn.

The wedding photo. My mother had been pretty, but to get to that essential prettiness, you had to dig through all that Happy Day bar girl makeup: lips iridescent with pink frost, eyes raccooned with heavy pencil, the liner extended perilously close to her hairline. A long ponytail pulled tight and unflattering bangs made her round face even more moon shaped. Of the two primary participants, she appeared the more composed. Sly even, with those Cleopatra eyes, this on-the-cusp-of-hooker Korean girl who'd won the heart of the rich American GI.

I had no doubt Irwin had wowed her with invisible assets and daydreamed prospects. He was four months out of the army with a freshly grown mustache and a sheen of applied confidence, as if he'd spent the ten minutes prior to the ceremony giving himself a pep talk in the men's room mirror. He held my mother's hand.

When they returned home as Mr. and Mrs., Grandma Roz literally rent her garment with grief (high drama, but it was an old sweater, already unraveling) and in her most memorable quote said to my father, "You were a schmuck in the crib. You couldn't find your own thumb. Once a schmuck, always a schmuck."

On page two—its dog-eared corners crumpled on my fingertips—we entered the Judith era. There was the card from Caledonia Hospital, which said, "Hi, Dad. You have a . . ." In the blank someone had filled in "girl" next to my tiny inked footprint. There was a photo from my first and only birthday party, the *tol* celebration with me in my *hanbok* and cake in my hair. I faced the lineup of symbols. A toy stethoscope had been placed front and center, but I'd had to reach to my right for the miniature violin. So that story wasn't apocryphal.

My father had written corny captions for these photos. *Anchors away!* for the one of me in a sailor dress handed down from my cousin Staci. *Quite a cutie!* for a junior high school shot of me, definitely not a cutie, playing the cello at a recital organized by Mrs. Beckersham. He even had my high school graduation photo, the one with the well-developed wariness in my eyes and the disastrous overdeveloped perm. Where the hell had these pictures come from?

And the clippings. From every concert starting with college, reviews from the *Baltimore Sun* and the *Washington Post* with my name underlined. Also my engagement announcement to Todd from the *Atlanta Jewish Times.* A few of the articles had scrawled dates in the margins. And the mystery was solved. Of course Aunt Phyllis's hand was all over the artifacts and Operation Never Forget. Uncle Arnold had snapped the photos and she'd sent them to Arizona. Newspaper pieces had been clipped and forwarded. Had Irwin asked her to do this or had it been her idea to keep her brother connected to the family he'd abandoned? Even if the child wouldn't see her father, the father must see his child. And who knows—I could hear that masters-in-social-work mind percolating—possibly one day?

"Maybe, yes, Aunt Phyllis send," my mother said. "She don't tell me. But it was your daddy who put together. He hold on to album all these years." She did not look up as she unwrapped the sweater. "Oh yes, very soft. Like very much. I think it fit perfect since my diet. Need to try on right now."

Then she had the sense and the grace to leave me in the fading afternoon alone with the album and my thoughts.

Chapter 29

❧

"**I**'m dying." Richard Tarkoff's somber voice came through my cell phone the next day, then sparked as he slammed me with the punch line: "Dying of boredom. Come save me, Judith. I'm at Hopkins, third floor, La Casa de Chemo."

Richard had made the final cut into a highly experimental trial of some magic potion that might buy him a few months. With one foot across death's threshold, it was worth it to him to spend three hours in a recliner, three times a week, shivering under a stack of blankets while an IV bag dripped hope into his veins.

He lit up at my entrance, even more at the sight of the gold and brown Godiva box I opened and placed in his lap. "Bless you, my child," he said, squinting over the selection of truffles.

Reluctantly, I shifted my gaze from the box to his skeletal face and arms, skin washed a bilious green. I forced myself to meet the eyes he opened after the first wave of cacao-induced pleasure. They glittered the peculiar feral fear that's a dead giveaway. Richard had been dying and resurrecting for months. This, I sensed, was the real deal. And it was close. I smelled its proximity the way I smelled the odious chemicals he gave off.

I'd kept my promise to see more of him. A few days after I handed over the bag of books to the housekeeper, I'd made it inside. But a drugged-out Richard had been barely coherent, so no point in staying. I'd also phoned.

"Not so hot," Sarah would tell me when he was sleeping or resting.

"Hanging in," Richard would say when he was up to talking.

At the hospital, I could see for myself. Not so hot. He patted the recliner arm, summoning me, and I rolled a footstool over and sat at his feet, where I'd always felt I belonged. For a half hour, with his untethered hand resting on my shoulder, I caught him up on the latest gossip from "the band," as he liked to call our ninety-seat orchestra. And I confessed my latest neurosis.

"I've always felt confident in my talent. Maybe not top league, but I knew I played well, sometimes very well. I thought I was ready to . . ."

I couldn't bring myself to say "replace you." He filled in.

"Move up. And you are ready, Judith. This panic thing? You've had a lot hit you all at once. A revolving door of men entering and exiting. Your father barreling back in. That lawyer friend reappearing. Don't look so shocked." He gave me a sly smile. "I get other visitors. You're not my only source of information."

I chewed a fingernail, wondering how I was going to break the news to him about the Inderal. My gut told me he wouldn't approve. But he had no idea how desperate I was.

"Well, don't pass this on to your other sources, please, but I was thinking about backing out of the audition gracefully. I have this image of freezing in front of the committee or, worse, totally losing it and being dragged off frothing at the mouth to Sheppard Pratt."

"Nonsense. You're not the frothing type. Besides, after all you've been through getting to this point, you want to give up a shot at my seat? You want to give up on the North Korea gig? I'd think that would be a deal maker for you."

"It is but . . ."

He waved a dismissal. "Angela's already working on the Korea program. And she's not bringing in a guest artist. She's thinking of having the principal cellist play Barber's Cello Concerto. Quintessentially American. How's that for a tour de force." His voice softened with longing. "This nearly was mine. Could be yours, Judith."

It would be a star turn for the likes of someone on a par with Eloise Flint, even Yo-Yo Ma. I envisioned myself alone under a spotlight center stage playing for the leaders of a nation that might have nuclear weapons and wouldn't hesitate using them at the slightest provocation. Talk about bombing.

This bit of news tipped me over the edge. I took a deep breath, winding up for the pitch, "There *is* one way I might be able to beat this anxiety thing."

A knowing smile curved his lips. I got it then. Richard had let me meander through the setup, waiting for me to crawl to the confession.

"*Might* be able. Might, as in contemplating? It's my understanding you've already played under the influence."

Damn that tattletale Geoff.

"Inderal. I'll be honest with you, Judith. I'm not thrilled you're on it."

Mortification mixed with desperation made the perfect formula for tears. I blinked against their sting.

"*On* it," I muttered. "You make it sound like it's heroin or crack."

"There's a danger in using a powerful prescription drug off label. Serious side effects. And yes, I personally know of a few musicians who'd be accountants without chemical assistance. I just don't happen to think you're one of them."

I looked up at him. "Well, if I'm not, I'm doing a hell of an imitation of a CPA. And say what you will, it got me through the other night."

After a moment's hesitation he said, "Ah, about that. One of my sources seemed to think your playing last Friday was . . . uh . . . emotionally flat. No fire. Lackluster."

"Emotionally flat," I repeated, in shock. "Geoff told you that?"

"Angela also stays in touch."

That gave me a jolt. "Jesus. She knows?"

"She knows what she hears from the podium. The rest is speculation."

"Oh, shit. Why do I think my career is on the line here?" I meant my life, but I couldn't say that to a dying man.

I think he picked up on it anyway. He reached down and took my hand in his ice-cold one. "Sweetheart, you're one hell of a cellist. I only wish you believed in yourself half as much as I believe in you. I wish there were some way I could *make* you believe it."

"Me too. Oh God, me too."

Maybe all that emotion was too much for him, because he shifted into practical mode. He drummed my shoulder with one finger. "Now you listen to me. You've got wonderful technique and no shortage of passion. The only concern I have in the entire audition repertoire is the tempo in the middle of the *Don Quixote*, where you tend to rush. We've talked about that before. If you don't let your nerves sabotage you into hustling through that passage, you'll ace it."

I leaned my damp cheek against the back of his hand scarred with needle punctures. What I said next surprised even me. The mind can be quick to rationalize when it's backed into a corner. "Would it be the worst thing in the world if I stayed in the second seat? I've been happy where I am."

He blew an exasperated breath. "*Been* happy. Note the tense, please. You and I both know you'd be miserable taking direction from someone who got the place because you forfeited it. You'd never last. You'd be out of there like a shot. And then what? No, my dear. It's your time and your place." He waited a half measure. "Sure, the audition is a risk. But life itself is a risk. It's over too damn soon whatever you do, so you may as well live it with passion. If you don't, I'll come up or down from wherever I land and haunt you."

He unlocked our fingers. "All right, lecture over. The patient needs a shot of sleep. I'm sending you home. Up, up, and away."

I got to my feet.

"Now give a kiss and know that I love you."

Was that the first time he had ever said that to me? *I love you.* Yes.

I bent to kiss his cheek. "I love *you*, Richard." I was sure that was the first time I ever told him. And I must have known it for years. How big was the sarcophagus that held my feelings? And how deep was it buried?

Still, I made the deadline, I told myself. I got to tell Richard I loved him. And I did it with time to spare.

Chapter 30

"Ladies and gentlemen, may I have your attention please."

Our well-disciplined orchestra hurried the process of resuming seats after the first rehearsal break Wednesday morning. Clutching a balled tissue in one hand and the edge of the podium in the other, Angela Driscoll waited for silence.

"I'm afraid I have sad news. I just received word that our beloved colleague and friend Richard Tarkoff passed away early this morning at his home in Roland Park."

I felt a stab of anguish at the announcement, a spasm of sorrow that took my breath away. *Richard's gone,* I thought, trying to absorb the finality of it. But I wasn't surprised. Before dawn that morning, I'd been roused by the problematic passage in the *Don Quixote,* the one he'd said I took in too much of a hurry. Wide awake against the pillow, I'd heard the phantom music playing in my head. *Of course* my tempo was off. Strauss wrote the cello to represent Quixote as a visionary and I played the poor wretch as if he were only a madman. He was a dreamer, so slow him down. How had I missed that? How had I found it? In the dead dark, I heard Richard say, or made him say, "There you go, Judith. You've got it now, sweetheart." I had looked at the clock. It was four thirty-seven.

I knew I'd never ask Sarah to pinpoint the exact moment Richard passed. Let me think what I wanted to think. Needed to think. But I'd seen him the day before and I'd heard him that morning and I'd expected Angela's announcement. But not so soon. Too soon!

Angela worked to pull herself together. "We can take comfort in the knowledge that Richard's passing was peaceful and that he was surrounded by his loving family. Arrangements for the funeral haven't been finalized yet. When I have more information, I'll pass it on. Before I share Sarah Tarkoff's personal message to all of us, I'm asking for a minute of silence in memory of Richard."

I bowed my head, wishing I knew the kaddish memorial prayer to recite for him. I gave him what I had.

Dear Lord, *Baruch attah Adonai eloheinu melekh ha'olam, borei peri hagafen*— Wrong . . . That was the prayer over the wine Uncle Arnold recited at Passover. But I was pretty sure God and Richard would take it for a blessing.

As the minute of silence drew to a close, a soulful sound emerged from the back of the stage. Taps played on a trumpet is as moving as on the traditional bugle, and the way Geoff uncoiled it made my skin prickle. We all knew his distinctive sound. And who else would perform such a spontaneous loving tribute to a fallen comrade?

As the last sorrowing note faded, we looked to Angela for a cue. She waited a respectful beat before saying, "All right, everyone, we'll continue with this rehearsal as Richard would have wished. Sarah told me his message to us was 'Play on.' So let's pick up with the *Frühlingsstimmen*."

This week's program was "An Evening in Vienna." Richard had thought the "Voices of Spring" waltz was kitsch squared. Nonetheless, we played our hearts out.

. . .

Geoff was standing in the circle of mourners I slogged past on my way to the storage locker to stash my cello. Earlier that morning we'd had the briefest encounter backstage. He'd said, "Ah, Judith. How was the weekend?"

Something in his tone had told me he knew the Maine attraction had been Charlie. It wasn't hard to pinpoint the source: my mother, the formerly shy flower who'd blossomed into a big-mouthed senior.

"Cold," I said, wondering whether he'd work that one word over, plumbing it for meaning. I hadn't hung around to take questions.

Now as I walked past, head down, he peeled off the circle and caught up with me. "So sorry about Richard. We're all going to miss him, but you . . . Well, standmates have a special connection, don't they?" We halted simultaneously and he moved around to lift my chin with his forefinger. "Hey," he said, checking me out as if emotional bruises showed up black and blue. "Any way I can be of help?"

"Shit," I said, and in the process of removing his finger I found myself holding his hand. "I don't know. I don't think so. Shit!" The initial pain had converted to a dull ache. "It wasn't as if we thought this would have a happy ending."

"True. But until the very end, there's hope. And now that's gone."

The smallest sob escaped my throat.

"Ah, Jude," Geoff crooned, and that did it for me. I moved into my old comfort zone and laid my head on his chest. He stroked my hair, which I took as permission to cry. Except I didn't. Couldn't. My stoic Korean side backed off quietly from a public meltdown.

"It's okay. Let it go. It's good for you to let it go," he encouraged. Geoff was a full-out kind of guy. He choked up when Queensland won the regionals. A really good Barossa Shiraz brought tears to his eyes. For this favorite colleague, his voice crackled with emotion. "You do know Richard was ready. Oh, I'm not saying he didn't want to live. But not the way he'd been living for the last year or so. I think he'd had enough of the pain and decided it was time to exit stage left. He just had to make sure all his t's were crossed, that Sarah and the boys were ready to let him go. And he wanted to make sure you went for his seat."

"As if I could fill his shoes." My heart sank with this new obligation.

"You have your own shoes. About thirty pair, if I remember correctly." He eked out an indulgent smile; then his gaze shifted to middistance. "Uh-oh. La maestra. You're being summoned."

I turned to see Angela taking a call while beckoning me with a crooked finger. Geoff poked his chest and she mouthed no and pointed at Ernst Leonard, our pianist. Geoff said, "She wants Ernie too. Go. We'll talk later."

Angela adjusted her earpiece, nodded at Ernie, then at me. "That was Sarah. The funeral is scheduled for Friday at two at Temple Beth Zion on Park Heights Avenue."

"Not Levinson's?" I asked. Sol Levinson & Brothers mortuary was the preferred final venue for most of Baltimore's eternally frozen chosen.

"Levinson's was booked with other services and the synagogue has a piano."

Ernie rocked on his heels at the mention of "piano." A positive Pavlovian response. For me, the word, which fell into the same genus as "cello," whooshed the air from my lungs. *Mudang* alert! Storm clouds on the horizon. Magpies racing for cover.

Angela, oblivious, chugged along. "Richard had specific requests about the service. Of course, he wanted music. He asked that you two . . ."

Oh God no, oh God no, oh God . . .

"He mentioned you by name . . . requested that you two perform the 'Meditation' from *Thaïs*."

"Beautiful selection. Perfect." Ernie was already flexing his fingers.

"This Friday?" I said, wondering if I committed suicide before the funeral, could they double up on the service? Boxed, with dirt shoveled over me, was looking pretty good about now.

"Correct. I understand the Jewish religion dictates that funerals be held as quickly as possible. But Richard had close friends around the world who will want to pay their respects. Sarah felt she needed to give them the time to get here. Yo-Yo is coming in from Paris."

"Really?" Ernie said, darting me a meaningful look.

"She thinks Lucian Landau will be flying in from Israel. He's trying to rearrange his schedule. Some of the best musicians on the planet will be sitting in those seats."

A month earlier, no big deal. I'd played with Yo-Yo, Lucian— name the best and the brightest and they'd guested with the Maryland Philharmonic. That teddy bear Slava Rostropovich liked to high-five me, rest his soul. I'd never been intimidated by the big guns. But now, with posttraumatic stress or whatever they called this seizure of confidence, my heart actually did falter a beat or two.

"Sarah says the synagogue has a stage that could house the Mormon Tabernacle Choir. So Richard could have asked for the orchestra. Or he could have requested Vijay." Angela was right— the "Meditation" was written for violin and our concertmaster was the logical choice. "But he specifically wanted you two, close friends as well as colleagues. That's a lovely tribute. An honor."

Oh God.

Ernie tried to look grim, but I felt his pride seeping out. I was also seeping. Little sweat beads of panic from every pore.

Come on, Richard—I sent my entreaty to heaven—*this is my inheritance?* Abject terror?

"The *Thaïs* shouldn't be a problem for either of you. You can work out any kinks when you run through it together. Judith, just make sure you don't rush those quarter notes around four minutes in. There's a tendency to push. And watch the level of intensity. Remember, this is meditative. You don't want to turn it into a tearjerker. No soap opera, please." Her voice had turned schoolmarm and she was talking to a spot over my head.

I nodded mechanically, wondering if there were enough Inderal in the world.

After she dashed off, Ernie said, "Think she's on edge? 'No soap opera, please.' Don't take it personally. She's got this bastard of a board meeting in an hour, when she's going to announce that the North Korea trip's—" He stopped. "Why the blank stare? You're telling me you didn't know about Korea? If so, you're the last."

Of course Richard's secret was out. Every orchestra was a hive of gossip. "I heard the rumor," I admitted.

"We all heard the rumor. Angela was delusional if she thought she could keep something this huge under wraps. One leak and *le deluge.* So we got pumped up for it and now it's hit a major snag and she's got to inform the board we may not go to Pyongyang after all. That on top of Richard's passing. A helluva day for her. For all of us."

"What's the snag?" Why did I think I wasn't going to like the answer?

"Something about one of the musicians and a background check is what I picked up."

Uh-oh. "You know who?"

He shrugged. "The only thing I can come up with is we've got twelve people in the orchestra who weren't born in the States. Maybe their papers are screwed up. You were born here, right?"

"In Brooklyn."

"There you go. Foreign country." He patted my back. "Seriously. It's all political stuff, way beyond us mere musicians. And Angela's laundry list for the *Thaïs*? Just go with the flow. Don't overthink it, Judith."

"But you overthink everything," Geoff pointed out when I told him. "Now you've got the notion that the snag in the Korean project is you."

"Who else? It's only Lyndon Shin and me who have Korean connections. And he's thirty-three and was born in Seoul. My mother's family was from the north. She could have lied on her application to get into the U.S. In fact, my father must have filled it out, so I'd make book they lied. That could be the holdup."

"Or maybe it isn't."

"I'm hoping. But Angela was—I don't know—cool to me this afternoon. I had the feeling she'd rather Richard had chosen someone else to play the *Thaïs*. *Anyone* else." I blew a puff of anxiety. "Me too, actually."

"Well, you owe it to the poor sod." Geoff was losing patience. Not that I blamed him.

Marti had her own brand of advice for my jitters. "I'm going to tell you what my mama used to tell me when I got the heebie-jeebies about speaking my piece in Sunday school. She'd say, 'Martha-boo, imagine your audience stark naked. Or sitting on the commode.' Okay, can you imagine Yo-Yo Ma . . ."

And Charlie said . . . Well, for two days nothing from Charlie. On the third, a strange e-mail popped up about a house in Georgetown on the market and would I check out the listing online. "Since you and I may be living there someday, I'd value your approval."

Typical Charlie bait, I recognized from our time back in Cambridge. He'd toss out that stuff to test his own feelings. You couldn't make too much of it.

Still, under my normal neurotic circumstances, it would have fueled sleepless nights. Now it would have to get to the back of the obsession line behind the clear front-runner: how I was going to get through a five-minute piece at Richard Tarkoff's funeral with two hundred world-class musicians in a position to titter, mutter, and (I could actually picture this in my twisted psyche) out-and-out heckle me. I could see—really, I could envision his frizzy halo in full quiver—the generally amiable conductor Zigmund Manheim launching one razzmatazz of a Bronx raspberry as I drew my last stroke ever on the cello's E-string.

Save me, O God of my forefathers.

Chapter 31

❦

Within minutes of Sarah Tarkoff's call to Angela, the orchestra's public relations and development departments leapt into action. Although at first the crassness of it made me cringe, I had to admit they brainstormed a brilliant coup. They turned the following evening's open rehearsal into a fund-raiser, a tribute to Richard that would bring tears to donors' eyes and pens to their checkbooks. "As he would have wanted it," an internal memo tried to persuade his colleagues.

Knowing Richard, I figured he may well have gotten a kick out of being made into a shill postmortem. And you couldn't expect PR to just ride out this perfect storm of opportunity, luck, and schmaltz. This was an event loaded with the Phil's most generous benefactors.

A few times a year they were invited to sit in as the orchestra rehearsed that weekend's program. It was a thank-you-for-your-support, you're-one-of-us occasion. The civilians loved open rehearsals. They got to watch the musicians screw up and cut up a little, and they got a taste of Angela's dry wit as she buffed us to a shine. Nobody loved to schmooze an audience more than Angela, or did it better. And nobody picked a donor's pocket with a more elegant sleight of hand.

The full-press court began in the lobby, where traditionally the guests sipped champagne and nibbled refreshments. We musicians circulated among them, glad-handing and making small talk, an exercise in forced intimacy that supposedly translated into more funding dollars.

Then, suddenly, the unexpected. The crowd hushed as Angela stepped front and center to announce that the evening was dedicated to the memory of—flourishing off the velvet drape over the easeled portrait of Richard in his prime—a shining light with the orchestra for more than four decades. Our principal cellist had passed away the day before, expressing a final wish that his beloved Maryland Philharmonic live long and prosper. "And so we are hereby establishing the Richard Arthur Tarkoff Foundation for Capital Improvements." (Ah, electronic eye toilets for the ladies' rooms.) It was a brilliant Lazarus moment that generated a rumble of sympathy and a collective nod of support.

In the past, I'd enjoyed working the reception with the orchestra groupies, but tonight swamping the undertow of grief were huge surges of gut-wrenching fear at the prospect of performing solo at Richard's funeral, an obsession best tended in private. (I could almost hear him *tsk-tsk*ing like a metronome in his coffin.) So my plan was to track a single figure eight through the crowd and head backstage. It was the last loop that snared me.

"Judith, over here. *Here*, Judith!" a familiar voice rang out, really *rang*, loud enough to temporarily dampen the chatter in the immediate vicinity. I stared at the woman who'd swept into my path, the one with the alien hairdo, a stranger wrapped in a purple jersey Diane Von Furstenberg rip-off as she metamorphosed into my mother.

"You surprise?" she asked, gold teeth gleaming. "I tell you she surprise, honey."

The honey was Irwin Raphael, looking as out of place as the pope at a klezmer concert.

"Winnie Chang donate much money all the time. She get invite but can't go. So she say, you take two ticket, Grace. Korean girl play. You like very much."

Our guest artist that week was Melanie Rhee, the talented young Korean-American violinist. Nice of Winnie. Stupid of me not to think of inviting my mother.

"I'm looking forward to it," Irwin said as he slipped my mother's hand in his.

Really? The few seventy-eight records he'd left behind in Brooklyn when he'd rushed off to pursue the chippie were of Sinatra, Ella, and Benny Goodman. These days, judging from the way he dressed, like a Jewish cowboy—that night in a plaid sport jacket with a bolo—I figured he liked country music. So this had to have been a reach for him.

"Winnie have much culture," my mother said. "Me, only when you play. But tonight I like, I think. You make duet with Korean girl, Judith?"

"No, *Uhm-mah*. She's playing solo, but the orchestra will be accompanying her."

Decibel level soaring, my mother announced to the neighborhood, "Judith play solo many night. Associate principal. Soon be principal. Highest cello in orchestra. My daughter make me very, very proud."

My accomplishments had always given her what my aunt Phyllis called *nachas*—proprietary pleasure. Grace had boasted about my first job, a part-time gig in a small-town orchestra, with as much gusto as she would about my later work with a major symphony. She really loved me for whatever I was.

She looked around to see if the immediate world was taking that in. "Ah, look near stairway." She waved. "Selma Frommer, Blumen House 7B. Such snob." She extracted her hand from Irwin's and pushed her nose into a snooty pug. "I need to say hello and brag too." Her eyes twinkled. "She always brag on her son, the big, famous doctor. Now my turn. Be right back. No more wine for you, Irwin. Two glass enough." She darted off.

I heard a hum come from my father, as if he were revving up to get through a conversation with me on his own. He began on a high note.

"She's a pip, your mother." His eyes followed her and his lips curled in a smile at the sight. "In her golden years, she's an outgoing person. Who would've thought she'd turn out this way? Not that I don't like it. That's what I saw of her personality when I met her. But then, when she came here, she hardly spoke English and she was shy as a cat. A totally different woman. And now she's back to the version of her I met in Seoul." He shook his head so the pompadour shimmered ebony in the lobby light. "Amazing how getting older changes you. Makes you better sometimes."

Was he leading into a commercial for the new and improved Irwin Raphael? If so, it would take a money-back guarantee to make me buy it.

One look at my caveat emptor face and he hitched his neck in the direction of Richard's portrait. "Sorry about your partner. Eight years younger than me. Poor bastard. Excuse my French, but your mom said he suffered a lot. In and out of the hospital." He fiddled with his bolo clasp in the shape of steer horns. "Personally, I hope I get hit by a bus."

A pregnant pause as I silently seconded the motion.

"I seen so many hospitals with Lorna. The late Mrs. Raphael. Lupus is a hell of a disease. She was in more than out in the last few years. 'Don't let me die in the hospital,' she always begged me. I promised she'd die at home. Another promise I didn't keep."

That lassoed my attention. We were heading down some yellow brick road here. Where it was winding I couldn't yet tell.

"Her sister called an ambulance near the end. Jesus, I hate hospitals."

At which point I found my Oz. "Is that why you didn't come to see me when I had the aneurysm?"

"Wha?" His jaw literally dropped.

This thought had been nudging me since Irwin had reentered our lives.

"You had to have known. If not through Mom, through Aunt Phyllis. You think people get better with age? My aneurysm was only a year ago, I could have died, and you *still* didn't show up."

"Now just one cotton-pickin' minute, kiddo. The hospital's not why—" he began.

"I don't tell him." My mother, whose timing was as good as any musician's, had threaded her way back. Now she edged in, facing me. "And I tell Aunt Phyllis to keep big mouth shut. Why? I tell you why. Chippie . . . Lorna very sick when you sick. Lupus make very bad time for her."

Grace laid a consoling hand on my father's arm. "And if I tell him you have aneurysm, he come run, run, run. For what? I know you won't see him. If I tell you, you be so mad. It make you more sick to see your daddy here. So I don't tell and I make Aunt Phyllis swear she don't tell."

He hadn't known. *He hadn't known.*

Just then, my watch alarm sounded and, as if the timer had set it off, my chest began to ache. Not the breathless clutch of anxiety. I knew the difference. And though I was swept by a cold sweat, not a heart attack. This, I suspected, was an event that would never show up on any cardiogram. A piercing of that membrane I'd toughened to protect my emotional center. Just a tiny puncture, but it hurt like hell.

Or it could have been gas.

"The orchestra is starting to warm up. I've got to go," I said just to my mother as the chest pain ebbed.

Her other hand flew out to capture my elbow. "When Irwin and I begin e-mail, I talk about you many things. Now back here, he get so upset when you have even little headache. He think your aneurysm come back. He go crazy, your father. He worry about you. He love you."

"Can we discuss this later, please?" I asked, needing air and my arm.

Even in the lobby, I could latch onto the muted sound of the musicians warming up onstage. The program was all-Prokofiev. I wanted to hear the carefree youth of Juliet in the Suite No. 2. That the runaway who messed up my youth loved me, this I didn't want to hear.

"Go." Grace freed me. "We eat at Matsuri restaurant after concert. You father say he don't like sushi but I like, so he eat it now. You come with us tonight. We eat, we talk."

The idea of a reconciliation supper with the old man turned my stomach more than squid sashimi.

"Sorry, *Uhm-mah.* I can't. I'm playing at Richard's funeral to-morrow and I need to practice with the pianist after the rehearsal."

I'd booked a half hour with Ernie after the stage cleared, one last session to make sure we were in sync with the "Meditation." Then home to go over and over my mistakes, real and imagined, and count down the hours until F-Day: Friday, funeral, fuck up. Take your choice. Take all three.

"Maybe tomorrow," my mother said. "After you come back from cemetery, I make us lunch. Yes, Irwin?"

Take four, if you counted my father.

My father, my father. I thought and rethought the new, un-modified word as I hurried off, leaving them silent behind me. Now that I had a father, what was I supposed to do with him?

Chapter 32

Richard Tarkoff, rest his soul, made his final appearance before a packed house. And what a house! Temple Beth Zion, a standout even in the cluster of designer synagogues on Park Heights Avenue, was a Walter Gropius paean to—well, whatever it was that Independent-Progressive-Reconstructionist Jews believed.

It took me five minutes to navigate the huge, crowded art nouveau lobby that could have passed for the first-class salon on the *QE2* in its heyday. And then there was a queue to sign the guestbook. When I finally got to the front, I thumbed through the preceding pages wanting to see who would be in the seats for the service. I swallowed a lump of fear as I found the sprawling, flourishing signatures of musical giants: Wasserstein, Sundergard. Lermontov, Chumsky. It would be just Ernie and me up there playing before the crème de la crème, a thought that sent my pulse rocketing. But soothingly, just above the line left empty for me to sign, Aunt Doris and Uncle Lester Rosenberg had written, "Richard, you were an inspiration to us all. Truly a man for all seasons." Truly.

I was bent over the page, about to add a bravado curlicue to the R in Raphael, when an arpeggio of prickles ran down my spine. I swear I felt her before I heard her. And then I did hear that unmistakable loud, grating voice that was chalk on blackboard to me. And the fake international accent. She was from Borough Park, Brooklyn, for God's sake. Eloise Flint. My nemesis from the New England Conservatory. My replacement in Charlie Pruitt's bed. Thief of honors in the Balakirev competition. A woman who could vacuum all the air from a room in a single sweep.

I checked and, damn, there she was off to my right, maybe twenty pounds heavier than the airbrushed book jacket photo, but definitely Eloise in a weird brown-striped caftan thing and too much artsy-craftsy jewelry. She was nodding like a parrot peck-peck-pecking as the violinist Lucian Landau whispered at her side. Then her beady avian eyes locked on my gaze, she waited a beat, and she waved. Not a socially acceptable full-handed dash of a hi, but an affected flutter to show off her superior fingering, I supposed.

And then I had an *Oh God* moment as I realized she'd soon be sitting in the sanctuary, up front, I was sure, following my every bow stroke, judging my every intonation.

Geoff materialized beside me. "You okay, Jude? You look a mite green about the gills."

Beyond him, Eloise eyed us with unabashed curiosity. I laid one hand on Geoff's arm, proprietarily. Strictly for her benefit.

"Feeling queasy," I said, accepting the small pack of tissues he pressed into my hand.

"Ernie alerted Joan as backup and she's standing by. But you can do this, Jude. I know you can."

As Eloise's inappropriate cackle split the air like a hen screeching out an extra-large egg, I said, "Right." What I needed was some pharmaceutical assistance. Richard would have thought I was cheating, but a half-full vial of just-in-case pills buried in my handbag jiggie-jigged a maraca rhythm against my hip when I moved.

Which wasn't fast enough for the woman behind me. "Nu already, sweetheart?"

She leaned in, giving me a tight, burgundy-outlined smile. "The book? You want to sign the book?" She tapped her Movado. "Hopefully before the Second Coming?"

I signed. Geoff signed, and took my elbow. "Now shall we pay our respects to Sarah and the boys?" he asked.

The condolence line stretched through the door of the reception room. As we inched along, I got a view of Sarah accepting sympathy hugs at the other end. She looked pale, but put together.

We were almost at the grieving family when she and I made eye contact. She held up a pause finger to me and leaned over to the older of her boys, the Stanford professor. I heard her say, "Joel, darling, I need a break. Give me five minutes. And keep the line moving. It's almost time for the service anyway."

She crooked the finger and beckoned me to follow her.

"Be back," I said to Geoff.

I had no idea why I'd been singled out or where we were going. It turned out it was to the sanctuary. There, she took my hand.

As she led me in I said, "Sarah, I'm so sorry. You know how I felt about Richard."

"I *do* know, Judith. And how he felt about you. Come, let's sit for a minute."

We took adjacent seats in the first row. If we'd been in Ghana, the deceased might have been buried in a coffin carved in the image of his beloved cello, but here he rested center stage in a simple casket of rich oak. The gorgeous Matteo Goffriller instrument was positioned five feet away. I still had no idea why I was here, but it had to be something important to pull the widow from the receiving line.

"Truthfully, I don't think you know how much Richard loved you and respected your talents, but you will soon enough." Sarah checked her watch. "I've had them keep the main doors locked, so we can have this talk. But as you can hear from the lobby, the natives are getting restless, so I'll make it quick."

Her voice thinned to a thread that seemed just about to break. "I can't believe he's in that coffin. Of course, he selected it himself. Which is just like Richard—in control to the very end." She gave a short, parched laugh. "They say you can't take it with you. Now, had he played flute, I would have tucked it in with him. But the Goffriller? That has to stay behind." Her glance flitted from the cello to me. She was dry eyed, sharp eyed.

"Can you imagine how much pleasure that cello has brought to the world over the last four hundred years? And how much more it has to give?" Then she said crisply, "Richard was very clear about its disposition after his death. Because it's a substantial bequest, he took all the necessary legal steps to make sure his intentions would be honored. The Goffriller would bring an astronomical price in a private sale, perhaps even more at auction. But he knew where he wanted it to end up."

Her grip on my hand tightened. Where she was heading had begun to seep in, but the destination seemed so implausible, so outrageous, my brain refused to go there.

"For Richard it was a purely emotional decision. On my part—and he wanted my concurrence—I felt a decision of this magnitude required some thought. Our sons have no musical inclinations. The gene doesn't seem to run in the family. Financially they're both well off. I will never be homeless. And the prospect of selling that gorgeous instrument, the possibility that someone like that detestable Eloise Flint—and this is hypothetical, of course—might empty her bank account, add it to the proceeds from her new book—Richard called it a grim fairy tale, by the way—and walk off with it . . . Well, that was unthinkable to both of us."

Her hand was trembling ever so slightly. Or maybe that was mine trembling in the cave of hers. "So." Sarah swiveled to seal the deal with a widow's sad smile. "It's yours, my dear. We'll get it to you in plenty of time to work with it for your audition. Oh yes—on that subject, Richard said to tell you that whatever doubts you had about *your* gift, this gift should put them to rest. I should remind you, Judith, that he was not only a brilliant musician, he was also an astute critic. I'd take his word for it."

She gave me a moment to let it sink in, this incredible legacy, this vote of confidence from the coffin. Of course, I was flabbergasted. Astounded by the sheer scale of the gesture. But that was in the first aftershock seconds. Then, very quickly, it all seemed to make perfect sense. Richard had been so generous to me from the beginning, he wouldn't let the end of him be the end of his goodness.

"One more thing. He left you an annual stipend to cover the insurance. Bottom line is you won't need anything but you and the Goffriller to make magnificent music. 'Nothing extra' were the precise words he asked me to repeat to you. Whatever that means, he said you'd understand."

I did. Although I swayed under the impact of the last few minutes, the pill bottle in my handbag had lapsed into guilty silence.

Confounded by the joy of owning this exquisite cello and the pain of not being able to thank Richard for it, I stammered, "How can I ever express my—?"

Sarah cut me off. "Just make the best music you can, Judith. Now you have no excuse not to."

How was that for a burden and a blessing?

"After Joel speaks, he'll move the cello center for you." She was on her feet.

I thought the echo in that vast auditorium had mangled her words.

"The Goffriller. You want me to play it today?"

My stomach plummeted so suddenly that my center of gravity shifted. Even on that awful night at the Berenson when the first panic attack had struck, I hadn't felt the crushing force to double me over. Now I fought to stay upright.

"Yes, of course. I want you to play it today." Sarah and her pearls shimmered too bright in my vision. "But more important, that's what Richard wanted. He loved what you coaxed from that Goffriller. And your new bow is also a beauty." Richard's François Tourte bow had an equally distinguished pedigree.

I watched Sarah pat my hand reassuringly, but hardly felt it. Most of me had gone numb, but shock and dread must have been readable on my face. "You've played the instrument before, Judith. A number of times. Always beautifully."

The Dvořák, when he was dying. Maybe five or six other times total. The first was a winter evening in the Tarkoffs' living room fifteen years before. Richard had rocked in his chair as though he were davening a prayer of thanksgiving as the cello exploded torrents of tone in Chopin's G Minor Sonata. My fingers flew and the Goffriller's heart nearly burst with emotion. An aristocrat, a peasant, a revolutionary—a superb instrument can be everything.

Sarah, the attorney, clinched her closing argument. "And now you have the opportunity to play one last time for Richard. That way the both of you can say good-bye to him."

• • •

Geoff was waiting for me in the lobby, arms folded, expression self-satisfied. "So how's that for a parting gift? Oh, Jude, wait until you get your hands on that Goffriller. It will be transcendent."

"What?" I snapped to incredulous attention. "You knew?"

"Richard couldn't keep it to himself. He was thrilled for you. Me too. He did the right thing, leaving it to you."

I flared. "And having me play it today? Unprepared? Unrehearsed with it? You think that's the right thing too?"

"Today? Here? Now *that* I didn't know." His laugh was so boisterous, it turned the head of an outraged mourner. "Why, that old fox. And yes, he did the positively right thing. Brilliant."

We took seats in the second row. It was like being strapped in a taxiing plane. Doors shut. Fate sealed. Too late to back out. We took off so quickly, I barely had time to think.

The rabbi recited the "time to sow and time to reap" passage from Ecclesiastes.

The cantor chanted.

I felt for the vial of Inderal in my right pocket. There was no water for a pill and had there been I would have choked on it anyway after Richard's coded command from the grave. I stared at the Goffriller, willing myself to absorb its centuries of confidence.

Joel, the older son, read the poem "Invictus," his voice cracking at the reference to the "unconquerable soul." When that was over, he carefully moved the Goffriller front and center and announced, "As my father wished, the 'Meditation' from *Thaïs* by Massenet will be played by Ernst Leonard at the piano and Judith Raphael on the cello Dad loved."

I walked the last yards, my heart thumping in sync with my

steps. Once seated, I allowed myself a moment to settle in. After all, Richard wasn't going anywhere except to heaven and, as Aunt Phyllis used to say, quoting maybe the Bible or maybe Warren Beatty, heaven can wait.

Ernie would also have to wait for my cue. Stop, smell the funeral flowers, my dearly departed mentor would have instructed. The Orthodox don't do flowers (no music either), but this synagogue looked like the Brooklyn Botanic Garden. I inhaled, giving myself ten seconds of sweetness. I embraced the Goffriller, *my* Goffriller almost, and breathed in its centuries-old promise of brilliance. As Joel exited stage right, I caught a glimpse of the exiled Tecchler cello that had served me well all these years and was about to be turned in for a new love. Which reminded me to look for Geoff's reassuring smile. Got it. Quickly scanned the house. Zigmund Manheim, at the end of the third row, eyes downcast, was thumbing through the program. Daniel Kassakov, probably my favorite living cellist, fidgeted next to him. Danny liked me too. His gaze caught mine and he winked. Inappropriate but appreciated. Lucian Landau, having escaped Eloise Flint's braceleted clutches, was two seats left of Daniel.

I found my nemesis on the aisle, fourth row. In spite of having given a command performance at Buckingham Palace and being descended, according to her auto-bogus-ography, from Priscilla Alden, Eloise was simultaneously and energetically chewing gum and picking her nose. Somehow, that indecorous image of Eloise short-circuited my anxiety. She was only human, my nemesis was. We were all only human.

With that reassurance, I nodded to Ernie, lifted Richard's legacy François Tourte bow, and drew my first stroke. Velvet. Then, in a miracle worthy of Moses himself, whose sun-drenched, stained-glass image cast vivid spotlights on the stage, I relaxed and let muscle memory take over. And then I did forget them all out there, except for Sarah and the family. And Richard, of course. I was playing for Richard in that zone that surpasses rational thought. My hands were detached at the wrists, moving on their own. I conjured up images of my old friend alive and healthy. By the last sixteen bars, it was Richard playing the "Meditation." The final chord stretched mournfully as if he and I couldn't quite say good-bye.

In the ensuing silence, pierced only by a single echoing sob, I returned to my place next to Geoff.

"Well done," he whispered as I slipped into my seat. "Richard would be . . . what's the word . . . kvelling. Ah, look at you." He pulled out his handkerchief and dabbed tears from my cheek. "I'll bet there's not a dry eye in the house." *His* eyes were glistening.

Limp with relief, back in the real world, I still needed reassurance. I whispered, "Was it too schmaltzy? Passion can edge into schmaltz."

"It was perfect."

"I didn't know I was crying up there."

"That's what happens when you're lost in the music."

After the prayer for the dead and the final amen, Geoff was called as a pallbearer to hoist the coffin with its shell of a cargo down the aisle and out the door. Sundergard and Chumsky were honorary pallbearers taking up the rear, and when the procession had passed, the rest of us peeled from our rows to converge in a single stream flowing toward the exit.

Somehow I wound up shoulder to shoulder with Zigmund Manheim and we picked up Eloise on our slow shuffle. "We're going to miss him," he said. "One in a million. By the way, you played superbly." That meant a lot to me coming from a musician of his caliber.

Eloise bit her lip and said nothing. She seemed to be waiting for Ziggy to move out of earshot. Honestly, with all the residual energy from the *Thaïs*, if she gave me a raft of critical crap, I wasn't sure I could restrain myself from reaching over, grabbing her bow hand, and squeezing her fingers into long-term disability. Except that among them was the one that had been playing dig to China with her nose. Ugh.

And then, with Ziggy taking a detour to catch up to Landau, it was just us two surrounded by a crowd of chatter. Eloise turned to me and I got a close look at what the years had wrought. Time was a real bastard—it brought you to your knees and then you needed to replace them. We were the same age, she and I, but she'd already had a rotator cuff repair and treatment for thoracic outlet syndrome, classic cellist's injuries, as well as some complicated ophthalmic surgery, according to the chapter in her bio titled "Falling Apart." No wonder she had dark circles under her eyes. Once, those hollow cheeks had been plump and dimpled. No more. Could you lose dimples?

This wasn't the pretty face that Charlie had looked into as they thrashed about in the Wendell Street bed. Well, I'd had him first, and I might have him last. And even when she'd had him—if he'd told the truth up in Maine—he'd been pining away for me. For the length of an eighth note, I felt sorry for her.

Her voice, when it finally emerged, was unexpectedly muted and barely abrasive so I had to crane to hear her. "He was right, Ziggy Manheim. The 'Meditation' seems easy, but it's deceptive. I always rush the passionate spots. Your pacing was faultless. In fact, the entire piece was well done. Very well done."

I was waiting for "You've come a long way, Judith" or some other snide tag. But no, that was it. *Finis.* After more than two decades of fuming over her laudatory reviews, switching channels when she was on PBS, and taking unwanted vacations to duck her when she played with the Maryland Philharmonic, my obsession with Eloise Flint ended right there with a whimper, not a bang.

So what did you say when you got thrown a compliment from a longtime nemesis? I responded with a simple "Thanks," astounded once more by the gifts life handed you if you lived long enough.

At the lobby doors, under the tablet crown that proclaimed "Teach Us to Number Our Days That We May Apply Our Hearts unto Wisdom," Eloise Flint and I parted ways.

Chapter 33

"Such sweet satisfaction."

I didn't know whether Marti McDowell was referring to my Eloise story or to the mocha rum brownie she was chewing, but the woman was in full-out ecstasy.

It was the following Thursday and we were spending the afternoon at the Belvedere's caterers for a tasting session of the food planned for my birthday party. We'd worked our way through the hors d'oeuvres and were into desserts, heavy on the chocolate. All that caffeine had tuned Marti's sarcasm to a twanging pitch.

"I, for one, am delighted you and Eloise played nice at Richard's funeral. Very mature of you both. Of course, it helped that she buttered you up like a baguette about your performance and that Charlie Pruitt said she was the worst kind of skank going after him lo those many years ago and so defused your jealousy." Marti licked her fingers delicately.

I gave her an offended glare. "I was never jealous, just ticked off. It was a vile thing she did, going after a dormmate's ex. And 'skank,' by the way, is not a word Charlie would ever use."

"Yeah, well, shut my lower-class mouth because The Judge is presiding. Speaking of whom, you haven't been making puss-in-heat noises about him for a while. Has the sizzling romance cooled? I thought by now you'd at least be pinned. Sig Chi, of course." She gave me a snarky smile. "So the final Jeopardy question is: Where's Charlie?"

I wouldn't give her the satisfaction of admitting I was a little miffed at what I interpreted as his neglect. I'd phoned the afternoon of the funeral to tell him about the service and Richard's gift of the Goffriller and ended up mortifying myself by sobbing and babbling into his voice mail. Out of control was not the best approach with Charlie, but I'd been keeping the grief tamped down so far and just lost it.

There had been no answer from him that night, but the next one, as I was about to sit down to a solitary dinner, my doorbell had rung. I'd opened it to find a delivery person just about hidden by a suffocatingly enormous bouquet of yellow roses and purple irises.

"He's flower fixated." Marti dabbed crumbs from her lips. "It's the easy way out, you know, to say it with flowers. You tell your administrative assistant to write something appropriate on a card and you don't have to deal with all that messy back-and-forth that we call communication. So what did his AA have to say?"

I'd memorized the card. " 'Ju-ju. Forgive not calling. Swamped here. Major case exploding. Sorry about Richard. What is Goffriller? We need to talk. See you soon. All best, Charlie.' "

"*All best.* Well, if that isn't 'as dictated to.' Okay, soon is when?"

"Tomorrow night. *Need* to talk." I gobbled the mini cannoli in my right hand followed by the mini éclair in my left. "I hate that. Waiting for the shoe to drop."

"Hmm. Could be he's ready to go exclusive and invite you to move into that house in Georgetown he's considering buying." She licked a dribble of chocolate from her finger with her gossip's tongue.

I'd made the mistake of sharing Charlie's e-mail with her, the one asking me to take a look at the listing of a $4.2 million house with a conservatory and an indoor lap pool because I might live there someday. About as likely as my relocating to Mars, but Marti, being a writer and a drama queen to boot, always put the most sensational spin on any story.

"That's just Charlie doing his pie-in-the-sky, toe-in-the-water routine," I said. "I pay no attention. Besides, I'm nervous about the prospect of sharing the beltway with him, let alone a house. Don't even want to think about it."

"Really? Why? You want to try Charlie out for another twenty-five years? Most women would snap up this guy faster than Coach on clearance. This is a long-lost love returned, the dumpee's triumph, the stuff that Jennifer Aniston films are made of. So let's have a happy ending, please. And don't tell me you haven't thought about Charlie long term."

"Honestly, Marti, the performance anxiety and then having to play at Richard's funeral used up all of my obsessing time." I shuddered at the memory. "I was really on the tipping edge of crazy."

"Well, that's finished, right? The stage fright?"

"Don't I wish. I was back to my normal, such as it is, at Richard's funeral, but those were special circumstances. His vote of confidence with the Goffriller was still fresh. Sarah Tarkoff broke the news only ten minutes before I went up there. I was in a kind of shock that overrode the nerves, I guess."

"And now you've had time to work yourself up again."

"Auditions are stressful under any circumstances. And this one is a nightmare. I feel my whole life depends on how I do up there. My future is hanging in the balance. I could have another panic attack in front of the judge's panel. I could sit there like a frozen lump." My fingers were tingling just talking about it.

"Or you could sail through the nerves and knock 'em dead," Marti retorted. "Of course, after that you'll seamlessly cruise into whatever neurosis is next in line. Personally, I hope it's sexier than wanting to throw up into your cello. My prediction is something in the love department. I'm not saying now, mind you, but maybe down the line a piece, the judge will show up with something pear-shaped in five carats. And then—" She spun her voice into a sugary soprano and began to sing, "Sadie, Sadie, married lady . . ."

Even attached to Charlie, the M-word made me wince. It wasn't as if that particular state of the union had a brilliant success rate in my nuclear family, what with my mother and Irwin's ill-fated fiasco and my short, strange marriage to Rebound Todd.

Ending her song on a high note, Marti chirped, "How did that sound?"

"Off-key," I responded. "And from the quality of Charlie's attention, highly unlikely."

"His flowers starting to wilt?" Marti asked, archly.

"Holding up so far," I said.

"And you?"

"Ask me after this weekend."

My mother, had she been around, would have helped me sort things out. Pre Irwin's return, she'd been a reliable source of relationship wisdom. She dosed me with semi-Buddhist stuff about acceptance and patience, and with a calming cup of tea it usually set me on the right path.

On the other hand, she'd been a living example to me of what was in store for women who put all their eggs in one man's basket.

Amazing that despite her experience with Irwin, she never bad-mouthed him in particular or the gender in general. Even when her pain was fresh and she wasn't allowing him to wriggle his vermicular self back into our lives, she didn't say a word against him.

In my adolescence, when I cursed him with Bed-Stuy-groomed eloquence, she'd say, "Wash nasty mouth, Judith. Your father have reasons I don't know. Know only, you can't argue heart."

After I'd left Todd, she'd said, "Sure from start that marriage never last. You try to forget Charlie so pick up Todd. You can't argue heart, Judith."

I suppose her Can't Argue Heart theory proved out when Irwin made his encore appearance. This week, the two lovebirds were off on a gamblers' trek up the East Coast. They'd packed up the Jaguar (I'd begged her to rent something closer to a tank after I'd found out he'd memorized the eye chart to get his Arizona license) and stopped first in Atlantic City for a warm-up—at the craps table for him, baccarat for my mother. Next on to Fox-woods in Connecticut for an Elvis impersonator festival. Last stop was New York for the Belmont Stakes, third jewel in horseracing's Triple Crown. They'd be back in B'more Monday night.

Geoff was also mostly off my radar. We were onstage to-gether that week with no solos for me. We mouthed hi from a distance, chatted briefly a few times about the upcoming audition, but that was all. He felt we'd pretty much perfected the selections and he didn't want to move me from sublime to stale. Practice on my own for a few hours a day would be more than enough to keep me in top form.

We wouldn't see each other at all the following week. Neither of us was on the roster for the all-Mozart program. Wolfie com-posed for the limited number of instruments available in the 1700s and that's the way our philharmonic played him: with a reduced orchestra.

So the coaching sessions were finished, the Phil's season was almost over, and Geoff was taking the summer off. Which meant for two months we could steer clear of each other. By next fall, whatever we'd had beyond "hi" would be past tense. I'd be good with that, I told myself. I harbored no deep-seated need for someone who'd follow a ski whim to Colorado or take off last minute for a balloon ride over the Napa Valley. This was a man who only flirted with commitment, though he seemed to have perfected an annoying version of flirting with Deena, the blond goddess of the harp. Maybe she was the instigator, but he wasn't fighting her off. Admittedly, that smarted. And that wasn't me being jealous. Just me being my natural competitive self. No Geoff, no problem.

And then, a blip on the radar. At Friday evening's intermission, I wandered into the musicians' poker game to ask him a question about a tricky bit in one of the pieces we'd been working on one-on-one. He waved off my approach, eyes on the cards, mouth set to grim.

No big mystery what was pissing him off. He'd spotted Charlie Pruitt out front in the first half. Seated row D center, silver hair shining like a beacon, yellow bow tie flashing "caution" in the houselights, Charlie was hard to miss.

I never did get to ask my audition question because the second half ran late and then I had to rush to meet The Barrister at the artists' exit.

I did see Geoff later, though. *We* did. Charlie and I.

Chapter 34

Last-Minute Charlie. That had been my nickname for him back in Cambridge.

"He take you for grant," my mother used to tell me when I complained he was never on time for dates in the early stages, or for dinners that sat getting cold when we lived together. "You put up so much. So old-fashion, Judith."

When this was said, we were fifteen years post Irwin's defection, Gracie had been made a supervisor at the bathing suit factory, and the *New York Post*, which she read to improve her English, raised her consciousness as it banner headlined the shattering of some of the highest glass ceilings: Sandra Day O'Connor's appointment to the Supreme Court and Jeanne Kilpatrick's landing the UN ambassador job. Gracie might have been uneducated, but she was not stupid. She caught on faster than I did.

"That Mary Tyler Moore"—my mother insisted her favorite actress was part Asian ("her eyes very slant")—"she work big job. Smart. More smart than Ted Baxter. She not need man. You give in too much. Treat Charlie like God."

Gracie was right. But that was then and this was now, and when Last-Minute Charlie had phoned from the Washington beltway at six p.m. Friday to tell me he was on his way to Baltimore a day early, I'd said, "The orchestra's playing tonight. If you want to hear the best parts of *Candide*, I'll leave a ticket for you at the box office. Afterward I promised Marti I'd go with her to this jazz joint in Fells Point."

"We'll work it out," he said. "See you onstage."

He'd been late, of course. Fifteen bars into the Bernstein overture, I heard the rustle as he took his seat. His glance found me and he smiled. The core of me always thawed a little when Charlie beamed a smile my way. Love or approval or just charm radiating, it warmed me.

It was all ensemble work that night. I played effortlessly, with not a flutter beneath the breastbone. As we walked offstage, Joan Farley, the cellist one down from me, caught up to say, "I probably won't see you before the auditions, so I want you to know I'm pulling for you." And then I did feel the black butterfly spiral high in my chest.

Outside on Cathedral Street, Charlie took in the circus of light, color, and chatter as the audience spilled out of the lobby. Then he had eyes only for me, his hand slipped to my waist, and he pulled me to him. Before I went in for the kiss, I checked the immediate vicinity for stray musicians who carried gossip like birdseed. And for Geoff. He wouldn't pass the morsel; it would stick in his craw, and I didn't want to hurt him.

I looked around. No witnesses. No Geoff. Great kiss.

As we disconnected, Charlie curved a hand around the back of my neck and thumb-stroked the tensed muscles.

"I've missed you, Ju-ju. You've had quite a couple of weeks, poor girl. I'm sorry I wasn't more available, but my schedule was nearly as grueling."

Unless he'd lost a close colleague who was also a cherished friend, I doubted that.

"I can't tell you how eager I've been to see you and how much I'm looking forward to easing up for a day or two. Starting immediately, if not sooner. So home, Jeeves? My car or yours?"

"Both." I pulled away. "You'll follow me. And not home. I told you I had plans to meet Marti at the Bard on Thames. A jazz club? I did mention it."

"You did. That's still on the docket, is it? You know I like jazz, but it's been a long day, heavy on meetings, and I'm beat. What I'd really like is to put my feet up and spend the evening just you and me."

"Sounds wonderful. We can pencil it in for tomorrow night."

It was kind of nostalgic to watch Charlie rev up for the argument. His upper lip drew taut over the classic Pruitt overbite, his jaw tightened, eyes narrowed. I'd seen that expression enough times in my youth—at moot court, before finals, accompanying his recurring complaint about the way I stacked the Wendell Street dishwasher.

From my amused smile, I supposed Charlie realized this wasn't going to be the easy win he'd anticipated. He closed with a push. "Marti's just over the garden fence, so she gets to be with you all the time. I'm sure she'd understand."

Well, no. She'd be royally ticked off. She'd called twice that day to make sure I still intended to show up. It was half-price hamburger night at the Bard and the Benny Brown Jazz Quartet was on the bill. I'd love Benny Brown, she had promised. For whatever reason, this evening was important to her.

My Bed-Stuy experience hadn't been a total disaster. I'd picked up some major life lessons on the street. I might have let "watch your back" slip my mind a few too many times, but I always, *always* practiced "never dis a sister."

I said sweetly, "Tell you what, Charlie. I'll give you my house key—you can let yourself in and make yourself to home, as we say in Bawlmer. But I'm not going to bail on Marti."

It took him maybe ten seconds to process my intransigence and he became the Lance Armstrong of backpedaling. "Right. Of course, a promise is a promise." Charlie Pruitt stared at the stranger at his side—me. I decided I saw a flicker of respect spark his blue eyes.

"They serve coffee at this place? Great. A shot of caffeine with my scotch and I'll be powered up."

He took my arm—sweetly quaint and chivalrous even in defeat—and we began to walk toward the garage. "Jazz," he said. "Do you remember my collection of John Coltrane and—what was her name, 'My Funny Valentine'?"

"Carmen McRae."

"Carmen McRae, that's it. I think I've still got those tapes, eight-tracks, at the Maine house. Amazing how you lose touch over the years with something you love."

Amazing.

Thames Street—pronounced *with* the *h* and a long *a* because we defeated the hoity-toity British at the Battle of Baltimore—runs along the waterfront in Fells Point. A neighborhood of bars, restaurants, galleries, boutiques, and gentrified Federal-style row homes, it stays up late on weekends, and when we arrived at eleven its cobblestone streets were well lit and buzzing.

The Bard was packed. Marti was already seated in the main room chomping a burger. She halted midbite, took in Charlie, and sent me a curious look. "Well, this is a pleasant surprise." She wiped ketchup from her lip. "I thought you weren't coming in until tomorrow, Charlie. Not that I'm not over the moon to see you."

"Likewise. I was able to duck a dinner meeting."

The table was a small four. His shoulder rubbed mine. "How's that hamburger?" he asked. "I missed dinner and I'm starved. This was a good idea, Judith."

As a figure swaggered toward the table, I wondered how long he'd hold that thought. When Marti was pushing for this girls' night out, she'd mentioned she had a new romance in her life and Nora might join us. "I'm warning you. She's not my standard frilly femme."

Not even close. Lanky as a cowpoke in jeans, a maroon crew-neck, and tooled leather boots, Nora was a Ralph Lauren ad come to life. Where Marti's hair was a froth of curls and her delicate features seemed carved from alabaster, Nora looked like a cross between a marine drill sergeant and Brad Pitt. Androgynously handsome, even with the buzz cut, she had the grip of a steamfitter.

"Hey. Judith. Heard a lot about you. All good." She nearly dislocated my shoulder on the down stroke. "And this is . . . ?"

I filled in the blanks, introducing Charlie.

Marti bit her lip, holding back laughter as Charlie and Nora shook hands. He inspected her as if she were a brand-new species.

"I like the bow tie, Charlie. Harrods?" Nora had a nice open smile. "Very cool." She turned to Marti. "Hey there, babe," she said, bending down to kiss her full on the lips, then sliding a nuzzle to her neck. Charlie squirmed beside me. And that was just the start of the evening.

The actual consuming of food was done in relative silence. The conversation was, to put it asexually, a three-way. To his credit, Charlie tried to talk sports, but Nora was a fervent Ravens fan and Charlie was big on lacrosse; she was NASCAR, he America's Cup. So the chatter was polite but awkward, with me refereeing and Marti observing, amused.

Finally, the houselights were doused, a spotlight bloomed on-stage, and the Benny Brown Jazz Quartet—piano, bass, sax, and drums—launched its first set with "Stars Fell on Alabama." Nora tried not to look bored. She managed to entertain herself playing with Marti's fingers.

"And now, ladies and gentlemen, a special treat," Benny Brown's velvet voice at the mike announced. "Y'all know Baltimore has some fine musicians, and tonight one of them is doing us the honor of sitting in with the Benny Brown Quartet. This cat works the Maryland Philharmonic Orchestra for his day job, but my classical man's got a set of chops when he gets to wailing our kind of music. So now, playing his own composition for the very first time in front of an audience, let's give a big bad Bard welcome to Geoff Birdsall and his 'Suite for My Seoulmate.'"

In the pulsing dark—and yes, that was my heart whomping—Marti McDowell had to have been counting her lucky stars. Because she'd set this up, and if I could have seen her, I would have killed her. I swear.

Chapter 35

❧

"Is that who I think it is?" Charlie whispered after Geoff lowered his horn a quarter way through to give Benny space for the piano interlude. "Isn't that your . . . ?"

"Geoff. Yes. I had no idea," I whispered back. "Believe me."

Marti, known for her tell-all mouth, had managed to keep this unveiling a secret. And I knew exactly how she'd defend herself when I got to laying her out. I could hear her in high Southern dudgeon: "Did I know you were bringing Charlie? Hell, no. I thought it would be an all-girl gathering and you'd be happy as a dog with two dicks that Geoff's composition was finally finished and you'd hear it complete first time out of the box. It was written for you, after all. I thought it was going to be an ass-kickin' surprise."

That's what it turned out to be. As Geoff unraveled the exotic, erotic melody, my annoyance with Marti turned to gratitude. Imagine missing this. It was a fusion of sensuous American jazz and *sinawi*, the *mudang*'s rhythmic otherworldly ritual music, with Geoff's trumpet standing in for the Korean double-reed *piri*.

The first three movements were upbeat and intricately patterned, alternating sizzling and cool. I was sure the ending had been written since our breakup. Bittersweet and bluesy, it spun a heartbreaking requiem for lost love.

Thank God we were in the dark throughout—I didn't want Charlie to see me blotting my eyes with a grease-stained napkin and I didn't want Geoff to see me at all. Only when the last jagged flight of melody faded did the houselights come up and the crowd rise to clap and cheer and stomp. Our group stood, though I crouched down a few inches, hoping the big guy at the table in front would block me. Geoff bobbed a quick bow and immediately turned to acknowledge his backup squad. Then the room went dark, a milky spot spilled to light my ex, and he began to play "My One and Only Love."

I got a whiff of Charlie's scotch-smoky breath as he leaned over to whisper, "Okay, I've had it. I'll wait for you outside."

It's discourteous and unprofessional for one musician to walk out on another's performance and I would never walk out on Geoff. Musically, that is. I stayed until his final mellow note.

"Leaving. Bye for us both," I said sotto voce to the silhouette of Marti and Nora, which had become a single shadow, and threaded my way through tables and out to the street.

Charlie was propped against the Bard's Tudor facade, turning his idle BlackBerry over and over in his palm, his version of worry beads. His eyes, when he looked up, were fuming red in the neon glow.

" 'My One and Only Love.' I had the Sinatra version. That was your song, right? Yours and Geoff's?"

Do people in their forties come up with "our" songs? *Only if they write them*, I thought.

"Actually, we didn't have one."

He fumbled with his BlackBerry. "I apologize for walking

out on you, Judith, but honestly, I couldn't take one more moment. That guy was playing just for you."

"You were rude," I replied. "Not just to Geoff, who didn't know. To Marti and Nora, who did."

"I doubt they noticed," he said. "They were otherwise occupied."

"Oh, Charlie," I said, sadly. "You were right. Your message with the flowers about needing to talk? We do."

He nodded, nostrils at full flare. He took in my face, which was not pretty. It seemed to inspire second thoughts. "Look, Judith." His nostrils relaxed. "I'm exhausted. My sense is we'd both be better served by a postponement. Let's sleep on it, shall we?"

We did that. And nothing more. Charlie was in the next room Skyping a colleague in Japan for I didn't know how long. By the time he slid in next to me, I was socked into sleep.

When I awoke Saturday he was off on his run, so the first time I laid eyes on him was when he walked onto the patio, where I'd laid out breakfast.

Out earlier to set the table, I'd noticed the blinds were still drawn over at Marti's. Two cars in her driveway meant a sleepover for Nora, I supposed. Good for them. I was glad somebody in the vicinity had gotten laid.

I poured my houseguest a cup of coffee and then a cup for myself. He took a fortifying slug and said into the mug, "I'm sorry if I was a jerk at the jazz club."

Not I'm sorry I *was* a jerk at the jazz club. *If* marked the spot. It was a debater's ploy, a lawyer's sleight of words. Theodora Gottlieb, MD, would have pointed out how it revealed resistance to assuming personal responsibility for one's own actions.

"Well, you *were* kind of a jerk." I dialed down to just above a whisper, which had always worked better with Charlie. "Yes, the suite was written for me. Geoff started it several years ago, ran into some snags, and I thought he'd abandoned the project. But obviously—" I stalled to a halt, stricken by the idea that he hadn't. Abandoned it. We were over, but the melody lingered on.

"I had no idea," I resumed, "that he was going—"

The BlackBerry gonged.

I wanted to take the Zen monk trapped inside that freakin' BlackBerry and wring his gonging neck.

Charlie reached into his pocket and pulled out the device that worked best for him. "E-mail." He checked. "My law clerk. A moment." He pushed a few keys and placed the crackberry on the table, screen up. Back to me. "You were saying . . ."

"When I was so rudely interrupted." I glared. "I was saying I had no idea he was going to play 'Suite for My Seoulmate' last night. I was surprised he'd even finished it. Marti set it up so Geoff wouldn't know I was there and she sure as hell didn't know you were coming. But I'm glad I went. It was beautiful. As far as 'My One and Only Love,' it's a standard. Purely generic."

Charlie gave that notion a going-over while picking apart a honey bun with his fingers. Kiki would have been appalled. He said finally, "Yes, right." He laid his sticky hand over mine. "I am sorry, Ju-ju. I'll apologize to Marti next time I see her so she doesn't think it was personal, my walking out. You know, misinterpret it as an insult to her sexual orientation. I don't have a problem with individual homosexuals even if I don't subscribe to the gay rights agenda promoted by the radical fringe."

"Of course you don't. You subscribe to the *Wall Street Journal*." I cracked a smile. "Look, you and I have always had political differences, but we've always respected each other's point of view. Still, that was college and this is all grown-up and I suppose we should try to figure out where we both stand before you take over the Washington office and unleash me on your new Capitol Hill colleagues. I really don't want to give the D.C. branch of Pruitt, Bryce and Summerville a collective heart attack."

He seemed to be considering his reply when his BlackBerry launched into a clickety-clack shimmy on my tempered-glass table. A nearby squirrel, spooked, made a mad dash for cover. "I turned it to vibrate only, but this is a call coming in." He snatched the damned thing up and read. "Ah, one I must take. It's a situation. Excuse me."

I nodded, quickly loaded up my tea tray with breakfast dishes, and headed into the house.

I was in the music room, taking pleasure from just looking at the Goffriller cello, when I heard him come up behind me.

I turned. He was wearing his somber face. "Sorry about that. There seems to be an issue regarding jurisdiction . . . There's an important distinction between—" He flicked off the thought as if I wouldn't have grasped the legal fine points anyway. Or maybe I was shortchanging him, because he reached around to pull me close and whisper, "But not as important as we are."

After freeing me, he took a seat on my sofa and patted the space next to him. Obediently, I planted myself, but not so close that our thighs were touching.

He cleared his throat. "You mentioned the Washington office, my potential colleagues there." I nodded. He coughed a second clearing. "It seems there's been a change of plans. After considerable thought, I've decided not to take the reins at K Street after all."

It took me a minute of staring at his profile, which could have been stamped on the nickel with those classic features, except Jefferson wasn't nervously biting his lower lip. And then I put it all together.

"You're not moving to D.C." He wouldn't turn his head, didn't dare meet my eyes. "But you were shopping for houses in Georgetown." *For us,* I refrained from adding. Not that I'd had any immediate plans to move in. Not when I wasn't in panic mode anyway. It was more symbolic, the move closer to me. Geographically equals emotionally. So I must have scowled.

He sighed. "I can't expect you to entirely understand, Judith. It was a complex decision driven by multiple factors. Professional ones. First, I love my work. A judgeship had always been my ultimate objective, and to give it up now?" He shook his head.

"As I gave it more thought, it became clear to me that, in spite of my grousing about the workload, I wanted a few more years on the bench. Also, I haven't been a practicing attorney for thirteen years. How fair would it be to the team to have someone as rusty as I am in a leadership position, especially in the nation's capital?" He searched my eyes for understanding. I blinked a few times and he continued. "And speaking of fairness, I'd be bumping the fellow who rightfully earned the job and that sends a bad message about nepotism in a family-founded firm."

I stopped blinking and narrowed my eyes. "But you knew this before you'd opted for the move."

He leapfrogged that statement. "And then some personal considerations have arisen."

Ah-ha.

"Chloe has decided against the colleges in D.C. She's zeroed in on Columbia."

"Columbia University. In Manhattan."

"Umm. She thinks Columbia's program is more suitable for where she wants to go in her life."

Or where she wants you to go in yours. The light, which tended to dim when I was in Charlie's presence, was beginning to dawn.

I said, "And one of your motives for moving to Washington was to be nearer to your daughter." Why hadn't I thought of that before? What a schmendrick I was.

"Yes." There was a pause. "And to you, of course."

"Maybe, but I'm an afterthought. Again." Whiny, but true.

"Not true, Judith." I was Judith now. We were out of Ju-ju territory. "I'm not sure you can empathize, not having children." Ouch. "After a divorce, you feel you're losing them, and now here she is telling me that with both of us in Manhattan we'd have an opportunity to grow our relationship."

That turned me into the Incredulous Shrinking Woman. All I could do was shake my head in awe of the power of Pruitt females. At the same time, although I didn't have kids, I'd *been* one, and I understood firsthand—thank you, *Uhm-mah*—that they came first. *Should* come first. Even the likes of Chloe, who'd probably emerge from her ugly pupa stage to become a halfway decent butterfly, especially if her father hung in through the metamorphosis.

But there was more.

"And then there's the matter of my mother. Kiki is failing. Precipitously."

For that I found voice. "According to Chloe, it's an act. She thinks Kiki's sharp as ever."

"My mother compensates, and that's what Chloe sees. But I see major changes. Kathryn Van Tiller Pruitt never pleads. When I told her about the Washington move, she pleaded with me to stay. She told me she needed me. She didn't know how she could make it without me close by. She wept. She didn't weep at my father's funeral, for God's sakes."

"Is that right?" Since showing any kind of emotion stronger than a condescending sniff was just not done in Kiki's set, she must have been terminally desperate to get him out of the clutches of the Oriyenta yet a second time. And Charlie caved. Again. *Mazel tov, Kiki*, I thought. Marti was right. You're two for two.

Now that he'd unloaded his ammo into my gut, Charlie relaxed. "This doesn't have to put a major crimp in our relationship," he said. "Under three hours on the Acela train, New York to Baltimore. And Amtrak runs both ways. You'll come up to visit."

"Long-distance romances rarely work, Charlie."

The Harvard lawyer who'd made a seven-figure living by persuading and negotiating went full throttle. "Sweetheart, it's only for a short time. College whizzes by. Mother is in her nineties. For the time being, we can *make* it work. We can pull this off if we try hard enough."

Maybe, but I was almost fifty and, dear God, I was tired of trying so hard with things that should be easy.

When he registered my skepticism, he fixed me with those magical blue eyes that could be ice, fire, or, as they were now, simmering warmth. He pulled me against him, stroked my cheek, nuzzled my neck, traced the outline of my lips with his pinkie, and kissed me. Not a three-button-with-vest kind of kiss either. My heart went haywire. It was an idiotic organ.

"Damn you," I murmured, which was his cue to unbutton my shirt and tug at the zipper of my jeans. Cursing, fumbling, he finally unhooked my bra and pitched it across the room, toppling an empty music stand. Undistracted, he focused on what had always been hot buttons for both of us. Charlie was a breast man—that hadn't changed—and now I saw his eyes widen, heard him groan. "So beautiful." He kissed, he licked, his tongue drew rough circles and I was on fully automatic, spiraling from purring idle to roaring ready in twenty seconds. Then, in a flash of lucidity, I realized he was actually planning to make love on the sofa, really more of a love seat, which, though it sounded appropriate, was too short and too structured for comfort. Also I thought—back to crazy—*Not in front of the Goffriller.*

"Upstairs," I whispered, taking off, trying to outpace the doubts, screw them out of my head the way sex and only sex could do. Charlie was still sweaty from his run and wanted to shower. I allowed him a pee. Then we made love. At the beginning, the action was frenzied, but the pace slowed due to a wilting problem on his part—*in* his part—and we probably had what was the longest foreplay in the history of arousal. In the end, though, it was as good as the best we'd had back in Cambridge.

I had a pops concert that night. "An Evening with Rodgers and Hammerstein."

"You don't mind if I skip that, do you, Ju-ju?" Charlie asked.

Mind? I was relieved. Who needed Geoff scanning the audience to find Charlie, possibly smirking at his victory?

The night before, as Geoff had played the "Suite for My Seoulmate," I'd felt a deep stirring. But it was only nostalgia, I'd told myself. Only Judith doing her romantic dithering routine. More work for Theodora . . . eventually.

The cello didn't have a solo in this performance, but the trumpet did. Geoff played "If I Loved You" without his usual passion. Or maybe it was me, *my* passion that was off.

When I arrived home near midnight, Charlie was sprawled on my bed, his laptop beside him. His head lolled against the pillow and he was in full snore and dribble. What my husband might have looked like after two and a half decades, I thought. And felt old.

In the bathroom, brushing my teeth, I saw his pills lined up like toy soldiers in the battle against the fifties. Something for high cholesterol, something for high blood pressure, something for stress-induced asthma, and one more, not in the lineup but half buried in his toiletry kit, its white plastic cap calling to me to step over yet another boundary as I took a peek: Viagra. Which, I supposed, I should be thanking for the afternoon's revival meeting. I felt really old.

All my qualms came flooding back in with the morning sunlight. Charlie took three calls during breakfast, including one from Kiki, who must have been going deaf, because I could clearly hear her fortissimo fury about her latest nurse, someone named Rosalita who was a simpleton and was, Kiki was adamant, stealing money from her purse. The other calls were business related and long.

The last one halted Charlie's fork midair. Lots of legalese, and when it was over he stared into his coffee, then at me, his forehead wrinkled. It seemed that the "jurisdictional problem" was rearing its ugly head again. He apologized for having to cut out earlier than planned, but he really needed to address this in person.

Ten minutes later he was at my front door, juggling his suitcase, briefcase, and laptop case. He read my face. "Oh jeez. You're pissed again, right? Repissed?"

Repissed, depressed, angry at him, angry at myself, and freakin' confused. "I don't know about us, Charlie."

His sigh was tinged with impatience. "Well, then hang around and find out. And don't make any hasty decisions. I know you, Ju-ju. You're prone to overreact in the moment. Remember back in school when you were ready to sign that communist petition until I read you the fine print?"

"Dammit, that is the most patronizing—"

He overrode me. "All I'm asking is you give this—us—your studied consideration."

Studied consideration. Not *I love you madly. Don't break my heart, my darling.* Okay, over the top. But studied consideration? Dry as a mother superior's snatch, as Marti would have said.

He checked his precious Patek Philippe watch. "Sorry. Have to go. I'll call you in a few days."

"It's going to be a jammed week," I responded frostily. "I have the audition for principal on Tuesday."

He treated me to a blank stare. He'd forgotten already. But he was quick to recover.

"No heavy discussion. Just to wish you success with the audition. To tell you I'm cheering for you."

He kissed my cheek. His breath was sour cherries from the breakfast Danish, but his voice was syrup. And the words? The Barrister aka His Honor surprised me once again. "Don't give up on us yet, please. Now that I've found you, I don't want to lose you again."

Not bad for an exit line.

Chapter 36

My mother and Irwin, the gypsy gamblers, weren't supposed to be back at Blumen House until early Monday evening, but I'd picked up a ready-made lasagna at Whole Foods to drop off for their dinner. A welcome-home gift so Gracie wouldn't have to cook.

In the lobby, I got tackled by my least favorite resident.

"Not in service. Only one elevator is working, thanks to your mother." Miriam Botansky, as in buttinsky, seized my wrist as I pushed the "up" button. "Very inconvenient and I told her so."

It took me a moment to process before I said, voice spiraling, "Told her? What, my mother is home? They're back this morning? Is she all right?"

"Depends on your definition of 'all right.'"

I didn't have time to debate semantics with Mrs. Botansky. Swept by a wave of panic—the ambulance crew had frozen the elevator in the Pikesville building when Grace fell in the bathroom there—I shook her off and raced up four floors and down the hall to 4C. The door was ominously open. Wide. I skidded to a halt at the threshold, surveyed the interior, and muttered, "Dear God."

The living room was empty. No furniture. No knickknacks. I walked through to the kitchen, which had been cleaned out except for two cartons stacked near the refrigerator. The bedroom—stripped.

As I stood considering the implications, I heard the sound of a toilet flushing and a shaky baritone launch into "Strangers in the Night," the Sinatra version with the scooby-dooby-dos.

"Irwin!"

The music stopped and the old man emerged from the bathroom wiping his hands on his trousers. He was wearing a pair of ratty chinos and a striped pajama top tucked haphazardly into the waistband. His hair was overdue for a session with Grecian Formula—a half inch of silver gave way to a fading beaver color. No Dapper Dan this morning.

His eyes bugged at the sight of me, but he recovered fast, pulling composure from his salesman's sample case. "Judy—" His voice was as silky as top-of-the-line nova salmon. "How ya doing?" The smile was bold, but I caught a nervous twitch in the lower lip. "We weren't expecting you."

"No, I'll bet you weren't. All I want to hear is that my mother's not moving out of Baltimore."

"Never. Would we leave you?" The "we" didn't get by me. "Not a chance. Just upstairs two flights. Before you blow your stack, talk to her. She'll give you the details. Sixth floor, across from the elevator. Door's open, 6E. Beautiful place. Cross ventilation."

Apartment 6E was the largest, poshest unit in Blumen House. The oak-floored living room was flooded with light from wraparound windows. The kitchen was eat-in, the powder room had a soft toilet seat for seniors' bony bottoms, and the built-ins lining the den had mini spotlights to showcase Irwin's kachina collection.

I found Grace in the bedroom, wearing jeans and a T-shirt

emblazoned "Poker Diva ~ Atlantic City." She was getting to be quite a chippie herself, my mother. Arranging throw pillows on the bedspread of a California king, she startled when I barreled in and she covered her mouth like a kid caught in the cookie jar.

"Huh? You scare me, Judith! What you doing here? I told you not home till tonight."

"I thought after the ride you might be too tired to cook, so I brought dinner. I left it in your fridge. Your new one that's the size of a walk-in closet."

"Nice, yes? Sub-Zero. I make lots of *yukgaejang* to freeze for you. You can have all time now."

Oh no—she wasn't going to suck up, up, and away this betrayal. Moving her whole apartment, her entire life, without telling me, her only child.

"You lied to me, *Uhm-mah*. And we're not talking a little white lie here to avoid hurting my *kibun*." Out of politeness, to keep harmony, Koreans will sometimes stretch the truth to avoid having someone lose *kibun*—face, or pride. *Kibun* was my mother's favorite excuse for keeping me mis- or disinformed. "But let's work our way up the line to the big lie. Let's start with your telling me you weren't coming home until tonight. So when did you really get back?"

"Yesterday morning. But I have good reason to not say when."

I looked around the room. The bed was either new or—I bought the next thought an express ticket through my brain—the chippie's hand-me-down. Either way, it had to have been delivered. There was a chest of drawers in Southwestern style draped with a Native American blanket. A butt-ugly rustic mirror, its frame fashioned of twigs, already hung on the near wall. Both were from Irwin's Tucson house, probably. On my mother's old dresser—so old, she'd once shared it with him back in Flatbush—sat a television with a screen sized for cataract patients, the Best Buy tag still on. Sixteen hundred bucks. One could assume Bonnie and Clyde had been on a shipping/shopping spree. So this plan had been brewing for a while. Behind my back.

"Your reason better be very good," I said.

"Best good." By the set of her jaw, I knew she'd been training for this big reveal. "I don't tell you about move because you tell me no don't move. Hundred reasons no." Grace counted off on her fingers. "Irwin bad man, bad father. Leave once, leave again. His money pay for apartment. I take his money mean I forgive everything. You say I be his maid. I work too hard. *Aigoo!*" She smacked her forehead. "I know what you do next. You throw fit. Try to stop us. Speak to Emma, try to call it off."

Emma Lewis was the recently hired, exceedingly young residence manager. And why *hadn't* she notified me? She'd thought I approved, of course. I'll bet that's what they told her, the two-faced twosome, and since they were above the age of consent, with a hefty check of Irwin's to back up the contract, there was no apparent problem.

"And always, if I do what *I* want, not what *you* want, you walk around like . . ." My mother made the face of a gargoyle. "You act like brat. Make me crazy."

I couldn't deny it. I would have thrown myself in the path of a runaway train to stop the Irwin juggernaut.

"You need to change tune. Yes, Daddy do bad things. But I do too. He try to see you when you were little girl. I say no, no. You forgive me. But you don't forgive him. Why?"

"It's different. You wouldn't understand."

"Not understand because you"—she waggled her head and singsonged—"are only one so smart. My daughter always so right about everything." I couldn't believe she was scolding me as if I were ten. Using sarcasm yet. With finger pointing. "Even if what you say true, I ask big question: you rather be right or be happy, Judith?"

"What?"

"Dr. Phil ask on TV show. 'You rather be right or be happy?' Irwin make me happy. I love him. He love me. Now together. No marriage. Your father want to, but I say who need marriage? Better to shack up."

In the silence that followed my groan, we avoided each other's gaze. We both fixed on my mother's shoes. Strappy red sandals. With sexy heels just high enough to twist an ankle on a seventy-eight-year-old woman. I banked that worry for later as a male voice, with an accent as far from Irwin's Brooklynese as you could get without falling off the planet, called out, "Grace, I got the hammer, darlin'. Now I need you in here to tell me where you want these pictures hung."

Geoff Birdsall poked his head in the bedroom, did a subtle double take, and said, "Ah. It's you, Jude." His greeting didn't quite make it to lukewarm. "What are you doing here?"

"What am *I* doing here? What are *you* doing here?"

He presented himself full length in his grungiest jeans and a ratty Maryland Phil sweatshirt, hammer in hand. "Obviously I'm helping move your parents into their new digs." Geoff had always been quick to read my moods, a trait I used to treasure. I was brewing up a storm. He studied me for a few seconds before turning to my mother. "Grace, darlin', why don't you trot down to the maintenance office and see if anyone there has a tape measure?"

She scurried off, sending me an alarmed look in transit. I couldn't blame her for wanting to be out of the suddenly frigid environment.

When we heard her heels click against hardwood, he said, "Is there a problem, Jude? Because I know we've discussed that although you and I are, shall we say, divorced, I claim visitation rights with your mum. And now with your dad, since they seem to be a package." He had the unmitigated chutzpah to attempt an innocent smile, Aussie skunk. In the mirror behind him, though, I saw tension arching his back. Dead giveaway.

Why is it when you least want tears to spring, they trickle out to remind you of how little control you have over your emotions?

I struck first this time. "I can't believe you. It's one thing for them to pull off a stunt like this. Keeping me in the dark because they don't want to deal with me and face the truth. But you— Okay, we're over, but I've always trusted you. And believe me, I appreciate all you've done for me professionally. But intruding on my personal life here . . ." Geoff stared at me as if I'd escaped from a locked ward on a psych unit. "I never made it a secret how I felt about my self-styled father oozing himself back into Gracie's life, trying to seep into mine. And for you to be an accomplice in this total disregard of my feelings, this nose-thumbing of my status as a daughter . . ."

"Whoa. What are you saying?"

"You know exactly what I'm saying. They never mentioned a word to me about the move. How long have they been up to this? How long have you known? Is this some kind of revenge for Charlie? Because if so, you've stooped to a level that's so beneath—" As soon as I heard myself say it, I knew I was wrong. As soon as I saw the pain in his face, I knew I'd made the biggest blunder since stammering "I do" to Rebound Todd. I knew I'd do almost anything to take it back. But it was too late.

The reference to Charlie had pulled the pin in Geoff's grenade. In a flash, his face flamed, his brow lowered to Neanderthal, he gripped the hammer and swung. From my angle, it looked as if he were aiming to fling it on the bed and get the hell out of Dodge fast. But halfway through the rotation, the hammer head separated from the wooden handle and hurled itself into the ugly mirror. *Crash!* The silvered rectangle exploded. Shards rained down like ice crystals; twigs cracked and flew in a terrifying blizzard. I ducked, covered my eyes, and only looked up when I heard him gasp, though where he found air in that vacuum I had no idea. I was holding my breath.

Geoff's horrified triple take swerved from the headless handle he was still gripping to the shattered mirror to me. When he spoke, it was a blast to the ceiling. "God*damn* you, Judith!" Shouting my name, his voice broke.

I backed away as he stormed from the room. I heard the apartment door slam behind him. It sounded like the bang at the end of the world.

"Oh, crap. Look at my beautiful mirror, all in smithereens. That piece is irreplaceable. It's an heirloom, in Lorna's family for years."

Irwin stared balefully at a twig that had come off in his hands.

"I'm so sorry," I said. "I'll have it fixed."

It was fifteen minutes later and I was still trying to pull myself together after Geoff's meltdown.

Irwin was saying, "Here, let me take a look at you. You didn't get cut, did you? Sometimes these little bits of glass get stuck . . ." He adjusted his reading glasses, peered at my face with magnified frog eyes, and rotated my jaw to inspect my skin.

He'd never before laid a finger on me and I was about to shake him off when I noticed the row of dimples lined up in the flesh above his top knuckles. Just like mine.

For the first time, I realized I bore some resemblance to the Raphael side of my family. With my mother's people, I could see it vividly even as a kid, when I'd compared my round chin and chubby cheeks to the faded black-and-white photo that was all she had left of the Ryang grandparents. With the Jewish clan, I'd never felt that visceral connection that comes with recognizing yourself in someone else. Which of these big-boned, light-eyed white devils did I resemble? Certainly not Grandma Roz, who looked like she was descended from a long line of walnuts. Or my aunt Phyllis, with the blond bouffant and the size ten feet. Or my cousin Staci, who had her auburn hair chemically straightened at an upscale African-American salon in Far Rockaway. But now, as he moved in to inspect me, I could see that I had my father's high-bridged noise, a schnoz perfectly suited to a Talmudic scholar, and his ears, C-shaped shells with the lobe deficiency—genetic anomalies handed down from Moses.

Incredible. I looked like Irwin. A little. And because of that millimeter of tissue and bone bumped up here or shaved down there, something inside me shifted a millimeter.

"Nah, you're fine." He picked up the hammer. "But that Geoff went off his rocker, didn't he? I took him for an even-tempered guy. Go know. You have to wonder what could have set him off like that."

"It was an accident," I said, sure of it. "Though he was furious with me."

"What did you do?"

"I thought he was in on the scheme you and Mom cooked up to hide your move. I couldn't believe he'd keep a secret like that from me. We used to be close."

"Yeah, your mom told me you dumped him for the Park Avenue lawyer. The guy who broke your heart all those years ago, which told me, Ivy League or not, the lawyer was a dummy." Irwin bestowed what could only be described as a fatherly smile on me. "Personally, I liked this Geoff guy up till today. He's a real man's man. As to whether he screwed you over, pardon the expression, I can tell you without a doubt he did not. No way."

Had Irwin Raphael sworn on a stack of Bibles, I would have checked to see if they included Leviticus and all the Psalms, because he'd probably picked them up half price at a fire sale.

"Your mother told him that the upgrade on the apartment had your stamp of approval. She said you were playing house with the old boyfriend this weekend, which is why you couldn't help us get the new place set up."

"She said *what*?"

"Something about your being with the lawyer, which you were supposed to be, right? So she stretched the truth a little. No big deal. She told me if the Aussie knew the real setup, he'd never be able to keep it from you."

Why, that old conniver. She was even slicker than Irwin. Credit, though—she understood what Geoff was and wasn't capable of. She'd always been a good judge of character, with the notable exception of her ex-husband. If *I'd* ever had the touch, I'd lost it. Irretrievably.

"Oh God," I said, eyeing a scattering of glass shards on the bedroom carpet. "I accused him of . . . He'll never forgive me. I need to find him. Right now. I've got to apologize." Even as I babbled my remorse, I knew Geoff couldn't have any mercy left for me to throw myself on.

"Hey, calm down, sweetheart. This ain't the end of the world. Besides, he's long gone. Took off like a shot. Best settle it by phone, anyway. Seriously, I wouldn't get too close to a guy with that kind of a temper. You could have fooled me. He never came off as a nutcase before."

"He's not a nutcase. *I'm* the nutcase."

"Nah, you're a Raphael. We're all very stable. Look at your aunt Phyllis. Eighteen years of therapy and she still can't drive the Long Island Expressway." My father winked. "Come on. Let's get out of here. I'll have housekeeping clean this up. See, that's the beauty of living in a place like this. No cleaning. And now that I've taken over the cooking, it's like your mother's on vacation. She can play keno online all day long if she wants."

"You cook?"

"Like a Frenchman, though I specialize in Mexican. There's a lot you don't know about me, kiddo. But you'll learn."

His arm found its way around my shoulders as we walked together out of apartment 6E. I let it be. I was grateful for the support. For a lapsed second or two, I let myself lean against him. It felt good, dammit.

Chapter 37

I'd deal with my criminal of a mother later. Geoff was top priority. I called him from my car. He didn't pick up, so I left a tearful apology. Not enough, I decided. I needed to present myself at his high-rise so he could see for himself my sackcloth-and-ashes penitence. Halfway there, I decided against it. That was after calling Marti, who'd said, "Wow, you've just set some kind of record. Driving two men out of your life in the space of four hours. One goes quietly. One goes crazy. Good job, Judith. No, in my opinion it's not the best idea, you going to Geoff's flat. Why not give him a little time to cool off?"

When I got home, I found his message waiting. He could have phoned my cell, so I figured he wanted his response on record and he didn't want to talk to me.

"Judith . . ." Deep sigh. "Please know I'm sorry about the mirror. I left a message for your mum that I'd pay for the repair, and I got hold of the building's handyman. He'll hang her pictures. Of course, I apologized to Grace and Irwin. As for us, if need be, we'll hash this out at a later date. Right now you must put everything out of your mind except the audition tomorrow. The rest is secondary. Focus. Concentrate. You'll do yourself proud."

Typical Geoff. The Aussie with a heart as big as the outback. Sweet, even at the bitter end. And then, for whatever we'd had that we had no more, I buried my face in my hands and wept.

At eight o'clock the following morning my mother showed up at my front door, Tupperware bowl in hand. I could see my father at the wheel of the Jaguar idling in the driveway. Obviously he wasn't coming in.

Just as well, because we might have lost whatever gains we'd accrued from our short but sweet bonding experience of the day before. I was cranky after a bad night. My mind racing with reruns of the day before and qualms about the day ahead, I'd grabbed only snatches of sleep, getting up twice to brush up the selections I'd be called upon to play.

I'd expected a longer period of adjustment to the new cello. Cellos have personalities, cellists have idiosyncrasies, and by some stroke of fortune the Goffrillers and the Raphaels fit well together from the start. I had to tweak my technique somewhat, and with me it didn't give off the dense, luxurious sound Richard had coaxed from it but, if it was different, it was equally sublime. Most of the time. There were a few bumps I wished Geoff had been around to help me smooth out. More to the point, I wished Geoff had been around.

My need reminded me that I'd always taken his got-your-back presence lightly. But lightly was how he'd wanted to be taken, right? Lightly was what we'd both wanted, yes? My confusion had triggered a second cleansing cry earlier that morning. I'd watched the sun come up on my patio and sobbed into my coffee. Not a good way to start a demanding day.

My mother, examining my red-rimmed eyes with her worried ones, made no move to cross the threshold. "Not inside visit today. Only stop to bring breakfast. Just make on new stove.

Doenjang. You love *doenjang.*" I did love the soup of soybean paste and greens. "Not heavy. No garlic, so you won't stink at audition." She pressed the container into my hands. "I know you, Judith. Big deal today, so you get nerves and don't eat. But must eat. Give you strength to play best."

"Thank you, *Uhm-mah.*"

What was the use? I could never be cross with her for long. I should have confronted her about the moving violation, but it had been Grace and me against the world for my entire childhood and since our last estrangement the thought of an angry distance between us had made me uneasy.

"Also, I got something from your *ap-ba,*" she said, using the Korean word for "dad." This was the first time she'd ever called him that. "He want you to put in your pocket for audition." She laid a chunk of bling on the lid of the soup container. "Money clip. Solid gold. For good luck. See horseshoe? Mean good luck."

I'd take my luck where I could get it. I held the clip up and waved my thanks toward the Jag. Irwin hesitated for a moment, as if caught off guard by the gesture. Then he waved back. "Tell him I'll carry it with me." Oh, why not? What did the wave and a few words cost me? And the payoff was the delight on my mother's face.

"Very nice. Sure, I tell him." Her smile narrowed to reassuring. "Don't worry about nothing, Judith. You do good. Lulu Cho say she have dream about you. You play cello and pig dance to music. Dream of pig very good luck in Korea."

"So is dreaming of a big turd."

"What is turd?"

"*Ddong.*"

"Ah-hah-hah." Grace laughed uproariously, showing gold. "Yes, Korean think good to dream shit. True. My mother, grandmother used to say same. But funny, yes?" She swiped her eyes.

"Listen, Lulu Cho very fine *mudang*. Never wrong. You believe. You win principal."

I nodded. God knows, I was trying to make myself believe.

"I want you, I want you not." Leaning against a wall of a toilet stall in the women's dressing room late morning, I chatted with a hexagonal blue pill, twenty milligrams of Inderal balanced on the Mound of Mars, site of courage, on the palm of my hand. "Yes or no. Talk to me, baby."

Recently I'd been getting it on with my confidence game. But minutes away from the showdown, my self-doubt had come flooding back.

Tucked in the bottom of my handbag was a full bottle of the meds I'd popped before my last symphony solo to conquer my performance anxiety. Now I stared at the little pill of salvation, weak with desire, murmuring, "Want you. Oh God, do I want you."

My body was reeling from crashing weather fronts. A hot flash rolled across my chest. Rivulets of perspiration trickled from my forehead, threatening my eye makeup. My hands were ice.

A swallow of serenity was just what the doctor ordered, but I gagged on the idea. Above the flush of toilets, I could hear Richard's disembodied voice making a last stand.

Drugs are appropriate when the anxiety is deep-seated and untreatable by any other means. That's not so in your case. Don't start what you don't need. Goddamn it, Judith, I promise you— you've got what you need.

So playing his fabulous Goffriller mellowed by my tiny blue friend here would be a betrayal, wouldn't it? I couldn't dishonor Richard's memory that way, could I?

And then there was Geoff, proxying for the dearly departed on the Just Say No ballot. When I'd mentioned to him in the synagogue parking lot after the funeral that I was thinking about calling on pharmaceutical assistance for the audition, he'd given me a stricken look.

"But why, Jude? You didn't need it today and you won't need it then. You just played that *Thaïs* piece as if it were a lament over the death of God himself, and you pulled that passion out on your own in front of all the celebs. Ach, you don't get it, do you? You've broken the anxiety chokehold."

"Today was different," I'd said. "I had no time to think. The vote of confidence was still fresh. But the audition—that's a whole different game. The panic could sweep back in, Geoff. The pill takes the edge off."

"Maybe too much so. To be blunt, the night you took it I thought your playing was crap. Yeah, you got through it. But as your aunt Phyllis would say, *Feh!* My opinion? Go commando. Everybody's strung out at auditions anyway. That's the point, isn't it? It's the quaking on the edge that tips you over into the transcendent."

Now I slipped the pill into the pocket of my skirt, where it nestled next to my father's horseshoe money clip. If I felt my luck running low, I could always reach deep down for backup.

I could hear Richard call down, "Brava!" and Geoff—wherever *he* was—say, "That's my sheila." Except I wasn't his sheila anymore, was I? I'd made sure of that.

Geoff. Since his message the day before, there had been no sign of life and no promise of seeing him soon. I wouldn't run into him in the next few hours because on audition days the concert hall was cleared of extraneous musicians. Only those competing and those judging were allowed on the premises.

A part of me was ready to grab my cell phone and punch in his speed-dial number to hear his rich baritone insisting I was good at this, I knew the pieces, I'd done the work, I wasn't going to screw up. Then my left brain kicked in, reminding me what acting on impulse had led to the day before. It wasn't a good time for us to talk about my perceived deficiencies, a subject that might stray into relationship territory. No, I needed to remain focused.

The crowd of contenders did nothing to reassure me. The scuttlebutt was that the principal posting had turned out an unprecedented number of responses from first-class musicians. In a lousy economy, smaller orchestras were closing shop, major ones weren't promoting so fast, and principal seats were scarce as magpies' teeth.

There was no way I could tell the exact size of the contestant pool from what I saw milling about in the bowels of the Berenson. Of more than two hundred applicants, sixty had made it to the initial round the day before. Scheduled five or six per hour, given maybe ten minutes apiece onstage to do their thing, they'd been told their fate and had gone back to their hotels to pack or stay another night for their crack at the next level. As the Philharmonic's associate principal, I'd been able to skip the first cattle call. By now, the herd had been culled, leaving maybe ten or fifteen serious rivals. If I made this morning's cut, I'd be competing in the afternoon's final against the top two or three, very likely including Vincent DeGrassi, who'd ambushed me in the hall to say hello and size me up. And psych me out, the ever ambitious Vince.

Musicians are a collegial bunch. Our report cards could read, "Plays well with peers." There is hardly any backstabbing in the profession, but Vince had a reputation for doing what it took to advance his career.

His cologne—a vapor of cloying sweetness—preceded him. "Hey, Judith." The smile below the pepper-and-salt mustache was too broad to be true. "I was wondering when I'd bump into you. How long has it been? Jacob's Pillow, right? Ten years?" He took my cold hand in his warm one. Not a lot of nerves in play for him. "You look great. Burt says you've got the big five-oh coming up." The timpanist was on the party list. "I have to say you look amazing for your age." The first shot landed wide of the target— he wasn't *that* much younger. The second found its mark. "Sorry about Richard Tarkoff. Terrible loss. For you especially. Gonna be rough without him out there, huh?"

Very skillful. Under the guise of sympathy, he'd reminded me that my mentor had been on the judging committee when I'd tried out for associate. Up to the final round, candidates played behind a screen and judges were scrupulous about objectivity. However, just knowing Richard was there had given me a boost.

"So sad. I always liked the man. And I think the feeling was mutual."

No, not really. Richard had thought Vince was a prick.

"He once said, 'You remind me of me when I was young, Vince. Incredible focus combined with impeccable technique.'"

Richard would never have said that. He was far too modest for self-aggrandizement.

When I didn't bite, Vince bumped it up a notch. "You heard Cynthia and I are divorcing? No children, thank God, but she's being a witch about the settlement. A very controlling woman. The quintessential concertmaster."

He gave me a calculating look before firing his next shot. "There must be something in the air because I heard you and Geoff Birdsall split . . ." He fiddled with his tie, wondering, I suppose, if he'd hit the bull's-eye.

Slightly off center. I'd known the news would make the circuit. Nothing was sacred in the musical community.

". . . and that he's taking it hard."

That rocked me a little. Geoff wearing his emotions on his sleeve. That wasn't like him.

I checked my watch. Vince was in the audition slot before me. His predecessor had just been escorted upstairs to the stage. That gave me maybe twenty minutes to get in my warm-up and do my breathing exercises. This conversation wasn't doing my pulse rate any favors. I'd taken one step toward my escape when he hooked me back.

"I can understand his wanting to move. I'm doing the same thing, trying to put California behind me. Get some distance from the disaster. But London! Jesus. I suppose it's not such a stretch for an Aussie, but to be away from the—"

My feet, suddenly lead weights, locked me to the floor. Good thing, too, because from the ankles up I swayed like bamboo in the wind. My brain, on the other hand, had braked to a halt at the mention of London. It took Vince's smirk to jump-start it.

Of course I'd chased Geoff off. Been a bitch. Beyond self-absorbed and into selfish. Taken him for granted. Told him—by words and actions—to get lost. So I could hardly blame him for refusing to wait in the wings while I dallied with my old boyfriend. Geoff wasn't an understudy type of guy. Okay, I tried to soothe myself, maybe it *would* be better with us oceans apart. Better for him, certainly. For me, right now I wasn't so sure. Wasn't sure at all.

I nervously jiggled the cello charm, Geoff's gift to me. "He's moving to London." I tried to make the question a statement, but my voice was vibrato and Vince was sharp. He caught on.

"Oh boy, you didn't know. I had no idea. I figured he might want to keep management in the dark, but you . . . Well, now the cat's out of the bag. The UK Concert Orchestra is looking to fill an open principal trumpet. Burt says Geoff flew over last night to check it out. I'll bet they won't make him go through this fucking rigmarole. My understanding is he'll have it if he wants it. Smaller ensemble. Lighter schedule. Cushy job." He licked up to his mustache like a tomcat relishing a dinner of broken bird. "Goddamn, I feel awful about laying this on you, Judith. Especially now."

No, he didn't. He'd done what he'd set out to do. Rattle me. Make my stomach clench and my hands tremble. Joke (mine, made up on the spot):

Q: "What do you call a cellist with the shakes?"

A: "I don't know, but you don't call her a cellist."

I reached into my pocket to feel for the happy pill. Still there. Not for long.

This time Geoff *had* deliberately held out on me. I suppose for a decent man it made sense not to tell me just before I went on to win or lose the rest of my life. But look how it had turned out: me facing Vince DeGrassi, who was knitting his bushy brows in ersatz sympathy.

Except what screws people like Vince is their arrogance. A limitless ego never knows when enough is enough. He'd knocked me out with the Geoff bombshell, so the jerk could have bounded off with a spring in his step, convinced he'd put away the competition. But he had to push. He had to make sure the body wasn't twitching.

"Judith, I almost forgot . . ." *Almost forgot.* What a crock! It was obvious from the anticipation on his face, whatever he had up his sleeve was going to be the coup de grâce. He'd planned on saving his best for last, but what could be worse than his news that Geoff was moving to London? A parry that caused me exactly what he was aiming for, a swift stab of agony that still throbbed, soon to be followed by a distracting soreness. Right now, I had to blank it all out. Hurt, angry, sad are not a combination plate you want to carry with you into an audition. Vince was unable to hide his satisfaction at the outcome of his ploy. Though he worked on keeping a straight face, his gray-streaked mustache made little rays above the sunny arc of his mouth.

Maybe this was about the North Korea trip. Vince was a notorious gossip. Maybe he'd heard it really *was* me who'd wrecked the negotiations. Maybe something Grace had done or not done on her paperwork sixty years before had screwed up a history-making international cultural exchange. With Angela out there, if I was the spoiler, I'd be lucky to keep my current seat, let alone move up to principal.

"Congrats on the Goffriller."

Ah. So the Goffriller was his ace in the hole. I wondered how he was going to play that hand. As it turned out, dirty.

"That must have been a staggering surprise. It was for your friends and colleagues. You and that priceless cello of yours are the hot topic of the week. Everybody's talking about it. And I mean everybody."

Of course they were. If my Baltimore colleagues knew, the woman who mopped the stage at the Bangkok Symphony knew.

"I'm sure you've seen on Google that the last Goffriller put up at auction went for a cool million five. Now that's one hell of a parting gift."

Crass. But not deadly. Deadly was coming, I could tell from the cattiness that had crept into his voice. "You two must have had a very special relationship."

So there it was. Overcome by revulsion, I backed up a step.

In case I'd missed the lack of subtlety, he drove the knife home again with a redundant twist in the singsong of a taunting five-year-old. "Unusually close, even for stand partners."

Richard and I had an affair. And the Goffriller was a gift to a mistress from her dying lover. That's what he was saying, what everyone in every symphony orchestra in the world was thinking. And didn't that imply I hadn't, *couldn't* make my way up the professional ladder on talent alone? I had to rely on the trading of sexual favors for success? Therefore I was a weak slut sister and an alpha male like Vince DeGrassi could mug me for the principal spot.

As he took in my offended, teeth-gritting silence, he straightened the knot of his tie. *Tighter*, I urged silently. *Tighter, until your eyeballs pop and your evil swollen tongue flops like a limp dick under your silly mustache and the coroner pronounces you DOA.*

But he was alive and he wasn't finished. "Fabulous instrument you inherited. Up there with the best. But you do know it's going to create unrealistic expectations. You playing the Goffriller, there'll be no excuses for a less than perfect performance. No room for the slightest mistake." Bastard. I wanted to jab my knee into his balls. Hard.

I took a deep, cleansing breath, trying to pull up Dr. Gottlieb's words at our second appointment the week before. *Before your audition, think confident, think calm. Remember, serenity is not freedom from the storm, but peace amid the storm.* Had she been quoting Mahatma Gandhi? Al Roker? The session had been devoted to my terror onstage, which tellingly took place only when I played solo. "Alone again. Does it feel something like abandonment?" she'd suggested. "But you're never alone, Judith, when you fully trust yourself."

Facing Vince, I pulled up one of Theodora's self-soothing exercises. You couldn't risk closing your eyes on that weasel, but I unfolded my clasped fingers and breathed to a calming rhythm. *Peace. Inhale. Peace. Exhale.*

Sorry, Doc. Peace was the farthest thing from my mind. Victory occupied every vigilant brain cell.

Then I said, because it was true, and also because I knew it would throw him, "You're right, Vince. I appreciate your reminding me. That was just the push I needed. Really, thanks." I gave him a grateful smile. Swallowing my loathing for the greater good, I topped the smile, à la mode, with a peck on his nasty, cologne-soaked cheek.

And that's how it should have ended. But his ear—large, lupine, and springing a bramble of kinky hair—was so close. And telling him off would be so satisfying. Self-destructive, maybe, but satisfying. Oh, the hell with it. I couldn't resist. I whispered into his hairy ear: "I hope you crash and burn, DeGrassi. Now go screw yourself!"

There's a Korean proverb my mother liked to quote: "Even a fish wouldn't get in trouble if it kept its mouth shut."

I left Vince standing there gaping like a flounder.

Chapter 38

Ｔhere was no way I was going to sit in second chair while DeGrassi in principal called the shots till death or retirement did us part. No way in hell I was going to sit shoulder to shoulder with him as stand partner, suffocating in his stinky cologne Eau de Smug. And after my kamikaze screw-off, he'd have it in for me with a vengeance. To stay with this orchestra in any capacity, I knew what I had to do.

I must have looked as fierce as I felt because our personnel manager, who'd come to escort me upstairs, gave me a curious look. "You okay?" He really wasn't supposed to communicate with me beyond clarifying procedure. As I patted my new side-kick of a cello, I curved a smile. "Fine." Which I was close to, now that I had a mission.

Onstage, I took the candidate's chair, spread the same long black skirt I'd worn to audition for associate principal, my lucky skirt with the lucky horseshoe money clip and the Inderal still in its pocket. My music had been placed on my stand in the order I'd be playing the selections. Muted voices and the rustle of evaluation forms floated in from behind the concealing screen.

The committee was made up of colleagues, some of whom were also friends. In my mind's eye I envisioned the lineup:

Angela, then the concertmaster, second violin, principal viola, principal bass. Principal cello, dear Richard, absent. The next row was smudged. I had no idea which members of the cello section had accepted the invitation to sit in on the audition as I'd done many times myself.

A coughing fit broke the silence. High pitched with a soprano whistle at its crest, it erupted from Lauren Symonds, I was sure. Our principal viola had been out for two weeks with pneumonia. I'd chipped in for the get-well plant the string section had sent. Lauren was unaware that the person who'd insisted on a gardenia bonsai rather than a cactus dish garden was candidate number seven, at that moment drawing her bow on the first note of the opening to Prokofiev's Symphony No. 5.

I played that and bits and pieces from the two Strauss *Dons*— *Juan* and *Quixote*—as well as I'd ever played them. I gave Bach his glory, nailed all the crescendi and decrescendi in the scherzo from Mendelssohn's *A Midsummer Night's Dream*. Yes, I faltered on the *Tännhauser* overture—it was in my blood to ride that anti-Semite Wagner too hard. The personnel manager poked his head around to convey the committee's request that I replay the last two lines a bit slower. I thought it was still off. But the solos that dipped into Tchaikovsky's Rococo Variations and the Dvořák concerto, an emotional kaleidoscope, soared and shimmered in all the right places. Sum total, my mother and Geoff would have been pleased. I wanted to think that Richard Tarkoff's witty ghost and Florence Beckersham's beautiful spirit high-fived each other in heaven.

A half hour later I learned I'd made it through to the final round.

It should have been easy. I was charged with lightning from the morning's competition. And I loved the afternoon's set, was relieved the committee had chosen the William Tell rather than the excerpt from the Brahms Concerto No. 2, the piece that had sparked a panic attack the last time I'd played it in public. For this deciding round, the screen would come down and I'd be able to make out my colleagues on the judging panel. I knew they'd be tempted to lean over backward, tipping away from me to prove objectivity, but I was familiar with the process, had felt what they'd be feeling, and trusted them to find the perfect balance of fairness.

My two competitors were Vince, whom I dearly wanted to arm wrestle for this position, and a young cellist from Pittsburgh noted for the precision of his technique. The only time I'd heard him, I'd detected a deficiency of heart. An audition for principal *anything* demanded a grand passion. So it should have added up to victory for me.

Should have. As I began to warm up—disaster. The François Tourte bow, the one that partnered the Goffriller, failed me. There was a tiny eyelet that tightened the horsehairs to an exact tension, and when all was well you heard a faint click that told you, *Done.* Over time, though, those eyelet threads wore out, and, when they did, the strings didn't respond. You got zilch, zero. Flabby-bow syndrome was a death sentence. The bow was useless.

Every cellist carried a standby for just such an occasion. Lucky for me, I had my Sartory bow, which had worked beautifully with my trusty Tecchler cello but had never been up against the exalted likes of a Goffriller. Richard's bow had a particular heft, a sparkling yet adaptive personality that I'd quickly learned would handle whatever I asked of it. My bow, I'd discovered over the years, was more temperamental. It had its favorites. It loved Mozart, but it didn't have a taste for, say, Elgar. The solo I'd signed on to play in the final was Elgar's Cello Concerto. So I was worried.

Vince DeGrassi, with an animal lack of shame and a nose for prey in trouble, stopped by to congratulate me on my first round, but really to check me out. He poked his head in the door, baring his teeth in an approximate smile, showing no sign he'd registered my final furious whisper. He had to be playing some higher-level mind game to freak me out. No need. I'd freaked myself very proficiently without any help.

He found me examining the injured bow and could barely contain his joy. "It happens . . ." He smirked, ecstatic it had happened to me, for him, at this perfect time and place. *Grrrr*, the man made me want to kick ass. I knew I could have kicked his fat one with the Tourte bow in hand. But now?

With no Geoff close by, I conjured up a conversation with him.

Me: "My Sartory bow isn't as good a match for the Goffriller."

Geoff: "With all due respect, Judith, based on your recent behavior, you know very little about good matches. Your old bow has worked perfectly well for you for years."

Me: "But it's not part of the package Richard left to me."

Geoff: "Ah, I get it now. You think this gift from Richard—the cello, the bow, the whole kit and caboodle—holds some kind of magic, don't you? Come on, Jude. You know better. The magic isn't in some old instrument. It's in you, luv. You make the magic."

Then he recited his favorite saying: "The best musicians don't play cello; they play music. So forget the details, go for the big picture. You're number one. Rock on, babe."

Even far away, when called upon, Geoff was . . . inside me, I realized with a shock. *Inside me*, and not just in the usual place he inserted himself so brilliantly. He'd found his way to my . . . God help me . . . heart, soul, and kishkes. Oh, perfect timing, with him in London forever.

Then Charlie materialized. Not in person. Or even by

phone—I hadn't heard from him since the weekend. He arrived via Teleflora, of course. The bouquet was huge, formal, and symbolic: predominantly yellow roses, our flower, and baby orchids, maybe because they were exotic, which is the way he thought of me, or maybe just because he could afford them, and stephanotis, which I knew from all the bridesmaiding I'd done was the wedding flower. Still, until I read the inscription I thought, maybe (my heart going arrhythmic), *Geoff from London*. But the typed message was definitely Charlie. He must have ordered it by phone on the fly between hearings, or he'd told his secretary to call it in, because it read:

"Here's to your success. You deserve the best. The orchestra does too. Sending much love to you, Jew-Jew."

Jew-Jew.

That launched me into a fit of hysterical laughter that was just what I needed to break the tension. Of all people, after all these years, Charlie Pruitt in his own screwed-up way came through for me.

Second bow came through, too. That afternoon it sucked up to Mama and gave its all.

The Elgar was an intimate exercise shot through with yearning and despair. My adolescent idol Jacqueline du Pré, RIP, had owned the piece. I took my inspiration from her, but in that audition I made it mine. Really mine. With no ghosts haunting it, no pills taming it, the music emerged incandescent, spiritual, painful, and sweet under the striving bow.

"Thank you, Judith" was all Angela said to me before I got shipped back downstairs to await the verdict. But I heard the congratulations in her voice. I could read music, and I knew.

Chapter 39

⌇

As soon as the results were made official, I called my mother.

"*Aigoo!* Principal cellist! I knew it. So sure you win. Everything worth it. The school. The practice. All bring you to today. Very proud, Judith. You never know how proud."

Irwin hollered in the background, "Me too. Tell her I'm proud too."

My mother's joy was expected, deserved. She'd earned it with every stitch she'd sewn at the Slimline Swimsuits factory, every necessity and small luxury she'd denied herself so I could have whatever it took to get me out of the projects and onto the stage. But the pleasure of the old man with the pompadour and the mentholated-cigarette breath, what had he shelled out to own a share in the moment? Except—it rolled in as a wave of visceral recognition—to pay for my first cello and my music lessons, never knowing he'd done that, never knowing how much the checks he'd managed to send had changed my life. Funny how the wave knocked me on my keister.

"Have you told him yet that he paid for my lessons?" I asked my mother, aware I might be opening Pandora's box, but also that this was a secret I didn't want buried forever. He was on the far side of eighty. I was coming down fast and hard on fifty. If not now, when?

"Scared to tell. Afraid you be mad," Grace said. "You okay if I tell now?"

"Yes, *Uhm-mah*. He should hear that he did a good thing. It's only fair. And say thanks for me."

"Okay, but you say thanks yourself sometime, yes?"

"I'll get there."

"Soon, Judith. He has pacemaker and two stent. Nobody last forever."

My next call was to someone who knew that all too well. When I reported the judges' decision and, sniffling back tears, thanked Sarah Tarkoff again for the Goffriller, she said, "The Goffriller didn't hurt, but the truth is—and Richard used to say this all the time—talent will out. Judith, he'd be thrilled."

I phoned Charlie. He didn't pick up. He was in court or chambers or, for all I knew, tending to Kiki or Chloe. I left a message thanking him for the flowers and giving him the good news.

I got hold of Marti at home, interrupting her writing a review of a seafood house in Fells Point. She was so excited by my news that she nearly (as she so elegantly put it) peed herself.

"Champagne mixed with unadulterated glee does that to me. I've been hitting the Piper since three, celebrating in anticipation. Because I never had a doubt in Dixie you'd finish off that De-Grassi turkey with a fork to the pope's nose." She choked for a second on bubbles or emotion, then recovered to ask, "So no stage fright? No turning into a gelatinous mass of quivering terror?"

"Just the normal pre-big-audition jitters. As soon as I lifted the bow, they disappeared. Honestly, there was nothing even approaching performance anxiety. I think I've knocked the son of a bitch out for good. The consensus seems to be that I'm a pretty good cellist. Who's my subconscious to argue?"

"Now that's the attitude! You got through this audition, you can get through anything," she slurred rapturously. "Stop off here on your way home. I'll break out another bottle and we'll toast your victory. Oh, hon, those magpies are dancing their mother-loving wings off."

And then there was Geoff. Or, more precisely, there wasn't Geoff. Except in my head. Despite my best efforts to play Whac-a-Mole with thoughts of him, they'd been popping up since I heard he'd probably be moving to England. I envisioned him strolling down Sloane Street arm in arm with Deena the harpist, imported expressly for this excruciating fantasy. I imagined him stretched out on a blanket spread against the banks of the River Cherwell canoodling with a thirty-year-old duchess named Lucinda. I kept this craziness from Marti, of course, but she had a *mudang*'s sixth sense for the awful truth.

"I can't believe you haven't called him. Your mother brought you up better than that," she said later that afternoon, waving her champagne flute, spilling bubbly down the front of her shirt and onto her dining room table. "He hung in there with you, swallowing his pride and a shitload of pain to make sure you aced the audition. Stuck with you through thick or thin, babe or bitch, even after you threw him overboard for Charlie. And you say he can't be depended on to be around when you need him."

I took a sip of the champagne, hoping it would dull the ache in my chest. "Well, he's not sticking around anymore. He's moving to London."

"So you've told me three times and counting. Good for him. He may be devoted, but he's not a wimp. You can't hold on to these men of yours forever, Judith. Now be a menschette. Call and tell him the news. And thank him."

I ran my finger around the rim of the crystal flute. The last time I'd seen Geoff was when he'd stalked out of my parents' new apartment. It was going to be one uncomfortable conversation. "It's nearly midnight in London."

"Geoff Birdsall hasn't gone to sleep before midnight since he was six months old."

I stared at the phone, wanting to share the news with him, most of all longing to hear his voice. Marti gave me a piercing look. "Stop torturing yourself. Call, dammit."

He picked up on the first ring. "Judith! Good God, woman, I've been waiting to hear from you. I was afraid to call in case . . ." The phone magnified a deep intake of breath. "How did it go?"

"I got it."

There was a whoop at the other end. "You did! That's smashing news. Well done. Well done. I knew you'd pull it off. You would have done it without the Goffriller, but that clinched it. Yessss!"

He couldn't contain his exuberance. Imagine, having a friend or whatever who took that much pleasure from my accomplishments. He seemed to have put aside all the bad feelings.

"It's pretty exciting. You're in England." My voice was flat.

That quieted him down. "I am that."

"I found out from Vince DeGrassi, of all creeps, ten minutes before my audition." I let that skitter its way across the Atlantic.

"Oh, shit." He drew an audible breath. "Well, that brilliant plan backfired, didn't it?

"What a dunderhead I can be, and without even trying. The thing is, you and I weren't on the best of terms for a sit-down and I thought this . . . uh . . . situation might take some explaining. I was worried it might play with your head right before the tryout."

"Yeah, well, it's after the tryout now," I said, cuing him on.

"And it's midnight in London," he countered.

I could almost hear the gears grinding as he considered how he was going to break the news of his defection to me, the poster child for abandonment issues.

"It's a tad complicated, Jude, and there are lots of details yet to be resolved. How about I tell you all about it when I see you?"

"Fine." Not fine, but who was I to say so? The next question I did have a right to ask, but it would let him know I cared too much about the answer. Yes. No. Yes. I succumbed. "Which will be when?"

"In time for your party, of course. Ah, Jude, I'm happy it worked out. Never had a doubt, of course. Everything's coming up roses for you, isn't it?"

"I suppose," I said. "Yes, of course. It's been a great day, though I'm glad it's over."

There was a pause. Then I said, suddenly swamped by exhaustion and an inability to make sense of all the flotsam churning in my emotional whirlpool, "I guess I'll let you get some sleep."

"Now that I know you brought it off, I'll sleep like a baby. Wonderful news. Good night, Jude."

Did I want to tell him I missed him? Yes. No. Yes. No. No.

"Good night, Geoff. Safe travels."

"Nice and ladylike," Marti said after I clicked off. "Very Aunt Penelope in the parlor with her needlepoint. Miss Manners would give you an A."

I couldn't seem to put the phone down, dead though it was. (How symbolic of the way I managed my love life.)

Marti pried it from my fingers. "So? Second thoughts? Or, knowing the way your obsessive mind works, second hundred thoughts?"

I adopted a casual tone and chose my words carefully. All Marti needed was ammunition and she'd be shootin' advice with both barrels. "Well, I miss him. You know, to hang out with. We have common interests."

"Common interests. Uh-huh. That's got to be top of your list, chitchatting about Beethoven's Ninth and all that." She managed to snort and smirk simultaneously.

"And he's fun to be around."

"Now that's more like it. Fun is *fun*, isn't it? Much better than abject misery. Glad you picked up on the notion before it's too late."

I shrugged and emptied my champagne glass in a gulp. "It's too late already."

"Could be," she said. "If so, I guess you'll just have to suck it up. You'll survive. You're good at that." And she poured us both a refill.

Chapter 40

M y party was held on a warm afternoon that promised to stretch sunlight into evening so the band could play on and on in the gilded spotlight streaming through the Belvedere's Beaux Arts windows.

According to the Korean calendar, my birthday and the celebration of it exactly fifty years later fell on a golden day. June 22 sits at the very beginning of the tenth solar term, which follows the summer solstice, *haji*. Nothing could be better, Lulu Cho had told my mother shortly after my birth, than for a child to emerge when the earth itself was at the peak of its life cycle, when yin energy was at its height, when all the world was gold.

Fifty years later, as my party guests circulated around the elegant cream and blue ballroom, my aunt Phyllis looked up from a plate heaped with shrimp to give me the once-over.

"You're half a century old. Incredible. And I was there when you were born. You were so tiny. Only five pounds, ten ounces. When Grandma Roz saw you in the nursery the next day, she said, 'I've eaten chickens bigger than that.' And now look at you. Look at this party. It's amazing you even made it to this point with what you've been through, but this . . ." At a loss for words for once, she flourished a gesture that took in the scene.

It *was* quite a scene, a fantasy of crystal and silver, music and flowers. Not a mai tai or a tiki cocktail umbrella in sight. Marti's theme was, she explained with a grin, "plain ol' elegance—think Versailles, only toned down a smidge and without the heads rolling."

She had arranged hydrangeas and pink roses from her garden, huge bunches of them in baskets centered on the fuchsia-clothed tables. Waiters threaded through the crowd with trays of hors d'oeuvres. On the bandstand, four of my colleagues from the orchestra—keyboard, bass, clarinet, and drums—were going to town on Cole Porter. At the back of the room, a bartender poured wine with a generous hand and gave out bottled Foster's wrapped in linen napkins, Marti's little nod to Geoff, whom she was currently championing. I scanned the room for the umpteenth time. His beer might have been there, but Geoff wasn't. His absence didn't escape Aunt Phyllis's eagle eye.

"So it's over between you and the Australian. You traded him in, and for what? For him, right? That's the judge over there?" She cocked her head toward a dark-suited figure standing off to one side, tapping furiously into his BlackBerry.

My aunt sent me a pitying look. "You never had a good eye for men, Judith. From college on. First with *that* one, who left you flat. Then with the rabbi, who was a huge mistake from the start."

"Todd was a cantor."

"Todd was a goofball. With terrible table manners. He held his fork like a shovel. And just when I thought you finally acquired some judgment with Geoffrey, you start up again with the blue blood, which is a setback if you ask me. Look at him, in his own little world. All afternoon on his iPod or whatever. Not circulating. Not even a glance in your direction."

Not entirely accurate. He'd kissed me when he'd arrived. Perfectly appropriate, lip to lip, more than chaste.

We'd just broken apart when I got tugged off to greet my guests. As I moved among them I caught glimpses of Charlie making small talk with strangers—occasionally glancing my way to smile and shrug—until finally I saw him drift off to a corner with his always conversational electronic friend.

But now he must have felt the burn of my aunt's stare, because he looked up, broke out a decorous wink, and made his way toward us.

"A pleasure," Aunt Phyllis murmured at the introduction while making it clear it really wasn't, that she was more than ready to move on. "Look at your uncle Arnold, Judith, with the plate full of sliced sirloin. A triple bypass and the man is determined to kill himself with cholesterol. If you'll excuse me, I've got to go save my husband from himself."

"So that's the famous Aunt Phyllis," Charlie said as she trotted off. "Of the Magic Carpet stores. See, I remembered." Trying to score points.

"She's a retired social worker. Actually a pretty smart woman," I said as he guided me out of the crowd. My mother's searing beam of death followed us. She'd cornered me in the ladies' room earlier to tell me he'd introduced himself to her.

"No handshake. He make little bow like I'm Japanese person. He call me Grace, not Mrs. Raphael. I bet you never call his crazy mother by first name. So disrespect. What kind of name anyway, Key-Key? Now I think maybe big-time judge not good enough for you. Not worth your pinkie." She sniffed. "He is like *haepari*." Jellyfish. "Not bad man, but weak. No bone in back. Also too old. His hair more white than Uncle Arnold. And he walk bent, like he work in field whole life. Hunch over desk too much, I think. Reading, reading, all time reading. Man like that no fun. You only fifty. Just beginning new half. Best half, I know. Why you want someone like that?"

In that one over-the-sink lecture, my mother had given me two blessings. I was Good Enough. Which, after Richard's legacy and my own victories, was coming through at last. I didn't need Charlie or anyone else to validate the rest of what was going to be my new, better than enough, life. Grace had gotten it before I did—*it* being everything really: endurance, forgiveness, the triumph of time over pain, the power of love and of letting go when you should and holding on when you wanted to. It didn't hurt that she was there as a shining example. I finally got it too.

At a window facing Chase Street, in the harsh light of day, I stared fondly at Charlie. Fondness was my default feeling for the man I had once loved so fiercely. As the music played on behind us, he congratulated me on my birthday and my audition. Then he lifted my bow hand, turned it over, and ran a finger down my lifeline. "So talented. I'm very proud of you." He brought my hand to his mouth and kissed the palm. "And grateful we found each other again. You have no idea how much I care for you, Ju-ju."

"Me too, Charlie. And always will." What I had to say next caught in my throat. I swallowed hard. "The thing is, you and I aren't a good fit anymore. Maybe we were the only ones who thought we ever were. But now it should be obvious even to us. You're pretty much who you used to be. And I'm pretty much not. In case you haven't noticed, I've changed."

"Oh, I've noticed," he said in a mournful voice, as if it were a bad thing. "I turn my back for a paltry twenty-five years and—*presto*—you're a whole new person." His laugh was sardonic. "How the hell did that happen?"

It was only when I said it aloud that I realized the strength of its truth. "I made it happen, Charlie."

Charles Evans Pruitt was no dummy. His smile became a melancholy curve. "It's over, right?"

I gave myself a moment to say it the right way. After twenty-five years of fading bitterness and then the sweet reprise, it deserved the right way. I took a deep breath, as if preparing to draw across strings.

"It's over." My voice matched my feelings, soft with regret for my own wasted dreams as I put us to rest. "I guess our version of happily-ever-after turned out to be not with each other."

And that was it. No appeals, just a pat on the hand before he let it go, a smooth segue into his business voice and an unsurprising apology. He'd have to leave early. Soon in fact. He was due back in Manhattan for a cocktail reception for the parents of prospective Columbia students. Good thing I hadn't counted on him for forever after.

"So I'm afraid I won't be around when you open your gifts."

"The invitation specifically said no gifts, Charlie."

"Do people really mean that? In any event, you'll have to forgive me because I did get something for you." He extracted a small gray velvet box from his trousers pocket. "Actually, I planned to give you this when the world was young, but now seems as good a time as any. Consider it a farewell token from an old lover or a birthday gift from a new friend. Better yet, both."

I opened the box to find a pair of diamond and ruby earrings. Gorgeous, if your taste ran to heavy, ornate, antique, and exceedingly pricey.

"I can't accept these, Charlie."

"I know what you're thinking, but they're not my mother's. My aunt Honora left them to me. You'll be pleased to know Honora couldn't abide my mother. She thought Kiki was a terrible snob." He held the box up to catch the sun. "Look at those rubies. Have you ever seen such spectacular fire? They'll be beautiful with your dark hair, Ju-ju. You'll do them justice."

Well, it was all very flattering. I didn't have the heart to tell him that carting around those heavy gems on my earlobes was a weight I didn't want to carry. What I wanted—what I *needed*, I'd discovered lately—was lightness and joy. But my mother had raised me to be polite, so I accepted the wildly expensive jewelry. It was the least I could do, considering our history.

"I'll enjoy the thought of you wearing them." Charlie checked his watch, craned his neck to peer twelve stories down, and said, "Looks like my driver's here. Happy fiftieth, Ju-ju. Let's stay in touch, shall we?"

A BlackBerry gong set to deafening cut through the noise, precluding my need to respond. I gave Charlie's free hand what I knew would be a final squeeze. Then he went one way and I went another. But not quite forever.

As I was making my way to Marti to break the news, I was pulled aside by Angela Driscoll.

"Wonderful party, Judith. Big year for you."

If she only knew. "It has been," I replied.

"Actually, I meant the big five-oh. But yes . . . Richard. So of course it has been. Well, I think what's up ahead will be better. Much."

She handed me a fancy gift bag. Another flaunter of the no-presents policy, but she was my boss and I wasn't about to reprimand her.

"I wouldn't normally suggest this, but I'd like you to open it now." She was conducting this conversation. Her eyebrows rose encouragingly.

I parted a cloud of tissue paper and removed a blue lacquer box decorated with plum blossoms inlaid in mother-of-pearl.

"Gorgeous," I said, turning it to catch the iridescence in the light.

"It's Korean, of course. I understand plum blossoms signify new life, new beginnings, so I thought, Just right for Judith's fiftieth. New beginnings, exciting things on the horizon." She hitched her chin, cuing me to lift the lid.

It was a music box. With all the noise around us we had to strain to hear the first four bars of *Arirang*, the folk song that bridged the two sides of the Korean divide. The melody every Korean knew from the crib, the one my mother used to sing to me.

"I thought that might hold special significance for you," Angela said, smiling. I bobbed an assent, overcome, eyes welling. She paused. Angela Driscoll knew how to milk a dramatic moment. "What a haunting melody. I assume you'll be happy to play it next spring in Pyongyang?"

I looked up from the red-velvet-lined box. "You're kidding. Oh my God. We're going?"

"We're going. Contract signed. Of course, there can always be last-minute glitches, like nuclear holocaust. North Korea has tons of WMD and a short temper. And I admit, there was a time when I thought the concert would fall through. It was dicey for a while."

"Yes, I heard a rumor . . ."

"Honestly, the CIA should sign up the entire orchestra. Nothing is secret, nothing is sacred."

"I heard a rumor it had something to do with background checks."

"That got out too, did it?" Then she read my face. "Oh, Judith! It never even occurred to me—you thought it was about you, didn't you? No, no. Nothing to do with you. This isn't for publication, but the issue was Lyndon Shin." Our piccolo player. "Lyndon's uncle is vice president of South Korea. That was a sticking point for the North Korean culture minister. Touchy kind of stuff, propaganda-wise. But it got ironed out."

More proof of Geoff's Galilean notion that the world, especially when its orbit was off-kilter, didn't revolve around me.

"So Korea next April. How's that for a gift, huh? You won't get two of *them*." Angela gave me a hug, turned to leave, halted mid-pirouette, and turned back. The woman had mastered the art of stagecraft. "One other small item. We're not bringing in any guest artists on this trip. We're showing off our own. As principal, you'll be featured. You'll be playing *Arirang* solo in Pyongyang."

Ten seconds into my stunned silence, she placed her index finger under my slack lower jaw and pushed up.

"Much better. You're speechless. Good—that means you can keep the news quiet for a few more days. I don't want it to get out yet. I'll announce it to the troupe an hour before the official press release is e-mailed out. It really is a history-making moment for the orchestra."

I was still in shock. She filled in my answer. "And yes, I can only imagine, Judith. History-making for you too."

"Tell me the truth," Marti said, embracing the room with open arms. "Is this not everything you ever dreamed of for your second birthday party? The joint is jumpin'. Check out your parents or whatever you call them these days."

Irwin and Grace were doing a mean foxtrot to "From This Moment On." They'd been on the dance floor for most of the afternoon.

"Did you see that? He just dipped her like Fred and Ginger. Amazing. Irwin's eighty and his knees are better than mine."

"They look good together," I admitted. I was making progress accepting the new status quo, was no longer nauseated watching them exchange adoring glances. In fact, I found it mildly endearing. Maybe they were *beshert*, preordained to be a couple, as Aunt Phyllis contended. Who was I to buck fate?

"What a turnout!" Marti was saying. "I can't believe you pulled a ninety percent acceptance rate for this party. Who knew you had so many friends? Even Sarah Tarkoff came out of mourning for you." It had been a month since Richard's passing. Sarah had told me he would have wanted her to be there.

"And that one over there flew cross-country just for this." Marti nodded toward Tim Beckersham, engaged in earnest discussion with a woman I didn't recognize.

"He arrived at BWI this morning and afterward he's going to turn around and catch the red-eye back to California. He left a very pregnant wife at home and traveled twelve hours to be here for five. Now that's a tribute."

I'd known Tim since he was a kid and he'd been a good one. Mrs. Beckersham hadn't dragged him to Bed-Stuy on the days she navigated the New York City subway system to get to me for my lessons, but he'd sat through most of our recital rehearsals at the Brooklyn Academy of Music. While we played, he'd be down in the first row doing his homework or reading his book. Now he was a physician, a gastroenterologist with a wife and twin sons.

"The next baby is a girl," he'd told me excitedly in the few minutes we snatched to chat off to the side. He'd added with a catch in his voice, "We're going to name her after Mom. I just hope she has her character." My beloved Florence was going to have a namesake.

"Tim is a gem," I said to Marti. I squinted. "Okay, who's the woman with him?"

"That pretty young thing is my date. She and Tim are probably talking large intestines. Kendra's an OR nurse at

Hopkins. I went for my mammogram, the elevator was crowded, we two were jammed together like moles in a burrow, and the rest is not quite history."

"You've got to be kidding. What happened to Nora?"

"Nora is on a business trip. And I've decided commitment is one of those overrated systems like communism. I've overthrown it." She gave me a nudge in the ribs. "Uh-oh, check who's sashaying by . . . Hi, glad you could make it," Marti tossed off a greeting as Deena Marquis, flitting a wave, sailed by us, large fake boobs making a prow of her profile.

"Explain," I said when she'd passed. "What's *she* doing here?"

"Oh yeah, I meant to tell you about that bolt from the blue. Burt Silverman called me last night to ask if he could bring a date. The date turned out to be Deena. It seems a romance between the harpist and the timpanist has been in the closet for close to a year. Burt said musicians are a bunch of yentas and he wanted to avoid the gossip stirred up by an intra-orchestral romance. You know; you and Geoff had your share of it. Then your birthday reminded them they weren't sixteen anymore and they decided to make their official debut at your party." She gave me an impish smile. "I guess Geoff must have been a red herring, or a cover for what was really going on. And that, in turn, suggests the Aussie is, at this very moment, unclaimed."

"The Aussie is, at this very moment, unaccounted for. Or haven't you noticed?"

"Oh, ye of little faith, don't despair. It's only four o'clock. On the other hand, four o'clock means a big surprise." She scared me when she got that Machiavellian glint in her eyes.

I groaned. "No more surprises."

"Don't be a whiny baby. Of course more." Marti grabbed my hand and began tugging me toward the bandstand. Then she stopped.

"Now pull yourself together, because your guests are about to sing you the Happy Birthday song." She made her eyes *Sesame Street* wide. "Are you ready for cake and ice cream and other goodies beyond your wildest dreams?" I allowed myself a small whimper. "Excellent. You're going to love this. I pulled out all the stops."

Chapter 41

T he cake's inscription—"Happy 50, Judith. Tempus Fugit"—had been Marti's idea, of course. Clever, but not outrageous. You always had to worry about outrageous with Marti.

"What 'tempus fugit' mean?" my mother asked, staring at the letters in red icing.

"It's a saying in Latin. Time flies. You know, life goes by very fast."

"She put this on cake? Hahahaha. Very funny woman, Marti."

What happened next was nothing less than inspired. A waiter rolled out a trolley cart draped in a tablecloth. For one exquisitely normal moment I thought the cloth was hiding maybe a make-your-own-sundae bar. Then Marti produced a hot pink sequined blindfold, secured it over my eyes, and I knew I was in for it.

"Go along with this," she hissed in my ear, "or I swear I'll have you barred from every halfway decent restaurant in Baltimore."

Whatever she'd concocted involved my mother, I deduced, inhaling the scent of Shalimar at my right shoulder before I heard the crinkle of paper unfolding and Grace begin to read. Marti must have written the script, because it had appropriate tenses throughout and a full freight of articles.

"Many years ago— Okay, not so many because I say 'many' she be very mad," my mother improvised, to the crowd's amusement. "Judith had a first birthday party called *tol* in Korea. In this tradition, the baby chooses the symbol of how her life will turn out from a *toljabee* table. Judith chose a musical instrument. Today she plays principal cello with the Maryland Philharmonic Orchestra." Much cheering from out front. "Now, for the second half of her life, she will choose again. What she picks will decide the course of her future. Good luck, my dear daughter."

Caught between laughter and tears, I swung my arm right, trying to grasp my mother's waist, and nearly lost my balance.

"Stop fooling, Judith. You act like child. You fifty-year-old now." My mother's mike was on and the audience whooped with delight.

I felt a breeze under my chin as someone whipped the drape from the cart.

My mother urged, "Go, Judith. Now."

As I groped the air, shouts from the audience directed me. "Warm," someone yelled. "Warmer." "Cool."

Oh no—mere mortals directing my life would anger the gods. I spun around, reached out, and grasped . . . what? Marti snatched off my blindfold.

I held a heart in my hand (better than the toilet plunger she'd positioned dead center). A doctor's anatomical model of a human heart, one of those awful four-chambered breakaway replicas with the auricles and ventricles in living color.

"Life size, I'll have you know. On loan from my cardiologist," Marti said into the microphone.

"Judith made the very best choice," Lulu Cho, edging in, pronounced to scattered applause. She was no spring chicken and her voice magnified was tremulous, but still commanding. "The heart is the symbol of love. This means Judith will have love forever in her life, to give and to take. And now let us sing happy birthday to her in two languages. English first, then Korean."

The cake was presented, I blew out the candles, and my guests sang the English rendition. For the Korean version, waiters threaded among the guests handing out the traditional sweet rice cakes. Then, with the lights dimmed, the words projected on the wall, and the band reprising the tune, I was serenaded with:

Sang-il chookha-hapneeda
Sang-il chookha-hapneeda
Jul guh woon sang-il ulh
Chookha-hapneeda

Forty-nine voices sang out—no, fifty. In the front row, standing next to and towering over my father as the old man blotted his eyes, was Geoff Birdsall. He must have just slid in. He let loose in his lusty bass *Chookha-hapneeda!* And as the last note faded, he touched his fingers—those elegantly long, sublimely supple fingers—to his lips, and released a greeting kiss.

The butterfly beneath my breastbone soared at the sight of him. The bewildered moth that shared its habitat bashed around in the dark wondering what the hell was going on. Hi-Jude kisses to start. Bye-Jude kisses no doubt at the finish. Well. I wasn't kissing so fast.

Oh God, even if only for the length of my party, Geoff was back.

"Glad you made it before the cleaning crew arrived," I grumbled preemptively as we seated ourselves at a corner table out of the Electric Slide line of fire. Irritation was a stand-in for the sadness I felt just below the surface. I shoveled in a forkful of Fugit. I needed a sugar hit to get through what promised to be a depressing conversation.

Geoff looked up from toying with his cake. "Sorry. Getting home turned into something of an adventure. My original flight was canceled last minute and then there was a mix-up with . . . Well, in the end, I'm here and happy to be. This is a spectacular party."

"Thanks to Marti and my mom," I said. "They put it together. Always there for me." *As you used to be before your defection to the redcoats* was the implied and extremely unfair accusation.

Geoff didn't or wouldn't pick up on it. Instead he said, "Jude, you've got an entire cheering section these days. Starting with your colleagues. Vijay told me you had a brilliant audition. He said the *Don Juan* was the best he'd ever heard it played. The bloody Phil can count itself lucky to have you in the principal seat."

And there it was on a silver platter, my lead-in. I took it. "And I'm sure the UK Concert Orchestra is busting its braces to know Geoff Birdsall will be on trumpet. Sounds like a dream job," I said, doing my damnedest to sound sincere, not quite pulling it off.

He must have caught the rough edge on my voice. "It wasn't something I initiated," he said. "I got an e-mail from an old friend who plays with the UKCO—"

I interrupted. "You don't owe me any explanations, Geoff."

"No, I want you to know how it went down. My friend said the trumpet seat was about to open, he'd already spoken to management about me, and I had a leg up. Their vetting process is not nearly as structured as ours. I told him I'd think about it. Next thing I knew, management was on the phone. They needed to fill the seat in a hurry and asked would I hop over."

"So you hopped." *For God's sakes*, I scolded myself, *cut the attitude. Make your exit with some dignity.*

"I thought it might be time for a change of scenery," he continued. "After all, you and I were over and done with. And I didn't want to be the mourner at the wedding feast." He swiveled to take in the room. "Where *is* Charlie, by the way?"

"Been and gone," I said. "Very been and very gone." But Geoff was fighting jet lag and the inference zipped by him.

"Yes, he's a busy man, no doubt." He resumed: "So I thought perhaps it was time for a move. I'm always up for a bit of adventure—that's what I told myself. And it was a plum of a job. Odd coincidence, but the same day you were auditioning here, I was giving them a little sample there. And I reckon I wasn't half bad."

"They made you an offer on the spot?"

"They did."

Had that five-pound plastic model of a heart fallen off the *toljabee* cart, it couldn't have plunged any faster than my own flesh-and-blood heart. *Get a grip*, I told myself. My white-knuckled hand was already clutching the edge of the table.

Always sensitive to my moods, Geoff's *uh-oh* detector must have gone off. "Something wrong?" Those stunning hazel eyes were cloudy with confusion.

"No, fine. You were saying?"

Only I realized I didn't want to hear what he was about to say. At that moment, whatever Geoff and I had over the last three years—a liaison so light it couldn't help but take off in the first ill wind—turned heavy. Not the kind of heaviness you couldn't lift. Not a burden to be shouldered or a cross to be borne. This was a weight like a bundle of feathers—lightness multiplied infinitely—that anchored you in place so you didn't get blown away, didn't even think of running. You stayed and allowed whatever it was to find you and wrap itself around you. *Love*. The breathtaking, in addition to the heavy-breathing, variety.

We'd had it all along, but who knew? I didn't, until Geoff's absence defined its presence.

He was still talking. "So I auditioned, they offered, and we spent a long afternoon haggling over the contract. I had some reservations about the benefits package. I asked for a night to sleep on it. Then you called, Judith.

"I heard your voice—that's all it took—and the whole deal came apart. I asked myself, Who was I kidding? I couldn't get far enough away to erase what the sound of your voice alone did to me. The adventure excuse was bullshit from the start. The truth was I just didn't want to witness your happiness with Charlie. Selfish of me, I know, but I was afraid I'd be hurt beyond healing seeing you with him." He pushed his plate away. "It's never a good idea to run away from your fear, is it? I could tell myself that I was moving toward a new start in London, but I knew it was really running away. And that never works. Ask Irwin."

As if on cue, we both turned to follow Irwin the runner, who was walking very slowly and carefully toward us, balancing a tray of full champagne flutes.

"I know to you he's half bastard, half buffoon," Geoff said. Actually, not quite anymore; he hadn't been updated. "But it took a lot of courage for your dad to try to make amends. Anyway, I spent most of that night thinking through the move. It sounded ideal. But there was an awful lot of Mahler on the concert calendar. So depressing. And the Brits are a bit stodgy for this Aussie. Also, English weather really does suck. It rained for the entire week I was there. I'm a fan of sun, as you know. Bottom line, I told them thanks but no thanks."

I thought I'd misheard him. The band was loud. "You said no?"

"Yes, I said no. I declined the offer."

Which is when the world, or maybe it was just my heart, stopped for at least ten seconds.

"So it appears I'll be hanging around a while longer. At least until something better comes along. Which isn't bloody likely. Don't worry, Jude. I've pretty much made peace with the new order. I won't get in your way."

I want you in my way, I thought. Didn't say. Couldn't talk.

"With the symphony season just about over, I can make myself scarce. Maybe I'll visit my folks for a start. And I've been thinking Tahiti would be just the ticket to take the chill off after that."

I found my voice, but nerves made me babble. "Tahiti, really? I've always wanted to go to Tahiti. Since I saw my first Gauguin at the Brooklyn Museum, I've dreamed about Tahiti."

"It's a good place to holiday." He went glum. "I have a feeling even Charlie could stand a week there if he was guaranteed reception for his BlackBerry."

"Honestly, I can't see Charlie wearing a pareo." The image of the distinguished judge wrapped in a sarong made me giggle. At that moment, almost anything would have made me laugh.

Geoff had turned seriously somber. "In any case, I've come to terms with the situation. I wish you the best, Jude. Whatever makes you happy."

The band had just gone on break, and in the sudden silence it all came in loud and clear. "*You* make me happy," I blurted, astonished to hear myself say what I realized I'd been feeling, tamping down for a while now.

He gave me a searching look. Vamped three beats. "No kidding? You're saying *I* do? Me, not Charlie?"

"The Charlie fling is over."

"It was a fling, was it? That's all it was? And you've sent him packing? Really? Poor bloke." Geoff looked remarkably cheerful for a man expressing sympathy. "He's going to take it hard."

"I think he'll be fine." He would be, too. Oh sure, it might sting for a while, but that would be pride more than love. Not the kind of love I needed, anyway. "He's got a rich, full life, Charlie does. More than he can handle."

"Well, I can tell you *I* missed you. Those weeks without you were like someone lopped off my right hand. And you know how important a right hand is to a trumpet player."

"Me too. My bow hand. It was only after it was gone that I realized how much I needed it . . ." My voice was shaky. ". . . to make music."

"Really?" He couldn't quite get over it. "Isn't this a corker? Me, not Charlie." He took a long pull of beer. "Fortifying myself." Then he planted the beer bottle on the table, took my hands in his, and said, very formally, very adorably, "I may be presuming here, but I've got to chance it." He cleared his throat. "You do know I love you, Jude. And . . . if you want to get married, I'm willing. More than. There, I've said it and I'm still standing. Marriage is a definite option. I'm up for it, if that's what you want."

"Not necessarily," I said.

Taking the "necessarily" off the table made me feel suddenly, incredibly free—free enough so I could foresee a day when "possibly" might find room at that same table.

On a wing and a prayer I said, "I love you too." Softly, because it scared me so. As I'd been recently reminded, I didn't have the most sterling record when it came to picking men. But Geoff heard it, I could tell by his hard swallow. And then because, what the hell, I was risking my ass anyway with this conversation, I reached over and stroked his jaw, bristly with the red-eye flight stubble he hadn't stopped to shave. "My love," I said, and again, "My love."

"Ah, Jude." His voice was tender. "I love you so much. I am one lucky bastard." Then the big Aussie grinned and changed key. "Okay, got that settled. Now, what's next?"

"Tahiti for hang gliding. Do they hang glide in Tahiti?" I was high on the moment, half talking, half laughing.

"If they don't, we'll teach them." He slowed the tempo. "But first, winter in Sydney. You'll love it there and I can introduce you to my mum, my family, and the best of my mates. They'll fall head over heels for you, the lot of them. Then the week in Tahiti and home." His glance turned merry, mischievous. "Crikey, maybe we ought to figure where home *is* exactly. You have space for my didgeridoo collection at your place? I'm thinking long term. Curator accompanying, of course."

Geoff moving in with me? Those didgeridoos, huge aboriginal horns, required a room of their own. "We'll manage," I whispered.

He reached over, drew my hand toward him, and pressed his lips against my palm.

Marti, standing nearby in a chat circle with my mother and Lulu Cho, caught the move. She issued a loud, exaggerated "Ahem" and sent me a cartoon wink.

I nodded to her, then turned to the shuffle of my father inching toward us with three flutes of champagne.

Arriving with a smile, he handed me a glass. "Hey, Geoff, here you go. And one for me." I had a feeling it wasn't his first. "Happy you made it, young man. I see you didn't get a tan in London. Lousy weather those limeys have. Judith, beautiful party, beautiful birthday girl. I gotta tell you, when you blew out those candles with the spotlight on you, it struck me how much of your mother you got in you. The Korean genes combining with the Jewish genes make you a real knockout. Ain't she a looker, Geoff?"

"She is that, Irwin. An absolute stunner."

I stared at another birthday surprise, the freshly grown gray smudge under Irwin's classic Raphael nose. "And I like your mustache," I remarked. It was the nicest thing I'd said to Irwin Raphael since he'd turned up a month earlier. My version of "We're okay."

"Something new," my *ap-ba* responded. "When you're old, it's good to try something new. Just for the heck of it." He flashed his caps at Geoff. "But not too new, if you know what I mean."

"I'll drink to that," I said, my voice taking on a melody I recognized as joy.

It was on that note that the party ended for me and the rest of my life began. Then again, the rest of my life had the promise of turning into one long party.

Geoff and my father lifted their glasses.

The old man said, "Here's to you, Judith. Happy fiftieth, kiddo."

Geoff chimed in, "Cheers, luv."

My mother, who'd strolled over from the women's circle, slipped in next to me. "Don't forget best Korean toast." She lifted her glass in the traditional fashion, supporting her right arm with her left hand. "*Gun-bae.*"

"*Gun-bae,*" we all repeated.

But I had the final word over the Piper-Heidsieck, "*L'chayim.*"

To life. Whatever it brings.

Chapter 42

It brought me the greatest gift in all my nearly fifty-one years the following April.

Seated on the flower-banked stage of the East Pyongyang Grand Theater, I peered into the audience. The theater seated twenty-five hundred. That night they were mostly North Korean men in somber business suits and women in gorgeous pastel *hanboks*. Also a contingent of U.S. State Department representatives.

We played the "Star-Spangled Banner" and "Patriotic Song," the national anthem of the Democratic People's Republic of Korea. Then an all-American program: Aaron Copland's *Appalachian Spring*, a medley from *Porgy and Bess* in which Geoff got to show off on trumpet, and the New World Symphony. As Dvořák's final notes of tribute faded and the hall exploded with applause, I moved with my cello to the podium that had been placed for me up front, center stage. I took my chair, Angela raised her baton, and the orchestra behind me flooded the theater with the first stirring chorus of the national folk song, *Arirang*.

My nerves were the right kind of strung for that night's concert. Calm enough so I didn't have to call up the tranquil image of the beach where on winter break Geoff and I had blissfully stretched out after windsurfing the waters around Maui. Taut enough so I would give the performance of a lifetime and remember every shining detail.

I could see clearly to the fifth row. The first row lined up the country's highest party officials. Backs straight, hands folded in their laps, they sat with expressionless faces. The second row showed sparks of emotion. As the lushest violin passages of the folk song soared, an older man dabbed tears and a few women mouthed the words they had known from childhood. In the middle of the third row, my mother and father never shifted their stare from me. The principal flutist played a melancholy interlude, Deena shone on the harp, my parents' stare remained unwavering.

Amazing. The old guy had shelled out a hundred thousand dollars of the chippie's money to the Maryland Philharmonic's Richard Arthur Tarkoff Foundation to earn the title of patron and secure the trip and the seats for him and my mother.

Grace was dressed in her own mother's now antique *hanbok*, a gift from her sister, my aunt Min Sun. The two women separated by war when barely out of their teens held hands. Next to my aunt were her husband and six of my cousins, who'd been discovered at a cooperative farm in Hwanghae by who-knows-what means by who-knows-what American agency under pressure from Secretary of State Eleanor Aldridge as a favor to her cousin Charles Evans Pruitt. Charlie had connections and he had class. It had taken a single phone call from me for him to set the wheels in motion. His final gift to his lost love was my lost family. Better than rubies.

Angela led the violins to a soaring transition as the first chorus ended and a spotlight bloomed over me. I took a deep, steadying breath—*Remember this, Judith; remember this until your dying day*—and gave an infinitesimal nod to my parents. My father sent me a wink and nudged my mother, who blew me a kiss.

The signal from Angela and I lifted my bow, drew it across the historic strings of the Goffriller, and made it weep the music of *Arirang*.

As I played, I sang the song's familiar lyrics in my head. Their absolute meaning is lost in the mists of time, but most Koreans agree they have to do with love and abandonment. And, some say, hope.

Photo by Fern Eisner

Toby Devens has been an editor, public information specialist, and author of short fiction and articles for national magazines. She has lectured worldwide about writing and women's issues and has led writing workshops. Her first published book was a humorous and poignant collection of poetry that was excerpted in *McCall's* and *Reader's Digest*. In 2006, she published her first novel, *My Favorite Midlife Crisis (Yet)*. She lives halfway between Baltimore, Maryland, and Washington, D.C.

CONNECT ONLINE

www.tobydevens.com
www.midlifepassions.blogspot.com
facebook.com/tobydevensauthor

Happy Any Day Now

Toby Devens

A CONVERSATION
WITH TOBY DEVENS

Q. What inspired you to write Happy Any Day Now?

A. I've always been interested in the theme of return and how the past cycles into the present. When old friends and former classmates reconnected with me through social media, I recovered some who had been lost to me for decades. In several cases, there were reunions. The idea that people who had played a role in my life were suddenly back to make magic or mischief (or both) was fascinating. I wanted to explore that.

Also, the roots of family have become more important to me as I've grown older. Not long ago, I did a bit of genealogical research and turned up the ship's manifest for my maternal grandmother, who left Austria for America, all alone, to start a new life. She died before I was born, so I bombarded her generation of the family with questions about how she'd adjusted to the new world. That led to my fascination with the immigrant experience in general and the ways people adapt to transplantation, how they wilt or bloom in new soil. With America welcoming unprecedented numbers of newcomers from Asia, I decided to make my main character Korean-American, but Grace's story has much that's universal about it.

Judith's relationship with Grace is another narrative thread. Mother-and-daughter dynamics are tricky to manage under the best of circumstances and Judith and Grace perform the special, precarious balancing act of a single mother and only daughter. Judith has always walked a tightrope between love for and independence from Grace. I thought it would be interesting to follow up with the two adults to see if that relationship landed on its feet.

Q. *This is your second novel. Can you tell us a little about your first one and how it compares to* Happy Any Day Now?

A. *My Favorite Midlife Crisis (Yet)* is a novel about women who reinvent themselves after their tidy worlds are shaken up. The narrator, Gwyneth Burke, MD, walks in on her husband of twenty-six years in the arms of their male interior decorator and—*bam!*—life as she's known it is over. From then on, she's on her own. But not alone. She's got friends: never-married business-woman Fleur Talbot and widowed fiber artist Kat Greenfield. We follow this witty and resilient trio as they take on career issues, aging parents, truculent children, difficult men of course, the occasional hot flash, and a delicious plan for revenge.

Each writer has a personal voice and mine pervades *My Favorite Midlife Crisis (Yet)* and *Happy Any Day Now*. Both stories are set in Baltimore and spotlight protagonists who are dedicated to serious work. Gwyn is a surgeon who deals with cancers specific to women; Judith is a classical cellist. Gwyn and her pals are in their mid-fifties; Judith is rapidly approaching the big five-oh. One lead is a physician, the other an artist, so their personalities are quite different, but at the core is a similar latent strength just waiting to be tested.

The stories share my preference for plots with twists and surprises, a focus on character, and lots of dialogue because I enjoy writing it and think it reveals even more than description does. Both have a healthy dose of humor, sizzling sex scenes, and love. Blissful, painful, complicated love.

Still, the books are very different from each other—the way siblings from the same mother can be—and my labor with both novels was considerably longer and significantly harder than with my daughter.

Q. Judith's Korean/Jewish background gives so much richness to the novel. How do you happen to know so much about both cultures?

A. I have Asian cousins and a second generation that blends the Asian and Jewish strains. A family Christmas letter a few years ago with photographs of their beautiful babies sparked my thinking that this combination offered interesting story possibilities. *Happy Any Day Now* took off from there.

The Jewish experience is something I grew up with and continue to be surrounded by. The Asian component required more extensive research. I live in a community between Baltimore and Washington, D.C., that hosts a rich cultural mix, a very diverse population that includes a large number of immigrants from Korea. I started by chatting with my neighbors. I visited Koreatowns in various cities. I also read books by Korean authors and did research online. Korean-American blogs were my go-to source for all kinds of information—the women traded recipes and childhood reminiscences, exchanged advice about how to deal with their parents, wrote about preserving the meaningful traditions of their ancestors for their own kids. The more I came to know, the more I was impressed by how many qualities and values the Jewish and Korean cultures have in common.

Q. Through your depiction of Judith's and Geoff's roles in the orchestra, you bring classical music down to earth and make me want to listen to many of the pieces you mention. How did you choose the selections you made? What would be on your ideal playlist for listening while reading Happy Any Day Now?

A. I come from a musical family. My mother and her brother both played piano, her twin sister played violin, and a first cousin was an Academy Award–winning composer/conductor. Saturday afternoons, our apartment was flooded with music from the Metropolitan Opera radio broadcast.

Later, for a New York magazine, I reviewed concerts at Lincoln Center and Carnegie Hall and became hooked on the serious stuff. I've listened to the local classical music stations for years, so I felt reasonably comfortable matching the selection to the situation in *Happy Any Day Now.* When in doubt, I consulted musician friends in California and London, who made suggestions.

A playlist . . . what a great idea!

1. We first meet Judith at cherry blossom time in Baltimore, so the perfect accompaniment to the beginning of the story is "Spring" from Vivaldi's *The Four Seasons.*

2. From the Manhattan rooftop scene: France's iconic Édith Piaf singing her haunting rendition of "Non, Je Ne Regrette Rien" is available on numerous CDs and as an MP3 (as are many of the selections I note). Also from that scene, a reference to the theme from the PBS drama *Brideshead Revisited.* The score from Charlie's favorite show when he and Judith were together in Cambridge is available on CD. And there's a wonderful sequence on YouTube with music and still photos.

3. The work that freaks out Judith onstage, Brahms' Piano Con-

certo No. 2, is at times meltingly beautiful, at others stunning in its intensity. Many consider the version recorded by Maurizio Pollini with the Berlin Philharmonic (Claudio Abbado conducting) a masterpiece.

4. Dvořák's Cello Concerto, mentioned a number of times in the book, may bring tears to your eyes as it does to mine. Some think it's the greatest concerto for the instrument ever written and it's been recorded by almost every major cellist. CD versions are available by Mstislav Rostropovich, Yo-Yo Ma, and Jacqueline du Pré, among others.

5. The two *Dons* by Strauss—*Don Quixote* and *Don Juan*—which figure prominently in the story, can frequently be found paired on CDs. Also, look on YouTube for the complete performance of *Don Quixote* by the Chicago Symphony with Daniel Barenboim conducting.

6. Richard mentions one of Paganini's *Twenty-Four Caprices* as being a lifelong challenge. Hear all twenty-four in their original incarnation for violin played by Itzhak Perlman in EMI Classics Great Recordings of the Century series. Also, don't miss a masterful playing of that dastardly difficult cello adaptation in the CD *Portrait of Yo-Yo Ma*.

7. A touching moment is Judith playing Massenet's "Meditation" from *Thaïs*. My second favorite performance of this piece (after Judith's, of course) is by Yo-Yo Ma. Check it out on YouTube. Or listen to it tucked in among Bach's "Sheep May Safely Graze," Piazzolla's "Libertango," and other compositions for cello on the highlights CD *The Essential Yo-Yo Ma*.

8. And finally, Mozart's Horn Concertos—just because they never fail to lighten my heart.

Korea's keening shamanistic music, which sometimes serves as background to *mudang* readings, is strange to Western ears at first, but may grow on you. If you want to experience it, there are at least two CDs out there featuring the double-reed *piri* as well as the two-stringed fiddle called the *haegeum*. Search online for "*sinawi* music of Korea" and you'll come up with samples.

Of the popular songs mentioned, two stand out: "My One and Only Love," which Geoff plays at the Bard in Fells Point—the Sinatra version is the gold standard—and "Stars Fell on Alabama." In a CD simply named *Ella and Louis*, Ella Fitzgerald sings the latter like she's unwrapping velvet, and when Louis Armstrong joins her, his rasp is uncharacteristically mellow.

Now you have the best in the book. So, as Richard Tarkoff would say, "Play on!"

Q. Grace is one of my favorite characters in the book. She's funny and courageous and has great common sense. Can you tell us more about how you came up with her?

A. Oh, I loved writing Grace. Inspiration? There used to be a Korean woman living on my street who took her grandson—about four, I'd say—out for a walk on weekday afternoons. Occasionally, she'd stop at my front garden to point out tulips or the cherry tree in bloom. She was gentle and funny with the little boy. Later, she walked for exercise with her husband. She scolded the old fellow with many fierce hand gestures, then broke out a gold-toothed smile. I modeled Grace's physical appearance on this woman and perhaps picked up the little bit of her personality I observed. The rest was drawn from my own mother's sometimes unaware sense of humor and her fund of hilarious superstitions, an aunt's perseverance in the face of difficult circumstances, a friend's . . . Gosh, I don't know. It's always a jumble. I may lift a gesture here, a pattern of speech there, a snippet of circumstance from way back, but the composite bears no resemblance to, as the legal disclaimer goes, anyone, anything, or any event living or dead. I haven't a clue about the creative process and, truth is, I don't want to know. I'm afraid if the mystery is revealed, it will vanish. Even if I tried to replicate a real person, I'm sure what would emerge wouldn't resemble the original in the slightest. I don't try. I just let it come together on the page. Memorable characters—and I hope Grace is one—really do take on a life of their own.

Q. What are your favorite parts of the novel? What parts were the most fun to write? Which were the most difficult?

A. I always have a great time writing about relationships—but that's also the most difficult material to get down. Dissecting how and why human beings behave as they do is challenging because it's frequently unpredictable and inexplicable. But that is the way people act in real life—sometimes against their better judgment, better interests, better nature, and, God knows, logic. As the writer I'm charged with making those you've-got-to-be-kidding decisions and actions of the characters believable. And when love enters the picture, especially romantic love, all bets are off.

I got a kick out of writing Kiki, also Irwin and Marti—the more outrageous characters. After a while, they became like family. I knew them too well to like them unreservedly, but there was no doubt I loved them.

On the other hand, Judith's performance anxiety episodes were difficult because as a child I acted professionally and experienced stage fright. It was painful to recall that stomach-churning fear, but also cathartic for me as an adult to write about it.

Getting the music part right was challenging. The big find for me with regard to that segment of my research—and I did lots of the standard probing and poking around—were the online musicians' forums, open to all. Here I picked up facts about the audition process, debates over the use of antianxiety drugs, wonderful small details that enrich a story. It's amazing how generous people are with information, how much they share online. Thank you, anonymous musicians. You know who you are. Really, only you know who you are.

Q. Are you a big reader? Can you imagine a life without books?

A. Life without books would be, for me, life without air. I come from a reading family. My mother made sure I had a library card as soon as I qualified. Asking a factual question of my dad usually prompted the answer, "Look it up, sweetie." On languid summer days, you could find me socked in our apartment, reading about ancient Egypt in a tattered Book of Knowledge encyclopedia or gobbling up all the Sherlock Holmes stories. Eventually, my mother would extract the book from my hands and chase me with, "Enough reading, Toby. You're getting a bedroom tan. You need fresh air. Go outside and play."

Early on, I learned that books expand your universe like nothing else can. I still believe that and I still—no matter how busy I am—read for pleasure daily.

Q. Would you share some of your own life story and what led you to writing?

A. Brooklyn born and bred, as a child I performed as an actress on-stage and in television. But even then, I had a craving to write. I kept a notebook with me in rehearsal halls and behind the scenes in TV studios. I turned out poetry and fairy tales, then the adventures of a detective, à la Nancy Drew. By thirteen, having "retired" from acting, I resumed a conventional childhood. In high school, my English teacher commended my writing and urged me to keep at it. In college I was editor of the literary magazine, and after my return to New York, I earned a master's degree in English literature while working my glamour job as a writer/reviewer and then editor for *Where* magazine. From there I went on to an editorial position with Harcourt Brace publishers and my future husband, whom I met when I interviewed him for an article.

After we married and our daughter was born, I used chinks of time to write articles and short fiction, which, to my surprise and delight, were published in national magazines. As Stewart's struggle with a chronic illness grew more intense and my daughter turned toddler, there was hardly time to think, let alone write. I prayed a lot, however. Prayers that, late into the night when the needs around me settled, I wrote down. Some were funny, some poignant, and they turned into my first book, *Mercy, Lord! My Husband's in the Kitchen*. It came out the week my young husband died.

Eventually—after emerging from the initial swamping wave of grief, and bolstered by good reviews for *Mercy, Lord!*—I was ready to write again. But I had a child to support and care for, and over the next decades, even after my second marriage, my time and energy went to the family and job I loved. Still, ideas brewed, and eventually I left my job to write a book that literally demanded to be written, *My Favorite Midlife Crisis (Yet)*. After that, another I couldn't turn away—it had my heart—*Happy Any Day Now*.

Q. *What do you most like about the writing life?*

A. When the work is going well, you get something like a runner's high. I assume serotonin or another pleasure hormone is surging, because everything around you fades and you're totally absorbed in the joy of writing. Also, when things in the real world are falling apart and you feel helpless to change them, your ability to shape a fictional world, steer your characters' destinies, give them satisfying resolutions to their problems can be sanity-saving.

The feedback from readers is incredibly fulfilling. After *My Favorite Midlife Crisis (Yet)* came out, I received so many revealing and touching e-mails via my Web site. Readers identified with the characters and thanked me for giving a voice to women "of a certain age." One wrote that her husband had walked out of their marriage earlier that week and she'd been despondent. Finally, she forced herself out of the house, wandered into a bookstore café for a cup of tea and a browse, and picked up *Midlife Crisis*. She said that the book gave her hope that there could be happiness ahead for her. For an author, it doesn't get better than that.

On the practical side, it's nice to be able to work in sweats and slippers and make your own schedule. And I like the balance of the solitary—it's just you and the laptop when you're writing—and the camaraderie with other writers.

Q. *What writers have you particularly enjoyed and been inspired by over the years? And are you a member of a book club?*

A. The first who made an indelible impression was Louisa May Alcott. I loved *Little Women* so much that, as a preteen, I wrote a mercifully short play based on the story and drafted my friends to act in it.

Later on, I became a big fan of the three Johns: Updike, Cheever, and O'Hara, who did such a wonderful job of vividly capturing specific times and milieus. Dorothy Parker is an idol. She displayed amazing versatility: short fiction, poetry, screenplays, book and film reviews. Everything was clever and frequently, in the case of her stories and poems, heartbreaking.

I love Susan Isaacs's voice. *Compromising Positions* was to me a breakout novel. Her savvy, witty woman protagonist was a new phenomenon and readers were captivated by her. Since I tend to write about bright women who use humor to brave their way through crises, that first Isaacs book was a personal inspiration.

There are certain authors whose talent transcends their genres. I'm addicted to Daniel Silva's Gabriel Allon series, Elizabeth George's Inspector Lynley novels, and Laura Lippman's Baltimore-based Tess Monaghan books. These writers are masters of the spy and detective formats, but, bottom line, they're simply fine writers.

Among the younger crew, I'm especially impressed by Tana French, whose Dublin-set stories are riveting. I have a review of her *Faithful Place* at the salon page on my Web site, at www.tobydevens. com. Maggie Shipstead made a marvelous debut with *Seating Arrangements*. Karen Thompson Walker's *The Age of Miracles* is a stunning first novel.

As for nonfiction, Nora Ephron is a hands-down, thumbs-up favorite. In a tribute to her in my blog, midlifepassions.blogspot.com, I try to explain why her work resonates so deeply with women of all ages and backgrounds. Other nonfiction writers I'm always eager to read: Anne Lamott, Doris Kearns Goodwin, and Erik Larson.

I am a member of a couples book club, which is a hoot. The mechanics of coming to a consensus about what we want to tackle next is always fun and surprising because we try to move outside our comfort zone. We chew over the books during dinner. Once I nearly slung the soup at a dear friend. He literally hated a novel I adored. The back-and-forth gets pretty heated. But a really rich chocolate dessert always produces the peace that passeth (mutual) understanding.

Q. What is your next novel about, and what might we expect from you over the next several years?

A. First, I'm heading to the beach. And not just to stretch out on the sand. I like to have my settings—the medical practice in my first book; the invented Maryland Philharmonic in my second—work almost as characters in my stories. And what's better than a beach town where an intruder from the past is about to make waves?

My protagonist is in her mid-forties, with an interesting history and a future in jeopardy because . . . Well, I'm in the early stages. I know it's going to be exciting and fun to write and, I hope, like my other novels, exciting and fun to read. Even when the roof caves in (as it does literally and figuratively in this one)—especially when the roof caves in—if you survive intact, you gotta laugh.

That's the immediate project. Over the next few years, more novels, because there are always stories percolating, and not writing is never an option.

QUESTIONS FOR DISCUSSION

SPOILER ALERT: The Questions for Discussion that follow tell more about what happens in the book than you might want to know until after you've read it.

1. First, did *Happy Any Day Now* make you laugh? What were the funniest parts for you?

2. What is your overall reaction to the novel? Does it seem fresh and original? Do you care about the characters? Is it the kind of novel you want to tell your friends about?

3. Judith Raphael is almost fifty and facing some major challenges in her life. Do you like her, even when she is obsessing about her situation? Her life circumstances might be quite different from your own, but can you relate to her anyway? Why or why not?

4. What do you think of Judith's mother, Grace? What do you most admire about her? Discuss her role as immigrant, garment worker, mother, and as her own woman. What has she retained from her Korean origins and what about her is purely American?

5. Judith has changed over the years, but Charlie seems to be the same man he was decades before. Think about your first serious

romantic relationship. Do you have regrets about the way it ended? How do you think your life would have been different if you had wound up with your first love?

6. Judith's grandma Roz was not happy with her son's choice of Grace for his wife. Kiki was determined Charlie wouldn't marry Judith. How much influence should a mother or father have over the choice of a child's spouse? Discuss guidelines for good relationships with daughters-in-law and sons-in-law.

7. Richard Tarkoff is Judith's beloved mentor, who has had and will continue to have, through his gift to her, a huge impact on her career as a cellist. Has a mentor of some kind, professional or personal, ever helped to shape your life?

8. Discuss Judith's experience while growing up as one of the few Asian kids in school. Did you know kids in school whose ethnicity set them apart? Were you one of them? Care to share stories of what you remember, or what your own children have gone through?

9. Why do you think Grace is willing to take another chance on Irwin? If you were free to accept him back in your life, would you welcome back a former husband or lover?

10. Do you find the resolution of Judith's relationship with Geoff satisfying? Why do you think they agree to move in together but not necessarily get married? How do you envision their future?

11. Judith develops a case of performance anxiety that threatens her career. How do you feel about speaking before an audience?

Do you (or does someone you know) have a phobia or fear that limits your life? What can you do about it?

12. Have you ever had your fortune told, and did the predictions come true? Do you think Lulu Cho is a fraud or the real deal?

13. The novel ends with a party. Describe the best party you've ever attended. What do you consider essential for a good party?

14. Grace tells Judith that the next fifty years will be the best ever. Whatever your own age, do you agree that life keeps on getting better?